Another Us

KIRSTEN HESKETH

Another Us

CANELO

First published in the United Kingdom in 2020 by Canelo

This edition published in the United Kingdom in 2020 by

Canelo Digital Publishing Limited
31 Helen Road
Oxford OX2 0DF
United Kingdom

A CIP catalogue record for this book is available from the British Library.

Print ISBN 978 1 80032 007 9
Ebook ISBN 978 1 78863 963 7

This book is a work of fiction. Names, characters, businesses, organizations, places and events are either the product of the author's imagination or are used fictitiously. Any resemblance to actual persons, living or dead, events or locales is entirely coincidental.

Look for more great books at www.canelo.co

Printed and bound in Great Britain by Clays Ltd, Elcograf S.p.A.

S

For John, Tom and Charlotte — with love.

Chapter One

'Mum?' Jack stopped stirring his Coco Pops and stared at the plumber. Chocolate milk dripped from his spoon and Jack blotted it with the forearm of his sweatshirt. 'Mum, why is that man so ugly?'

The moment hung, poised, like the one droplet of brown milk about to plop off the edge of the table.

Of course, it had to happen now; on a Monday morning when I hadn't engaged my brain and there was breakfast to finish, teeth and hands to clean and bags to gather before school. And it would be *this* particular Monday morning, September 14th. The date that had been eyeballing me from the calendar for weeks. At least Freddie, our teenager, had already taken himself off to school. He would have cackled with loud, delighted laughter and made the whole thing twice as bad.

If that was possible.

What were the options?

Think, Emma.

Think!

Plan One: ignore the question and move on. But eight-year-old Lily was rigid with appalled fascination and the plumber was staring at me in mute humiliation, so this was unlikely to do the trick.

Plan Two: the whispered apology. 'So sorry. Jack tends to blurt stuff out. Tells you how it is.' No. *No.* Definitely not an option. Jack was right; the plumber was – how could I put this nicely? – aesthetically challenged. Bald pate. Receding chin.

Protruding teeth. How on earth could I say anything without making it twice as bad?

Plan Three: 'Jack, sweetie,' I said. 'You must stop calling everyone ugly. It's getting very boring.'

That was quite clever.

But Jack just screwed up his face. 'Don't lie, Mum,' he said. 'I've never said it before.'

The plumber gave us all a 'look' and went upstairs without a backward glance.

There was no Plan Four.

There was still no Plan Four when I got back from dropping Lily off at school. In the end I fudged it. I gave the plumber freshly ground coffee, chocolate biscuits and my best apologetic smile but I didn't actually *say* anything. Then Daniel got back from his run, I cajoled Jack away from the computer and we were off.

Daniel and I didn't say much in the car, but Daniel put a hand on my thigh and the space between the words was warm and comforting. After a while, I turned to look at Jack. Cross-legged on the back seat, he was playing *Wizard World* on Daniel's iPad, fingers and thumbs a-whirr. I tried looking at him dispassionately – a small, slight boy with a broad face, a freckled nose and tousled strawberry-blond hair. His striped blue sweatshirt was decidedly grubby, though; how long had that faint white stain been there? Wrestling Jack's current favourite item of clothing off him was hard because he liked to wear it all the time – even in bed – but that was no excuse. I should have been supervising him rather than fretting about the plumber.

Oh *God*.

Would the stain count against him?

Against all of us?

'How's it going, Jacko?' I asked, leaning over and scrubbing at the stain with my nail.

2

''K.' Jack swatted me away. 'Can we get a McDonald's after?'

Despite my nerves, I couldn't help smiling. 'Chancer,' I said. 'Let's see how the meeting goes.'

Jack looked up. 'How does it have to go to get a McDonald's?' he asked.

Good question.

'I just meant it depends how long it goes on,' I said. 'We need to get back for Freddie and Lily.'

Jack gave a grunt and turned back to his game.

I hadn't meant that at all.

I wished I was somewhere else.

Anywhere but hurtling along the M40.

I wished it was that morning, before the plumber arrived. Or yesterday, when we were slumping at home in a lazy Sunday fug. Or, better still, drifting along the river on *Frejalily*, the scruffy little cabin-cruiser we'd bought in a moment of carpe-diem-ness and allowed the kids to name.

Yes, take me back three weeks to our overnight jaunt up the Thames. Take me back to navy-blue water and wavelets capped in silver. Long shadows along the banks, the heady smell of mown grass and a little island dense with oaks and willows…

'Someone's tied a rope to the big tree,' shouted Freddie, momentarily forgetting his teenage cool.

Minutes later, all three children were taking it in turns to swing over the river and drop, shrieking, into the water below. I couldn't wait to join them. I rummaged in the holdall for my costume, pulling out handfuls of clothes in increasing frustration. It wasn't there. Of course it wasn't. I'd forgotten to pack it.

I considered the alternatives.

Plan One: skip the swimming.

Plan Two: bugger that.

I was wearing sensible black knickers and the kids would never notice the difference. I slipped off my shorts and wrestled my bra from under my T-shirt. A girl has to have a dry bra to come back to – even if she's in danger of two black eyes in the meantime.

'Officially bonkers,' said Daniel, reaching for the *Guardian*.

'Come in with me?'

Daniel gave me his what's-she-asking-me-to-do-now? expression. The one where he put his head on one side and his eyes went all squinty-sexy. He'd come in with me. I knew he would. He just needed a moment to get used to the idea. Sure enough, here he was, peeling off his T-shirt to reveal his reasonably tanned and toned dad–bod. At least he was wearing his trunks.

Coaxing the kids out of the river for tea an hour later was a challenge.

'Hop on board, guys,' said Daniel for the fourth time. 'Time for tea.'

Jack hauled himself out of the river reluctantly. 'How can I hop all the way up there?' he demanded. 'I'm not a kangaroo.'

'Don't be weird,' said Lily, pushing past him and climbing on deck.

'You're the weird one.' Jack kicked out at her departing bottom.

A pause.

Then Daniel laughed. 'Who said you can't hop on board, Jacko?' he said. He climbed ashore and stood behind Jack on the bank. 'Let's go. One, two, three – hop!'

Jack hopped and Daniel swung him into a fireman's lift and deposited him on the deck.

'There you go. One kangaroo safely aboard.'

There was silence and I held my breath. Which way would Jack go today? Would he laugh or scream? There was no way of telling.

4

Jack began to laugh.

And thank goodness for that!

As the sun teetered on the horizon, Daniel and I sat at the bow with a bottle of red. I liked how our body language was mirrored; knees hugged to chests, cheeks resting on knees, glasses dangling. Just two grammar school kids who found each other way back when and got lucky.

Daniel put his arm round me. 'Look at what we've got,' he said. 'What we've *made*.'

His other arm, sweeping around, took in the two of us, the kids bickering companionably in their sleeping bags in the cabin, the boat…

'The adventure's just beginning,' I said. 'One day we'll take *Frejalily* all the way to Marlow.'

Daniel grinned. 'Think big, Em,' he said. 'Oxford…'

'London…'

'Calais…'

'Gibraltar…'

'Transatlantic…'

I looked at valiant little *Frejalily* with the moss around her windows and burst out laughing.

Daniel hugged me closer. 'Give us a kiss,' he said.

And I obliged.

Slowly.

Sweetly.

And we sat together and watched the sun go down.

–

Daniel braked as a white van pulled in front of us. I was back on the M40 and heading into the unknown.

That last boat trip seemed a lifetime ago.

Another family.

Another couple.

Another us.

Chapter Two

The meeting took place in a shabby Georgian building in a scrappy part of Aylesbury.

We were shepherded along a warren of tatty corridors and into a utilitarian room with a one-way mirror. It reminded me of work, except there I was the one doing the interviewing, the one in control. A psychiatrist called Grant with a bald head, a bushy red beard and a soft voice greeted us and launched straight into questions. 'Does your son overreact to situations?' 'Does he find it difficult to interact with other children?' 'Does he avoid eye contact?' Whatever happened to not leading the witness? I was tempted to say that if *I* asked such closed questions in *my* interviews, I'd be sacked and quite rightly too, but a lady called Maggie with a long, dark plait and a nose-piercing was taking notes and I was afraid it might count against us.

Jack didn't stand a chance.

Then Grant moved on to an exercise. A test in all but name. It was all a test at the end of the day, wasn't it? Judging us, judging our son. Grant read out groups of words and Jack had to say what linked them.

'Apple, orange, banana?'

'Fruits,' said Jack cheerfully. He liked games like this.

'T-shirt, trousers, jumper?'

'Clothes.'

This was better.

'Nose, eyes, foot?'

'Parts of the body.'

'Fingerprint, signature, face?'

6

Whoa...

'Don't know,' said Jack with a frown. He hated getting caught out.

'Not to worry,' Grant said cheerfully, getting to his feet. 'It's identity. A tough one.'

Daniel and I exchanged a grimace.

Grant returned with a piece of paper.

'Have a look at this,' he said, putting it on the table in front of Jack. It was a black and white picture; the kind you get in a child's colouring book. In the background, rolling fields and a sky full of birds and, in the foreground, a little girl pushing a baby in a pram at the top of a steep hill. Look a little closer and the girl had let go of the pram.

'So, Jack, what's going on here?' asked Grant.

Jack looked at the picture and then gave Grant a fleeting glance. 'How d'you mean?' he asked.

Come on, Jack, I urged. The pram might roll away and the baby might get hurt. The pram might roll away. The baby might get hurt. Come *on*, my beautiful boy. You can do this.

'Say what you see, Jack,' Grant said encouragingly. 'No right or wrong answers.'

Of course there was a bloody right and wrong answer.

Jack scratched his head. 'There are three tractors and one is bigger than the others,' he said.

The tractors were microscopic. Seriously, I could hardly make them out without my glasses; I'd thought they were smudges or hedgerows or something. *That's* how small they were.

But Jack loved tractors. They were one of his 'things'.

It wasn't fair.

Maggie asked Jack to show her his iPad game and Daniel and I were ushered into a little meeting room with Grant. Grant put his hands into a steeple and I almost expected him to pull on a black cap.

'Jack meets the criteria for an autism spectrum disorder diagnosis,' he said.

And that was that.

It wasn't even noon.

—

Grant left us alone and Daniel and I stumbled to our feet and into each other's arms. I was crying, I realised. So was Daniel.

Daniel never cried.

'I think I already knew,' he said.

'I think I've *always* known.'

We looked into each other's eyes, defences down.

'Oh, Dan,' I whispered, scratching my scar. 'I don't want Jack to have Asperger's.'

I didn't want history to repeat itself.

For the family genetics to play out in exactly the same way.

I didn't want Jack to become another Teddy.

There. I'd said it.

Thought it.

Daniel stroked my hair. 'I love you,' he said.

'I will always love you.'

'I know you're upset,' said Daniel, 'but try to keep it together for Jack.'

Words and tears and heartbreak and love.

—

'I've got Asperger's,' Jack announced cheerfully, ten minutes later.

'You have,' replied Daniel, jollity personified. It was like they were discussing a Wycombe goal. 'It's OK. It's... great, in fact.'

'Is it great enough to get a McDonald's on the way home?'

8

McDonald's was packed.

Daniel and Jack grabbed a table, leaving me to queue up.

'Having a good day?' asked the cheery cashier when it was finally my turn. Her golden curls were tumbling out of her cap and she didn't look much older than Freddie.

'Lovely, thank you,' I replied. As you do. I mean, how much worse did my day have to get before I said, 'Shite, thank you'?

When I got back to the table, Jack was absorbed in a booklet called *Asperger's and Me*. There was a cartoon of a smiling boy on the front and I took an instantaneous dislike to it. I'd had more than enough of cartoon children for one day.

'Mum, do you know the difference between a meltdown and a tantrum?' said Jack.

'Um, not really,' I said, doling out the Big Macs (no mayo, lettuce or gherkins for Jack).

'Toddlers have tantrums. But *I* have meltdowns. I'm being another me.'

'Right.'

Who knew?

'So, from now on, you mustn't tell me off when I shout. OK?'

'OK.'

I needed to read that leaflet. All the leaflets. I needed to find out how best we could help our lovely boy. I fought the urge to fold Jack into my arms. Not that he would let me. He winced if I ruffled his hair. Flinched if I patted his shoulder.

'I've found a good bit, too,' said Daniel, brandishing a leaflet at me. 'Apparently we need to have lots of Mummy and Daddy time. Meals out, that sort of thing.'

'Sounds good to me,' I said cheerfully. 'We haven't been to the Crown for ages.'

'The *Crown*?' Daniel put his arm round me. 'Come on, Em, you can do better than that.'

'Ha! Silly me,' I said. 'How about Il Cantina?'

'Oh, I think the Manoir aux Quat'Saisons at least.'

I giggled and snuggled against Daniel. It was all going to be OK. We'd get through this, just like we got through everything else. Together...

'Don't forget weekends away,' I said. 'I'm thinking Paris. *Special* Mummy and Daddy time.'

'That's my girl,' said Daniel with a grin. He pulled me closer and kissed me lightly on the lips. 'Special Mummy and Daddy time sounds exactly what the doctor ordered.'

'What's special Mummy and Daddy time?' asked Jack, cramming in a handful of chips.

Daniel and I shared a conspiratorial smile. 'It's just an expression, Jacko,' I said.

Jack grunted.

'Something that will help us beat that statistic,' added Daniel, nuzzling against my neck.

Er...

'What statistic?'

Daniel didn't answer. I felt his arm stiffen against my shoulder.

'What statistic?' I persisted, pulling away to look at him.

'Nothing,' said Daniel. 'Talk about ruining a lovely moment.' He gave an embarrassed little laugh and started singing. 'And then I go and spoil it all by saying something stupid...'

The first chill of unease ran up my spine. 'Tell me, Dan,' I said. 'Please.'

We both glanced at Jack, who had lost interest in the conversation and was fiddling with Dan's iPhone. We turned back to each other.

'OK,' said Daniel. 'But I promise it's nothing. I read somewhere that 80 per cent of marriages with an autistic child break up before the child is sixteen.'

Oh God.

'Was that in these leaflets?' I asked incredulously. Talk about a double whammy. Your child is on the spectrum and…

'No, no. Online somewhere.'

'Where online? What were the sources?'

'I don't know. I shouldn't have mentioned it. It's clearly bollocks.'

And yet he'd stored the information. Mentioned it.

Suddenly his arm wasn't so reassuring. It might not be able to protect us, after all.

Maybe it might not all be all right.

'Can I have a McFlurry?' asked Jack.

It was the same girl behind the counter. Her curls were a health and safety issue this time.

'How's your day so far?' she asked. She smiled at me in a friendly, blank way that showed she clearly didn't remember having served me already.

I couldn't lie again.

I just couldn't.

'It's shite, thanks,' I said. 'My son's on the autism spectrum and my marriage is heading for the skids. Crunchie McFlurry, please.'

'Lovely. Would you like to super-size that?'

I was quiet on the journey home.

I'd thought 'all' I had to worry about was Jack, but that statistic had really rattled me. Eighty per cent of marriages was a shockingly high figure. And the trouble was, you couldn't argue with numbers. The touchy-feely qualitative stuff was all very well for developing hypotheses and providing colour but numbers – especially statistically significant ones – just happened to be the truth. That's what we said at work, anyway.

The numbers *were* the truth.

What chance did Daniel and I have against those odds? Oh sure, we were close. We loved each other to bits. Always had done. But now we *knew*, had that percentage looming over us, it might tempt fate. Make it a foregone conclusion.

I sat in the car, eyes half closed, thoughts freewheeling, out of control. How had it come to this? Not that I'd have changed anything, even for a heartbeat. But it all seemed so *random*. So arbitrary. All those crossroads and sliding doors and seemingly tiny decisions that had brought me here today. What if I'd jumped into the fountain after Roger Whatshisname at the May Ball? Or Mark. Lovely Mark. What if I'd followed him to the States? What if I hadn't insisted on playing the Nineties career-girl card?

What then?

'This has been the best day ever,' announced Jack from the back.

It hadn't been the best day ever.

Because, oh sod it, I'd known. Of course I had. I'd known ever since Jack was a baby. Call it a mother's intuition, call it paranoia, call it whatever you like; I'd known. Even when Daniel and Mum had muttered darkly about post-natal depression, I'd almost hoped it was but knew it wasn't. Something about Jack's eyes. The lack of a guileless baby-stare. The way he'd flick his eyes away from me, as if in pain.

Jack was different.

I'm his mother and of course I'd known.

I just thought we'd got away with it.

Chapter Three

The next day, I was back at work in leafy west London and it was like nothing had ever happened.

I worked in market research, in a small consultancy that specialised in moderating focus groups. My job was interviewing small groups of consumers in a lot of detail using fancy interviewing techniques and psychological exercises. And bloody brilliant it was too. I loved it all: the interviewing, sure, but also the office banter, the camaraderie, the shared moments of triumph or horror. No children Velcroed to me, no unexpected interruptions, no unpredictable meltdowns.

Bliss.

A few days later, I was interviewing a group of empty-nesters in our in-house viewing studio. It was a big, brightly lit room fitted out as a lounge, the only unusual note being the one-way mirror, like the one at Jack's diagnosis. This time, there were lots of executives from a skincare company behind it. They'd be taking notes, eating pizza and, no doubt, commenting unfavourably on the size of my arse. Fortunately, this particular group were readily offering up the sort of pithy bons mots about ageing that would have them drooling. I could moderate it pretty much on automatic pilot.

Then my phone vibrated. I took a sneaky look.

Joyce: Would it be convenient to pop over? Jack very distressed.

Joyce was our childminder. Lily and Jack went to her house every day after school with a bunch of other children. 'Pop' and 'convenient' were not exactly words that sprang to mind while moderating a focus group but I couldn't unsee a text that said 'very distressed'.

It was time for Plan One – an exercise to buy me time to text Joyce back. I always had a Plan Two – often I had a Plan Three too. Today's Plan Two involved flicking through magazines and selecting a picture that described getting older. The women duly shuffled forward and set to work. I pulled my phone onto my lap, shielded behind the discussion guide and texted Joyce.

Emma: What's happening?

Joyce: Jack is hysterical.

What was the betting she didn't mean funny-hysterical?

The respondents had finished their task, so I couldn't reply immediately. I asked them to explain their pictures and the first lady on my right held up a sheet of black paper.

'This is the future when you're old,' she said. 'Just a void.'

She looked as though she might cry and I felt a bit mean. The poor woman had thought she was coming along for a cup of tea and a nice chat about moisturisers and here she was exposing her darkest fears. I smiled sympathetically and, while the next lady was talking, I did a quick mental calculation. Joyce was meant to have the children until 6:30 p.m. but, if I pushed it...

Emma: I can be with you by 5:30

Joyce: I'll do my best until then

I could almost hear the sniff in her voice.

The next picture was a ball and chain. The one after a gorilla with sorrowful brown eyes. Every single respondent had come up with something deep and meaningful. By the end of the group, they were *all* nearly in tears but the clients were ecstatic and I was the hero of the hour.

Phew!

My boss, Belinda, drew me to one side. 'Great projective exercise,' she said. 'Was it inspired, by any chance, by the text you received halfway through the group?'

Texting while moderating was obviously a complete no-no. Belinda – with her efficient white shirt and glossy dark bob – would never contemplate such a thing.

'I just thought it would be useful for the respondents to express themselves indirectly,' I replied demurely.

It wasn't a total lie.

Belinda laughed. 'It was fab, whatever it was. Let's thrash through the findings...'

I took a deep breath. 'Would it be OK if I ducked out? It's an emergency. Jack...'

Belinda hesitated. Then she said, 'Of course. Go. *Go*.'

I scarpered before she could change her mind.

—

For once, the traffic was on my side and I was at Joyce's redbrick semi on the outskirts of Hambley by 5:40 p.m. Lily was doing handstands on the side lawn with another little girl, but there was no sign of Jack. I knocked on the front door and Joyce swung it open immediately. Tall and thickset, she had short dyed-blond hair and today her lipstick was bleeding into little disapproving lines. She barely said a word as she led me to the dining room. Jack was ashen-faced, his eyes rimmed red.

My precious boy.

I crouched beside him and touched his shoulder. I know, I know, not the brightest thing to do when I knew full well he didn't like it. Jack duly shrugged me away and stared up at the ceiling.

'What's up, Jacko?' I asked.

Jack didn't answer.

'There was an altercation in the garden,' said Joyce. 'I haven't got to the bottom of it, but Jack had an almighty tantrum.'

'Meltdown,' I clarified.

15

'Pardon?'

'We prefer to say meltdown.'

Joyce's mouth almost disappeared. 'Whatever it was, it's taken me an hour to calm him down. I can't be having this. In fact, could I have a word?'

I thought we were already having a word, but Joyce obviously meant alone because she led me down the hallway and into the lounge. She didn't offer me a seat.

'I think Jack should stop coming here,' she said, pushing the door closed behind her with a leopard-print mule.

'What?'

I was utterly gobsmacked. Joyce had been looking after Jack for years and this was far from his first meltdown.

Then the penny dropped.

'Is it because of his diagnosis?' I asked.

I was outraged. Scared, too. Was 'it' starting? People starting to behave differently because Jack had a diagnosis. A label.

'It's nothing to do with that,' said Joyce. 'It's due to the fact he can be disruptive. Lily's welcome to stay, of course.'

'*No.*' Suddenly Joyce was the enemy. The future I didn't want to face. The whisper from the past I didn't want to hear. 'It's both or neither.'

—

'What on earth happened?' I asked as I reversed out of Joyce's drive. My heart was going like the clappers and my vision had blurred. Not the best state in which to be driving.

'Nothing,' said Jack, calm as you like.

'He was screaming and screaming,' said Lily with a world-weary air.

'Yes, but I wasn't being me,' said Jack.

From the noise that ensued, I deduced that he'd poked Lily and that she'd whacked him back.

'Stop it!' I said sharply, pulling up at the lights. 'And it *was* you, Jack.'

'It was *another* me,' said Jack. 'And the real me can't remember what happened.'

That was convenient. Turn everyone's life upside down and then claim it was someone else.

Must try it sometime.

'Well, the "other you" has upset Joyce and now she doesn't want you to go there any more.'

Finding a new childminder would be hard. They were in hot demand. Worse, they were all in cahoots with each other. The news of Jack being 'fired' would already be doing the rounds.

'Good,' said Jack. 'I hate Joyce's.'

Anger morphed to a choking guilt. What a terrible mother I'd been, expecting Jack to conform after school as well as during the day. I'd known he hadn't particularly liked going to Joyce's – of course I had – but it had just been one of those things. I needed to work.

I swung the car into our driveway. Home. Seventies, detached, with a low roof and lots of dormer windows. It was far from the smartest in town, and much smaller than the Victorian villas it was sandwiched between, but despite all its faults Jack wanted to be *here* after school, not at someone else's – probably tidier – house. And in all honesty, I wanted him here too. I didn't want strangers judging him, rejecting him. Rejecting *us*.

I wasn't going to farm Jack out.

Not now.

Not any more.

'Right, from now on, you two will only have to go to a childminder twice a week,' I said firmly.

There were cheers from the back seats.

'Promise?' said Jack.

'Promise?' said Lily.

'Promise.'

Somehow.

'Bugger Joyce,' said Daniel later, when we were curled up on the sofa together. 'Maybe I could offer her a bit of how's-yer-father? She'd be powerless before my charm.'

'She'd eat you alive,' I said with a snort of laughter. 'Anyway, her mind was quite made up.'

'Then we'll have to find someone else.'

I poured us each another glass of wine and took a deep breath. 'How would you feel if I went part-time?' I said. 'Worked school hours three days a week?'

I wasn't sure how Daniel would take this. He was the major breadwinner (management at a biotech company – to be honest, I wasn't sure what he actually *did*) but we'd always been a two-income family.

'Please, Daniel,' I persisted into the silence.

If I could make Jack's life easier, something good would come out of his diagnosis.

'Of course,' said Daniel at last – but I couldn't really interpret his tone of voice. 'We'll manage.'

'Thank you, thank you.' I buried my head into his neck. He smelled of washing powder, of shaving foam, of Daniel.

'D'you reckon your work will go for it?'

I thought about it. I thought about how delighted the clients had been today. I thought about how complimentary Belinda had been.

They'd buy it.

They'd be mad not to.

Chapter Four

They were having none of it.

The next morning Belinda explained – in a way I'm sure carefully avoided falling foul of employment law – that it wasn't possible. Hours were long. Turnarounds were tight.

Part-time didn't work.

It was full-time or not at all.

I knew all that. Rationally at least. I'd just thought they'd make an exception for me.

Daniel was sanguine. 'Hint you might resign,' he said. 'Call their bluff.'

So, the very next morning, it was handbags at dawn.

I knew it was going to be tough when Belinda brought along Penny from HR. Actually, Penny *was* HR. She was Finance Director too and she'd never taken kindly to my expenses being late…

Belinda and Penny put their lattes down. They'd both gone for extra-large and their cups loomed over mine. Belinda always went for medium. *Always*. They'd obviously planned it.

Bugger.

Belinda smiled sympathetically at me and opened a packet of M&Ms. A real chocoholic, she was *always* opening packets of M&Ms. 'I'm so sorry we can't meet your request to go part-time,' she said.

'But *why* can't you?' I blurted out.

Stay calm, Emma. Stay cool.

'*None* of our researchers work part-time,' said Penny. Her little round glasses magnified her eyes and I found it difficult to meet her gaze. 'It's nothing personal.'

It *felt* personal. Really personal. Damn them both for making this difficult. I put my coffee cup on top of an upturned glass for a bit of height superiority and sat up as straight as I could.

'If you can't offer me a part-time position, I'm afraid I'm going to have to resign,' I said.

That should do it!

Penny and Belinda exchanged a glance.

'If I was in your shoes, I'd do exactly the same thing,' said Belinda.

Huh?

'You would?'

'Absolutely,' said Penny. 'You've got to put your children first, haven't you?'

Penny didn't *have* any children.

'Do you *want* me to leave?' I asked. I was totally perplexed.

'Of course not,' said Penny. 'You're one of our best researchers.'

'So how do you feel about... this then?' I said.

That was a great question. Open, neutral, non-judgemental. Hopefully it would make them realise how silly they were being.

But Belinda just laughed. 'You're forgetting I know all the tricks of the trade,' she said. 'Next you'll be asking me what type of plant your job is!'

'No, I won't.'

'Well, I think it's a vine that's choking you,' said Belinda. 'You're finding it difficult to commit...'

'No, I'm not.'

'You had to leave the skincare groups early...'

'What?' I spluttered. 'Everyone was really pleased with those groups. And my son was being diagnosed with autism!'

Oh God. More evidence 'it' was starting?

Penny put her hands into a steeple. 'As you're resigning, there's no redundancy as such. But, as a goodwill gesture, we'll give you three months' pay. And, obviously, should your circumstances change, you're always free to come back to us. How does that sound?'

I didn't know.

I had a horrible feeling I'd been outmanoeuvred but I wasn't quite sure how. Did I *want* to leave? I didn't. Not altogether. But I'd promised Jack I'd go part-time and if they weren't going to budge…

My coffee cup wobbled and fell off its plinth, the liquid skidding and pooling across the polished surface.

Messy.

Out of control.

My life.

I left soon afterwards. I had a couple of projects to finish off, but – for now – there wasn't much else to say. As I drove home along the M4, my mood lifted. A real first-day-of-the-summer-holiday exhilaration. A fresh start.

I was free!

On a whim, I turned off the motorway at Maidenhead. I'd tell Daniel face to face. I hated the phone anyway. I pulled into the car park of his sleek glass and steel office block and texted my arrival.

I'd barely got through the revolving doors when the lift doors opened and Daniel came striding across the lobby.

'What on earth's going on, Em?' he snapped, voice staccato with anxiety. 'The kids?'

'All fine.' Had this been a mistake? 'Coffee?'

'Coffee? Jeez, Em. I'm *working*.'

Yup. Definite mistake.

'Well, d'you want the good news or the good news?'

'Please don't play games.' Daniel ran a hand through his hair and left it standing on end. It looked quite cute.

'Sorry. Well, the first good news is that I've got three months' pay-off.'

Daniel paused. 'And I presume the other "good" news is that you've handed in your notice?' he said.

'Yep.'

There was a silence. The kind of silence that made me curl my toes in my kitten heels.

Finally, Daniel said, 'Christ, I need that coffee.' He shepherded me over to the cafe in the corner of the lobby. 'Latte?'

'Please,' I said. 'And biscuits.'

I was obviously going to need them.

By the time Daniel got back, I was on the attack. 'We *discussed* this,' I said. 'You *said* to tell them I'd resign.'

Daniel sighed. 'I said to hint at it,' he said.

Hmmm. Maybe I *had* been lighter on the hinting than I'd planned.

Maybe I'd actually bypassed the hinting part altogether.

'They weren't going to budge. But I'll make it work. I'll walk everywhere. I'll buy the value brands...'

Daniel almost smiled. 'The money's one thing,' he said. 'The other is if you can hack it.'

'Hack it?' I took a large bite of shortbread.

I was a good mum. A *great* one...

'You like work,' said Daniel. 'You were desperate to go back after maternity leave.'

An attractive blonde in a tight pencil skirt minced over. 'Ready for the clients, Dan?' she said in a husky, mid-Atlantic drawl. She leant over and patted down Daniel's unruly hair. 'That's better,' she said with a laugh. Then she turned to me. 'I don't think we've met?'

'This is my wife, Emma,' said Daniel. 'Emma, this is Nicole.'

Nicole had the grace to flush.

'Nice to meet you,' we said at the same time.

'Just give me ten, Nicky,' said Daniel 'And then I'm all yours.'

'Sure thing,' said Nicole. She winked at me, patted the side of her mouth and sashayed off toward the lifts.

I turned to Daniel. 'Have I got crumbs round my mouth?' I demanded.

Daniel glanced at me. 'A few,' he said.

'Fantastic!'

Just fantastic.

What had *that* been all about?

And nothing in Daniel's manner had been remotely flirtatious but Nicole was definitely interested in *him*. I couldn't blame her. Daniel was a good-looking bloke by anyone's standards: dirty-blond hair, high cheekbones, sexy, slanted green eyes. Sometimes I wondered how I'd snagged him. Then, of course, he'd be an arse and I'd tell myself that he was lucky to have *me*…

But, hang on.

Maybe I *should* be worried.

Maybe I should be on my toes.

Maybe it was The Statistic in action and this was how 'it' started.

No.

Stop it Emma. Don't be daft.

Daniel won't have given The Statistic another thought.

Daniel stood up. 'I'd better be getting on,' he said. We walked to the revolving doors and he gave a perfunctory kiss on the cheek. 'Just remember we're meant to be pulling *together*, Em.'

Oh!

'What's that supposed to mean?'

A warning? A prediction? An omen?

'Nothing,' said Daniel. 'It just is.'

I went through the doors and turned round.

Daniel had already disappeared.

Chapter Five

You'd have thought it would be easy, wouldn't you? That, a couple of weeks in, the photos would be in albums, the light outside the front door would work and I'd be the proud owner of a washboard stomach. But it wasn't quite like that. I was seriously out of practice at being a full-time mum and it was wonderful and boring and stressful and complicated all at the same time. And nothing had changed since Jack's diagnosis. We were apparently in various 'systems' for Jack to get help at home and at school, but nothing had actually happened. It probably wouldn't happen for months.

Take the school playground, for example.

In many ways I loved the school run. It was the anchor in my otherwise unstructured day and I'd probably have turned up even if both kids were off sick. But Jack could be tricky. Really tricky. He came out of school like a coiled spring and any false move meant we'd be on a one-way ticket to Meltdown Central. It hadn't happened yet but, for some reason, this petrified me more than anything.

Anyway, about two weeks after his diagnosis, Jack ran up to me after school and thrust his book-bag into my hands. Then he pulled my face down so that our eyes were level.

'Can Luke come to ours tomorrow?' he demanded. 'Can he? *Can* he?'

I hesitated. Jack had been chewing his polo shirt; the top button was cracked and the surrounding material was slick with saliva. If he was this stressed anything could happen. The trouble was my car was booked in for its MOT the next day. It was an engineering certainty that it would fail and we'd have to walk home across several busy roads and if Jack decided to—

'*Can* he, Mum?'

Right. Plan One…

There was a tap on my shoulder. It was Sian, uber-mum and chair of the PTA.

'Did you get the letter about the meeting tonight?' she asked crisply.

Jack ignored her and put his hands on my face again. 'Can. Luke. Come. Round?' he demanded.

Oh God.

Which was worse? Pissing off the chair of the PTA or dealing with a Jack in meltdown?

No contest…

But Sian had turned to Jack now. 'I just need to have a quick word with Mum,' she said with a tight smile.

Jack drew himself up to his full height. '*I* was talking first,' he said. He didn't bother smiling. 'Don't you know that it's very rude to interrupt?'

Sian's eyes widened. Her daughter Abbie's hand shot to her mouth in shocked surprise. Abbie's shirt was, of course, bone-dry, the button intact. Her sleeves even had neat creases in them.

Oh God, oh God…

My mouth opened by itself. 'Of *course* Luke can come round tomorrow,' I said.

Maybe my car would pass its MOT. Maybe pigs might fly.

Jack gave a fist-pump and ran off without a backward glance.

I turned to Sian. If she gave me a parenting lecture, I'd run off without a backward glance too.

'Sorry about that,' I said. 'What letter? What meeting?'

'Special needs,' said Sian. Neither of us smiled at the irony. She pulled a piece of paper out of her blue folder and handed it to me. 'Do come. I'm sure you'll find it helpful.'

And they were off, Abbie glancing over her shoulder as they walked away.

'What a cow!' said a voice behind me.

I turned round in relief. It was my best friend Ness, all cascading brunette curls and killer curves. We'd been friends ever since Freddie and her daughter Bethany started school together and one of the very best things about leaving work was getting to spend more time with her.

'Oh *God*,' I said. 'Did you hear what Jack just said?'

Ness gave an unladylike snort of laughter. 'I love Jack,' she said. 'And he was right. Sian *did* interrupt.'

'I know. But...' A thought occurred to me. 'D'you think they've arranged the meeting *because* of Jack? Maybe everyone's been holding their breath, waiting for him to be diagnosed.'

'Don't be so paranoid,' said Ness, giving me a little shove. We rounded up our children and started to make our way toward the gate. 'Anyway, you get a night out. I could do with one of those.'

Five years ago, Ness had had a surprise son, Noah. Shortly afterwards her husband, Bastard, had buggered off with a woman who didn't even have the decency to be ten years younger.

Ness was in dire need of a social life. So was I, for that matter.

'Yeah, but not talking about other people's problem children,' I said.

It was more than that.

Jack's diagnosis was still too raw. I didn't want us becoming defined by his Asperger's; '*you know, the ones with the little autistic boy*'.

There was so much more to him – to all of us – than that.

Once home, I pottered around our kitchen-cum-playroom making a casserole from a Waitrose recipe card hoping that crème fraiche past its sell-by date would do a similar job to sour cream. Jack and Lily were playing harmoniously. With the lights on against the grey evening, I imagined we looked quite the perfect family – two children lolling on the rug together and Mum fixing the tea.

That wouldn't have happened if I was still at work.

Our mythical observer would see a teenager in football kit pad into the kitchen and head for the fridge. They would note that, while said teenager dodged out of Mum's reach when she tried to kiss him, he did so with a smile.

'Good day?' I asked.

'Awesome.' Freddie poured himself a pint of orange juice and downed it in one. 'I've been chosen for the A team.'

'Freddie, that's wonderful!' My second attempt at landing a kiss also failed.

'Come and watch on Saturday.'

Lily stood up and wrapped her arms round her big brother. 'Can I come too?' she asked.

'Nope. No flowers,' replied Freddie with a grin.

Lily pouted. 'Not even one tiny Lily?'

'Absolutely no Lilys, Roses, Tulips or Poppys.'

Jack looked up. 'Tulip's not even a girl's name,' he said.

–

After supper, Freddie went upstairs to do his homework and Lily and Jack carried on playing. I chucked things into the dishwasher, trying not to think of work. I missed it. And Belinda would be missing me too. Maybe I should message her. No sooner had I had that thought than I grabbed my laptop and settled into the battered leather armchair. Belinda was online. I knew she would be.

Emma: Resist the M&Ms in the interviewing room!

No reply. I pressed 'refresh' a couple of times. Still nothing. I began to feel miffed – I could *see* she was online.

Then a new message arrived.

You'll never guess what the blighter's done now!

It was Mark. My ex. We mixed in the same work circles and were still on friendly terms. Occasionally we'd ping each other with amusing or horrific anecdotes. Mark's tales were usually so outlandish that I suspected they were only loosely based on the truth.

> **Emma:** Go on

Just a heads-up: it was usually to do with sex.

> **Mark:** Lucia caught the missus giving me a blow job. Told us it wasn't the right way to do 'sexual intercourse' :-o!

Ha!

Lucia was Mark's ten-year-old daughter and, no matter what she'd been taught in her sex education classes at school, there was no way she'd have actually said that. Mark was just clearly playing it for laughs.

I was about to reply with something equally outrageous when I paused. Should I be indulging in such banter with another woman's husband? What about The Statistic? Then I laughed at myself and started typing. It was only Mark…

> **Emma:** *Splutters with laughter* I bet Mr Small made a very quick appearance

I liked that. It was quite witty.

> **Mark:** Yep. Right pisser, especially as it's only an annual occurrence! How's the wacky world of the unemployed?
>
> **Emma:** Not sure I'm cut out to be a domestic goddess

28

Mark: Oh, I don't know. I can just see you in pearls and stirring a porcini risotto

Emma: Stop it!

Mark: I didn't say or imply only pearls

Emma: You didn't have to. How are things with you?

Mark had gone for empire-building and now owned a medium-sized market research agency.

Mark: My new project involves looking at the impact of financial legislation changes on catalogue shoppers... says it all really!

Emma: You must have done something very bad in a former life to get that...

'It's the Grindstone Cowboy!'

Daniel had arrived home. I hadn't heard his car and I slammed the laptop shut just as he came into the kitchen. Not that I was doing anything wrong...

Daniel gave me a kiss. 'All OK?' he asked.

'Fine, thanks.'

Lily give Daniel a hug. 'Guess what, Daddy?' she said.

'What, flower?'

'Jack told Dylan Briggs that he's a bastard!'

Wham! As soon as Daniel was through the front door.

'Thanks, Lily.'

Daniel raised an eyebrow at me. 'Did you know about this?' he asked.

I shook my head. 'Nope.' I'd never heard of Dylan Briggs.

Daniel turned to Jack. 'Is this true?' he demanded.

'Yes,' said Jack, matter-of-factly. 'Dylan *is* a bastard. He hasn't got a dad.'

I fought a deeply inappropriate desire to giggle. And failed.

'Give me strength,' muttered Daniel. 'That was really naughty of you, Jack.' He opened the fridge and grabbed a beer. 'How long have these two been on electronics anyway?'

'It's fine, Dan. They're cooperating really nicely.'

'Yes, I've transferred Lily's *Wizard World* account from the DS to the Wii,' said Jack. This from the boy who couldn't yet tie his own shoelaces. 'So, now I can use your portals, Lily.'

'No, you can't,' said Lily.

'I'll just delete your account then.'

'*No.*' Lily kicked out in Jack's general direction and he lunged at her, hitting her on her arm. Cue loud sobbing and clutching of slightly reddened limb.

Calm to nuclear in two seconds flat. Familiar territory.

'Yes, cooperating *really* nicely,' said Daniel. 'Right, electronics ban for the rest of the day.'

Jack scrambled to his feet and stood in front of his father, no regard for personal space. 'It's not *fair*,' he shouted. 'Lily started it.'

'You were both as bad as each other.'

'Then you're an idiot!'

'How dare you. No electronics tomorrow as well.'

'What about Lily?' Jack was shouting now, the veins on his neck bulging.

'You're the one who's answering me back.'

'You're answering me back too! I hate you.'

And Jack thumped upstairs.

Dan gulped down the rest of his beer. 'Shit. Can't I *ever* come home to a quiet house?' he muttered.

I thought about biting my tongue. I really did.

'It *was* a quiet house before you got home,' I said, 'and now our son's upstairs having a meltdown.'

'Jack's been insulting half of Buckinghamshire and you were on bloody Facebook...'

Freddie appeared at the door. 'How can I do my homework when everyone's screaming?' he demanded.

Statistic or not, I'd had enough. It was really hard being at home with the kids and trying to keep everything calm and then Daniel came home and just *ruined* it all...

'I'm out of here,' I said.

Everyone stared at me.

'Where are you going?' Daniel asked.

I considered the gym. I considered a run.

Nope.

It was going to have to be the Special Needs meeting after all.

Chapter Six

I regretted my decision straight away.

The meeting was in an anteroom near the back of the church. St John's was a C of E school and *lots* of meetings took place in the church. A rubbish decision in my view; it was chilly even though the electric heaters suspended from the ceiling were glowing gamely and it was gloomy despite the harsh strip lighting. Worst of all, the only drink on offer was an industrial-sized tin of own-label coffee next to a belching water urn.

It all felt like a rebuke for daring to have a child with special needs.

There were about a dozen women there and they all seemed relaxed and cheerful. No one looked like they were comparing this to cocktails in London or even wine in the pub. Maybe this was as good as it got when you were a stay-at-home mum to a son with Asperger's. Maybe this was the highlight of the day, the week, the month. Maybe one day I would look back and say wistfully, 'Remember that wonderful meeting in the church.'

I was tempted to slink back home but several acquaintances were smiling at me. I smiled back weakly and sat down. The plastic chairs were obviously designed for people who went to at least three Zumba classes a week and I confess there was a tad of overspill on either side.

This was grim.

Then a woman with one-toned copper hair and a heavily zipped biker jacket dropped heavily into the chair next to me. She had wide, hazel eyes, a heart-shaped face and, like me, she was wearing jeans and Ugg-style boots and clutching her mobile phone like a toddler's comfort blanket. Unlike me, she had a large butterfly tattoo on the inside of her wrist.

'Are you Jack Healey's mum?' she asked without preamble.

'Yes?'

'Thought so. You look really alike. Anyway. I thought you'd like to know your son called mine a bastard the other day.'

Oh God. Dylan Briggs' mum. Could this evening get any worse?

What to do?

Plan One: apologise.

Actually, that was the *only* realistic option.

'I'm so sorry...' I duly began.

A warm gurgle of laughter escaped from Dylan's mum's burgundy mouth. 'Don't worry about it, mate,' she said. 'Asperger's?'

'Yup.' I smiled at her.

'Thought so. I've got one of my own at home. I'm Mandy by the way.'

'Emma.'

We headed over to the coffee urn. As we waited our turn, I discovered Dylan was an only child in the school year between Jack and Lily. They'd moved to Hambley three months ago after Mandy had split with Dylan's dad. Mandy was a receptionist at the doctor's surgery and had started dating a guy who did marketing for Wycombe Wanderers. Freddie and Jack would like that. They loved Wycombe Wanderers even though Jack had spent at least a year thinking they were called Wycombe-Wanderers-Nil.

Anyway, thank goodness for my interviewing skills. They made small talk much easier.

'Have you heard of The Statistic?' I said, when she'd finished talking.

I had to ask.

'What statistic, mate?' Mandy looked a bit nonplussed.

'The one that says eighty percent of marriages with an autistic child break down.'

Was that a weird thing to be asking?

'Oh, that one,' said Mandy. 'Yeah – did for me and Dylan's dad. Not that we was actually married.'

Wonderful. Absolutely bloody wonderful.

Mr Berry, the headmaster, arrived. He was accompanied by a woman I didn't recognise. Tall and willowy, she had glossy brown tresses straight out of a Pantene ad and an exquisitely pretty face. She was wearing a petrol-blue dress cinched in at the waist and a superior smile. An old country song sprang, unbidden, into my mind; one that talked about taking an instant and irrational dislike to someone based on absolutely nothing. I pushed the thought away, appalled by my shallowness. I wasn't usually that nasty.

'Who's the milkmaid?' Mandy suddenly whispered.

'I don't know,' I replied, stifling a giggle.

Maybe Mandy was battling similar thoughts about the newcomer herself.

Mr Berry called for silence. 'Thanks for coming, everyone,' he said. 'Virginia Kennedy suggested this meeting,' he added, nodding at the milkmaid. It would be Virginia, I thought; not Ginny or some other diminutive. *Virginia*. 'I think a group for parents of children with special educational needs is an excellent idea.'

There was general murmuring of approval and then Mr Berry invited us to introduce ourselves.

Mandy went first. 'Dylan's nine,' she said. 'He started having problems last year. I was quite relieved it wasn't just him being a little bugger and me being a crap mum.'

We all laughed easily together and it broke the ice.

My turn. Frankly, it was a touch scary. It's one thing talking to a boardroom of people, but quite different when it's so up close and personal. I could feel my neck and chest growing hot as I stood up.

'Hello,' I said. 'Jack's in Year Six and he's just been diagnosed with Asperger's.'

I wasn't sure what else to say. They probably all knew already. They were probably wondering why we'd taken so long to get a diagnosis.

A latecomer walked in; a dad this time. He was boyish looking, a little scruffy, pretty gorgeous. Nodding a 'sorry' to Mr Berry, he crossed the room. Then he clocked Virginia and did an almost cartoonish double take. His subsequent attempt to look disinterested was such an utter failure I couldn't help smirking. He caught my eye and, interpreting my smirk correctly, grinned self-deprecatingly. He had a lovely smile that creased up his face and I felt a little ripple of interest.

Virginia's turn. When she stood up, I could see that she wasn't actually that tall, but she had that effortless good posture that makes you look as if you are. And God, she was *so* pretty: neat little upturned nose, huge brown eyes, wide sensuous mouth. A Rachel Weisz sort of vibe.

'Hello,' she said with quiet confidence. 'We've moved here from Clapham. My son Joshua is seven and has mild autism. As soon as we realised it was a possibility, we enrolled onto the Early Bird Programme...'

As she carried on speaking, I felt my hackles rising. Daniel and I had spent months kidding ourselves Jack was just a late developer and I'd spent that time gorging myself to a fifteen-pound weight gain. Virginia had obviously not only been proactive about the whole Asperger's thing but had kept to a sensible, calorie-controlled diet all the while.

It wasn't fair.

The introductions continued; children with dyslexia and others with generic learning difficulties. Then the late-arriving dad stood up. I took in his comfortable faded jeans and soft, navy pullover. He had thick, wavy mid-brown hair with a hint of grey at the temples and that smiling, curving mouth. My kind of sexy, boy-next-door looks to a T. I could almost hear

The Statistic sniggering. Ha, I sniggered back. If you think a handsome stranger is all it will take…

'Hi, I'm Paul Archer,' said Cutie. 'We've just moved here from London too. We must compare notes some time, Virginia.'

Yup.

He definitely fancied her.

'I feel like an imposter,' Paul continued. 'I'm the only dad here and Gabriel hasn't actually been diagnosed with anything. I think he may be on the spectrum but I'm not really sure where to start.'

I felt a surge of empathy that had nothing to do with soft jumpers and sexy mouths. Virginia obviously felt the same, because she leant forward and touched him gently on the arm. The little minx.

Introductions over, the meeting moved on to discuss one-to-one help in the classroom. Jack didn't need any, so I zoned out and started to feel guilty about stropping out earlier. It had been pretty unforgiveable to dump the kids on Daniel after a hard day at work and with no word of warning, even if he had been being pretty unreasonable.

'Well, that was pretty dull,' said Mandy when the meeting was over and Mr Berry had left.

'It was,' I agreed. 'About as relevant to my life as bird-watching.'

Paul had come to join us. 'Not a twitcher, then?' he asked.

'Only when I'm really bored,' I said. 'I twitch a lot then.'

Paul's smile widened. He really was very cute.

'Can I catch you Aspie parents before you go?' Virginia asked, joining our group and giving her hair the Pantene swish. 'Joshua only really needs help in the playground and I was wondering if we should try to set a Lunch Club for our kids. Somewhere they can escape to when it all gets too much.'

'Great idea,' said Mandy.

'Absolutely,' I agreed.

In fact, it was an *excellent* idea. It was the playground where things always went tits-up for Jack. If there'd been a Lunch

Club equivalent at Joyce's, maybe Jack wouldn't have got into an altercation.

'Fab,' said Virginia. 'What about you, Paul?'

'Count me in,' said Paul. 'The playground's the place Gabriel comes unstuck too.'

'Great,' said Virginia. 'I'll try to catch Mr Berry tomorrow.' She touched my sleeve. 'By the way, I love your top, Emma.'

'Thank you.' I'd been wrong about her. She was lovely. I must learn not to jump to instantaneous judgements about people—

Virginia smiled at me. 'When's your baby due?' she asked.

I arrived home thoroughly confused.

On one hand, I was spoiling for a fight and there were certainly grounds for one. The kitchen was still a tip and Matt the Mog was on the table scavenging the remains of the casserole. Daniel had his hip wedged against the kitchen island; head down, he was absorbed in his bloody phone and oblivious to the chaos around him.

On the other hand, I really shouldn't have walked out earlier. And I certainly shouldn't have been having flirtatious thoughts about a handsome stranger. Maybe we were evens.

'Hey,' I said tentatively.

Nothing.

I don't think Daniel had really registered my arrival.

'Hi, Dan,' I said, more loudly.

Dan raised his head a centimetre. 'What? Sorry, the shit's hitting the fan at work.'

Daniel's head office was in Texas, which meant the action often kicked off in the evening. But was that really any excuse for ignoring me?

I'd been about to say *sorry*.

'Are the kids asleep?' I asked instead.

'Not sure.'

I stomped upstairs. In the interests of honesty, I should admit I scoffed three chocolate digestives on the way up. Because I was outraged. *Outraged!* I might have stopped work, but did that really give Daniel carte blanche to bow out from having anything to do with the house or the family? Honestly, I might as well be a single parent, sometimes!

And, more to the point…

Pregnant indeed!

—

None of the children were asleep.

Lily was at least in bed. 'I stayed awake for you,' she said. 'Are you still cross?'

'Cross?' Oh God. I'd completely overlooked how my storming out might have affected Lily. 'No, I'm fine, flower. Sorry about earlier.'

'OK. Something worrying has happened. Hellie's invited me round tomorrow.'

Helena was Lily's BFF. She was also Jack's friend Luke's sister. The same Luke who Jack had coming round to play the next day. No doubt their mother Caroline had planned this double play-date on purpose.

'Why's that worrying?' I asked. It seemed jolly sensible to me.

'She's invited a new girl too and I'm worried they'll go off together.'

I looked at Lily's earnest little face and her squidgy little cheeks and my heart swelled with tenderness. I hugged her to me fiercely.

'They won't. Who couldn't love you?' My precious flower.

I tucked her into bed and sat with her for a while and then went in search of Jack. I found him slumped in front of the computer in the office: a grand title given it also masqueraded as the guest bedroom and (when it couldn't be avoided any longer) the ironing room. Did Daniel know Jack was flouting his electronics ban? Did Daniel care?

'Hey, Jacko. Off the computer please.'

'Oh, *Muuuum*. I'm on *Wizard World*. Come and watch.'

Wizard World was Jack's current obsession – a fantasy medieval world with monsters to defeat and quests to complete. I liked to kid myself it was helping Jack's social skills. Frankly, I quite fancied playing it myself.

A few minutes' bonding wouldn't hurt, even at this time of night. I pulled the piano stool up to the computer and put my arm round Jack, nuzzling my face into his hair.

My beautiful boy.

Jack's avatar was fighting with a purple wizard. 'Who's that?' I asked, gesticulating with my spare hand.

'Dragon-Slayer.' Jack wriggled away from my grasp. 'He's pretty advanced.'

'No, I mean in real life. Do you know him?' Or was my ten-year-old being groomed by an online perv? Bad mother, bad mother.

'It's Jamie Kennedy. From my class.'

Kennedy. Virginia's son?

'Does he have a brother called Joshua?'

'Dunno. He's new. He has a little brother with a dark blue coat.'

Interesting. Virginia had a son in Jack's school year. It was somehow reassuring that he was also online at 10 p.m. on a school night.

Jack was typing.

My mum is watching ATM. Invasion of da mum!

The reply came back quickly.

Dis is a mum-free zone. I have 2 go. Cya 2moro.

39

Jack didn't return the goodbye. He just carried on playing. I decided to bounce the Lunch Club idea off him while he was a captive audience.

'I've been to a meeting in the church,' I started.

'Why? Were you praying?' Jack's eyes didn't leave the screen.

'No.' Sigh. 'It's just where the meeting was.'

'Why was it there?'

'It doesn't matter where it was.'

'So, how come the first thing you said was that it was in the church, then?'

Jack gave me fleeting eye contact, along with an expression suggesting I was a couple of sandwiches short of a picnic.

'Let it go, Jack!'

He understood my tone of voice all too well that time.

'What did you want to tell me about?' he asked.

Through slightly gritted teeth, I outlined our plans for the Lunch Club.

Jack didn't answer immediately. 'OK,' he said finally, as if he was doing me a huge favour. 'But we have to be able to have our lunch there. I find it really stressy when people watch me eating.'

Really? Jack had recently started nagging me to eat his meals in the lounge but I'd put it down to the lure of *The Simpsons* rather than an Aspie trait.

Jack was still talking. 'And we don't have to do any work if we don't want to, even if it's "socialisation skills".' He used a silly voice for the last two words and held up his fingers in mock quotation marks.

'But apart from that?'

'Sick. I'm fed up with Alex Field being a dick in the playground.'

I took that as a positive.

Once I'd packed Jack off to bed, I closeted myself in the en suite. Stripping down to my undies, I surveyed myself side on in the mirror. Slim-ish hips, even when carrying excess weight.

Long legs, and full breasts that could probably still pass the magic marker – if not the pencil – test. Between the two it did go a bit belly-up. Actually, it went a tiny bit belly-down; any further and my tummy would soon be facing its own pencil test. My midriff had never been my best feature, even before kids, and it was certainly a little rounder than it used to be.

But did I really look *pregnant*?

That night, I couldn't sleep.

After all our years together, I was used to the peaks and troughs of married life but this seemed different. Daniel and I had barely spoken before we went to bed and now there was a careful gap between us. And why was it tonight – of all nights – that I'd met the first man I'd fancied in ages? Coincidence? Or maybe it was inevitable. Maybe that was how The Statistic worked?

Stop it, Emma!

This is Daniel you're talking about.

The lovely boy you've known since you were eighteen.

Yin to your yang.

My head was pulsating with the rumblings of a headache. I felt in the bedside drawer for the painkillers, ripped open the paper wrapper and let the tablets plop into my glass of water. Then I lay back, waiting for the tablets to dissolve.

I could remember the dress I'd worn the night I met Daniel as if it was yesterday. It had tiers of turquoise and gold and a wide sash to showcase my still-waspish waist. I'd spent ages blending coordinating tiers of eyeshadow and my lips shimmered in Rimmel's Twilight Teaser. All that effort to go to a Cambridge May Ball with a chap called Roger who had offered to pay the extortionate thirty quid for my ticket. I still have a photo of us somewhere, my arm linked with his and half-smiling at the camera. Nineties fashion aside, I looked heartbreakingly young and lovely, staring at the future with confidence and poise.

I had no idea I was about to meet my future husband.

Roger had got a first in his finals and tradition dictated he be thrown into the fountain in the middle of the quad. I stood to one side and watched proceedings impatiently; after all, I hardly knew the guy and I wanted to party. Roger squelched off to change out of his DJ and I'm ashamed to admit I never made it to our arranged rendezvous. Roger exits stage left; a cameo role.

Sorry, Roger.

Left alone, I headed for the disco and pushed to the centre of the throng. I've always adored dancing and the throbbing music and exuberant atmosphere was sexy and hypnotic. I was really happy to dance on my own but soon I was aware of a gorgeous blond boy in jeans and T-shirt dancing nearby. Had it been a decade later, I might have thought he looked a little like Daniel Craig. As it was, I was just aware of a frisson of excitement and adrenaline as, eyes locking, we danced ever closer. Ridiculously quickly afterwards — we were both very drunk — we were snogging shamelessly on the dance floor before beating a hasty retreat to Daniel's room. Daniel had crashed the ball, hence the non-regulation clothing, and it all seemed very racy; I'd never have dared do such a thing.

Daniel and I were inseparable during those heady, dying days of the academic year. It was a glorious early summer and we squeezed the last drop out of every day. We partied and picnicked and punted, sometimes with my friends, mostly with Daniel's. There were quiet times too, curled up together in Daniel's narrow bed, listening to Bruce Springsteen and letting the world carry on without us.

More than anything, there was an urgent poignancy to our time together. It was like a holiday romance. Daniel was a couple of years older than me and, while I would be returning to Cambridge come October, Daniel was going down for good. I don't think it seriously crossed our minds to try to keep the relationship going. Everyone knew May Week romances didn't last. Better Daniel was going down now. Better than seeing him on a miserable November morning struggling to lectures in a cagoule.

So, we ritually swapped telephone numbers and addresses without any real intention of using them and I went home to Sussex for the summer with the bittersweet broken heart that has you sobbing to sad songs into the small hours.

And that was that.

Chapter Seven

'She asked when your baby was due? No! I hope you decked her one.'

The next day, Ness and I were shuffling along the river, trying to work up the enthusiasm to break into a proper jog. My 'baby' clearly needed the exercise.

It was a beautiful morning; the air was damp and pungent with waterweed and the gentle hills a palette of the palest yellows, browns and greens. Although it was past nine o'clock, there was still a mist hovering low over the silvery water, making ghosts of the rowers on the river.

'Oh Ness, it was awful,' I said, swerving to avoid a rowing coach tearing down the towpath on his bike. 'I was tempted to invent a due date.'

'Please tell me you didn't.'

'I didn't. But only because I couldn't think of one off the top of my head. There was a dad there too. He heard *everything*.'

'Oh no,' said Ness. 'A cute one?'

'A new one. Paul Archer?' I chose not to elaborate on his cuteness factor.

'Oh, yes. Definitely cute. He's got a boy in Noah's class who keeps trying to escape from school. A couple of days ago, he made a break for it with Mrs Hatch in hot pursuit!'

We both collapsed in giggles. Let's just say Mrs Hatch, the reception teacher, wasn't a natural candidate for the hundred metres' dash.

'So, how's domestic bliss?' asked Ness.

I debated whether to tell Ness about The Statistic. I decided against it. The fewer people who knew about it the better. It was less likely to tempt fate.

'Is it terrible to say I'm a little bit bored?' I said instead.

'I'm not surprised,' said Ness 'What you need is a challenge.'

'I have a challenge,' I replied. 'I have a Jack.'

'No, I mean something for *you*,' said Ness. 'Something to put a zing in your step.'

'It'd have to be a cheap challenge,' I said. 'I've got to eke out my pay-off.'

I couldn't even buy a lipstick nowadays without feeling guilty.

'What about a 5k run?' asked Ness. 'I'd join you. I need to do *something*. My arse is the size of Buckinghamshire.'

It wasn't, of course; Ness had a figure that undulated in all the right places. I wasn't quite the ugly friend, but I just had a boring, messy dark blond bob and I'd been piling on weight at an alarming rate since Jack's diagnosis.

'I'll think about it,' I said. 'Can we turn round now?'

'Yes please. My hip's killing me.'

We duly turned and started shuffling back toward Hambley. The jumble of old houses propping up the Norman church looked horribly far away. Ness was running with a limp and, even wearing the obligatory two sports bras, my breasts were doing a workout of their own. It must have been a pretty gruesome sight. Thank goodness for the mist.

Then a slender figure appeared, running gracefully toward us.

'Oh God,' I said, grinding to a halt.

It was Virginia, swinging chestnut hair in a high ponytail. She was breathing heavily and covered in a light sheen of sweat. It would be how she looked after sex, I thought incongruously.

Virginia stopped, putting her hands on the small of her back and arching backward with a grimace. I had a brief vision of doing a quick set of press-ups in return but, as I'd probably need a mobile crane to get upright again, I stayed put.

'Emma. Hi,' said Virginia.

'Hi.' I smiled back. I could be mature about these things.

'I'm glad I've bumped into you. I wanted to apologise for yesterday.'

Oh God.

'Please don't.' What was she planning to say? I thought your spare tyre was a baby?

Virginia sighed. 'OK. But I *am* sorry. Oh, and I'm seeing Mr Berry before pickup. Paul's coming too. Maybe Mandy. Join us?'

Everything about this woman pissed me off. She'd only been at the school five minutes and she was already taking over.

'I'll try,' I said.

'Lovely,' said Virginia. 'By the way, my son's having a party this weekend. Just football and back to ours for lunch. We wondered if Jack would like to come?'

I hesitated. 'This weekend' and 'we' suggested Jack was a late addition to the guest list and at Virginia's behest. It would have surprised parents to know how quickly Jack could suss out sympathy invites and how offended he could be by them. *And* it was a football party. Jack loved football but he wasn't always a popular player because he had no intention of passing the ball to anyone else. Football parties often ended in tears.

And yet I could think of at least four reasons to say 'yes'. Jamie and Jack had been playing *Wizard World* yesterday, so they were clearly friendly. Virginia had an Asperger's child herself, so she'd be understanding if anything went wrong. She might think I was being stroppy if I said no and it was important to keep the moral high ground. And it would, of course, be an excellent opportunity to nose round her home.

The last reason clinched it.

'Lovely,' I said.

'Wonderful.' Virginia tripped off lightly.

'Cow,' said Ness.

I went to the meeting.

Of course I did.

I had nothing better to do.

It seemed no one else did either because, in the end, all four of us were wedged into Mr Berry's tiny office. I noted that Paul had lost none of his boy-next-door charm in the cold light of day. I tried to ignore that fact.

After Pregnancy-Gate, I clearly should have had liposuction. Failing that, I should have wrestled myself into Spanx pants and worn my most waist-creating wrap top. I should have ensured I looked so obviously *not pregnant* that Virginia would realise what a ridiculous faux pas she'd made.

But I hadn't done any of those things. My car had duly failed its MOT, I'd totally run out of time and I'd ended up flinging on the same clothes as yesterday. The ones that had made me look pregnant.

Virginia, perched on a filing cabinet, was unrecognisable from the morning in a tightly belted fuchsia coat, the perfect foil for her blow-dried curls.

Anyway, the good news was that Mr Berry loved the idea of the Lunch Club. Really loved it. The bad news was that the school didn't have the money it would need to get someone in to run it. It looked like the whole idea was a non-starter.

Of course, the likelihood of failure made it suddenly seem really important.

'Could we raise the money ourselves?' asked Virginia.

'Don't forget we'd need to do it *every* year,' said Paul.

'Oh yes.'

Gloom descended.

'I've an idea,' said Mr Berry. 'This is confidential but a couple of senior teachers are retiring soon and it'll free up some funds. If you can find the money to get the scheme up and running this year *and* it proves to be a success, I'll see if the school can take over the funding next year.'

46

We smiled round at each other and, full of renewed enthusiasm, started lobbing fundraising ideas at Mr Berry.

PTA funds? Already commandeered to upgrade the computer system.

Paying for it ourselves? Any initiative needed to be fully inclusive, regardless of ability to contribute.

A school lottery? Gambling was frowned upon in faith schools. The vicar already considered the Pumpkin Party dangerously pagan, so a lottery would be akin to sacrificing virgins at dawn.

'What about a ball?' I suggested. I loved balls. At least, I did when I was thin. All that dressing up and twirling around.

'Brilliant,' said Paul.

'Great idea,' said Mr Berry.

'Excellent,' said Virginia. 'I organised one at my sons' last school, so I know the ropes.'

By the time the school bell rang, it was settled. We were no longer a random set of parents brought together by the unusual wiring of our children's brains.

We were the Lunch Club Committee.

Ball Planners extraordinaire.

A force to be reckoned with.

It felt great to be part of something again. To be on a mission to make things easier for Jack. To *belong*.

There was a spring in my step as we trooped outside.

Luke and Hellie's mum, Caroline, was waiting for me in the playground, a vision in a spotted Boden skirt and high heels, auburn hair in a casual up-do.

'All set for the child swap?' I said cheerfully.

Caroline started fiddling with her chunky necklace. 'I'm afraid Luke won't be coming to yours today,' she said.

'Oh no! Jack's so looking forward to it.'

'I'm sorry,' said Caroline. 'Was it a firm arrangement? I mean, I know the boys had a brief chat about it yesterday but I'm not sure Luke agreed to it. It's still fine for Lily to come and play with Hellie, of course.'

'No!'

Out before I could stop it.

'No?' repeated Caroline with a frown.

'*No.* It's a package deal. If you don't want Jack, you can't have Lily.'

Caroline pursed her lips. 'Suit yourself,' she said and wriggled off to join her cronies. One put her arm round Caroline's shoulders. As if it was Caroline who needed the sympathy...

Deep breaths, Emma.

It doesn't matter.

Only it *did* matter and I minded terribly. For Jack, of course, but also for me. I suddenly felt lonely. Lonely, isolated and very sad. And I couldn't help hoping Caroline would turn up tomorrow with her prissy little skirt tucked into her prissy little white cotton panties.

—

Lily was livid when she found her playdate was cancelled.

'*Please* let me go,' she begged, eyes full of tears.

'I can't, flower. I'm sorry. Luke doesn't want to play with Jack.'

'But Hellie *does* want to play with me!'

'I know. And we can do that another time,' I said. 'In the meantime, there's pizza for tea...'

'I don't care! Hellie's going to go off with Izzie and I won't have anyone to play with.'

Absolutely bloody marvellous.

And here was Jack, running toward me. By the look on his face, he'd already discovered that Luke wasn't coming to play. He so wasn't going to take *that* lying down.

I wasn't wrong.

Well, strictly speaking, I *was* wrong, because Jack absolutely did take it lying down. Prone on the asphalt, the shouting started.

'I want Luke to come. I want Luke to come.'

Over and over again.

It was exactly like a toddler having a tantrum except, at ten years old, Jack was simply too old to get away with it. Instead of indulgent – or, at least, understanding – smiles, people looked horrified. A couple of people shepherded their children away, glancing over their shoulders as they did so. Even Lily slunk away. Not a single person came over to support us. Not one.

It was Sod's law Ness had gone to the physio.

What to do? What on *earth* to do?

I crouched down beside Jack and rested my hand lightly on his shoulder. 'Come on, Jacko. There's pizza and dough balls for tea.'

'No!' Jack rolled onto his side and hit the ground with a fist. 'I want Luke to come.'

'Come *on*, Jack!' My voice high-pitched with stress.

'*No!*'

Oh God.

A wriggling Jack – slight as he was – would be impossible for me to carry. I was running out of options. I stood up, trying to gather myself. This was pants. Absolute *pants*. I loved Jack with all my heart, but I didn't know what to do with him. It didn't matter how many worthy committees I joined, how many fancy balls I helped to organise. Whatever way I tried to dress it up, Jack had autism and I'd seen how that played out once before.

I couldn't stop the inevitable.

———

That summer of '76 was a belter. So many heavy, hazy days you couldn't remember when they'd started and you began to think they'd never end. It was the year my cousin Teddy came to stay for the last

49

time. We had three days together. Things to do. Places to go. The pit to explore.

They'd just knocked down a big old house round the corner from us. Mum said they were going to build a block of flats there – the same as the two I could see from my bedroom window. But for now there was just a big hole in the ground. Teddy loved it. I knew he would. The first day we were having so much fun we didn't bother to go in for lunch. We just ate the squashed-fly biscuits we'd grabbed on the way out. Then Teddy said we should build a den in the lilac bushes. I swept the floor with a handful of leaves while Teddy made a pathway of stones. Each stone had to be exactly the same size so it took ages, but, by the time he'd finished, the whole den was perfect. We lay on the beaten earth and looked out through the tangled boughs and lacy flowers and watched the sun getting bigger and lower until it was balanced on the very edge of the world. Teddy talked about the sun and the moon and about how space worked and I thought I'd never been so happy in my whole life...

Then Dad and Uncle Robert arrived.

We heard them first, calling us. Teddy said not to call back but I did anyway and then we could see their faces through the branches. They both looked very cross. We'd missed lunch and tea and everyone was worried and when we got home there was to be shepherd's pie but no pudding and then we were to go straight to bed.

Teddy wouldn't come out. He just wouldn't move and I didn't know what to do. So the dads came in, pulling the branches aside and messing up the stones, and everything went wrong. The sun started jumping around, and the flowers were sickly sweet and the shouting was so loud I had to put my hands over my ears. Teddy was shouting too and then he started picking up the stones and throwing them at me. Pick. Throw. Pick. Throw. Pain in my head and stickiness on my face and metal in my mouth and suddenly the screaming was coming from me...

By the time my head had been stitched up, Teddy had gone.

I never saw him again.

Oh God.

What a time to be thinking about Teddy.

Here. In the playground.

At my most vulnerable.

And now I was about to cry.

'Emma?'

A man's voice behind me. Just what I needed. Maybe it was Mr Berry about to ask me to remove Jack from the playground. From the school...

I turned around reluctantly, rubbing my Teddy scar, which had begun to itch.

It was Paul.

'I'm taking Gabe to the new trampolining place,' he said. 'We wondered if you guys would like to come along?'

Chapter Eight

I'd barely cried since Jack's diagnosis.

But I cried now. As soon as Paul had issued his invitation, I dissolved into messy, snotty tears and stood there gulping like a fool.

Jack scrambled to his feet and ran over to Paul.

'Do you mean Bounce?' he demanded, running the back of his hand under his nose. 'Has it opened? Can we go?'

Now, you might think that a child already inconsolable because his afternoon plans had changed wouldn't take kindly to those plans potentially changing again. But that would be too easy, wouldn't it? Jack started jumping up and down and pulling on my sleeve. To be fair, he'd been talking about the imminent launch of Bounce for weeks and this obviously kicked cancelled playdates into touch.

Lily came running over to find out what was going on and soon she, too, was spinning around with excitement. So, it really didn't matter what I wanted – and to be honest I didn't really know *what* I wanted.

I was outnumbered.

'We'd love to,' I said, finding my – rather shaky – voice.

I followed Paul across the playground, trying to compose myself, and it wasn't until the kids were clambering into the back of his scruffy silver estate that I began to doubt the wisdom of spending the afternoon with him. For the first time, I properly acknowledged the kernel of raw attraction that had been there ever since I'd first set eyes on him the day before.

I fancied the pants off him.

'You OK?' asked Paul, as I hesitated on the kerb.

'I hardly know you,' I said. 'You might be a mad axeman.'

No, I don't know why, either.

Paul considered me, head on one side. 'Well, yes I might,' he said. 'But equally, *you* might be a mad axe-lady. I wondered why your handbag was so large.'

'Ha!' Almost despite myself, I could feel a smile tugging at the corner of my mouth.

'Anyway,' added Paul. 'Your kids are already in my car. You'd be a very irresponsible mother if you let me drive off with them.'

'Believe me, it's tempting!' I said and Paul rewarded me with a lopsided grin.

I got into the car. So what if I fancied him? It wasn't against the law and it was hardly as if I was going to do anything about it. And it certainly beat walking home with a couple of kids in meltdown.

I took a sneaky look in my phone mirror. Could have been worse. My hair was hardly sleek but it was tousled rather than frizzy. My eyes glittered, my cheeks were flushed and my mascara was smudged, but it wasn't quite the blotchy, puffy-eyed mess I'd feared. Not that it mattered...

'Hellie said Bounce doesn't open until next week,' announced Lily from the back seat.

Now she told us. I glanced at Paul, embarrassed for him, dreading how Jack was going to react.

'Strictly speaking, your daughter is right,' said Paul.

'O-K.'

I should have listened to my instincts. Maybe he really was a mad axeman.

'Today is a preview for the great and the good.'

'Right,' I said. And exhaled deeply.

'What does that mean?' asked Jack.

'It means,' said Paul, 'that for one day only, we are Very Important People.'

'How come?' Jack sounded sceptical.

'Because I *am* very important,' said Paul, grinning into the rear-view mirror.

'No, you're not. You're just a boring dad.'

'Jack!' I exploded. God, he could be so *embarrassing* sometimes—

'It's OK,' said Paul. 'Gabriel would say the same. I'm a writer as well as a boring dad, Jack.'

I was impressed. Suddenly Paul seemed even more attractive. Unless he wrote the instructions for flatpack furniture. 'Are you a *real* writer?'

'No. A plastic one.'

'Sorry. I meant, what *kind* of writer?'

'Novels.'

Wow.

'Children's books?' I asked. 'Is *that* why you're invited today?'

'No, actually. Sci-fi. Well, sci-fi meets historical.'

'Jane Austen with spaceships?'

'Ha!' Paul shot me an appreciative look. 'Romans with aliens. I've written three. The next is out in the New Year.'

I was full of questions but we'd arrived and the kids were squealing with excitement. Bounce was just a boring old ware-house, but today it was decked out in bunting, the press was out in force and the mayor was strutting around in full ceremonial garb. There was even a slightly dog-eared red carpet. Something like this was big news in our little town.

Once inside, the children were presented with grippy socks and led away by staff in bright purple T-shirts. After all the upset earlier, Jack disappeared without a backward glance. Paul and I were shepherded upstairs to a large, open mezzanine over-looking the dozens of interlinked trampolines and presented with glasses of bubbly. *Bubbly!* At four o'clock on a Tuesday. We grabbed a table with a good view and surveyed the scene. Lily was already in her element, bouncing high and flipping herself over and over. And there were Jack and Gabriel, suddenly thick as thieves, wandering over to join a supervised game of dodgeball.

Sorted.

I took a sip of my bubbly and exhaled deeply.

'Feeling better?' said Paul.

'Yes, thanks.' Suddenly I felt embarrassed. 'How much of a tit did I make of myself?'

'You didn't,' said Paul. 'It was a horrible situation to be in.'

The easy tears threatened again. 'It's not Jack's fault,' I said. 'Better just to say I'm a tit. A great big tit.'

'A blue tit, maybe,' said Paul. 'Especially if you're cold.'

I laughed, almost despite myself. 'Boom, boom,' I said. 'The old ones are the oldest.'

Paul smiled. 'Anyway,' he said. 'Enough of all that. Tell me about yourself. What do you do for a living – when you're not wrestling overwrought sons, that is?'

I took a sip of my bubbly. 'Marketing consultancy,' I said. 'Or at least I did until recently but I've just been laid off. In fact, maybe I'll write a book or two now. I've always wanted to.'

Paul narrowed his eyes. 'So now you've time on your hands, you're just going to knock out a couple of bestsellers, are you?' he said.

'No. I never said that. I just said I wanted to write a book.'

Paul started clinking his car keys against his champagne flute. It was plastic, so it made a thud rather than a ding. 'OK,' he said. 'Suppose I said I'd always wanted to be a management consultant?'

'*Marketing* consultant. I'd be fine with it.'

'Ah. But how about if I said I hadn't had time to squeeze it in? That when I got bored of what I was doing at the moment, I'd make it my next project?'

I shrugged. 'Fine. Naïve maybe. You have to train, get a name, build up a client list.'

'Exactly! Everyone thinks they can write a book if they put half a mind to it. It's actually bloody hard. You have to learn your craft like anything else. And don't you dare ask me if I've won any awards or been top of the bestseller lists.'

It had been my next question. I kept schtum.

'Everyone thinks unless you're a household name, you haven't made it,' said Paul. 'But no one asks you how many awards *you've* won. They just accept you're a management consultant.'

'Marketing. And I never asked you about awards.'

Although I should have. He was very sexy when he was riled.

'But you thought it.'

'Certainly not!'

'You definitely thought it.'

'Even if I did, it's not the same. You're not the thought police.'

'Yes, I am.'

Hang on… Were we *flirting*?

'Room for one more?'

I'd been so absorbed in our conversation that time had fallen away and I hadn't noticed anyone approach our table. It was Mandy, already plonking down a glass and pulling up a chair.

'You're a bigwig as *well*?' I said, shuffling around and trying not to look – to *feel* – too disappointed at the interruption.

'No, you're all right,' said Mandy. 'I just blagged a lift here with Sian.'

'Phew!'

The three of us sat and shot the breeze. Normal stuff. Silly stuff. Stuff people say when they're getting to know each other. And do you know what? The 'A' word wasn't mentioned at all. Not once. I used to assume parents of kids with special needs would talk about nothing else but it wasn't like that at all. Mandy was a hoot and Paul had a brilliantly dry sense of humour as well as being stroppy and sexy.

This was *fun*.

Mandy raised her glass of fizz. 'Here's to the Lunch Club,' she said. 'If Virginia was here, we could have our first meeting.'

'Let's fix something up while we're still keen,' said Paul. 'Thursday morning?'

Mandy shook her head. 'Single parents' coffee morning. Virginia's down for it an' all.'

'I didn't know Virginia was divorced,' I said.

Damn. Another victory for The Statistic?

'She's not,' said Paul. 'She's a widow.'

Oh! Divorcees were ten a penny at St John's but a *widow*. That was something else. An exotic creature to be objectified, discussed, pitied...

'Poor Virginia,' breathed Mandy. 'And with an autistic child too.'

'Was it an illness?' I asked. 'An accident?'

'A stroke,' said Paul. 'I gather he was much older than her.'

I rolled this new information around my mind, teasing and prodding it. Suddenly I was sorry I'd had such uncharitable thoughts about Virginia. I should really try to be kinder.

'Mum?' It was a very pink Lily. She put her arms round my neck and rubbed her cheek against mine. 'I'm thirsty.'

'Oh, she's yours!' said Mandy. 'I've been watching *you*, Bendy-Wendy. Fantastic flips.'

Lily beamed. 'Thank you,' she said shyly.

'You must belong to a club?'

'No,' said Lily. 'I just practise on the field at school.'

'Well, you're brilliant. Make sure Mum signs you up to a club.'

Lily turned to me with shining eyes. 'Can I, Mummy? There's one starting here.'

'Absolutely, flower.' I planted a kiss on her hot little forehead.

And here was Jack accompanied by Gabriel and Dylan – all red in the face and demanding refreshment.

'Hey, Mum,' said Jack once we'd distributed cups of water. 'You know pie?'

'Pie?' I was nonplussed. 'You mean like apple pie?'

'No, pi. The number.'

'Oh.' That was random. 'Well, I must have done a long time ago. Not so hot on it now.'

'It's never finishes,' said Jack. 'And look what Dylan can do.' He grabbed my phone and started tapping. 'Go, Dylan.'

Dylan smiled. He was a tall, slightly overweight lad with an obliging air and, at Jack's command, he stood on tiptoe and reeled off about a hundred numbers without hesitation.

Jack's face was a picture. 'Sick,' he breathed. 'Every single one is right. Mum, is pi an odd or an even number?'

Mandy and Dylan left soon afterwards. Paul didn't seem to be in any hurry to follow them and neither was I. The afternoon had turned around in a most pleasing manner. The kids went off to carry on bouncing, Paul bought coffees and we carried on shooting the breeze.

Then Paul said, 'Some of the parents are having a go!'

I glanced over into the hall. Numbers were thinning out and some of the trampolines had now been set aside for adults. One mum was even doing a backflip.

'Shall we join them?' Paul was already standing up and holding out a hand.

I could think of nothing worse.

My dad used to call me Bambi because as a girl I was all awkward, gangly limbs. And although said limbs had since filled out, I was still horribly ungainly. I often had bruises from where I'd bumped against something or misjudged a space, so I was hardly going to impress Paul with my prowess. I'd probably trip over and break my leg, taking out a couple of kids with me. Or the trampoline would give way under my weight and we'd plummet into the abyss…

'I'm all right, thanks,' I said, staying firmly seated.

'Come on,' Paul persisted. 'It'll be fun.'

Unlikely. But there was just something about Paul's crooked grin and boyish enthusiasm that made me go against my better judgement.

'Oh, go on, then,' I said with a little groan, letting him pull me to my feet.

Paul rewarded me with a full-on crinkly smile and we went downstairs, got ourselves kitted out in the right kind of socks and headed into the bright, echoey hall.

I felt horribly exposed.

I hadn't been on a trampoline since I was a child. I'd always refused to get one for my kids after all the horror stories of broken limbs and cracked skulls. At first, I stood there flexing my knees. Then I did a couple of little hops.

Paul was watching me, head on one side. Then he laughed. 'Come on,' he said. 'You can do better than that.'

He took hold of my hands and started jumping. I had little choice but to join in. Higher and higher we went, until we were both grinning like idiots and my hair was flying behind me. Paul's hands were warm and dry in mine. Who cared if I looked like a Heffalump on speed? This was fun!

'Knees,' shouted Paul suddenly and we fell to our knees as one. Up we came again, eyes meeting, full of laughter.

'Sit,' I yelled and we let go, sat down and bounced up again. That was much harder and there was a fair amount of stumbling and flailing before we found each other again.

We carried on in this vein until I didn't care who was watching or what they thought. I hadn't felt this exhilarated in ages. Maybe we should try a flip...

'Oh, no. Collision,' said Paul, looking over my shoulder and coming to an abrupt halt.

I turned. Two little lads were clutching their heads and one was in tears. Paul was already there, comforting the boys, signalling to the staff. He had complete control of the situation and there didn't seem to be much I could usefully do, so I carried on bouncing, kicking my legs out behind me.

This was better than the gym.

Better than therapy.

It should be available on the NHS.

Paul jumped back onto the trampoline just as I was mid bounce and the trampoline came up to meet me and… suddenly we were both lying on our backs, hopelessly entwined. For a moment, I let myself lie there, head against his soft, navy arm. Then we both scrambled to our feet, weak with laughter.

The kids were standing there, looking at us in horror.

'You are *so* embarrassing,' said Jack.

'We can't take you *anywhere*,' sighed Lily.

'I want to go home,' said Gabriel.

—

Paul and I sat in comfortable silence on the way back. We wouldn't have been able to hear ourselves speak anyway because Jack and Gabriel kept up a steady stream of very loud conversation.

'What are you playing?' asked Jack. Gabriel was on an iPad.

'*Minecraft*,' said Gabriel. 'You like *Minecraft*.'

'Not really. I like *Wizard World* better.'

'*Minecraft* is your favourite game,' said Gabriel firmly.

'No, it's not. Why d'you keep saying that?'

I was confused too. Then the penny dropped. Gabriel was reversing his pronouns. *Gabriel* liked *Minecraft*, not Jack. Pronoun reversal was a classic sign of Asperger's.

'Thank you for today,' I said, when Paul pulled up in front of our house. 'It was…' I paused, trying to find the right words. 'It was a lifesaver.'

'I think you'd have been fine anyway,' said Paul. 'But I had a brilliant time too.'

We smiled at each other for a smidge longer than was strictly necessary and, in that heartbeat, I knew that he felt the same twitch of attraction.

But he just said, 'Watch out for mad axemen,' gave a wave that encompassed us all and drove away.

Daniel's car was already in the drive. I found him and Freddie at the kitchen table, poring over Freddie's maths books.

'Hi guys,' I said cheerfully, throwing my coat on the back of one of the chairs.

Daniel looked up. He didn't smile. 'You look interesting,' he said.

I glanced in the mirror above the fireplace. My hair was all over the shop, my cheeks were rosy and as for my mascara...

'I've had the most amazing day,' I said, dabbing under my eyes. 'I've been to the new trampolining place. And we've decided to form a Lunch Club for the autistic kids at school *and* we're organising a fundraising ball.'

Wow.

Such a lot had happened in one day.

Daniel still didn't smile. 'That's great,' he said, tonelessly. 'And, while you've been out gallivanting, *I* received a call from Freddie, who was locked out the house, and I had to leave work early to let him in.'

'Oh no!' I said. 'Freddie, if you'd forgotten your key, you should have called *me*. I was only five minutes away.'

Freddie stood up and picked up his school books. 'I did call you, Mum,' he said. '*Hundreds* of times!' He gave me a 'look', pushed his hair off his forehead and stomped out of the room.

'What's up with *him*?' I said, plonking myself down in one of the chairs and glancing at my phone. There were six missed calls. But I'd been... busy. I couldn't be expected to be on call every minute of every day, could I? Freddie had managed perfectly well being a latchkey kid when I'd been at work.

Matt the Mog jumped onto my lap and started kneading his paws into my thighs.

At least *someone* loved me.

'He's got a detention,' said Daniel. 'Maths homework – or a lack thereof. Look, Em, you're meant to be in charge round here. You should be at home when Freddie gets home from school – or he should at least be able to get hold of you. What happened today was unacceptable.'

'No, it wasn't,' I countered, hotly.

Daniel stood up. 'It really was,' he said. 'Freddie dragged me back from work just when there's a restructure brewing.'

'Oh, I see. It's all about *you*, is it?' I said coldly. 'Never mind me and the hideous time I had in the playground with Jack...'

We stood staring at each other across the table for what seemed like an age and then, at exactly the same moment, we both smiled ruefully.

'I'm sorry, Dan,' I said, rubbing my cheek. 'I should have checked my phone.'

Daniel blew out his cheeks. 'No, *I'm* sorry,' he said, coming round the table and giving me a hug. 'I totally overreacted. I bet the kids loved the new trampolining place.'

'They did,' I said, burying my head into his shoulder. 'It was a VIP preview *and* we went with a famous author.'

'Really? Who?'

'Paul Archer.'

I wanted to say Paul's name, get it out into the open.

No secrets.

'Never heard of him,' said Daniel.

'Me neither,' I admitted.

'Not that famous then,' said Daniel and we both laughed, the tension between us gone.

'So, is this restructure likely to affect you?' I asked, pulling away and going to the fridge.

'I don't know,' said Daniel. 'The rumour is they're closing some departments and moving them out to the States.'

'Oh.' I grinned. 'Well, a Stateside adventure could be fun.'

'It could be *brilliant*,' said Daniel.

'But it ain't going to happen,' I said. 'Not with the family. Not with Jack.'

'No,' said Daniel.

My phone pinged. It was Mandy, suggesting a Lunch Club meeting at hers the following morning. I'd no sooner accepted than the phone pinged again.

This one was from Paul.

> Fancy a quick coffee before the meeting tomorrow? I'd love to pick your brain about all things Asperger's? MAM

No.

There was going to be nothing that could possibly complicate things between me and Daniel.

Nothing that could complicate *us*.

'I've just received this,' I said, shoving my phone under Daniel's nose. 'Would it be OK with you?'

Daniel screwed up his face and read the text. 'Who is she?' he said.

'It's a *he*. That author.'

Daniel laughed. 'He wants to talk to you about *autism*, Em. Unless it's an elaborate code, I'd say I'm pretty safe.'

I laughed too. But, to be on the safe side, I texted Paul back:

> Tomorrow manic. Sorry. MAL

'What does MAM mean?' asked Daniel idly. 'One of those trendy acronyms?'

I paused, then shrugged. 'Dunno,' I said. 'Maybe it's a typo.'

As I slid the pizzas and dough balls into the oven, I wondered why I'd lied.

Chapter Nine

Mandy lived in a modern terrace near the railway line. It was what estate agents might call 'bijou' – a galley kitchen with a hatch through to an L-shaped living-cum-dining room. It was also absolutely immaculate; Mandy obviously lived by the 'a place for everything and everything in its place' maxim. (I'd never worked out the former so it was very hard to do the latter.) There was a comfy tan leather sofa, a couple of matching chairs and a low glass table with a vase of carnations on it. She obviously had Dylan well under control – a vase at that height wouldn't last five minutes at home.

I'd hardly sat down before Mandy said, 'How come you managed to wangle yourself an invite to Bounce with the rather gorgeous Paul Archer yesterday?'

Paul wasn't there yet. Nor was Virginia. But honestly! You couldn't get away with anything in our little town. Could you imagine the hoo-hah if I'd actually gone for coffee with Paul and turned up at the meeting with him?

'I think he felt sorry for me,' I admitted. 'He'd just seen Jack have the mother of all meltdowns in the playground.'

'Yeah, right,' said Mandy with a snort. 'Nothing to do with your long legs and your stonking boobs and your little-girl-lost look then?'

'*What?* Don't be ridiculous—'

Then I stopped, because the doorbell rang and the man himself had arrived. In he came, with his navy jumper and his tousled hair and his lopsided smile and, sorry, but Mandy was right. He *was* gorgeous. The way his eyes crinkled and his eyebrows lifted when he spoke. The blokeish way he sat down; legs apart, jeans moulded to thighs…

'How are you today?' he asked me with a grin.

I laughed. 'One big bruise,' I said.

'Me too. It was fun though, wasn't it?'

'Great fun.'

And here was Virginia. Armed with my new information, I couldn't help scrutinising her with new fascination. She didn't *look* much like a widow. Not that I'd have expected her to be beating her breast or anything, but there was nothing marking her out as any different to the rest of us. She was calm and in control and, as before, beautifully turned out. Today she was wearing a deep blue scarf that brought out her deep blue eyes. I couldn't help but admire her. If I lost Daniel, I'd wear the same manky leggings and sweatshirt for a year.

'What are you all doing on Saturday evening?' Virginia asked as soon as coffee had been distributed. 'I thought it'd be fun to kick things off with a social. Dinner at mine? With your partners?'

We quickly ascertained we were all free.

'But haven't you got Jamie's party that day?' I asked.

'Oh, that's a few boys back for lunch after football,' said Virginia.

My admiration was complete. Either activity would have me automatically reaching for the painkillers.

'Now, we don't want to bore your other halves by talking shop, so I'm making it a murder-mystery dinner party,' said Virginia rummaging in her bag. 'I've got invitations for you here. Details on your characters, ideas for your outfits…'

I felt a stab of excitement. I'd always wanted to have a go at a murder-mystery evening. And it would be infinitely better than making polite conversation with a bunch of people I hardly knew. I scanned the front cover of the invitation:

Early twentieth-century Egypt. The end of a successful dig. Dun Lutin, the internationally renowned archaeologist, has been found dead in his hotel room…

Ooh.

'Ha! I'm the world-famous writer, Barbara Carthorse,' said Mandy.

'I'm Brad Fitt,' said Paul with a modest bow. He didn't mention a wife or partner.

'Steve's Doug A. Trench,' said Mandy. 'He's going to love that. What about you, Emma?'

I read my invite aloud. 'You will be playing the part of Ainn Shent-Ruyn.'

I paused, working it out.

Gee, thanks Virginia.

We settled on a late Valentine's Ball to raise money for the Lunch Club. Not quite time to reinvent myself as an uber-slim goddess but certainly enough time to shift ten pounds if I got my skates on.

'Now, we need to elect a chair,' said Virginia.

It would be her. Of course it would.

'I'd like to propose Emma,' said Mandy.

What?

'Really?' Was she having a laugh?

'Really. I think you'd do a mint job.'

'Thank you.'

That would shake my life up. I could throw myself into it, use my business skills, make it a real project. *And* I'd be helping Jack.

Virginia put down her mug of coffee. 'I'm not sure if we're allowed to nominate ourselves, but I'd like to put myself forward too,' she said. She was smiling, but there was steel in her eyes. 'I know a lot about organising balls.'

Damn.

The fizzing morphed from excitement to anxiety. I didn't want a vote, a popularity contest in all but name. But neither did I want to hand it to Virginia on a plate.

Paul came to my rescue. 'Why don't we have joint chairs?' he suggested. 'You could have different areas of responsibility.'

Virginia cocked her head to one side. 'That could work,' she said. She didn't sound totally enthused.

'Fine by me,' I agreed, probably not sounding much happier.

'Great. We're set,' said Paul.

I couldn't help wondering who he would have voted for.

—

Our differences emerged as soon as soon as we got down to the nitty-gritty.

'It's got to be held at the Club,' I said.

'The Club?' echoed Mandy.

'Saxony Hall. It's a private members' club down by the river. It's got a gorgeous ballroom.'

I'd been to a couple of events there over the years and Daniel's company often used it for meetings and away days. It really was the obvious choice.

'Sounds pricy,' said Mandy. 'Why don't we use one of village halls and cater it ourselves?'

'Because we need the richest parents,' I said. 'People who are prepared to flash the cash.'

'If it's expensive, there'll be flak from the less well-off,' said Mandy mildly.

Now I was cross.

'Lots of parents never come to *anything*,' I said. 'They don't even come to the Pumpkin Party – and that's free. So, if they want to sit on their fat arses and moan about it, that's fine by me.'

There was a silence. I wondered if I'd gone too far. I hadn't meant to. I'd just wanted to get my point across, impress Paul and make sure we made as much money as possible.

Then Paul laughed. 'Love it,' he said. 'Profit-driven commercialism versus egalitarianism in a nutshell. Go girls!'

I stuck my tongue out at him. 'You're making it sound like I'm a money-obsessed *Torygraph* reader,' I complained.

'No, I'm not,' said Paul. 'I'm a fully fledged *Guardian* subscriber but I agree with you. We need people who are happy to spend money or we'll never reach our target.'

'Absolutely,' I said. 'We need to unashamedly fleece people.'

'We do. Until they're shorn naked.'

And we all laughed easily together.

'Actually,' said Virginia, 'in my experience, we'll only break even on the tickets wherever we go.'

'How come?' I asked.

'Well, I expect the Club costs a bomb, so even if we charge parents a packet we won't make that much profit. And the village halls might be cheap but people won't pay as much to go something there. It all evens out in the end.'

'What do we do then?' Mandy asked.

'We agree on a venue, make it clear to everyone we're there to fundraise and then set up a really good auction of promises.'

'Sounds great,' said Mandy. 'Well, it would do if I knew what an auction of promises was.'

'It's where people promise things like a night of babysitting or a lift to the airport,' I said. 'Then we auction the promises off to the highest bidder.'

'Right. But it'll take a lot of babysitting to make five grand,' said Mandy.

'We've got to persuade people to donate bigger things,' said Paul. 'Cooking meals or use of their holiday homes. I'd be up for sorting that out. Join me, Emma? A chance to bleed people dry?'

'I'd love to.' Suddenly I was all fired up. And not just because I would be working with Paul.

'Fine. I'm happy to head up the ball proper,' said Virginia. 'Venue, food, entertainment.'

'I'll join you,' said Mandy.

Paul and me on the fundraising together then. Somehow it seemed almost inevitable.

'OK,' said Virginia. 'We need to set the date and get it into diaries. We also need to tell people what it's in aid of and get them thinking about what they could donate.'

'Absolutely,' I replied, trying to sound similarly joint-chairwoman-ish. 'Why don't you get the date approved and Paul and I will draft something about the auction?'

Virginia nodded and there was a general swapping of seats. Paul eased himself onto the sofa next to me and I feared his proximity was unlikely to help my concentration.

Paul pulled out his laptop. 'Right, time to get our heads down,' he said.

'Sadly, I don't think it's that kind of meeting.'

Out of my mouth before I could stop myself.

The sort of thing I would say to Daniel without a second thought.

The kind of thing Ness and I would snort over all the time.

The kind of thing that was totally inappropriate to say to a man I hardly knew.

Paul looked at me but didn't say anything. I thought I saw amusement, surprise, a hint of embarrassment...

I tried again. 'We'll need to start with some bumf about the A word,' I said.

'Go on then. You're the expert.'

I took Paul's computer, opened Word and sat there for a moment. What I really wanted to type was that my cousin Teddy had had autism and that he'd been mad and bad and his parents had had to send him away to an institution. Their own marriage had disintegrated – the ties that bind as fragile as chiffon – and, now, every time Jack had a meltdown, I worried that history would repeat itself. Jack would turn violent, he would be taken away from us and Daniel and I would never speak again...

I didn't type any of that, of course. I just wrote:

> Asperger syndrome is a disability that affects how
> a person processes information and relates to other
> people.

Ugh. Dry as powder and about as palatable. I pressed delete and tried again.

> People with Asperger's have difficulties in three
> areas: communication, social interaction and social
> imagination.

Paul raised an eyebrow. 'What was that about wanting to write a book?' he said.

I laughed. 'It's actually really difficult,' I said. 'You try.'

Paul took the computer, stared at it for quite a while and then started tapping away. He made a final tweak, then rotated the laptop back toward me.

'What about this?' he asked.

> As soon as we meet a person, we make judgements
> about them. From their facial expression, tone of
> voice and body language we can tell whether they
> are happy, angry or sad and respond accordingly.
> People with Asperger syndrome find it hard to read
> the signals most of us take for granted.

'Not bad, sir,' I said with genuine admiration.

'Great. Let's just add on a couple of sentences about the Lunch Club,' he said. His mobile rang and he glanced at it. 'Sorry, I need to take this.'

'That's fine. I'll finish off.'

Paul sauntered off, phone already clamped to his ear. Right, one last chance to impress. I pulled Paul's computer toward me, accidentally minimising the document. Behind it was the website of an autistic charity. A quick glance and... Paul had copied his masterpiece word for bloody word. He strolled back

70

into the room a moment later and, as our eyes met, his face split into a huge grin.

'Why, you…'

I trailed off and, with a bubble of laughter and indignation, lobbed a crushed-velvet cushion across the room at him. Then I watched as, with ghastly inevitability, it missed and hit the vase of carnations on the coffee table. The vase wobbled and fell, a puddle of water flooding the table and splashing onto the cream rug below.

Oh God!

Why on earth had I done that?

The room went quiet. Several pairs of eyes stared at me with silent censure. With a twinge of humiliation, I realised my behaviour had strayed to the wrong side of appropriate.

'Plagiarist,' I said light-heartedly as I tried to staunch the flow with my sleeve.

'Rubbish shot,' Paul replied equally light-heartedly. But his eyes didn't quite meet mine and he turned his attention to Virginia.

My first thought, as I got up to get a cloth, was that I'd blown it. Whatever 'it' was or could have been. I'd been as unsubtle as a heifer on heat and probably as sexy.

My second thought was how inappropriate my first thought had been. What was I *doing*?

I'd knocked over a vase and, rather than apologise to my hostess, I was thinking about a man who shouldn't even be on my radar. I was a happily married woman, for goodness sake. At least, after tonight, I hoped I was.

'I'm so sorry,' I said to Mandy, who had followed me into the kitchen.

'No worries, mate,' said Mandy, tearing off some sheets of kitchen paper. 'But Healey…'

'Yes?'

'Be careful, mate. Be very careful.'

And I knew she wasn't just talking about a vase of carnations on a glass coffee table.

Chapter Ten

The day of the murder-mystery party rolled around quickly.

I woke to late-summer sunshine streaming through the gap in the curtains. Daniel was inert on the bed next to me. With his hand lightly curled above his head and a sunbeam highlighting his hair, he was the lovely, vulnerable boy I'd given my heart to all those years ago. Poor Daniel. I should be supporting him, not chucking cushions at random authors. With a wave of tenderness and guilt, I nestled into his side. He rolled away with a fragrant burp.

'Mum?'

It was Freddie, all rumpled jimjams and bed-head. I glanced at the clock. Nine o'clock.

'You all right, love?'

'Yeah. It's the match today!'

Match?

Match!

'Of course!' I said. 'My big boy in the A team.'

Freddie grinned. 'What time do we need to leave?'

'I'm not sure. Dad's taking you.'

'Aren't you coming too?'

'Oh Freds, I'd love to. But I've got to take Jack to a party and get some fancy-dress stuff for tonight.'

Daniel hauled himself to a seated position. 'Let's leave at ten to be on the safe side,' he said. 'And don't worry; I'll cheer loud enough for two.'

'OK.' Freddie turned to leave.

'I'll make pancakes for breakfast,' I called after him.

Freddie didn't answer.

I was quite nervous about dropping Jack off at Jamie's party. The local sports club had been the scene of many a disaster. But Jack disappeared happily enough into a gaggle of mini Rooneys and Vardys. My spirits soared. I was just a normal mum dropping her child off at a party...

It was time to start pulling my outfit together for that evening. A quick rifle through my wardrobe confirmed what I already knew. I had absolutely nothing by way of Edwardian glamour.

With a distinct lack of enthusiasm, I dragged Lily to Monsoon. Was it the ghastly lighting or my ghastly body that made trying on every dress so depressing? There was just one simple black number with a flattering neckline that looked halfway decent. Actually, it wasn't bad...

Stepping out of the changing room, I beckoned to Lily, who was trying on hair accessories.

'How do I look?' I asked, giving her a twirl.

Lily looked me over with candid, grey eight-year-old eyes. 'Hideous,' she concluded.

'Lily, that's not very nice.'

'Sorry. But you look like you've got a baby in your tummy.'

The second time in a week! I'd have to step up the running big time.

Grumpy as hell, I swept Lily out of the shop and down the street to Oxfam. If I couldn't pull off the drop-dead-gorgeous look, I might as well play it for laughs. A little browsing unearthed a beige corduroy bucket hat with dark brown flowers. It was about as flattering as tipping a saucepan of spaghetti over my head but it vaguely fitted the costume instructions. Then I unearthed a long brown cardigan that might pass as an Edwardian cloak and a brooch shaped like a rose.

Bish-bosh.

Sorted.

After lunch, I set off to pick Jack up from Virginia's. I thought I knew Hambley pretty well but I'd never been to this particular gated community on the outskirts. Stylish townhouses. A man washing his car. Another mowing his lawn. It could have been an artist's impression of Anywhere, Little England. Blandly aspirational. A touch disappointing for Virginia.

Round the corner, however, a magnificent nineteenth-century mansion loomed into view. This was more like it. There were crenellations, pillars, even a small tower. For a moment, I thought Virginia owned the whole thing. Then I realised, with no little relief, that it was divided into apartments.

I parked in a little visitors' bay and, feeling like something out of Jane Austen, pushed open the studded front door. The entrance hall was huge and hilariously over the top: more pillars, marbled walls, even a domed roof. Floor-to-ceiling mirrors gave the illusion of corridors stretching away into the distance. It was like being in a surreal costume drama, except my jeans, boots and Oska jacket, reflected ad infinitum, were defiantly twenty-first-century and my waist hardly a corseted handspan.

The entrance to Virginia's apartment was tucked round the corner. I rang the bell and the door was opened by a young man in his late twenties. Strikingly dark and handsome, his white T-shirt hugged his torso quite delightfully. Yes, I am aware of the 'half your age plus seven' rule, thank you very much, but there's no harm in looking. I wondered if he was Virginia's bit on the side. No wonder she played the merry widow to perfection.

Aware I was staring, I gave Hottie my brightest smile and thrust out my hand. 'Hi, I'm Jack's mum, Emma,' I said.

'And I'm Jamie's stepbrother, Harry.'

Right. Late husband's son from an earlier marriage, probably. Not the totty.

'Nice to meet you,' I said. 'And what an amazing place!'

'Fun, isn't it? Gives Ginny and the boys a chance to indulge their completely unjustified delusions of grandeur.'

Ginny?

I couldn't resist a discreet snort.

Harry stood back and ushered me in with an elaborate bow. A small inner hallway led to a huge drawing room complete with intricate coving and magnificent chandelier. There was a beautiful marble fireplace – the mantelpiece at head height – and French windows opening onto a large terrace.

The room was simply arranged with shabby-chic furniture and plump ivory sofas. Scattered pieces of driftwood, stacks of coffee-table books and artfully arranged large pebbles completed the look. On paper, it was probably a style clash with the coving and the chandelier, but even a horde of small boys jostling over Wii controls couldn't detract from what was undoubtedly a lovely space.

It was stunning.

Clever Ginny.

I spotted Jack immediately, hovering on the edge of the game-playing group. Very pale, his body language was even more wooden than usual. He came over to me straight away and started pulling on my wrist.

'Come on, Mum,' he said. 'Let's go.'

Virginia bustled over with Caroline. They were carrying party bags and a tray of oozing birthday cake slices wrapped in paper napkins.

'Gorgeous place,' I said. 'And thank you so much for having Jack. I'm sure he's had a wonderful time.'

Virginia smiled back. 'You're welcome,' she said. 'By the way, have you got a fondue set I can borrow? I think I might need two tonight.'

Of course we had a fondue set. Doesn't everyone? Ours was lurking, unloved, on a top shelf alongside a bread maker and a little hotplate for keeping Chinese dishes warm.

'Sure,' I said. 'Not the fuel though. I could pop to Robert Dyas?'

'Don't worry, I've got all that. Just the set would be great.'

'OK. I'm really looking forward to tonight,' I added, giving Caroline a sideways glance. That would show Mrs I-Won't-Let-My-Son-Play-With-Yours who was in and out around *here*, thank you very much.

'Me too,' said Virginia. 'The Ball Committee kick-off,' she added to Caroline. 'Always a gamble entertaining people you wouldn't necessarily socialise with.'

Ouch!

Jack gave my wrist another yank and reiterated his wish to leave.

'I'll let you go,' said Virginia. 'By the way, Jack had a bit of a tough time today. I hope it wasn't too much of an ordeal for him.'

My small, shiny bubble of contentment at Jack's inclusion quietly popped. I was a fool. Jack and I would always be on the outside, looking in, being judged. People would always rub it in with their casual smiles and careless comments. Damn Virginia for being that person today. She should have known better.

'Thanks,' I said coolly. 'I really didn't need to hear that.'

Caroline's mouth opened and Virginia flinched as if I'd slapped her.

'Yes, but surely you've got to *challenge* the child—' she started.

I didn't want to hear Virginia's child-raising theories. I didn't want to be made to feel any more inadequate than I already did. I just wanted to get out of there. And so, face burning, I pushed past Harry and stalked out of the apartment, Jack trailing along in my wake.

The mirrors in the hallway showed a thousand times over that my eyes were glittering and my décolleté stained a dark blotchy red. I paused, trying to compose myself. Jack, oblivious, amused himself by striking dramatic poses and admiring his many reflections. After a while, I decided that looked rather fun and we spent a pleasant few minutes trying to outdo each other creating silly illusions. I was attempting a particularly impressive

Harry Worth-style number that involved waving one leg in the air when Paul and Gabriel walked in. Gabriel was carrying an enormous birthday present wrapped in shiny blue paper.

'Fancy seeing you here,' said Paul, a smile playing about his lips.

Mortified, I snapped the offending leg back into position. 'We were just leaving,' I said.

'Right. And *we'd* better go and deliver this monstrosity before Gabriel's arms fall off,' said Paul. 'See you this evening.'

It was only as I was belting myself into the car that I paused to wonder why Paul was arriving at the end of the party. Why, indeed, he was arriving at all? He didn't have a child of Jamie's age, so there was no obvious reason for him to be there. Maybe Virginia had schmoozed on in there after my faux pas with the cushion. Yes, it was the only logical explanation. They were, most likely, both single, and I'd seen how Paul had looked at Virginia at the meeting in the church.

No, I really didn't like her.

Not one bit.

–

On the way home, I casually asked Jack if he had enjoyed the party.

'Three out of ten,' Jack replied flatly, pulling a Sherbet Dip-Dab out of his party bag.

'Oh dear. How was the football?'

'Bad. I was the last to be picked. No one wanted me on their team.'

'That's tough, little man,' I said. I ignored the shower of sherbet splattering over us both.

'That wasn't the bad part. I'm used to not being chosen.'

My heart silently broke.

'What then?'

'It was when they were all mucking about at Jamie's and I got a bit stressy.'

'Yes. Jamie's mum told me.'

'I asked her not to!'

'Then she shouldn't have.' Damn Virginia. 'But why didn't you want me to know?'

'I didn't want you to be sad.' So quietly I had to strain to hear it. 'I wanted you to think I'd be OK.'

For a moment I couldn't speak for the lump in my throat.

'I *know* you're OK, Jack.'

I should have gone with my instincts. I should never have trusted Virginia with my beautiful boy.

'I hate being me sometimes,' said Jack.

There was a little sob and, for a moment, I couldn't tell whether it was from Jack or from me.

—

Having handed over his negative feelings, Jack was buoyant again in no time. I wished the same could be said for me. Once we got home, I went in search of Daniel and found him in the lounge, feet up on the sofa, deep in the Saturday *Guardian*.

'Jack had a *crap* time at the party,' I burst out. 'It's so unfair. So fucking, *fucking* unfair.'

Daniel folded up the review section and gave me a 'look' over the top. I shrugged; meaningful looks were all well and good but I had no idea what this one meant. Then Daniel nodded at the armchair and I saw Freddie was there, curled up and reading the sports pages.

'Oh, excuse my French, Freddie,' I said. Mind, you, it was hardly the first time Freddie had heard me swear. And I had a *right* to be upset about Jack. It *was* upsetting.

Daniel put the paper down. 'Freddie played very well today,' he said evenly. 'He set up two great goals.'

Oh God.

The football match.

I'd completely forgotten.

'Wonderful, Freddie!' I went to ruffle his hair but Freddie squirmed away from my hand. 'So, did you win?'

Freddie stood up. 'Don't even pretend you care,' he muttered.

'Freddie! Don't be so rude.'

'Whatever.' Freddie pushed past me and ran out the room.

I put my hands on my hips. 'Did you see that?' I said to Daniel.

'Come on, Em,' said Daniel. 'He's upset you didn't ask about the match and, frankly, I'm not surprised.'

'I didn't see him there! Bloody hell, whose side are you on?'

'Freddie's, actually, in this instance,' said Daniel. 'I'd leave him to calm down if I were you, and then go and say sorry.'

Wonderful.

It seemed I couldn't do anything right nowadays.

I sighed and then set off for the supermarket. We had the parents coming round for Sunday lunch the next day. I liked Daniel's parents, even though his dad had early-stage dementia and could be tricky. I loved my own mum to bits, of course.

But cooking for eight? With a hangover?

I hadn't factored that in when I'd accepted Virginia's invitation.

Arse.

—

'Is tonight compulsory?' Daniel asked as we were getting ready that evening.

'Absolutely.' I was slightly worried my outfit seemed to lack a bottom half.

'Can't I play the joker?'

'*No*. You never know, it might actually be fun.'

What on earth had lady archaeologists worn in 1910? Had jeggings been invented then?

'So might extracting my teeth without anaesthetic. Theoretically possible but highly unlikely.'

79

'Come on. It's to help Jack.' What I needed was a tweed skirt. I didn't have one but – aha! – I did have a pair of PVC trousers I'd never had the bottle to wear. With my newly acquired weight, they were skin-tight but they might pass as leather chaps.

'I can't see how making a tit of myself pretending to be Ivor Trowel is helping Jack,' grumbled Daniel.

'You *know* why,' I said. 'It's to help launch the Lunch Club Project. God, do I look ridiculous in this outfit?'

'No comment.' Daniel almost smiled. 'Your hat is… interesting.'

'It's stunning! Can I give you a black eye?'

'Charming. Now who's being grumpy?'

'Out of eyeshadow, silly. You're meant to be an amateur boxer.'

'Am I? Do your worst then.'

'Fab.' I set to work, carefully blending greys, blues, a touch of ochre.

'By the way, who do I have to blame for this evening?' asked Daniel.

'Virginia Kennedy.' I sat back on my heels to assess my handiwork. 'A bit of a cow, actually.'

'Why? What's she done? Apart from subject us all to an evening of hell.'

I decided against sharing the pregnancy comment. I told him about the party that afternoon instead.

'Well, maybe Jack did struggle,' said Daniel matter-of-factly.

I was tempted to give him a real shiner and save on my Mac Trio.

Chapter Eleven

As eight o'clock drew closer, I began to get nervous. Despite jollying Daniel along, a murder mystery was well out of my comfort zone too. And stropping off earlier in the afternoon hadn't been the most mature thing to do. Justified maybe. But not mature.

There were two rules for the evening. Firstly, be polite to Virginia. It was important to claw back the moral high ground. And secondly, refrain, under any circumstances, from flirting with Paul. No bouncing. No cushions. Time to rein it in.

And, actually, there was a third rule, necessary if the others were to be observed.

Do. Not. Get. Drunk.

Endearingly tipsy was fine. Inebriated was not.

Virginia's apartment looked even more beautiful by night. All trace of small boy had been expunged and votive candles in pretty holders graced every surface. With the grandeur of the room, I could almost imagine I really was in early-twentieth-century Cairo.

Virginia was wearing a scarlet bandage dress that made the utmost of her not very ample assets. Daniel was no sooner through the door and a glass of bubbly pressed into his hand than he was a man transformed, laughing and complimenting his hostess on her home; it seemed only a matter of time before he also started complimenting her on her breasts.

Having charmed Daniel, Virginia relieved me of the fondue set. 'You should have stayed for a drink this afternoon,' she said silkily. 'We had quite the little party. Caroline didn't leave until six.'

'Lovely,' I said blandly. A couple of minutes in and she was already winding me up.

Daniel and I went and joined Paul, who was standing by the fireplace. Even sporting a monocle and a pork-pie hat, he looked good enough to eat.

'Hello, Emma,' he said, pecking me on the cheek. 'Let me introduce you to my wife, Hanna.'

Wife?

Wife!

I'd had no real reason to assume that Paul wasn't married. It was just that he had never mentioned a spouse and there had never seemed to be one around. Mind you, he could probably say the same thing about Daniel. And it made no difference. No difference at all. We were just two parents doing the best by our children. Nothing had happened. Nothing was *going* to happen.

So I smiled and offered my hand to the petite redhead by Paul's side. Pale and pretty, she was very thin, her bare arms all sinews and veins. She was wearing a black cocktail dress and an expression that could curdle milk. Either she didn't want to meet me or she'd rather pull her eyelashes out than take part in a murder-mystery party.

I decided I was glad she was a grump.

It would have been awful to have actually liked her.

We were spared having to make conversation by the arrival of Mandy and a bearded, smiley Steve. With all present and correct, Virginia summoned us over to the TV and a DVD designed to set the scene. Dun Lutin, the seriously dodgy archaeologist, had been found dead in his hotel room, apparently bumped off by an exploding mummy. It was up to us to work out which of our number had committed this ghastly deed. It was terrifically camp and cheesy — I think Michael Winner was involved somewhere — and there was a lot of laughter and heckling as the film played out.

This was going to be fun!

We made our way over to the dining table and took our seats. There were nametags and a booklet at each place setting.

'Have a read through your manuals,' said Virginia. 'Any of you could be the murderer at this stage. And from now on, let's try to stay in character.'

Virginia disappeared off to the kitchen and we smiled round at each other nervously.

Mandy, next to me, caught my eye. 'Looking mint, mate,' she said, absolutely *not* in character. 'That hat's hardcore.'

'Thank you,' I whispered back. 'You look pretty mint yourself.'

She did. OK, she'd overshot the relevant time period by twenty years and was channelling flapper-girl chic, but no matter. In her drop-waisted floral dress, wide matching headband and beads, she looked fresh and pretty. Downing her drink in one, she plonked the glass heavily onto the table.

'God, I needed that,' she said. 'Dylan had a massive blowout before we left. And we're talking *huge*.'

'Poor you,' I said, refilling her glass. 'What about? Not that there needs to be a reason.'

'Pyjamas!' Mandy took another hefty glug. 'The label said eight and he's just turned nine. Wouldn't wear them. Even when I snipped out the label.'

'Well, you're among friends here,' I said. 'We all know what it's like to have a child with Asperger's.'

'I don't,' said Hanna firmly. We turned to look at her. Hanna, in turn, glanced at Paul, who was deep in conversation with Steve and not listening to us. 'Paul *did* tell you that Gabriel hasn't been diagnosed with anything?' she added in a lower voice.

The reason for the bad mood of epic proportion became abundantly clear. Nothing to do with me. Nothing to do with the murder-mystery party. Hanna simply resented Gabriel being lumped in with a group of nutters. And, by the same token, she had no wish to associate with their parents.

83

Mandy and I reassured her Paul was in the clear. None of us had jumped to any wildly inaccurate conclusions about Gabriel. And we were all quite normal despite our deviant offspring.

Hanna gave us a tight-lipped smile. 'Not that there's anything wrong with having Asperger's,' she said, far too late in the day. She couldn't have sounded less convincing if she'd tried.

Virginia started doling out starters, heels click-clicking on the wooden floor. Conversation ground to a halt and dutifully, belatedly, we started studying our clue manuals until bold capitals forbade us from reading further. My character seemed to be painfully dull. Thank goodness for that. I really didn't want to be the murderer and spoil the evening by being rubbish and giving the game away too soon.

'What the feck is this?' whispered Mandy, prodding her starter with her fork.

'It looks like goat's cheese croutons with pesto,' I said. I took a nibble. 'Nice, actually.'

'Oh God,' said Mandy. 'I don't do goat.'

'Neither do I,' said Steve, on her other side. Without further ado, he picked up both their croutons and stuffed them into his pocket. Stifling a snort of laughter, I decided I rather liked him.

'Shall we make a start?' said Virginia, sitting down.

The giggles dissipated. The silence lengthened until it threatened to become awkward.

Then Mandy, bless her heart, cleared her throat.

'Jenna Regretrien, my love, what were you and Ivor Trowel discussing last night in the hotel gardens?' she said, speaking in an exaggerated accent of dubious provenance.

'I think you're supposed to be English,' said Virginia.

Everyone roared with laughter, the ice was broken and we were off, with Daniel trying to defend himself against whatever skulduggery Mandy was accusing him of.

It turned out, of course, that everyone's character was seriously dodgy and everyone had a motive for bumping off poor old Dun Lutin. As the wine flowed, we started to relax. Daniel and Steve were playing a couple planning to elope with the treasure trove and I was proud of him; this really wasn't his cup of tea and he was making a real effort to get involved and to camp it up. The star of the show, though, was undoubtedly Paul, deadpan, improvising wildly and absolutely hilarious. Everyone else was pretty rubbish but at least we were trying. Only Hanna refused to enter into the spirit, speaking in a monotone and oozing disdain for the whole thing.

There was a quick break before the main course and I popped upstairs to the loo. The family bathroom was already busy, so I wandered into Virginia's bedroom in search of an en suite. I'm never really sure if that's 'done' but, frankly, I was desperate. Anyway, that was occupied too so I sat on the bed and waited. How come Virginia's room was so pristine? I wasn't expecting dirty knickers on the floor, but where was the usual bedroom clutter – the discarded dressing gown, the permanently plugged-in hairdryer, the loose pile of change?

A photo on the far bedside table caught my eye. I crawled across the bed to take a look. At first, I assumed the man by Virginia's side was her father but, on closer inspection, he had his arm round her shoulder and his fingers entwined in her hair. He looked handsome and charming but his hair was completely white and the skin on his cheeks hung in loose, fuzzy folds. He must have had at least twenty years on Virginia.

'Emma?'

It was – it would be – Paul, coming out of the en suite, still doing up his fly, for goodness sake. Not ideal when I was sprawled on the bed and looking suspiciously like it was a come-on.

'Hi,' I said, scrambling to my feet. 'I was just waiting for the loo. So, now it's free…'

By the time we'd got stuck into the boeuf bourguignon, things were a-jumpin' in Old Cairo.

Everyone's alter egos had been wandering up and down random tomb tunnels with unfeasible alibis. Everyone had been shagging everyone else. Everyone's accents were dodgy and everyone was three sheets to the wind.

This was a hoot!

It got even better when I discovered my character was having a secret tryst with Paul's alter ego. I glanced at Paul and received the subtlest of winks in return. Then Steve looked up from his manual and raised his eyebrows.

'What have you two lovebirds been up to then?' he asked.

'Nothing,' said Paul innocently.

'*Absolutely* nothing,' I concurred.

Steve's brow creased in confusion. 'It says here you were spotted near the tombs,' he said, fluttering his clue manual at us.

'Ah, but that's where you're wrong, my friend,' said Paul. 'Somebody must have been impersonating us.'

'Yes. Clever use of accessories,' I added. 'Perhaps they borrowed my hat.'

'You're not allowed to lie,' Virginia reminded us gently.

'Shame,' said Paul. 'Then, yes. I must admit that Ms Ainn Shent-Ruyn and I were checking out each other's booty.'

'Were you indeed?' said Mandy with a snort of laughter.

'We were. And, let me tell you, she's got particularly impressive orbs.'

Excuse me?

Was I imagining it or was Paul talking about my tits?

'Is that actually in your booklet?' asked Steve, frown lines deepening.

'Absolutely. Two orbs. Classical dimensions. Well worth investigating.'

Yup. Definitely my tits.

Well, two could play at that game.

'Sadly, I found your one-eyed serpent a trifle on the small side,' I said demurely.

86

Mandy spluttered over her stew. 'Ha! What do you have to say about this, Daniel – I mean Ivor Trowel?'

Daniel shrugged. 'It looks like I've been too busy erecting my tent with Doug A. Trench here to either know or care,' he said.

Only I saw the slightly sour look he gave me.

I didn't dare look at Hanna.

–

Once the main course finished, Virginia faffed around with the chocolate fondue while the rest of us buried ourselves in our manuals for the final set of clues.

Hallelujah!

I wasn't the murderer.

Now I could really relax and enjoy myself.

'Well done, everyone,' said Virginia, pouring methylated spirit into the canister of each fondue set. 'And now for the dénouement…'

She struck a match and the table was bathed in flickering light. Given what she'd just said, I thought it was planned, maybe one of those fireworks you sometimes have on cakes. I clearly wasn't the only one; someone else laughed and there was even a little whoop of appreciation.

A moment later, the paper tablecloth swooshed up in flames and it was clear this was far from planned. Virginia picked up one of the fondue sets and rushed through to the kitchen. It was the worst thing she could have done; the fondue set was dripping and the flaming meths started a little blaze wherever it hit the rugs. In less than a minute, half a dozen small fires had taken hold.

Our reactions were severely slowed by all the booze we'd sunk.

'Help me,' Virginia shouted, lobbing a saucepan of water over the flames. She was almost hysterical – the first time I had seen her anything but perfectly in control – and her words shocked us into action.

We leapt to our feet and scattered in different directions. Blue-tinged flames were spreading across the table and a wine glass toppled and shattered. I snatched the hat off my head and started swiping at the worst of the fire. Far from putting out the flames, it ignited. I swatted it against a previously unaffected part of the paper tablecloth but succeeded only in starting another fire.

Steve materialised by my side. 'Get the hat outside, Ainn Shent-Ruyn,' he shouted, giving my shoulder a little push for emphasis. I toyed with reminding him of my real name – we weren't acting anymore, after all – but…

No.

Outside.

Definitely the right thing to do.

Gripping the hat by the brim, I wrestled with the terrace doors and rushed outside into the cool night air. It was like entering another world: the smell of the smoke mingling with cold, peaty earth; the moths dancing around the lights; the radio wafting through the open kitchen window. I started bashing the burning hat against the wall. It was all so surreal that when Paul appeared by my side, stamping on a handful of smouldering paper napkins, it felt almost inevitable.

'Drop the hat!' barked Paul.

I stared stupidly at the inferno engulfing my right hand. My bashing had made not a jot of difference. If anything, it had encouraged the blaze.

'Drop it! It's burning you,' Paul shouted again. And then, 'Christ, your trousers are on fire.'

I glanced down.

Thick black smoke was billowing from my right calf.

I was actually on fire!

Paul grabbed a large flowerpot full of rainwater. He lobbed the contents in my general direction. Most of it fell short, so he chucked another with slightly more accuracy. And then another. The water was freezing, stagnant and it shocked me into action. I dropped the hat and stamped on it while Paul swatted at my leg with a soggy, mildewed cushion.

When the flames and smoke had subsided, Paul gave my hat its *coup de grâce* by throwing it unceremoniously into a large terracotta urn.

'You OK?' he asked.

'I think so.' I paused. 'My hand hurts though.'

Paul took my hand in his. Every cell was aware of his proximity, his touch. Together we inspected the damage. A weal, livid even in the gloaming, was forming under my thumb.

'Nasty,' said Paul, releasing his hold. 'I think you'll live, though.'

I nodded, rivulets of water running down my cheeks and into my mouth. 'Thank you,' I said. 'Very novel way of putting out fires.'

'Ha! Wait until you see what was next in line to be thrown at you.'

Paul held out a green flowerpot and I peered inside. At the bottom were two, very soggy, goat's cheese croutons.

'Mandy and Steve's starter!' I said. I started to laugh and Paul must have heard the hysteria in it because he put his arm round me. Suddenly, I don't know how, I was properly in his arms and he was kissing the hell out of me. Wine and smoke and honey and stubble and his hand in my hair and the brick wall cold and hard against my back...

After a while, we pulled apart and gazed at each other. Paul smoothed my wet hair back with both hands. His expression was intense, almost grim. 'Mm, *eau* de mouldy water,' he murmured and kissed me again. Not the most romantic of endearments but the kissing still felt wonderful.

I should stop...

I *knew* I should stop...

Then someone stumbled out of the terrace doors. It was Steve, waving a smouldering jumper and oblivious to the little human drama grinding to a halt in front of him. The jumper came in for Paul's flowerpot method of fire extinguishment. Then Steve grabbed a garden hose. He was about to head back inside when Paul put a hand on his arm.

'Let's just check the lay of the land before we let rip with that, my friend,' he said calmly. He gave me a backward glance and the two of them were gone.

I leant back against the wall.

Oh. My. God.

I had kissed a man who wasn't my husband.

A flicker of excitement, quickly extinguished.

Shock. Guilt. Horror.

What the hell was the matter with me. What the *hell* had I done?

And what on earth should I do now?

I really should go back inside. For all I knew, someone had called 999 and they'd evacuated the building from the front. Or they were passing buckets of water along a human chain and just needed one more person to keep the fire at bay. Or, worse still, Steve had seen everything and was spilling the beans...

Time to face the music.

—

Disaster had been averted.

Fire-wise at least.

All the flames had been extinguished. The overhead lights were on and the air was heavy with smoke. Fragments of clue manual and paper napkin littered the floor, the rugs were burnt in several places and there was water everywhere. It was a mess but it could have been so much worse.

Better still, no one appeared to be looking for me. There were no pointed fingers, no angry comments, no averted eyes. In fact, there wasn't really anyone around. Mandy was stacking the plates on the table. Steve was slumped in a chair studiously studying his clue manual, even though it was burnt to charred lace. Everyone else had gone.

'Christ, Healey,' said Mandy, looking up and noticing me. 'What on earth happened?'

I was suddenly aware of how I must look. Wet, burnt, tear-stained, a smidgen of stubble rash.

Bloody hell.

'My hat... I burned my hand,' I said. I could hardly string a sentence together.

Mandy took a look. 'Ouch, that looks sore,' she said. 'Run it under the tap and I'll see if Virginia's got anything to put on it.'

'Thanks. Where *is* everyone?'

'Virginia's seeing to the boys. Josh was freaked out by all the noise. I think Daniel went up to help. I'm not sure about Paul and Hanna.'

'OK.' I went into the kitchen and ran water over my hand. It was cold. Soothing. If only it could wash away my guilt as easily.

I felt different. I *was* different.

I'd betrayed Daniel.

And here he was. Right on cue.

'I wondered where you'd got to,' he said, putting an arm round my shoulder. 'I hear you've hurt your hand.'

'Yes.' I couldn't meet his eye. 'I burned it on that stupid hat.'

'You idiot,' said Daniel, not without affection.

'I know,' I said.

I was. A fickle, feckless two-timing idiot.

'And I don't just mean your hand.'

I went stone-cold all over. So Daniel *knew*. My life, or at least my marriage, was over. Steve *had* seen Paul and me kissing and had spilled the beans.

'Don't look so shocked,' said Daniel. 'You didn't do it on purpose and luckily I don't think there's much damage done.'

What?

I couldn't keep up with this. What hadn't I done on purpose?

Did Daniel think my lips had fused with Paul's accidentally? And what was the bit about 'no damage' supposed to mean? He was being almost ridiculously understanding.

Daniel was still talking. 'I'm partly to blame,' he said. 'I should have realised it was ours, should have checked before she lit the bloody thing. But you could argue she provided the meths and filled the canister, so technically it's her fault.'

Oh, bloody hell.

It hadn't occurred to me to question how the fire had started. Nor even to wonder which fondue set had been involved. Too late, I remembered the little gel packs of fuel we used to use. The bloody thing wasn't designed for a liquid. I was, at the very least, guilty of neglect.

'Oh my God!' I said. Three little words encompassing both relief and horror. But what to do now? Wimp that I was, my first instinct was to do a runner.

But I mustn't.

Couldn't.

Wouldn't.

'I'll go and own up,' I said, turning the tap off.

'Don't,' said Daniel. 'Let's see to your hand and then we'll help clear up.'

'But I've got to say *sorry*,' I said. 'I've got to offer to pay.'

'Oh, Em.' Daniel put his arm round me and kissed my hair. 'Honest to a fault.'

I blinked at him. 'Isn't it a good thing to be honest?' I said.

'Yes, of course it is. But Virginia's pretty upset and her son's kicking off big time. I don't think it will help her to know how the fire started just now. Plus, the insurance company might not pay out if they know the fondue set was misused. So, you'd just be putting her in an awkward situation.'

I paused. 'Oh. I see.' It still felt wrong though.

'If, for whatever reason, her insurance company doesn't cough up, we'll come clean and insist upon paying. But not tonight. OK?'

'OK.' I leant against him. He wasn't the enemy. He wasn't a statistic. He was my lovely, warm, wise Daniel.

And I had cheated on him.

Mandy swept in bearing lavender oil and bandages and Daniel and I stepped apart.

'I'm going to make a start on the washing up,' said Daniel, turning the taps on full.

'He's a keeper,' said Mandy, leading me over to the light and inspecting my wound. 'Right, let's get this bandaged up. Good job I did a first aid course at work.'

She started dabbing away with the lavender oil and then she swathed my hand in bandages in a most professional way. By the time she'd finished, Virginia had reappeared.

'I've just been seeing off Paul and Hanna,' she said.

'Have they gone?' Daniel turned round, forearms covered in suds. 'Just buggered off?'

'Apparently Hanna has asthma,' said Virginia. 'The smoke wasn't doing it any good.' Her tone implied she thought it was a pretty poor show too.

I was just relieved. Hugely relieved.

What the *hell* had I been thinking?

–

Daniel took the offending fondue set out to the car and stashed it in the boot ready to be picked up the next day. Steve got up (with a little help from Mandy) and the five of us cleaned and tidied companionably into the small hours. We cleared the table and stacked the dishwasher, tidied the kitchen and swept and mopped the floor. Eventually there was nothing left to do except inspect the damage. The rugs had burn holes, the wooden floor and table were singed in places and several glasses had been broken. But, we all agreed, it could have been so much worse.

'Thanks for staying,' said Virginia when we were finally sitting round the table and drinking limoncello. 'I don't know what I'd have done without you.'

'We never found out who the murderer was,' I said.

'By rights, it should have been Hanna,' said Mandy. 'She certainly made a good job of murdering the script.'

'Shh.' I giggled. Poor Hanna really hadn't made herself any friends that night.

'Actually, it was me,' said Daniel. 'Apparently I'm quite adept at slinking through tunnels in the dead of night. My boxing skills came in useful too.'

Virginia laughed. 'I'm sorry to ruin your moment of glory,' she said.

Daniel grinned. 'Be careful never to double-cross me,' he said. 'Look at what happened to poor old Dun Lutin.'

Chapter Twelve

I woke the next morning with a thumping headache. I turned the pillow over and was about to snuggle back down to sleep when Daniel started muttering darkly about fires and insurance policies. Then I remembered the fondue set and the kiss and that both Mum and Daniel's parents were coming for lunch.

Time to get up.

'What a night,' I said, sitting up and rubbing my eyes.

Daniel mumbled something from the depths of the duvet. It sounded like, 'I feel crap.'

'Yeah, me too. We can't cancel the oldies though. They'll have been looking forward to it.'

I got the gist of Daniel's response.

I hauled myself out of bed. On the bright side, at least it was normal family life. Thank God I hadn't wrecked anything with my stupid drunken snog.

No harm done.

Move on.

I bunged the lamb in the oven, left instructions for Daniel and headed to the supermarket for the forgotten odds and sods. There was always something. Today it was paper napkins and carrots. It would be paper napkins. Paul stamping on a smouldering pile before he—

No, Emma.

Don't go there.

All three kids insisted on accompanying me. Jack wanted to make sure I didn't slip any untested products into the trolley. Lily was after the latest pre-teen glossy and its shiny freebies. I wasn't sure about Freddie's motives but I was pleased he was coming along. Maybe I was forgiven for not going to the football match. Sadly, it soon became clear he was just grabbing the opportunity to 'hang' in the town centre.

The supermarket was packed and overly bright and generally not conducive to hangover recovery. We chose napkins acceptable to Jack and I tried not to mind that they had smiley faces all over them.

Then Lily couldn't find her magazine.

'Get another one,' I suggested. 'They're all the same.'

I snogged a man who wasn't your dad last night and I haven't got time for this.

'I want the one with the "Discover Your Destiny" spinner.' Lily stuck out her bottom lip. 'Everyone's got one.'

'OK.' Sigh. 'I'll ask if they've got any more out back. Jack, be a sweetie and get some carrots?'

Jack perked up. He'd never been allowed to weigh stuff on his own before. 'OK. How much weight?'

'Oh... a kilogram?'

Jack ran off and I found a member of staff who – thank goodness – found an odd copy of Lily's magazine with its bloody spinner. Then Daniel called, reminding me to get cat food.

'Mrs Healey?' A member of staff; the teenage daughter of an acquaintance.

'Hello, Rosie.'

'Can you come with me please?'

Heart sinking, I followed Rosie to the fruit and veg. A queue of people snaking through the aisle and, at the head of the queue, a small boy utterly absorbed in a pile of carrots.

I plastered on my bulletproof smile. 'All right, Jacko?'

'Yup. But it's hard getting these to weigh exactly one kilo. If I put this one on, it goes to one point one...'

'Stop being weird, Jack.' Lily cast an anxious glance at two nearby girls larking about on a trolley.

'You're the weird one. But these ones are just under a kilo-gram and I can't find…'

The queue muttered and stirred. 'Hurry up,' someone hissed, just loudly enough to make absolutely sure they were heard. My tiredness, my hangover, my guilt… I threw a handful of carrots into the bag and, ignoring Jack's furious protests, swept him and Lily to the checkout.

–

Half of Year Nine seemed to be in the town square, posing in little grungy groups or mucking around on their skateboards. It seemed only yesterday we'd been holding their hands on the way to nursery.

Freddie was talking to a girl. A *girl*! There was much hair flicking and overemphatic laughter – and that was just my son. Oh God; were the uncharted peaks and troughs of adoles-cence upon us already? Not Steady Freddie: my firstborn, fuzzy bundle of joy.

The fuzzy bundle was not best pleased to be interrupted. He trailed behind us to the car, grumpy as hell.

'Is she your girlfriend?' Jack asked, as we set off for home.

'You don't say girlfriend,' said Freddie. 'You say you're "in a relationship".'

'Well, are you in one of those, then?'

'Yes, actually.'

Really? *Really?* How had that slipped under the radar?

'What year is she in, Freddie?' I chipped in. I'd only caught a glance but the girl had looked much older than him. And, frankly, a bit of a slag in her bum-grazing skirt.

'Muuuum.' All three children groaned and my mum-radar picked up eye-swivelling in the back of the car.

'What?' I asked indignantly. It had been a perfectly reason-able question.

'It's Bethany,' said Lily with exaggerated patience.

'Is it? My God!'

Ness's Bethany. I saw her from time to time, of course, but the last time I'd really registered her, she'd been in tears because her lunchbox had spilled over the St John's playground. Since when had she been such a curvy teen temptress?

'What makes you "in a relationship"?' asked Lily.

Yes. I wanted to know the answer to that one, too.

'Holding hands?' suggested Jack.

'Nah,' said Freddie.

'Kissing? Freddie and Bethany, sitting in a tree—'

'Shut it, Jack.'

Full sex behind the bike sheds, then. At least someone in the Healey household would be getting it.

By the time we pulled into our drive, Jack had established Freddie and Bethany were an item because both had set their Facebook pages to 'in a relationship'.

'Can I join Facebook?' asked Jack.

'No!' Freddie and I said in unison.

Once home, I checked the bedrooms looked OK. Silly, our desire to impress our parents, even in middle age. Illogical too; it was unlikely any of them would attempt the trek upstairs.

Lily's room was, as ever, very pink and reasonably tidy. Lily was lying on her bed next to a broken Discover Your Destiny spinner. No matter, she said; it was rubbish anyway. I didn't get into Freddie's room; he was on the phone and my appearance was greeted with much grimacing and urgent hand-flapping. I retreated. Jack was arranging football cards into lines. His room was a bomb site. Football magazines littered the floor along with the usual array of dirty clothes, comics and school books. He obviously hadn't read the chapter about people with Asperger's being obsessively tidy. Maybe I should show it to him.

'I'm sorry about the carrots,' I said. 'I'm just a bit stressed at the moment.'

You know, kissing random dads, setting fire to people's homes. That sort of thing.

'Have you got your period?' asked Jack.

'Jack! That's totally inappropriate.'

'Why?' said Jack. 'Don't you have periods any more? Maybe it's the menopause.'

'For heaven's sake. Just tidy your room before Granny arrives.'

'Granny won't mind. She likes it like this.'

'No, she doesn't.'

'She does. She likes to make me happy. And, anyway, I find tidying really hard. I think it's my Asperger's.'

I felt my guilt-o-meter rise, then spotted the smirk on his face. Lobbing a pillow at him, I headed downstairs chuckling.

By the time Daniel had fetched Mum from her flat, the roast lamb and apple charlotte were both vaguely under control and I'd even had the opportunity to slap on some make-up. Just as well because Mum was looking fabulous in a lovely lemon jacket, her hair freshly washed and set.

'Hello, poppet,' she said. 'You look a bit peaky.'

'Just a late night,' I replied, kissing her papery cheek. I could trust Mum with most things but, frankly, where to start?

'Tripping the light fantastic, were we? And here's my lovely Jacko.'

Jack gave his grandmother his trademark hug, which involved twining his arms round her neck and making sure there was absolutely no other bodily contact.

Daniel's parents pulled up in their red Honda. They disembarked slowly and shuffled to the front door. The overall effect was beige: sepia people in a technicoloured world. For the record, I never, ever want to get old.

'Who are these children and why are they blocking my way?' said Daniel's father, tetchily.

One look at Daniel's lovely, lost father and it was obvious he was at his most cantankerous.

'They're your grandchildren, Dad,' said Daniel. 'They've come to say hello.'

'Nonsense,' said Daniel's father. 'I don't have any grandchildren.'

—

Jack waited until we were at the lunch table to remind me he wanted to join Facebook.

'It's only to play games, Mum,' he said. 'Everyone plays Pets Corner.'

His timing was deliberate. He knew I was far more likely to capitulate in company — especially with the grandparents in attendance. But I really didn't want Jack on Facebook. The potential communication misunderstandings didn't bear thinking about.

'I'm sorry, Jack, but the answer's no,' I said.

'*Absolutely* no,' said Daniel. 'Not until you're thirteen.'

Thank goodness Daniel had my back.

Jack was outraged. 'Freddie wasn't thirteen,' he said.

'Well, he should have been,' said Daniel.

'What? How's that fair?'

'Don't talk to your father like that,' said Daniel's dad. 'When I played cricket for England, we respected our elders and betters.'

Believe me, Daniel's dad had never played cricket for England. I think he'd done a stint bowling for Portishead as a lad before he put his back out. Lily and Freddie knew this of course and were struck by a fit of giggles that resulted in Lily sliding so far down in her chair she was in danger of falling off.

'Sit properly, Lily,' I said sharply. 'You're not five.'

Lily hauled herself upright and smirked at Freddie. 'What's this weird stuff?' she asked, prodding her roasted beetroot swirled with cream; the token vegetable-with-something-interesting-done-to-it. 'It looks like something's bleeding.'

'It's a dead man's heart,' said Freddie.

'No, it's not,' said Jack firmly.

'It is.'

'Gross.' Lily giggled.

'And if you eat it, you'll turn into him,' added Freddie.

'I won't.'

'You will.'

'So, I'll grow a willy, will I?'

'Yup.'

'All hairy like—'

'Enough, kids,' said Daniel sharply. 'For goodness sake, can't you just behave for a couple of hours?'

'It's not really a heart, is it?' said Jack.

Bless him.

'Of course it's not,' said Mum gently.

'Is Freddie lying?'

'Joking,' said Mum. 'Just joking. This is delicious, Emma.'

'Thank you.'

If we could just have peace and quiet for a few minutes. My head was bloody killing me. My hand too.

'That young man's taken my Yorkshire pudding,' said Daniel's dad, jabbing his fork in Freddie's direction.

'No, I haven't,' Freddie protested, pulling his plate out of his grandfather's reach.

'I saw you.' Daniel's dad stared belligerently around the table, looking for support.

I glanced at Daniel's mum but she just gave a little shrug. Accusing people of stealing food was obviously a new development.

'Freddie, just give Granddad yours?' said Daniel. He looked rather like I felt.

'No way! Granddad's already had two,' said Freddie.

'I'll have you know I've not had *any*, young feller-me-lad.'

Daniel put his own Yorkshire on his father's plate without comment.

'*Please* can I join Facebook?' said Jack.

After a couple of glasses of Merlot, Daniel's dad became expansive.

'Do you remember July 1977?' he said. 'Best summer of my life. Five wickets for seventy-four against Australia.'

'I thought that was Ian Botham?' said Daniel mildly.

I gave him an old-fashioned look. Wasn't it best to humour people with dementia?

Daniel's dad rallied gamely. 'Oh, old Beefy was there, of course,' he said. 'But he couldn't have done it without me.'

Lily and Freddie snuffled with giggles. Jack looked mutinous.

'All finished?' I said brightly. 'Let's have pudding.'

I presented my apple charlotte with a little flourish. It had been a faff to make but its mosaic of sugared brioche had turned out particularly nicely this time. Sadly, no one took a blind bit of notice of either it or me. And where was Daniel? Taking a suspiciously long time to load the dishwasher, that's where. Probably feet up with the *Observer* in the kitchen.

'*Please* can I go on Facebook?' said Jack.

'No.' I was losing patience now.

'Why not? Everyone else is.'

'No, everyone is not, Jack. Don't tell lies.'

Jack leapt to his feet. '*Me* tell lies?' he shouted. '*Me?*'

'Sit down, Jack, there's a good boy,' Mum said gently. She really was the best mum in the world.

'Disgraceful behaviour,' muttered Daniel's mother.

'How can you tell me off for telling lies when Freddie told Lily she'd grow a willy?' demanded Jack.

'That was a *joke*,' I said.

'Well, why wasn't what I said a joke?'

'It just wasn't.' I couldn't get into what did or did not constitute a joke now. I wasn't sure I knew, anyway.

'Why not? And, anyway, Granddad said he played cricket against Australia and we all know that's a big, stupid, *bloody* lie.'

'Jack…!' I'd just started telling him off big time when Daniel's dad pushed back his chair and got unsteadily to his feet.

'How dare you talk to me like that, young man?' he said, thumping his hands down on the table.

Don't judge him!

Don't judge my son.

'I'm only telling the truth,' said Jack, standing up too and squaring up to his grandfather. Their profiles were really similar. I'd never noticed it before. 'You *never* played cricket for England.'

'You cheeky little blighter. Wait until I get my hands on you.'

'I'll call Childline—'

Daniel burst back into the room. 'What on *earth* is going on?' he demanded. 'The whole street can hear you.'

My mouth opened by itself. 'OK, Jack. Go and set yourself up on Facebook. But I need to know your password and…'

Jack was gone.

Daniel turned to me, an incredulous look on his face. 'I cannot *believe* you just did that,' he said.

'Neither can I,' said Freddie.

'I want to go home,' said Daniel's dad.

It was barely three o'clock when Daniel's parents left and, a short while later, I dropped Mum home.

Mum held my chin with her hand as she kissed me goodbye. 'Don't think for a second you were always a little angel,' she said. 'Or that your father and I were always singing from the same hymn sheet.'

Given she usually made out that her life had been perfect and that I'd never given her a moment's trouble, this was a major concession.

But she'd noticed that something was 'up' between Daniel and me.

103

That we weren't pulling together as we perhaps once would have.

And that felt a little scary.

—

Daniel was waiting when I got home.

'You've got to be *consistent*, Em,' he said. 'What sort of message does it send to Jack – to any of them – when you blow with the breeze?'

'Oh, Daniel.' I said. 'What else could I have done? It was *horrendous* in there.'

'You should've stuck to your guns. And as for shouting like that—'

'And *you* should have stuck around rather than buggering off to the kitchen at the earliest opportunity. You hardly win Parent of the Year yourself.'

'You're the primary parent, Em. You've got to have coping strategies for when I'm not around.'

'You *are* around. Stop dumping it all on me.'

Freddie came in with a face like thunder. 'Jack's put on Facebook that I still have Spiderman pants,' he said.

I very nearly giggled. I could have sworn Daniel's lips twitched too.

'*And* he's put that Jamie Kennedy's party was an epic fail.'

Neither of us laughed then.

Wearily, I headed upstairs.

Arse.

Chapter Thirteen

It had just been a silly kiss.

Paul and I had been high on booze and adrenaline.

No big drama.

No need for soul-searching.

I'd take the kids to school as usual and, if I happened to see Paul and if any mention seemed necessary, I'd just laugh and move on...

'I'll take the kids in to school this morning,' said Daniel as I was stacking the dishwasher after breakfast.

I looked up, surprised. Daniel had done the school run regularly before I'd stopped work, of course, but he hadn't done so since.

'Thanks,' I said. 'But don't be late for work on my account.'

I didn't want Paul thinking I was avoiding him or playing silly games.

'It's no big deal,' said Daniel. 'I've got a call with China and I haven't time to get into work beforehand anyway. And I wanted to apologise for yesterday. Bailing out at lunch and then having a go at you...'

'Thank you,' I said. 'And I'm sorry too. I *wasn't* being consistent.'

Was it just me, or did Daniel and I seem to be spending most of our time apologising to each other nowadays?

'Let's have a date night soon,' said Daniel. 'We're well overdue one.'

He blew me a kiss and started rounding up the kids. I made myself another cafetière of coffee and settled into the armchair with Matt the Mog on my lap. It *was* lovely to have a more leisurely start to Monday morning and I could always catch up with Paul at pickup if needs be. I shut my eyes and—

'You still here?'

I started awake with a little jump. Daniel was back already.

'Sorry,' I said. 'I*'m* about to get dressed.'

'It's not that. You're meant to be meeting Ness for a run. She said she'd texted you to meet on the bridge at quarter past since you weren't at school today.'

'Shit…'

I'd completely forgotten; the change of schedule had thrown me completely out of whack. I glanced at my phone; there was the message from Ness and – oh dear – it was already nearly nine fifteen. I ran upstairs and flung on my running kit and was out of the door within minutes. But it was the best part of a mile to the bridge and I wasn't the fastest runner.

Ness didn't smile as I ran up to her. In fact, she looked distinctly pissed off.

'All set?' I asked brightly.

'Emma, you are really, *really* late.'

'I know. I'm sorry. I'd completely forgotten and—'

'Great,' Ness interrupted. 'And I've been standing here for half an hour like a right twat. I'm freezing my arse off. I can hardly feel my fingers. And at least three lorries have honked me. Couldn't you at least have let me know you were running late?'

'Well, I would have done,' I said, 'but by the time I realised, I was already on my way.'

'Yes, but I didn't know that, did I?'

'Sorry,' I said again. I gave her my most beguiling smile. 'It was only twenty-seven minutes, to be precise. And wait until you hear about my weekend from hell.'

Ness gave a grunt but at least she didn't storm off. We set off toward the riverbank and I filled her in on the murder-mystery evening, the fire and yesterday's lunch. I missed out the Paul element. That had to remain an utter secret. Even from my best friend. Anyway, Ness made roughly the right repertoire of noises in roughly the right places, but I could tell her heart wasn't in it. I felt a tad miffed. Surely it was an impressive haul of news, views and juicy gossip by anyone's standards.

'What's up?' I asked, as we turned onto the towpath.

Ness wrinkled her brow. 'Did you know Bethany and Freddie are going out together?' she said.

Ah. My elder son's burgeoning love life.

'I did. But you don't say "going out" any more,' I said. 'It's "in a relationship". Get with the story, missus.'

Ness didn't smile. 'I'm uncomfortable about it,' she said.

'Are you?' I couldn't help feeling a bit affronted on Freddie's behalf. Surely he was a catch. 'It's all part of growing up,' I said. 'And their "relationship" seems to be conducted almost entirely on Facebook, so she's not exactly going to get knocked up, is she?'

'That's not the point.'

'Come on. You *know* Freddie. He's as sensible as they come. Now if it was Jack—'

'Yes, but it's not Jack. And it's not all online. They're wandering round town together.'

'You mean hanging out in the town square with the rest of Year Nine?' It was so ridiculous I wanted to laugh. 'I saw them on Sunday morning. It was hardly gang culture!'

'They're also going down to the river.'

'Good for them. Fresh air. Exercise. Vitamin D.'

'But supposing there's drink involved?'

Yes, that would be worrying.

'What makes you think there might be?'

'Nothing,' said Ness. 'There just *could* be.'

Now I did laugh. 'Ness, *listen* to yourself,' I said. 'If there was any suggestion of booze, you know I'd be down on Freddie like a ton of bricks.'

'OK, OK,' said Ness. 'Sorry. I'm just feeling a bit wound up in general.'

'Why's that?' I asked.

Ness stopped jogging and started plucking the heads off the tall grasses that lined the path. 'This is top secret,' she said. '*Top secret*. OK?'

'Yes. Absolutely.'

Ness leant over. 'Mega crush,' she whispered, even though there was no one else around.

'Fab,' I said. 'Does he feel the same?'

'I think so. And he's *gorgeous*.'

'So why the secrecy?' Then a thought struck me. 'He's not married, is he?'

'No. But he's a bit younger than me,' said Ness.

'You shady lady! How young are we talking?'

Ness made a face. 'Late twenties, I think.'

I did a rapid calculation. 'That's fine. The half-your-age-plus-seven rule means you're OK with anyone over twenty-eight. So, spill the beans. Who is it?'

'My physio.'

I knew Ness had trouble with a wandering pelvis. But...

'Jeez, Ness, you've copped off with your *physio*?!'

'Why not?' Ness flushed a deep pink.

'Isn't it a bit of a cliché?'

'A *cliché*?'

'Yes,' I said. '"My inner thighs need more attention" sort of thing.'

'It's not like that,' Ness spluttered.

'It might be "not like that" with half the town. Which physio is it, anyway?'

I'd worked my way through most of the local ones over the years and, believe me, there were no obvious candidates.

'Not here. In Reading.'

'Well, that's something, I suppose.'

I might have been more inclined to empathise if Ness hadn't spent the past few minutes slagging off my son. No one likes their children being criticised, do they? But I made an effort to look interested as she told me how Mr Golden Hands had put his hands on her shoulders to remind her of their correct position. And then he'd kissed her. Or she had kissed him. She couldn't quite be sure.

Either way, it sounded very unprofessional to me.

But I listened. And smiled. And nodded.

And I still didn't tell her about Paul.

As school pickup drew nearer, I began to feel a bit queasy. Even if I had no intention of doing anything else, kissing another woman's husband *was* quite a big deal – especially as I was happily married myself. I needed to make absolutely sure that Paul knew it had been a mistake, a one-off. I needed to make sure he had absolutely no intention of telling anyone else about it. But, of course, I had no idea how he was feeling about the whole thing. Horrified? Excited? Nonchalant? Why hadn't he called over the weekend to try to sort the whole thing out? Maybe it was of the 'if the phone doesn't ring, it's me' school of not calling. Maybe he'd sat by the phone all yesterday waiting for *me* to call. Maybe—

Enough.

Enough, Emma!

Think about something else.

Right. I should get Virginia some flowers.

How was that for 'something else'?

A 'thank-you' for a memorable evening, not an admission of guilt for the fire, so that Daniel wouldn't be annoyed. No sooner had the idea come into my mind than I was off to the florist. I ordered a bespoke bouquet with lilies and irises and other lovely things and it turned out to be gorgeous but absolutely huge and eye-wateringly expensive, so Daniel was bound to be annoyed anyway.

I wrestled the bouquet onto the back seat of the car and drove to the school. Virginia was standing at the far end of the upper playground talking to Paul and Mandy. It seemed a very, very long way away and a very, very large bouquet, and already people were smiling and pointing.

Deep breaths, Emma. Shoulders back.

'Are those to say sorry to me?'

It was Ness, appearing out of nowhere.

I paused.

Should I have bought her flowers? I mean, I *had* been very late for our run and I hadn't been very sympathetic about her crush. Maybe I should pretend the bouquet *was* for her.

Then I saw Ness was smiling. 'I'm kidding, mate,' she said, giving my shoulder a little push. 'I'm guessing they're for Virginia.'

Phew. 'They are,' I said.

'Lovely gesture.'

We said our goodbyes and I continued my lonely trek across the playground.

'You look like something out of *Macbeth*,' said Paul, as I finally drew near.

I peeked over the top. 'The advancing forest rather than a witch, I hope.'

Cue Paul's relaxed, boyish laugh. 'Debatable,' he said.

I lowered the bouquet again and stuck my tongue out at him. Dancing green eyes. Curving mouth. The mouth that had kissed me...

'I've no idea what you're talking about,' said Mandy, 'but those flowers are amazing.'

'They're for Virginia,' I said. 'To say thank you for such a lovely evening.'

Virginia looked genuinely delighted. 'Oh, how lovely,' she said. 'So kind of you. Well, it was certainly a *memorable* evening.

I've been doing insurance stuff this afternoon. Did anything of yours get damaged?'

There was a question. My peace of mind had been incinerated. My wedding vows charred. My marriage slightly singed...

'Only my very stylish hat,' I said.

Everyone laughed.

'Man, that hat was *badass*,' said Mandy.

'It is now an ex-hat,' said Paul solemnly.

'I believe it was laid to rest in a terracotta urn alongside two goat's cheese croutons,' said Virginia with a grin and Mandy had the grace to blush.

Lily ran over, handed me her book-bag and simultaneously dissolved into tears.

'What is it?' I asked, crouching down and taking her into my arms.

My poor little flower.

Lily stood there gulping for breath. 'Hellie's gone off with Izzie and now I've got no one to play with,' she said. She could hardly get the words out, she was crying so hard.

Bloody girls and their friendships. I could, unfortunately, remember it well.

'Oh, Lily.' I hugged her to me, fiercely. 'They'll be back.'

'They won't. They hate me.'

'They don't. They're just being silly girls. Now, what about an ice cream?'

There was usually an ice cream van parked outside the school gate, even in the autumn. So much for encouraging healthy eating at school. Lily looked at me from under her fringe and gave me the ghost of a smile.

''K,' she said.

I rummaged in my pocket for some coins. 'You could even buy one for Hellie and Izzie,' I said.

'No *way*,' said Lily.

I laughed and straightened up. Virginia and Mandy had moved off – I could see the flowers disappearing across the playground. Paul was still hovering and, for a second, we just stared at each other. Then my mouth opened by itself.

'I'm sorry, Paul,' I blurted out. 'I'm not that type of person.'

I regretted the words immediately. They implied I thought Saturday night had meant something to Paul. That it was more than an impulsive drunken kiss. That he wanted something more. That *I* wanted more.

But Paul just nodded. 'I know,' he said. 'I'm not that kind of person either.'

Our smiles filled in the space between the words.

'So,' I said. 'Nothing happened?'

'Nothing. But I want you to know I've never done "nothing" with anyone else.'

'Me neither.'

'Onwards and upwards?'

'Onwards and upwards.'

Gabriel arrived and Paul hoisted him effortlessly onto his shoulders. Another smile and they were gone.

Wrong place. Wrong time.

Wrong life.

Chapter Fourteen

I meant for that to be that.

I really did.

I meant to put the whole thing down to experience and to move on – my marriage and my honour intact and The Statistic thwarted.

And it all started out so well.

I'd taken Daniel at his word and arranged a date night. Family restaurant trips were usually limited to Strada because Jack liked the food but, for Daniel and me, Hambley was our oyster and I'd managed to snag a table at Pampas, the new Argentinian place everyone was talking about. I wasn't that keen on steak but it was Daniel's absolute favourite and I wanted to make amends. Indeed, tonight, I was going to pull out all the stops to be sparkling, witty and gorgeous; the woman Daniel had fallen in love with all those years ago. I'd even ordered some new undies for 'afters'.

We wandered down to town side by side, hand in hand. This was lovely. We really should do it more often now that Freddie was old enough to babysit. Maybe we could make it a weekly thing. We'd become au fait with all the best places to eat. People would come to us for advice. Maybe I'd even get a little column in the *Hambley Weekly*...

Pampas was in the centre of town where Pizza Express used to be. Now it was all roughly hewn wood and cow-related paraphernalia. Maybe I should grab one of the whips to go with my – frankly scratchy – new lingerie. *That* would give Daniel something to think about.

The place was *heaving*, romantic couples interspersed with boisterous groups. I spotted at least two tables of mums from school, their animated chat punctuated by shouts of laughter. Daniel and I were shown to a table slap-bang in the middle. The noise level was just the right side of bearable.

The menu was basically different cuts of steak. I'd known that. The trouble was that I only liked it well done and the default here seemed to be medium rare. Order anything else and you were obviously more Bognor Regis than Buenos Aires.

'This looks great,' said Daniel, scanning the menu. 'It's ages since we've had steak. Let's push the boat out and have the fillet.'

Damn!

Now I would be being a real party pooper if I went for the token pasta dish. So, when a gaucho with an intimidating accent came to take our order, I smiled confidently, said 'medium please' and I told myself I was imagining his answering sneer.

We toasted each other with Malbec and Daniel reached across the table and took my hand.

'Here's to my wonderful wife,' he said. 'It's lovely to spend an uninterrupted evening with you.'

We smiled at each other and there was a pause. Quite a long pause, actually. Then, I said, 'How's work going?' at the very same moment as he said, 'How are you finding being a full-time mum?' and then we both said, 'No you first,' and, for some reason, it was awkward rather than funny. Then I started telling him about the ball preparations and about how worried Paul and I were that no one had donated anything to the auction of promises yet and how embarrassing it would be if no one ever did. Daniel nodded politely but he didn't seem particularly interested or engaged. Then he told me an anecdote about someone at work who had slagged someone else off in an email, but the wrong people were on copy and the shit had hit the fan – but I didn't really know the people involved, so my laughter was forced. This was awful. Was Daniel bored in my company? Was I bored in his? Either way, I was relieved when the starters came and we could stop talking for a while.

Things didn't pick up with the arrival of the main course. My steak was horrendously underdone and, every time I cut into it, blood oozed out all over my salad. Usually I would have sent it back, but I didn't want to put even more of a dampener on the meal. Not that it made much difference. The conversation limped along and pauses became longer and more loaded. The Statistic may as well have pulled up a chair and got stuck into the skinny fries. Honestly, I would rather have had a massive great row than this… nothingness. It was easy to imagine the raucous laughter at the surrounding tables was directed at us. Easy to assume the intense conversations were passing judgement on our silence.

I tried again. 'How's work really?' I said. 'You know, with the lay-offs and everything?'

Daniel sighed. 'Not great,' he said. 'All the opportunities are in the States at the moment. They're really winding down in the UK.'

'That's a bummer.'

'It is. I might have to go to Austin in the next couple of weeks. That's if they haven't got rid of me by then. Would that be OK?'

'Of course.' This was better. At least we were talking. Then a thought occurred to me. 'What about Nicole. *Nicky.*'

Hadn't she come over from Austin?

'Turns out she's part of the hatchet team,' said Daniel.

'Aha,' I said with a grin. '*You* should be OK then!'

'What do you mean?'

'Oh, come on. She clearly has the hots for you.'

Daniel put down his cutlery. 'For God's sake, Emma,' he said. 'This is serious stuff and all you're doing is making facetious comments.'

'It was a *joke*, Daniel,' I snapped. 'Remember those?'

'Barely,' said Daniel. 'And don't think I haven't noticed you trying to hide thirty quid's worth of steak under your lettuce. And that you're wriggling about like a bored schoolgirl.'

Huh!

I wasn't going to tell him my new undies were getting acquainted with areas they had no right to explore. He could bloody well think I *was* bored. Which, come to think of it…

My mobile rang and I made a point of answering it in the middle of the meal. It was Freddie.

'Jack's put "Josh Kennedy is a bastard" on Facebook,' he said. '*And* he won't take it down.'

'Oh, for goodness sake,' I said. '*I'll* take it down. Thanks for letting me know.'

'What was that about?' asked Daniel.

'Jack's put something he shouldn't have on Facebook,' I said, trying to log into the offending account. 'Oh, God! The little sod's changed his password.'

'For heaven's sake, Em. You should have set it up so that only *you* know the password.'

'I know, I know.'

'*I'll* call Jack,' said Daniel. He called Freddie's mobile and asked him to put Jack on. From the resulting conversation, I gathered Jack was refusing to budge.

'I don't care if it's *true*,' Daniel hissed. 'It's outrageously rude.'

More babble from the other end of the line. Daniel's fist clenched. I took the phone from him and tried a different, more Jack-friendly approach.

'Actually Josh isn't a bastard,' I said, 'because, even though his dad has died, his parents were married when he was born.'

'Really?' said Jack.

'Yes.'

'Sorry,' said Jack. 'I'll take it down.'

'And say sorry to Josh.'

'OK.'

We said goodbye and I put my phone back in my bag. When I looked up, Daniel was staring at me with his brows pulled together.

'Jack should have taken that post down because it was the wrong thing to have done,' he said.

'We can explain that to him later,' I said. 'But, for the moment, shall we try to salvage what's left of this meal?'

'Did madam not like her steak?' asked a new gaucho in a heavy accent.

'Madam did not,' I said. 'Any less cooked and it would be mooing. And stop pretending you're Argentinian, Tom. I *know* you're Sian's eldest.'

We didn't bother with pudding. As we walked home – hands resolutely in pockets this time – I seriously wondered for the first time if The Statistic might win.

—

That night, we made love for the first time in ages. Or I should say 'that night we had sex'. I think we both felt we had to. And it was fine.

In a sticking plaster sort of way.

Chapter Fifteen

It turned out it hadn't even been a sticking plaster.

The next evening, I was in the bathroom checking Lily's hair for nits. We'd had the dreaded letter from school and Lily had complained her hair was itching. There was actually something quite therapeutic about parting small sections of hair and methodically pulling through the fine-toothed comb. Lily, swathed in a towel, was singing 'Let It Go' loudly and tunelessly into a hairbrush.

Then Daniel burst in, brandishing a passport. 'What's this?' he demanded.

'It's a passport,' said Lily helpfully.

'It's *Jack's* passport,' said Daniel. 'And it's out of date. Out. Of. Date.'

'So?' I said. 'It's not as if he's going to Austin with you.'

'That's not the point. We might want to do something spontaneous.'

'And we might not.' I wasn't having this. I hadn't got a job. Dan's job was precarious. And Jack hated spontaneous holidays. In fact, he pretty much hated all holidays.

Daniel was undeterred. 'We could go somewhere at Christmas,' he said.

Lily stopped singing. 'Can we go to Lapland?' she asked.

'No,' I said.

'Maybe,' said Daniel simultaneously.

'Yessss!' Lily did a fist-pump. 'Jack? *Jack!*'

Jack poked his head round the bathroom door. 'Wha'?' he said.

'Dad says we can go to Lapland at Christmas. It'll be like *Frozen*.'

'I don't want to go there,' said Jack. 'I want to stay at home.'

Freddie came in. 'What's this I hear about holidays?' he said.

'Nothing,' said Daniel. 'Your mother hasn't kept the passports up to date.'

'Cheers, Daniel,' I said. 'Oh Lily, your hair is *crawling* with nits.'

I smiled at Jack. *He* would back me up.

Jack looked back at me levelly. 'My head's really itchy,' he said.

—

Once all the kids were deloused, I stormed downstairs to where Daniel was working on his laptop.

'Don't *ever* show me up in front of the kids like that again,' I hissed. 'We don't even *need* the bloody passports at the moment.'

'But if you do it now there won't be a rush later. It's not as if you have much else to do.'

Huh!

I'd show him!

—

The next morning, I got up early, packed Jack and Lily into the car and set off for the photo booth at Tesco. A pep talk, a chocolate bar, a bit of gurning and four minutes later we were all set. The kids weren't even late for school. Somehow, overnight, I'd morphed into one of those super-efficient mums. Just call me Virginia.

Then it was all systems go to get the paperwork sorted before I lost momentum. A quick dash to the post office for the forms and then round to Sian's for a countersignature. By eleven, I was back at the post office – only this time, half the town seemed to be there. Naturally, there were only two cashiers and the queue snaked back through shelves of obscure packing materials. By the time I got to the front, I was more than a little shirty. It was hard work being Super-Mum.

'I'd like the passport checking service, please,' I said, shaking my bits and pieces onto the counter. The queue behind me muttered and stirred at my audacity in doing more than buying a stamp.

'There's a smudge where your witness has countersigned.'

I glanced up, registering the woman behind the counter for the first time. Brassy, blond, of a certain age. Clearly not having a good day.

'It's microscopic...' I protested.

'*And* she hasn't included her postcode.' The cashier's voice was far louder than necessary and the queue shifted again. I could feel the hate waves penetrating the back of my head.

'I'm sure I can find it for you,' I said. I started searching for St Mary's Hospice on my iPhone.

The cashier sighed. 'I've got it here,' she said, brandishing a laminated sheet.

'Then why are you being so stroppy?' I said. Two could do the playing-to-the-gallery thing.

'I'm not being stroppy.' Quieter now. All wide-eyed and conciliatory. 'I'm just pointing out possible reasons your application might be rejected.'

We locked gazes, battle lines drawn. She was determined to find a reason to reject Jack's passport application. I was equally determined not to let her.

The cashier declared her hand first. 'This photo is unacceptable,' she said, voice shaking with glee. 'He's not facing the camera full on. It's what we call a partial profile shot. *Partial profile.*'

Oh God.

She had a point.

'*And* his hair is partly covering one eye.'

Damn. Things were definitely swinging her way. There was only one thing to do. I took a deep breath and went unashamedly for the Asperger's card.

'The thing is,' I said, leaning forward confidingly but making sure I could be heard by the entire post office. 'My son is autistic. He *hates* having his picture taken. I don't think we'd be able to get a better one.'

The cashier looked deflated.

'It's hard for him to look straight at the camera,' I continued. 'I could *try*, but eye contact's tough for kids on the spectrum.'

Now the cashier looked crushed. *Crushed*.

Emboldened, I went for the kill. 'And the thing with the hair? That's Asperger's too. Some would say it'd be cruel to take away his security blanket.'

I wondered if I'd gone too far. But the cashier's hands fluttered and she glanced at the queue. 'Well, that's different,' she said. 'They tend to be lenient in these cases.'

Did they?

The cashier was all embarrassed smiles as she helped me make the necessary amendments. I could even sense a thawing in the queue behind me. Thank God being politically correct was so 'in' nowadays.

'There you go,' she said. 'Even if the powers-that-be are having a menopausal moment like us, they should wave it through.'

I ignored her implication. I had won and I could afford to be magnanimous. Bestowing a gracious smile, I gathered my stuff and turned to leave.

Victory was short-lived.

Second in line was Virginia, smiling and reaching an arm out to me. Suddenly I felt awful. What kind of mother used her son's Asperger's to get her own way? And lied to boot? Was there something wrong with me? Jack was absolutely fine with having his photo taken. It was *my* fault the photos didn't meet the regulations. I just hadn't bothered to check the rules properly.

I ignored Virginia and hurried out onto the street.

'Emma!' Virginia was striding after me, still clutching her parcel. 'Are you OK?'

'I'm absolutely fine,' I said. 'You didn't need to leave your place in the queue.'

Virginia gave me her parcel to hold. 'It's no problem,' she said. 'I've got something you might find useful.' She started rummaging in her bag and emerged with a business card. It was purple with a picture of a dahlia on it.

Ally O'Reilly. Child and adult psychotherapist.

'I don't think Jack needs any help at the moment,' I said stiffly. 'But thanks anyway.'

Bloody cheek.

'Maybe not. But sometimes we mums could do with some help as well.'

What?

No really – *what*?

'I'm fine,' I said, internalising fuck off and die. 'I don't need a psychotherapist.'

Did I really come across as that *unhinged*?

'I think you might find it useful,' said Virginia. 'Hang on to it anyway. Then if you change your mind...'

And, with a squeeze of my hand, she headed back into the post office.

I stood there gawping after her. How *dare* she suggest I see a shrink? Did she see herself as some kind of Lady Bountiful, bestowing business cards on inferior mortals who didn't have perfect lives and tight, high bottoms?

I stood there for a while. I didn't want to go back home and be by myself. I wanted to hang out, chew the cud, moan about Daniel, bitch about Virginia. The question was, who with? Ness, the automatic choice, was working. So was Mandy.

Paul?

No. Totally inappropriate.

There were a hundred and one reasons why I shouldn't call *him*...

So, I called him.

He answered immediately. 'Hi, Emma.' There was the sound of footsteps on floorboards, a door shutting. 'What can I do for you?'

Suddenly, I wasn't sure.

'Um, I was wondering if you wanted to meet up. Maybe go round the shops?'

Pause. 'You want to go shopping with me?' Was that a hint of incredulity in his voice?

'Well, not *shopping*, shopping. To ask for donations to the ball.' A pathetic trill.

'Oh right. Do you mean now?'

'No time like the present.' Stop *trilling*, Emma.

'Aren't we better off doing that sort of thing in writing?' asked Paul.

'D'you reckon?' He was right. Of course, he was.

'I do,' said Paul. 'I don't fancy trailing round the shops, badgering a load of assistants who won't have a clue what we're talking about. And it's bloody parky out there.'

The fight went out of me. 'Fair enough. Crap idea.'

There was a pause.

'Are you OK?'

'I don't know.' I scratched my burn scab and my Teddy scar, perilously close to tears.

'Tell you what,' said Paul. 'I've got to pop into town. If you can hang on a few minutes, I'll meet you in Café Rouge. We need to catch up about the ball anyway.'

'OK. Thank you.'

–

Fifteen minutes later, installed at a corner table in Café Rouge, I was wondering why on earth I'd been so stupid and impulsive.

We'd got a ball meeting in a week's time anyway and Paul was bound to be pissed off I'd dragged him out in the cold...

But, here he was, wreathed in scarves and smiles. A brief moment to marry fantasy with reality – face a tad rounder, a little older-looking – and I gingerly tested my attraction as you might an aching tooth.

Or a fragile scab on a burn.

Yup, still there. Stronger, if anything.

'So, what's up?' Paul asked once we'd got our coffees.

Hmm. I couldn't really tell him about the disastrous date and the passport row and the fact that I was probably trying to get back at Daniel...

I went for the easier option.

'Virginia suggested I see a shrink.'

Paul goggled. 'Not really?' he said.

'Really, really.'

'Under what circumstances?'

I told him what had happened in the post office and Paul threw his head back and roared with laughter.

'Good for you,' he said. 'I'd have done exactly the same.'

'Would you?' I took a huge swig of creamy coffee.

'Yes. Excellent, on-the-spot creative thinking.'

'So, you don't think I need to see a shrink?'

'I wouldn't go that far!'

I wrinkled my nose at him, feeling much more cheerful.

'I've got something to show you,' said Paul. He took an envelope out of his jacket pocket and handed it to me. 'I picked it up at school this morning. It's the first promise for the auction.'

'At last! How exciting. What is it?'

'I don't know. I was going to wait until I saw you this afternoon. You open it.'

'No, you.'

'I insist.'

'OK then.' I took the envelope and held it to my lips. It felt important, like exam results or tests from the hospital. Then I quickly tore it open and read aloud from the slip inside.

'A tray of chocolate-covered flapjacks.'

As one, we doubled up with laughter; breathless, snorting laughter punctuated only by the odd high-pitched comment. The kind of laughter that had been markedly absent from my date with Daniel.

'Not just flapjacks, but chocolate-*covered* ones.'

'A whole trayful!'

'Halfway to our target already!'

We carried on in this vein for quite some time and until my stomach muscles were beginning to beg for mercy.

'Oh God, I haven't laughed like that for ages,' said Paul, hauling himself up straight.

'Me neither.' I wiped under my eyes for stray flecks of mascara and glanced around the restaurant. A couple of acquaintances from school were glancing at us curiously.

'So,' I said, trying to switch my brain into 'sensible' mode. 'We won't be able to auction things like this. We'll have to come up with a Plan Two. Some sort of lucky dip, I guess.'

'That's a good idea,' said Paul, putting on his serious face too. 'Oh, and by the way, I've got an appointment through for Gabriel.'

'Wow. I didn't even know you'd applied. That's come through quickly.'

'It's private,' said Paul. 'Against my better judgement, but they said the NHS one could take months.'

'Ha! *Torygraph* reader...'

'How very dare you!' said Paul with a grin. 'Anyway, d'you think it's the right thing to do?'

'What? Going private?'

'Nooo. Getting a diagnosis.'

'Definitely. If he needs it. What does Hanna think?'

Paul sighed. 'She's having none of it. She denies there's anything wrong.'

'Ah. You do need to try to get her on board. But then, of course, there's The Statistic.'

'What statistic?'.

'The one that says 80 per cent of marriages with an autistic child break down.'

Paul laughed. 'Sounds like an urban myth to me,' he said.

'No. Daniel told me. And you can't argue with numbers.'

'Bollocks,' said Paul. 'You can't generalise about people and marriages. Everyone's got their own shit.'

'So, what's your shit?' I asked.

I felt rather bold saying it but, doing interviews, you always play back the respondents' vocabulary. It relaxes them, helps them to open up.

Paul smiled and shrugged. 'Wondering if I'm doing the right thing being a full-time writer,' he said.

'Really?' I was surprised. 'It sounds like you've got it made.'

'On paper maybe. But sometimes it feels like a big, indulgent wank. I don't earn enough to keep the family, so Hanna has to work more than we'd like. Sometimes I wonder if I should go back to advertising.'

'Maybe you should write a better book.'

Paul laughed. 'You're right,' he said. Then he pointed at my burn. 'Is that from your hat?'

'Yes.'

'It's taking its time to heal.'

'I know,' I said. 'I keep picking it.'

'Well, don't. It'll scar.'

'OK, bossy.'

'About that night…'

'Fondue-Gate.'

Paul looked confused. Then his brow cleared. 'Ha! I've been thinking of it as Fire-Gate,' he said.

I loved how quickly he'd 'got' it.

'Hey guys.' A dad I vaguely recognised, already taking off his mac. 'D'you mind if I join you? It's pissing down out there.'

Paul and I locked glances. Irritated. Resigned.

'Be our guest,' I said.

'Thanks,' said the dad, plonking himself down. 'So, counting on your help at the barbecue tomorrow, Paul.'

'The Pumpkin Party? Yup, I'll be there.'

Time for me to go.

'I'll love you and leave you, gentlemen,' I said, standing up.

'Don't leave on my account,' said the dad.

Oh, I am, I am.

'It's fine. People to see, places to go.'

My heart soared at the disappointment on Paul's face.

Chapter Sixteen

The St John's annual Pumpkin and Firework Party, the event
viewed with such distrust by the vicar, was one of the highlights
of the school year. It started with your typical apple-bobbing,
pin-the-nose-on-the-witch kind of party in the school hall and
then we all trooped out onto the playing field for the bonfire
and fireworks. I loved it all: the camaraderie, the overexcited
little witches and skeletons, the throbbing music, the smell of
gunpowder.

Am I the only one who finds fireworks sexy?

I was expecting Daniel and Freddie to stay at home. Freddie
was scornful of anything involving 'the little school' and Daniel,
frankly, found both the chaos and the kids absolute hell. Usually
I tried to persuade them both to come but, this year, I couldn't
be bothered. Perversely, this was the year they both decided it
was a really great idea.

I'd been roped in to help at the Terrifying Tattoo Tent with
Mandy so I left Daniel with the kids, resisted the temptation
to walk oh-so-casually past the barbecue and headed into the
school hall. Everything was getting under way and Mandy was
already applying temporary tattoos to a ragged line of wizards
and ghouls.

'Yo, Healey,' she said.

'It's not meant to have started yet,' I said.

'Yeah, and it's only going to get worse. But I think we've got
off lightly. Virginia's doing something disgusting with spaghetti
and jelly and Paul is freezing his nuts off outside.'

'Result!'

I sat down beside her and set to work. My first few tattoos were less than successful. The cat was minus a tail, the spider had no legs and the skull was horribly crooked. This was tricky. And messy. Rivulets of water ran down my arm and under my sleeve.

Must concentrate.

Then Virginia pitched up, resplendent in a swingy turquoise coat that didn't look like it was going to work with the spaghetti and jelly. She plonked some leaflets down on the table.

'Bumf about the ball,' she said.

'Great idea.'

I should have thought of that. We were co-chairs after all. Why did I always seem to be several steps behind her?

Daniel arrived, pint in hand. I must say he was looking pretty good, all rumpled and squinty after a morning watching Freddie play football and an afternoon slumped on the sofa watching Chelsea play football.

Daniel stopped short when he saw Virginia. 'Hello ladies,' he said, warily.

'Good evening, Mr Healey,' said Virginia, all dimples and smiles. 'Haven't seen *you* since the fateful evening.'

Was she flirting with my husband?

'Indeed.' Daniel paused. 'You must come back to ours for dinner sometime.'

Hmmm. Was *he* flirting with *her*? Well, he could forget about any squinty sexiness with me for quite some time, thank you very much.

Daniel and Virginia disappeared and I reapplied myself to my work. The blasted tattoos weren't getting any easier.

'Hi, Emma! I see Freddie's here.'

It was Ness, staring at me accusingly.

'He is,' I said. And then I cursed, because the broomstick I was working on seemed to have lost its handle.

'I wondered why Bethany was so keen to come,' said Ness.

'Relax, Ness. It's a primary school party, not an e-fuelled rave!'

'But they might be on the field doing goodness knows what!'

'I doubt it. It's all cordoned off until the fireworks.'

For a moment I wondered if there was really was an issue. Maybe Bethany and Freddie *were* necking neat vodka somewhere. Then I spotted Freddie across the hall with Jack and Dylan. Freddie was leaning backward, trying to eat a doughnut dangling from a string and laughing at his own lack of success. He looked the absolute antithesis of a teenage hellraiser.

'Ness, Freddie's over there,' I said. I tried to keep an I-told-you-so inflection out of my voice.

'Still…'

'No "still". Stop making out Freddie's such a bad influence. And while we're talking about people who may or may not be being badly behaved, how are your inner thighs?'

Ness, bless her, flushed, giggled and headed off. Mandy and I carried on with the tattoos and, after a while, Paul came over to join us. Honestly, that tattoo stall was like Piccadilly Circus…

'I thought you'd be in need of some refreshment,' he said, handing round polystyrene cups of mulled wine. It was sour and grainy and reminded me of teenage parties.

A woman, beautifully fitted out in caramel and butterscotch, propelled a tiny witch toward us.

'Could Tallulah have a black cat, please?' she said.

'Of course,' I said. I ushered Tallulah into the hot seat and set to work.

Tallulah's mum picked up one of the leaflets. 'Are you organising the ball?' she asked.

'Yes.' This tattoo was going to be perfect.

'And the Lunch Club is for your children?'

'It is.'

Don't distract me when I'm working.

'Well, I think you're absolutely marvellous. Of course, only very special parents get chosen to have such special children. I don't know how I'd cope if my child was so… different.'

Mandy, Paul and I stood up and faced her as one.

'Do you mean Asperger's?' I said.

'Don't worry about us,' said Mandy. 'Our kids are perfect as they are.'

'My son hasn't actually been diagnosed with anything yet, but I'm kinda hoping he is,' added Paul helpfully.

I stood on his foot. Hard.

'Too much?' he whispered.

'*Way* too much.'

'Excuse me one moment,' said Tallulah's mum and we watched her butterscotch bottom undulate across the hall. I'd just perfected Tallulah's tattoo – minus its tail – when she twinkled back with a man in beige.

'Hello,' the man boomed, pumping our hands in turn. 'I'm Nigel Hughes-Jenkins. I hear you're fundraising?'

We nodded. Was he going to tell us what special, handpicked parents we were too?

'We'd like to make a donation to the auction,' said Butterscotch-Bum. 'Would a week in our ski chalet be appropriate?'

Wow.

'I should think so,' said Paul with glorious understatement.

We kept it together while they were still standing in front of us, but let rip with loud cheers as soon as they were out of earshot.

'Brilliant,' I said, pumping my fist. 'We're on our way.'

'And some,' said Paul. 'Onwards and upwards!'

'I want to go home,' said a little voice.

It was Lily.

She sat down behind the table, elbows propping up her face, hands cupping butter-soft cheeks. She looked so adorable and so like one of those glum little cherubs you get on Christmas cards that I had to stop myself from laughing out loud.

'What's up, flower?' I asked as Paul melted away.

'My costume didn't win a prize.'

I wasn't surprised. There were loads of witty handmade costumes on display and Lily was wearing a nylon skeleton outfit from Tesco. At least she'd *come* in fancy dress. Jack had flatly refused to dress up. I hadn't even suggested it to Freddie.

'Never mind,' I said. 'There's always next year. Why don't you hang out with your friends?'

'I haven't got anyone to hang out *with*,' said Lily. She blew out an exaggerated sigh.

'What about Hellie?'

'She's with Izzie. Izzie came second in the competition.'

'Ah. What did she come as?'

'A Tardis.'

So that was Izzie. She looked a perfectly sweet little girl to me.

'A Tardis isn't very Halloween-y,' I said.

'It's better than this stupid skeleton,' said Lily. 'Why can't I have a *proper* costume?'

The guilt-o-meter pushed into red. Why couldn't she? It wasn't as if I hadn't had the time this year.

'Hey, Bendy-Wendy,' interjected Mandy. 'Want to help me put a tattoo on Harry Potter here?'

Lily perked up but tried her best not to show it. ''K,' she said.

She shuffled her chair closer to Mandy's and set to work, tongue protruding. The three of us worked in companionable silence. After a while, Lily starting getting 'clients' of her own and I couldn't help noticing her tattoos were infinitely better than mine.

'Hi, Mum.' Jack shuffled forward. 'I want a cat. Please.'

I smiled to myself. Typical Aspie directness with a learned social platitude tacked on the end. At least the platitude was there.

'Right you are, Jacko,' I said. 'One cat coming up.'

I did my best but it was tricky. Jack just wouldn't keep still. He was always a wriggler but today he was worse than usual, twisting and turning and jumping whenever there was a loud noise.

'It's wonky,' said Jack, when I'd finished.

'A tiny bit,' I said. 'But it looks cuter like that, doesn't it?'

'No. And where's the tail?'

'It's a Manx cat,' I improvised. 'Very rare. Everyone will want one.'

'No, they won't.' Jack yanked his arm away. 'I hate it,' he said. 'Get it off me...'

'OK. OK. Just give me a second.' I grabbed a sponge and started scrubbing away but it remained stubbornly in place. Jack started to howl.

Lily gave me an agonised look. 'Everyone's looking at us,' she hissed.

They were too. We were on a one-way ticket to Meltdown Central in the middle of a packed school hall and I had absolutely no idea what to do.

Plan One: 'Come on, Jack, let's go outside and get a hot dog.'

Loud wails.

Plan Two: 'Let's go and see if we can find Dad.'

Louder wails.

Plan Three: just get out. Get out *now*.

I stood up and put my arm round Jack's shoulder to encourage him up. Jack lashed out violently and knocked over the bowl of water. It went *everywhere*, all over the table, the sheets of tattoos, Mandy's lap...

'Oh, *God*!' I yelled.

I picked Jack up and carted him bodily across the hall and out of the French doors. Only a matter of weeks ago, I'd doubted my ability to carry him – especially when he was struggling. It was amazing what stress could do.

The cold, dark playground embraced us with non-judgemental calm. I carried Jack over to the far end and put him down away from the noise and bustle of the barbecue. I thought he might run away but he simply sank to his knees and then lay on his back, hands over ears, still shouting.

'Stop it, Jack!' It was Lily, tears running down her face. She kicked out at Jack without making contact. 'Why do you always spoil things?'

'Lily!' I said sharply. 'He's your brother. He doesn't spoil things.'

'Yes, he does. You know he does. That's why you're crying too.'

And Lily spun on her heel and marched away.

I crouched back down beside Jack, one hand resting on his shoulder, and let the tears run unchecked down my cheeks. *Everyone* had seen us. *Everyone* had heard me shout. *Everyone* would think that I was a terrible mother. And everyone would be judging Jack, writing him off, mentally consigning us all to a future of...

And, in the meantime, exactly what was I supposed to do now?

'What's going on?' It was Daniel, striding toward me across the playground, Lily in tow.

Thank goodness.

'He had the mother of all meltdowns,' I said. 'Oh, Daniel, it was *awful.*'

'Yes, Lily said there was merry hell and that you lost it,' said Daniel. He said it matter-of-factly rather than unkindly but the hurt cut through me like a knife through butter. 'What on earth happened?'

'Mum put the tattoo on wrong and Jack got cross,' said Lily.

Come on Dan, I willed.

Tell me it doesn't matter.

Tell me it's not my fault.

But Daniel just gave me a look I couldn't read in the darkness and crouched down on the other side of Jack. 'All right, mate?' he said, helping Jack into a sitting position. 'All get too much?'

Jack took a deep breath and nodded his head. 'Yeah. Sorry. I wasn't being me.'

He was as white as a sheet.

A small, vulnerable, precious ten-year-old boy.

I really shouldn't have shouted.

'Right, let's get you home,' said Daniel. 'I think the Healey family has made quite enough of a spectacle of itself for one evening.'

Charming!

I wanted to go home. I really did. I wanted to go home, have a cup of tea, be with Jack... be with them all. But I couldn't just abandon Mandy.

'The tattoo tent—' I started.

'Oh, for goodness sake, Emma,' said Daniel. 'Does that really matter at a time like this? OK, *I'll* take Jack and Lily home and you stay with your precious PTA.'

Before I could answer, he was gone, Jack and Lily trailing behind him. I stood there staring after them all.

Was I really that useless?

Was it really my fault?

Then I turned and walked slowly back across the playground.

A wave of noise and light almost winded me as I approached the hall. I felt exhausted, overwhelmed... helpless.

'Emma. Are you OK?' It was Paul, appearing at my side.

'Not really,' I said. I didn't even have the energy to pretend that everything was all right.

'Yeah, I saw you come out with Jack,' said Paul. 'I was going to come over but then Dan pitched up. Where are they all now?'

'Gone home,' I said. 'I've got to stay and do the bloody tattoos.'

'No, you don't,' said Paul. 'Mandy will understand. Oh, Emma, love, you're *shaking*. Come here.'

He pulled me into his arms. It was a friendly, comforting hug rather than anything else but suddenly I was weeping against his shoulder.

'Oh God, I'm so bloody useless,' I sobbed. 'I'm a *terrible* mother.'

I felt Paul smile against my hair. 'No, you're not,' he said. 'You're a lovely mum.'

'I'm bloody not. I have no idea what do to when Jack gets like that.'

Paul stroked my hair. 'That's because it's *hard*,' he said. 'And it's not only Jack. Hanna's taken Gabe home because he lost it after sticking his face into the flour and Virginia's gone because Josh couldn't hack the spaghetti.'

'Really?' I said, pulling away and looking up at him.

If Virginia couldn't control Josh...

'Really. It's a crap evening for kids on the spectrum. Too loud. Too much going on.'

'But everyone heard me shout. *They'll* all think I'm a terrible mum.'

Paul shook his head. 'No one will have taken a scrap of notice,' he said. 'They're all too busy with their own evenings to worry about yours. Look, why don't I pop inside, grab your coat and explain what's happened to Mandy and then we'll go up onto the field. There's nothing like fireworks for cheering you up when the world seems against you.'

—

And so that's what we did.

We followed the throng onto the school field, pushed into the heart of the crowd that had already begun to assemble and stood together in the darkness, hidden, protected.

The world carried on without us in slow motion. There was Freddie, happy as a sandboy and mucking around with Bethany. There was Ness with Noah, no doubt looking for Bethany. There was Mandy, hoisting Dylan onto her shoulders.

It all felt irrelevant and so very far away. My world contracted to the patch of ground Paul and I were occupying, both of

136

us facing forward, shoulders touching. It would have been the most natural thing in the world for him to reach out and take my hand. Except that that would have been really naff.

'I meant what I said about you being a super mum,' said Paul apropos of nothing.

'Thank you,' I said, simply.

'The way you've accepted Jack's autism diagnosis and, more than that, the way you've given up your career – which I'm sure you were brilliant at. It's… lovely. And impressive.'

Until Paul said those words, I'd had no idea how much I needed to hear them. My eyes filled with tears.

'Can I ask you a favour?' said Paul suddenly.

'Of course.'

Anything.

'It might sound weird, but would you come to Gabriel's diagnosis meeting with me? Hanna won't come and I could really do with someone on my side on this. Someone who… understands.'

I thought of a thousand replies. I thought of saying no. And then, knowing exactly how it felt to be left alone to deal with all of this, I could only say 'Yes.'

'Thank you,' said Paul. 'It's a date.'

He reached out and took my hand and the sky exploded into a thousand sparkling lights.

And, actually, it wasn't naff at all.

–

Paul dropped me off and I let myself into the house in a bit of a tizzy. But holding hands didn't have to *mean* anything, did it? Just a friendly gesture between friends who were going through a tough time.

I'd expected to find bedlam but all was quiet. I pushed open the lounge door and there they were, all of them, watching *The Polar Express* in the dark. Lily was in her jimjams and snuggled up to Daniel on the sofa. Freddie was sprawled out in the armchair. And Jack was lying on the floor, feet up on the sofa, watching the TV over his shoulder.

Perfect domestic harmony.

I sat down next to Lily and put my feet on the coffee table. Twenty minutes ago I had been holding hands with Paul. I felt a pinch of guilt. How easy it was to lead a double life.

Then I laughed at myself.

Double life?

I'd been watching the fireworks with a fellow dad.

In public.

Begone, Statistic!

My marriage wasn't in trouble.

Was it?

Chapter Seventeen

I was worried Jack would be wary about going back to school on Monday but drop-off was exactly the same as usual. Lily ran to the play apparatus to do somersaults over the beams. Jack hovered near a group of ten-year-old boys mucking around on the climbing frame; a hopeful, hopeless satellite orbiting the most popular posse in the year. Neither welcoming nor hostile, the other lads simply ignored him and I was relieved when the school bell rang and they all shuffled indoors.

Business as usual.

Except, here was Hanna marching purposefully toward me. Hanna, in grungy greys and blacks and looking characteristically ill-pleased with the world.

'Leave. Off. My. Husband,' she said without preamble as she drew close.

Correction.

Ill-pleased with *me*.

Indeed, she had every right to be furious – I had held hands with him a couple of days before, kissed him before that. Icy fear coursed through my veins. The repercussions could be huge.

Please don't tell Daniel.

Please don't tell Daniel…

'I'm so sorry,' I said contritely. 'It was only—'

'It wasn't "only" anything,' snapped Hanna. 'It was actually quite unhelpful.'

Unhelpful?

Not the word I'd have chosen to describe tonsil tennis with her husband, but I suppose it was one way of looking at things.

Quite understanding, though, all things considered. Maybe she didn't consider a drunken kiss much of a big deal. Maybe it wasn't that big of a deal in the Archer household. Daniel, on the other hand, would be heartbroken—

'All that pressure on Paul to get Gabriel diagnosed,' Hanna was saying. 'Are you trying to press-gang him into joining your little group?'

Oh.

That sort of cross.

Thank God for that.

'Of course not,' I said, hoping my expression hadn't changed. 'And I haven't got a "little group".'

Hanna leant toward me, Titian hair flopping forward, blue eyes ice-cold. 'Yes, you have,' she said. 'Trying to find a new recruit, are we?'

'I'm really not,' I said. 'But wouldn't it be a good idea to get Gabe some help if he needs it?'

'There is no evidence to suggest *Gabriel*'s got *anything*,' said Hanna.

No doubt she emphasised her son's full name to stress I had no business claiming intimacy with her family.

'Maybe not,' I said. 'But Paul's worried about it. Maybe you should—'

'Don't tell me what I should do. Paul is wrong. You'll see.'

She swung away from me across the playground and I stood there staring after her. Poor thing. I remembered the helpless, hopeless feeling I'd had when the school first suggested Jack was on the spectrum. I couldn't add to her woes.

Wouldn't.

I whipped out my phone and texted Paul.

Emma: Does Hanna know I'm coming with you
to Gabriel's meeting?

I'd driven home by the time the reply came through.

140

Paul: Not exactly

Emma: She should be going. Not me

Paul: She won't

Emma: Ask again

Paul: OK. But if she keeps refusing?

Say no, Emma. Just say no.

Emma: Then of course I'll come

At lunchtime, as planned, I went over to Mum's for lunch.

Her compact flat in the sheltered housing complex was, as ever, warm, cosy and spotlessly tidy. The living room always depressed me; north-facing, it had a mean little view over the car park flanked by municipal shrubs and a wooden fence. But the kitchen was light and airy and opened onto a shared courtyard with wrought iron tables and chairs drawn into inviting little groups. Mum had used her share of the patio to create a container garden filled with flowers and herbs. Even in November there was a lot of stuff growing there and the scent drifted delightfully into the flat.

'How's my Jacko?' asked Mum as we put together a salad for lunch.

Oh God. Don't remind me.

'Pretty bad,' I admitted. 'He totally lost it at the school do.'

'Poor poppet.' Mum paused in her chopping, resting her mezzaluna on the wooden board and wiping her hands on her pinny. 'Did you see that article in the *Mail*?'

'What article?'

Dan and I made a great show of never having the *Daily Mail* in the house, but I regularly got a guilty fix online.

'The one that said Asperger's is almost certainly genetic.'

'Oh well, I'm sure that's true,' I said. 'One of the more sensible theories.'

'Yes,' Mum agreed. 'Back in the day, they said autism was caused by a cold mother.'

'No way!'

I'd never heard that one.

'Oh yes,' said Mum. 'Refrigerator mothers, they were called.'

'God, how dreadful. Don't you think that theory must have been dreamt up by a man?'

We both laughed but a voice started whispering in my ear. A horrid little voice suggesting maybe, just maybe, there was no smoke without fire. The faintest shiver ran down my spine. Had I been a cold mother? *Had* I? I'd been a stressed one to be sure; Jack had been such an unsettled soul. But had I been *cold*?

Mum was attacking a bunch of basil, its pungent smell brightening the kitchen. 'It's ridiculous,' she said. 'The genetic link makes much more sense. I've always thought it came from your dad.'

'*Dad?*' I was shocked. It had never crossed my mind.

'Yes.' Mum laughed. 'He was the original train spotter, wasn't he?'

'Was he? I never, ever heard him mention trains.'

'No, silly. I mean his cricket.'

Ah. Of course.

Dad's passion. But it was hardly unusual. In fact, back in the day, Daniel and I had been enchanted by the fact that both our dads were cricket fanatics. It was one of the things that bound us together, made our relationship seem preordained.

I said as much.

Mum stood up. She put her finger to her lips as if Dad was listening and beckoned me to follow her to the small second bedroom. Grandly dubbed 'the library', it housed floor-to-ceiling oak bookshelves, neatly stacked with the detritus of several decades of family life. It was an eclectic collection that included my old school books and a rubbish clay snail I'd made in Year Two. As ever, I was touched by the things Mum had chosen to keep when she'd packed up the family home.

Anyway. Mum pointed to a collection of meticulously labelled lever arch files next to the photo albums. I pulled one down and flicked through the wafer-thin pages. Column after column of batting averages, bowling scores, league tables. Created in the days before Excel, every digit handwritten in Dad's spidery hand. A real labour of love. Of obsession. Of something. Back in the day, Dad had been defensive, even secretive, about his hobby and the files had been kept hidden away. Even now, I felt a little guilty looking through them.

'Interesting,' I said. 'You know, this does remind me of Jack and his football. Except Jack isn't so neat. Bloody football cards and random bits of paper all over his room. It drives me bonkers.'

Mum laughed. 'Your dad wasn't neat either,' she said. 'I was forever clearing up after him.'

I slotted the file carefully back into place.

'It's quite cute that Jack and Dad were both obsessed by sport,' I said. 'At least you can't accuse me of that.'

Apart from Wimbledon, the Boat Race and watching England get knocked out of the World Cup, sport bored me silly.

Mum ruffled my hair. 'Holly Hobbie?' was all she said.

In case she passed you by, Holly Hobbie was a cartoon of a girl in a patched dress and an enormous flower-sprigged bonnet, popular among pre-teens in the 1970s. Holly Hobbie notecards were the 'in' currency one summer. And that Christmas, my nan had given me one of those cross-stitch sets and I got to know every patch and every sprig intimately from that.

But that was all.

Hardly an obsession.

Not in the league of Dad's cricket.

Mum was laughing. 'Do you remember the hanging wall plate and the candles?' she said. 'And the hideous little pitcher on your windowsill? I was quite pleased when that got broken.'

'Really?'

'And then there was the mug and the lunchbox. The instamatic camera. The trinket box, the ceramic egg…'

OK, OK.

Maybe, with hindsight, I did buy a lot of dodgy Holly Hobbie stuff.

'You even pestered me into buying you a matching curtain and valance set. And they all had to have exactly the same image of her. Side on with a tuft of hair peeking out. God forbid if it was different.'

'But lots of little girls have crazes,' I protested. 'What about those girls in my class who were mad about ponies? Or liked *Starsky and Hutch*? Or Lily liking One Direction, for that matter?'

Mum smiled. 'True,' she said. 'I had a pash on David Cassidy. And I was in my thirties!'

Phew.

'For a moment there, I thought you were suggesting *I* was on the spectrum,' I said.

'I wasn't suggesting anything, poppet,' said Mum. 'I was saying that as a little girl you were quite similar to Jacko, which isn't surprising as you're his mother. Now, would you like to take some of these toms back with you? Silly, I grow them because they were your dad's favourites. I don't even like them.'

'Thanks.' Suddenly I had a lump in my throat. About Dad and Daniel and Jack and – well – everything. 'Oh, Mum, do you think everything's going to be OK?'

Mum patted my hand with hers, all veined and age-spotted and vulnerable. 'Of course it is, darling. Look at how things have turned out. Daniel. Your lovely family. Everything's rosy.'

Everything was far from rosy.

My phone rang almost as soon as I got home.

'Mrs Healey? It's Mrs Sharp from Meadowlands.'

Freddie's school. Oh God.

'Is Freddie OK?'

Maybe he'd had an aneurysm on the football pitch. Whatever that was.

'Frederick's fine. But I'd appreciate a quick word. Would you be able to pop up to school?'

By the time I'd driven the short distance to the modern comprehensive the other side of town, I felt much more cheerful. I'd worked out why Mrs Sharp wanted to see me. Freddie must have been invited onto the school's Gifted and Talented scheme. It *must* be that. Freddie was bright but he was so good-natured and straightforward, it was easy for him to slip under the radar. The school must finally have seen his potential.

I hadn't met Mrs Sharp before. With her pointed chin and slightly sour expression, she certainly suited her name.

'I'll not beat around the bush, Mrs Healey,' she said. 'We're thinking of removing Frederick from his current class and teaching him in a smaller group for a while.'

Wow!

I'd been led to believe the G&T programme only extended to one subject and maybe to a class or two a week. So much for government cutbacks. This was *fantastic*.

'Well, if you think that's best for him,' I said, trying to look suitably modest. It wouldn't do to come across as an insufferably pushy parent.

Mrs Sharp looked surprised. 'It's not forever, of course,' she said.

'I know. I'm just so pleased Freddie's been chosen.'

Mrs Sharp gave me a strange look. 'This is *Gateway* we're talking about,' she said. 'For pupils with behavioural problems?'

If this was a movie, the soft background music would stop abruptly in a clash of discordant chords.

'*Gateway?*'

I was utterly shocked, but Mrs Sharp explained that Freddie hadn't been himself recently. His work had dropped off, he hadn't been concentrating in lessons and he'd been skipping his homework.

A thought occurred to me.

'He's not being bullied, is he?'

Mrs Sharp gave a snorting sort of laugh. 'Frederick? Goodness me, no. He's always in the thick of things.'

'So, he's popular?'

'With a certain set, yes.'

'That's good, isn't it? My younger son has Asperger syndrome and he'd *love* to have that sort of problem.'

'Mrs Healey, we're here to talk about Frederick. What's he like out of school?'

'Fine. Lovely.'

Easy, compared to Jack.

'No issues at all?'

'No. I mean, now he's a teenager, we try to give him his space...'

Couldn't have Mrs Sharp thinking I was a helicopter parent.

'Some boundaries and discipline are appropriate at any age,' said Mrs Sharp. 'Any experimentation with drink? Drugs?'

'*No.*' Now I was getting pissed off. 'He's fourteen. We're a nice, normal middle-class family.'

'Mrs Healey, let me assure you that behavioural problems at this school are by no means restricted to one social class.'

'I know. It was a joke. Please don't put Freddie in Gateway. I'm sure this is all a storm in a teacup.'

Mrs Sharp didn't answer for a few moments. 'Very well,' she said finally. 'We'll put him on report for a week and see how we go. But please make it absolutely clear that this is his last chance.'

'Thank you.'

I was out of there.

I collared Freddie as soon as he got home from school.

'What's going on at school?' I asked as he headed for the fridge.

'Nothing.' Freddie's eye contact was suddenly as elusive as Jack's.

'Mrs Sharp seems to have it in for you. She called me up to school today.'

'Oh my *God*.' Freddie kicked the skirting board in disgust. 'I *hate* Mrs Sharp.'

'She doesn't seem too keen on you either, matey.'

'She isn't keen on *anyone*. Must be the menopause.'

I tried not to smirk. Mrs Sharp was late twenties if she was a day.

'She's says you're slipping behind on your work and you're not doing your homework.'

'That's so unfair. Half the time they never tell us when it's due in.'

'Oh, it's the teachers' fault, is it? Nothing to do with you and your application? Freddie, she's talking about *Gateway*!'

'She talks about Gateway with everyone. She had Sam's mum in a few days ago.'

'Really?' Sam was a swot by all accounts. Maybe I was worrying unnecessarily.

Freddie pushed home his advantage. 'Honestly, Mrs Sharp is a nightmare. Everyone's saying so.'

He gave me a half-glance and suddenly I noticed a look of the young Daniel about him. Blond, earnest, oodles of under-stated charm. My God, Daniel had been only seven years older than Freddie when I'd first met him...

Freddie was sidling out of the room.

'Be a good boy and stay out of trouble.'

My lovely Steady Freddie.

Chapter Eighteen

It wasn't a date.

How could it be with Gabriel in the rear seat of the car? A small boy with curly brown hair whose very future depended on what happened today.

Paul was taciturn and monosyllabic from the moment he picked me up and I started to think this had been a seriously bad idea. Gabriel was going to get diagnosed and it would all be hideously sad and embarrassing and I wouldn't know what to say and Paul would never talk to me again—

'You *wanker*,' shouted Paul, slamming on the brakes as some guy in a sports car cut us up.

I touched him lightly on the arm.

Calm down. Keep it together.

'Wanker,' said Gabriel from the back.

'Thank you, Gabe,' said Paul.

'*Wanker*,' repeated Gabriel, with more emphasis.

Paul met my eye with a rueful grin. 'He's going to say that in the meeting, isn't he?'

'Of course,' I said.

Echolalia. The repetition of words and sounds.

A sign?

'Christ, I'm so stressed. I think I'm going to lose it,' said Paul.

'No, you're not,' I said reassuringly. 'And if you do, I still have the psychotherapist's card that Virginia gave me.'

'Your granny's called Virginia,' said Gabriel.

'No, she's not,' I replied. 'My grannies were called Dot and Bea.'

Both sadly missed.

'Yes, she is,' said Gabriel firmly. 'Granny Ginny.'

Ah.

The old pronoun reversal trick again. How had I got caught out a second time?

'You mean, *your* granny's called Virginia,' I corrected him gently.

'Yes. Daddy doesn't like Virginia.'

'OK. But your granny's a different Virginia to the one we're talking about. There are lots of people called Virginia. Just like there are lots of Gabriels.'

'No. Virginia. Granny Ginny,' said Gabriel. He kicked the back of Paul's seat in frustration.

'Let's leave it, shall we?' said Paul, tetchily.

I left it. But I couldn't help chuckling at the thought of Virginia as a granny. There was no one less like a granny that I could think of.

Grumpy Paul made his reappearance as soon as we arrived at the hospital. He strode ahead of us along corridors with automatic doors and signed us in with a grim expression, mouth set. This really had been a mistake of monumental proportions.

After a couple of minutes, a grey-haired, urbane-looking man in jeans and a black jumper came up to us.

'I'm Dr Poole,' he said affably. 'Mr and Mrs Archer?'

'Yes,' said Paul.

'No,' I said simultaneously.

Dr Poole raised an eyebrow. 'You are or you aren't?' he said.

'I am. She's not,' said Paul.

'I'm a friend,' I said. 'I've got a son on the autism spectrum too. No, I don't mean "too" because we don't know if Gabriel is—'

'Very good, very good. Are you joining us for our meeting?'

I hesitated. Suddenly it seemed a preposterous idea.

Paul didn't suggest otherwise.

'I'll stay here,' I said.

The two men disappeared with Gabriel and I sat down outside the office.

Well, that was great.

What a monumental waste of a day. And it was only going to go downhill when Paul received the inevitable bad news. What was I going to say when he emerged? Should I sympathise? Reassure him Gabriel would now get the help he deserved? Remind him of all the famous people who allegedly had Asperger's?

Meanwhile, what on earth was that noise?

'Nee-naw-nee-naw-nee-naaaaaw.'

A high-pitched, eerie wail from the room Paul and Gabriel were in. Was it Paul, losing it as predicted? No, it must be Gabriel. It sounded like he was imitating the ambulances. It was unlikely Dr Poole had specifically asked him to do this, so maybe it was another example of his echolalia. It couldn't be long no—

The door to the consulting room opened and Paul came out.

'Would you mind keeping an eye on Gabriel while we finish off?' he asked.

'Of course. Is it going OK?'

'Fine,' said Paul non-committally. He ushered Gabriel out and went back inside.

Gabriel started running around, still making siren noises. Several other children were making odd noises too, so I figured I didn't need to hush him. But I did take a seat near the entrance in case he decided to go walkabout.

The ping of a text and a number I didn't recognise.

> Hi Mum. This is Lily. I've borrowed Evie's phone to let you know that I don't have anyone to play with.

My heart lurched.

Emma: Poor flower. What about Hellie?

Lily: She and Izzie hate me

Emma: No, they don't. Buddy bench?

Lily: That's for weird people

The siren noises had stopped. The good news was that Gabriel was still in the waiting room. The bad news was that he was standing by a large rocking horse that already had an incumbent. Gabriel started shaking the horse's reins aggressively. The rider, a fragile-looking chap, burst into tears. Taking advantage of his lofty position, he grabbed a handful of Gabriel's hair.

The little boy's mum and I swooped at the same time.

'James, let go at once.'

'Gabriel, take turns nicely.' It's always difficult with other people's children, isn't it?

James and Gabriel took no notice of us.

'You want to go on the horse,' Gabriel yelled. 'Nee-naw, nee-naw.'

'You're on it. Yours!' the other boy shouted.

PC or not, I couldn't help laughing. James' mum prised her son's fingers from Gabriel's hair and started laughing too. Then she mouthed 'Asperger's?' at me with a friendly smile.

'Finding out today,' I answered. 'But I don't think there's much doubt.'

'Oh, sorry. I didn't realise it was diagnosis day. You seem very relaxed.'

'He's not my child. But I've got one of my own at home.'

The door to Dr Poole's office swung open and Paul emerged. He strode over to us, picked up Gabriel and kissed the top of his curly head. Then he slid his other arm round my waist and kissed me square on the mouth. I felt like the girl in that famous poster. Except we weren't in Paris. And it wasn't wartime. But you know what I mean.

'He's not got it,' Paul said, voice shaking. 'He's not bloody got it!'

James' mum shot me an openly sceptical look. But this was too important for flippant exchanges with strangers, so I ignored her and kissed Paul back.

'I'm absolutely thrilled for you,' I said firmly.

And I was. Of course, I was. But I was also very, very confused. Because how on earth had Gabriel *not* been diagnosed when his symptoms were so much more severe than Jack's? Jack had never reversed his pronouns or repeated words. It all seemed so random, so arbitrary. So *unfair*. And, worse, Paul's happiness and my congratulations suggested we thought Asperger's was the worst thing in the world.

And that felt rather like betraying Jack.

Paul put the struggling Gabriel down but kept his arm round my shoulder all the way back through the hospital. I made a conscious effort to banish negative thoughts and not to dwell on what the arm might mean.

A relieved dad.

A friendly gesture.

Halfway home, Paul turned off the motorway and stopped at a chocolate-box pub with a thatched roof and mullioned windows.

'Spot of lunch?' he said. 'Maybe something celebratory to drink?'

We shouldn't.

We *really* shouldn't.

But part of me wanted to and a bigger part didn't want to spoil his day.

'Why not?' I said.

Despite its exterior, the pub was modern inside and it had a huge play area for children – all multi-level tunnels and slides and poles. There were even people to supervise the little darlings. I liked. I liked a *lot*. And, after two huge glasses of wine and an equally generous plate of fish and chips, I felt relaxed and expansive.

'So, what did Dr Poole say?' I asked when Gabriel had scampered off to play.

Paul shrugged. 'He waffled on a lot. The gist was that when Gabriel gets stressed he can seem autistic-y. But not enough to be diagnosed at this stage.'

Hmmm.

Surely that was different from saying Gabriel didn't have Asperger's. In fact, it sounded suspiciously like a fudge.

Maybe that's what happened when you went private.

'Well, I'm delighted for you,' I said, banishing such uncharitable thoughts. 'Really delighted. Not that there's anything wrong in having Asperger's—'

Paul reached out and took hold of my hand.

'Emma, Emma, Emma,' he said, jiggling my fingers. 'What are we going to do with you?'

I didn't say anything – couldn't think of anything *to* say.

I just picked up Paul's hand and felt the weight of it in both of mine.

I couldn't help it.

Paul pulled me closer and kissed me gently on the mouth, his mouth cool and fragrant from his beer.

'I remember the first time I saw you,' he said. 'You were sitting in the church looking very stroppy. Then you saw me and laughed!'

'Ha!' I said. 'I wasn't laughing *at* you. I was laughing because of your unsubtle gawp at Virginia.'

'I wasn't gawping.'

'Yes, you were,' I said. '*I* gawped the first time I saw her.'

'Was not—'

'I need a poo, Dad.'

Paul dropped my hand and morphed into dad-mode in the blink of an eye. Off he went to the loos with his non-autistic son. I took a sip of my wine and tried to re-engage with the real world. How long had we been in the pub? Surely it must be nearly time to leave. I got my phone out to check. There was a voicemail from Daniel and, with a stab of guilt, I put the phone to my ear.

Daniel's voice was flat, his message succinct.

'It's happened. Three months' notice to work out. Happy days.'

Chapter Nineteen

For some reason, my first reaction was irritation.

Irritation that my lovely lunch had been interrupted.

Irritation that Daniel wasn't a successful author like Paul.

Irritation with Daniel in general.

I know, I know – none of that makes me a nice person.

I'm just trying to be honest.

A couple of seconds later, the angst, the worry and the *guilt* kicked in. What the *fuck* was I doing, sitting in a pub in the middle of nowhere with someone else's husband and child?

I shouldn't be here.

I should be at home.

With *my* family.

By the time Paul and Gabriel got back, I'd paid the bill and was hovering by the door.

'We need to go,' I said.

'Of course,' said Paul. 'Has something happened?'

I blinked back burning tears. 'Daniel's lost his sodding job,' I said.

We were on our way within minutes. Paul drove in silence, face expressionless.

'I'm sorry,' I said. 'None of this is your fault. I'm sorry I've spoiled your big day.'

'Don't be daft,' said Paul. 'You've made it better. Now, where I am dropping you?'

'Home please. I need to collect my car to fetch Jack and Lily from Mandy's.'

'Well, why don't I take you straight to Mandy's and then drop you all back home.'

Oh, he was lovely.

Lovely.

'I'm off to the States for work in a couple of days,' said Paul. 'I'm sorry to leave you in the lurch with the ball.'

'That's fine,' I said. 'I'll cope.'

'I know you will. And, when I get back, I think you and I need to talk.'

I didn't answer.

I didn't know what he meant.

I didn't know what to say.

Jack and Lily were just settling down to *Finding Nemo* and weren't best pleased to be picked up early. Lily, in particular, was pale and pinched and at odds with the world in general.

'I *told* you how sad I was at school, but you didn't do anything,' she complained from the back seat.

'I'm sorry, flower,' I said. 'I was in Oxford looking after Gabriel.'

'You shouldn't be looking after Gabriel,' said Lily crossly. 'You're *my* mummy.'

She had a point.

'Your mummy's got a baby in her tummy,' said Gabriel.

'No, she hasn't,' said Jack. 'She's just fat.'

Daniel *was already* at home. He was sitting at the kitchen table flicking through the *Guardian*.

'Where have you been?' he asked.

I hesitated. The guilt was unbearable. But had I really done anything so terribly bad? OK, so the hand-holding and kissing bit hadn't been ideal, but why *shouldn't* I accompany a friend to the hospital?

'I went with Paul to his son's Asperger's diagnosis,' I said casually, snapping on the kettle.

'Paul? The writer guy?'

'Yes.'

'Why didn't his wife go?'

'She doesn't think Gabriel's on the spectrum,' I said, getting the mugs out.

'Oh. And?'

'And what?'

The *guilt*!

'Is he on the spectrum?'

'No,' I said. 'Apparently he's not. But never mind that. I'm so sorry about your job.'

We took our coffee to the sofa in the lounge. There was a time when we would have snuggled up together, limbs entwined, but now there was a careful space between us.

Another us.

'What happened?' I asked.

Daniel shrugged. 'They're moving the whole department to the States,' he said. 'It's nothing personal.'

So much for Nicky being his Fairy Godmother, then.

'So, that's that then?'

'Yep. Unless you fancy moving to Texas.'

I thought about it. I was all for an adventure but...

'That's not going to happen, is it?' I said.

'Nope,' said Daniel. 'Not with Jack.'

'So, what next?'

Daniel puffed out his cheeks. 'No idea,' said Daniel. 'The redundancy won't be up to much. I haven't been there long enough. We can forget about that holiday for a start.'

Never mind the holiday. More to the point, what about the mortgage? The bills? We looked at each other, tired and defeated. This was not how it was meant to be. What had happened to the dynamic man I'd married? Come to think of it, what had happened to the feisty woman *I'd* once been? What a couple of washed-up has-beens we'd turned out to be.

No, Emma.

Enough of the self-pity.

We weren't at the end of the road.

Not yet.

'I'll ask for my old job back,' I said, thinking aloud. I moved across the sofa to hug Daniel but he stiffened and turned away.

'You're enjoying this, aren't you?' he said.

'Enjoying it?' I echoed. 'No, of course I'm not.'

'Yes, you are. Good old Emma picking up the pieces now Daniel's screwed up.'

'Oh Dan. That's so unfair.'

Daniel slumped back in his seat. 'OK, then,' he said. 'Do what you like. You always do anyway.'

'Come on. We're meant to be a team.'

'A team?' said Daniel. 'Ha! That's the biggest joke I've heard all year.'

He stalked out of the room and I could almost hear The Statistic give a deep-throated chuckle.

—

I waited a couple of hours and then I emailed Belinda asking to be re-employed.

Daniel was being overemotional.

It was the obvious thing to do.

Maybe I should take the opportunity to ask for a raise.

Chapter Twenty

'I'm sorry,' said Daniel the next morning. He was standing by my side of the bed holding a cup of coffee. 'I was bang out of order. Peace offering?'

'Thank you.'

I should have been the one saying sorry. After all, I was the one playing Russian roulette with The Statistic. With our marriage.

'I'm so... pissed off,' said Daniel, sitting on the side of the bed. 'I loved that job. And I'm pissed off with myself for wanting to be the breadwinner. I thought I was further up the evolutionary chain than that.'

I laughed. 'You are,' I said. 'You'll get something else soon.'

'Maybe,' said Daniel. 'It's tough out there. And you're right, of course. Go ahead and reapply for your old job.'

I thought it best not to mention I already had.

—

I didn't have long to wait for the reply.

I was in the school playground when my phone beeped with an email from Belinda. That was quick! They were obviously desperate to snap me back up.

I scanned the message.

Dear Emma. Thank you for your email...

Faint alarm bells started to ring. It seemed surprisingly formal. Surely, '*Hi Em, fab to hear from you,*' was more Belinda's style.

159

On the other hand, maybe it was best to be business-like when rehiring someone. Even if that someone was me.

I carried on scanning.

> Unfortunately... current business climate... unable to offer you...

I was stunned.

Stunned.

I called Belinda. How *dare* she fob me off? She might have been my boss on paper, but we both knew she'd only been the more senior because I couldn't be arsed with boring office politics and dreary management stuff. I was probably the better researcher.

No answer. I retied Jack's shoelace for him and then called again, on a whim making my call anonymous by prefixing 141. It was probably a coincidence Belinda picked up straight away that time.

'Bel, it's Em.'

I half expected her to laugh, to say sorry about the formal flim-flam, a couple of hoops to jump through before we can offer your job back. But there was a pause and then Belinda launched into a précis of her email.

'Excuse me,' I interrupted. 'You *said* I could reapply...'

'It's not that simple...'

Why was Belinda treating me like this? I was a *great* consultant. I'd won a couple of industry awards. Clients specifically asked for me to work on their projects. And, OK, maybe I'd taken a lot of time off with Jack and maybe it had been irritating and inconvenient for my colleagues. But anybody would have done the same. Anyway, things would be different now because I was going to be the main breadwinner. No matter what was happening at home, I'd be free to concentrate on my job.

Silly me. I hadn't actually told Belinda that.

'I forgot to tell you the good part,' I said. 'Daniel's been laid off. Well it's not good, per se, of course, but I'd be able to focus on the job *one hundred per cent*.'

'Emma, I'm sorry. We're not going to offer you your job back.'

'Shouldn't you at least put it to the rest of the board?'

'I have.'

Oh!

That stung.

We said a frosty goodbye and I disconnected, the sour taste of failure almost palpable. What price an Oxbridge degree and fifteen years building up a loyal client base? It was so unfair. I'd show Belinda. I'd... I'd set up my own consultancy. I wasn't stupid; I knew exactly how much profit management creamed off each and every project.

'Not looking good,' said a voice behind me.

I spun round. It was Hanna in a shapeless dark coat, hair tied back into a severe ponytail.

'I'm sorry?' I said.

What wasn't looking good?

'Your phone call...'

'Oh.' The cheeky mare. 'That was only Round One.'

'Well, I wonder if I could have a word after Round Two?'

Belinda was openly impatient when I called her back. 'Emma, I've nothing to—' she started.

'Actually, I wanted to thank you,' I said.

A pause. 'Why's that then?'

'Because it's about time I launched my own agency,' I said. 'And this will give me the little push I need.'

'Will it now?' said Belinda. 'Can I remind you about the non-compete clause? You're not allowed to contact any of your clients for a year.'

Shit.

I'd completely forgotten that.

The kiss of death to any new venture.

'Of course, I remember the non-compete clause,' I said, with a peal of carefree laughter. 'I was getting tired of the same old companies anyway. Time for something more cutting-edge.'

'Good luck with that,' said Belinda.

A second frosty goodbye. Round Two had hardly been a resounding win for Team Emma. But, come to think of it, I didn't really *want* to go back to work full-time. I liked the idea of being the master of my own destiny.

I turned to Hanna. 'Sorry about that,' I said. 'How can I help you?'

Hanna gave me a tight smile. 'Paul took Gabriel to meet an autism specialist yesterday,' she said, 'and, as I thought, he is not on the spectrum.'

He so is.

'OK.'

I couldn't bring myself to say congratulations.

'So, can I assume we'll hear no more about it from you?' said Hanna.

'Of course not.'

'Good. And the non-compete clause thing? They're usually pretty binding, so take it seriously. You'll need to milk any old contacts and get your foot in the door of some new ones. For the first year, at least.'

She made it sound like the easiest thing in the world.

'It'd be tough,' I said.

'You'd make it work. I have every faith in you.'

'Do you?' I looked at her in surprise. Maybe I had misjudged her.

'Yup,' said Hanna. 'You strike me as the type of person who doesn't stop until they've got exactly what they want.'

And that didn't make me feel very good about myself at all.

–

That evening, Daniel went out on the lash with his fellow reduntantees. I was a little upset he wasn't choosing to drown his sorrows with me, but maybe I'd use the time to explore setting up in business on my own. So, once the kids were fed and otherwise occupied, I grabbed a nearly full bottle of Chablis and installed myself in the office.

I started off by sending a message to Mark.

> **Emma:** I'm reinventing myself as a freelancer. Any projects going?

No point in beating around the bush.

The reply came back quickly.

> **Mark:** Thought you'd reinvented yourself as a lady of leisure?
>
> **Emma:** I had. But Dan's been given the boot
>
> **Mark:** Sorry to hear. Not going back to your old gaff?

No! They won't bloody have me...

> **Emma:** I fancy striking out on my own
>
> **Mark:** Good for you. Well, funnily enough, there might be something

Really? That was easy.

> **Emma:** Brilliant!
>
> **Mark:** You might not say that when you hear it's on body grooming
>
> **Emma:** ?!

For some reason, I had a vision of gorillas carefully picking fleas out of each other's fur.

Mark: Shaving and trimming the pubic hair to you and me

Emma: Ah. I've done stuff on the bikini line before

Mark: Not just the bikini line. Think more along the boxer short line

Right.

Emma: Very metrosexual

Mark: And probably very itchy

Emma: Ha-ha! Well, I'd love to get involved.

Mark: Great. Better go. Am mid cheddar focus group in Leeds ATM

Emma: What? Right now? You can't type while you're moderating!!!

Mark: Want a bet?

Emma: I bet you fancy the one third from the left

Mark: I do actually. I'm going to see what she'll do for a block of cheese. Over and out.

I felt quite triumphant after this exchange. I had a project! But I needed more. I'd be the sole breadwinner soon.

I started off by pootling around on LinkedIn for potential clients. LinkedIn didn't release this gold dust easily, at least not without making you pay a huge subscription, but I persevered and, within an hour, I had the names and contact details of a dozen insight managers. I poured myself another a glass of wine and toasted myself in the mirror.

I was on my way.

The trouble was, what to do now? There was no way I was cold calling these people. Far too embarrassing. Half-heartedly,

I started to outline a letter but it was hard. I had a quick shufti through my competitors' websites. *Everyone* promised strategic findings. *Everyone* was enthusiastic and full of integrity. *Everyone* had ridiculously impressive testimonials. In fact, everyone had such a super–duper client list that you had to question why they were on the lookout for more.

Jack appeared in the doorway. 'I want to go on the computer,' he said.

'Not now, Jacko.'

'But I want to go on *Wizard World* and destroy Freddie's base.'

'Freddie's base is safe a while longer, then,' I said. 'Why don't you read a nice book?'

Why was it always a 'nice' book? It was like calling the cashier in the motorway tollbooth the 'little man' – even if he was huge.

Jack started twisting the door handle around. 'Why are you on the computer, anyway?' he demanded.

'I might be going back to work,' I said. 'I need to get my foot in the door of some new companies.'

Jack looked at me quizzically. 'I'm guessing that's an expression?' he said. 'Cos it wouldn't be very practical to actually *send* them your foot, would it?'

He doubled up with laughter and started hopping around on one leg.

'Oh, Jack. I do love you,' I said.

'Don't go back to work,' said Jack. 'I like it when you're not working.'

That was lovely. It was worth it. All the worry, all the sacrifice...

'What do you like about it?'

'That you're not on the computer when I want to go on *Wizard World*.'

Jack scampered off.

I puffed out my cheeks and poured myself another glass of wine. Jack was gorgeous but every time I relaxed, Teddy popped into my mind, reminding me how quickly, how devastatingly it could all go wrong. I rubbed the scar that Teddy had left on my temple. Even now, after having a *laugh* with Jack, my heart was pitter-pattering with anxiety.

Suddenly, without meaning to, I tapped *Teddy Miles* into Google. I hadn't planned to. I just did. The letters looked forbidding but they were just letters. Just a name. And I could always delete them.

I sat there for a while and then I closed my eyes and gently pressed search. Believe me, *that* felt scary. Slowly, I cracked open one eye and then the other...

Nothing.

Well, not *nothing*, of course. It was a reasonably common name. There were actors in London and plumbers in Kettering and everything in between. But not what I was looking for. Although, what *was* I looking for? Teddy was a couple of years older than me so he'd be in his mid-forties now. The last I heard, he'd been institutionalised. He probably still was.

My interest piqued, I googled 'autism in the 1970s'. People on the spectrum seemed to have been labelled psychotics back then and interventions typically included removal from the family home. So, I hadn't remembered wrongly.

I read on. 'Treatments included D-Lysergic Acid Diethylamide Electroconvulsive therapy.' Bloody hell. Whatever that was, it sounded horrific. I could just see the medical table, the wide straps, the strip lighting. Was it legal? It certainly didn't sound ethical. Poor Teddy. Whatever he'd done, he didn't deserve that.

But what now? There was nowhere else to look. Teddy's parents were dead. I didn't want to stir up a hornets' nest by asking Mum. Teddy had always been Not-To-Be-Spoken-About. Something to be bundled up and hidden away. A shameful secret.

It was all so sad.

Enough, Emma.

I took a large gulp of wine and turned back to my letter.

Still no inspiration. Zilch. Zip. Nada.

Hang on, though.

What if I *did* send potential clients a foot? Not a real one, of course, but something foot-shaped. A doorstop, maybe. *That* would stand out from the crowd! I downed another glass of wine and hit Google. Chocolate seemed to be where it was at and it was a lot more fun than fretting about what had happened to my autistic cousin and what might happen to Jack. There were solid chocolate feet so realistic they probably tasted as cheesy as the idea. Perhaps not. The chocolate *shoes* looked far more enticing and there were dozens to choose from. There were sophisticated chocolate stilettos filled with truffles. Gorgeous polka dot slingbacks with matching handbags. There were even 'urban grunge trainers' for the guys. By now, I was quite excited. I was particularly thrilled by the website that gave helpful hints on matching shoe type to recipient personality. This would, admittedly, have been more useful had I actually known my recipients but I wasn't going to let a small detail like that rein in my enthusiasm. Oh no! I only had to make an educated guess based on their name and company. So, Fenella from a trendy London advertising agency was matched to 'quietly quirky' leopard print, while Joanne from Eden Vale was paired with 'cute and smiley' cow patches.

Corny? Moi?

Before long, I had successfully matched up twelve prospective clients with suitable edible footwear. This was fun! Why hadn't I thought of doing it before? An accompanying card with my name, contact details and 'I'd love to get a foot in your door' and *voila*! Who could resist?

I pressed the purchase button with a jaunty flourish and went to bed feeling very pleased with myself.

Chapter Twenty-One

Monday morning, standing in the school playground, I had second thoughts. What on earth had I been thinking? What on earth had I *done*? Talk about desperate. Talk about pathetic. Talk about chucking the best part of £500 down the drain.

Daniel would be *furious*.

Wait!

I'd cancel them as soon as I got home. They wouldn't have seen the order yet, let alone processed it.

I arrived home just as Daniel was getting into his car. The other us would have given each other a proper goodbye kiss. The current me was just relieved Daniel wouldn't be there to hear the call. But, as I shut the front door, I saw Daniel's phone was still on the hall table. I picked it up and ran outside but Daniel was already pulling out of the drive. I shouted and waved but it was to no avail. The dark blue Audi headed off down the street.

Damn!

Daniel would be lost without his phone. I really should be a good wife and take it to the office. Only, it was a long drive and I *needed* to cancel those shoes…

As I stood there, dithering, Daniel's phone pinged with an incoming text.

> Sorry. Need to cancel our meeting at the Club this
> am. Will call to rearrange. G.

That made my mind up.

The Club must be Saxony Hall, our ball venue. It was barely a ten-minute drive from home. Daniel had spent the weekend putting out feelers for a new job and must have arranged to meet 'G' – whoever he was – there this morning. I could cancel the shoes when I got home. There was still time.

I jumped into the car and drove to Saxony Hall. Yup, Daniel's car was in the visitors' car park and he was rummaging around on the passenger seat. I walked over and rapped on the passenger window. Daniel looked up with a smile, which morphed to surprise when he saw me.

I opened the door. 'Sorry to startle you,' I said.

Daniel stared at me blankly. 'I'm completely confused,' he said. 'What are *you* doing here?'

'You left your phone at home. And then "G" texted saying he couldn't make your meeting.'

Daniel got out of the car and took his phone from me. 'You're a lifesaver,' he said, scanning the message. 'I don't deserve you.'

The guilt-monster reminded me it was still there.

I ignored it and accepted Daniel's hug.

'What are you two lovebirds up to?'

We both swung round. It was Virginia, emerging gracefully from her cream Mini and grinning at us with amusement. Maybe she thought we'd booked a room at the Club for a bit of how's-yer-father. Maybe I should pretend we *were* there were for a little tryst. I linked my arm with Daniel's and smiled at her in a coquettish fashion.

'I'm meant to be here for a business meeting,' said Daniel. 'But it got cancelled.'

Spoilsport!

I unlinked my arm.

'What are *you* doing here?' I asked.

Virginia leant into her car and pulled out some slim orange files. 'Meeting the catering team about the ball,' she said. 'Why don't you join me, Emma? Mandy can't make it.'

'Sure.' Better than going home and making the beds.

'Daniel?' asked Virginia.

'I'd better head off. Thanks again, Em.'

He waved casually to us both and got back into his car.

Virginia and I set off across the gravel car park and up the front steps of the Club. Inside the large lobby, overstuffed sofas and armchairs were clustered into little groups and waiters in traditional black and white were scurrying around dispensing tea and coffee. Given the average age of the clientele, it was a bit like a very posh care home.

Virginia announced our arrival and we grabbed a couple of armchairs.

'It's weird being back here,' said Virginia.

It was weird *being* there with her. Not at all how I'd thought today would play out.

'Are you a member?' I asked.

Virginia shook her head. 'No. Andrew used to be,' she said. 'It's a great setting but everyone's so *old*. Andrew was in a croquet competition once and he got through to the final because all his opponents died!'

We laughed easily together.

How strange this was.

'I'm sorry about Andrew,' I said.

'Thanks.' A sigh. 'It's hard.'

'You're doing brilliantly,' I said. I meant it. 'You always seem so in control.'

Virginia grimaced. 'I'm trying to be,' she said. 'Some of the time it's OK, but then I go and do something stupid. Like with the meths.'

Oh God.

Tell her, Emma.

Tell her.

'Mrs Kennedy?'

A stocky man straining out of a black suit was approaching our table. It was Sam the catering manager and the moment to come clean about the fondue set had gone, because we were plunged into a detailed discussion about menus and decorations and wine lists. Salmon mousse or vegetable tartlet? Chicken chasseur or sea bass? Profiteroles or cheesecake?

Then we toured the ballroom. Sam suggested having a tree of promises for any small auction donations like the flapjacks. There was even a potted bay tree outside the front door we could use.

It was all rather thrilling. I left feeling efficient and accomplished and much, much warmer toward Virginia.

It was only when I got back into the car that I noticed I still had my slippers on. They were quite smart tartan ones — but they were very obviously slippers.

I'd been wearing them all morning.

And Virginia hadn't said a word.

–

It wasn't until I got home that I remembered about the chocolate shoes.

'Hold on a wee moment,' said a breezy, Scottish voice. 'Right, got you; quite a substantial order.'

'Yes…'

'And all dispatched over the weekend.' Satisfaction in her voice. 'We're really busy at the moment, so they obviously worked on getting it out on Saturday. They'll be delivered today.'

Relief was snatched away. Like when a late bus finally turns up and it's out of service.

'How can I stop them?' A hint of panic. I tried to quash it with a few Jaffa Cakes.

'You can't.'

'I have to.'

'It's impossible.'

I hung up and ate several more Jaffa Cakes. Sadly, they failed to do much quashing on the panic front. Tasty though.

What to do now? Word was bound to get around about what I'd done. There'd be a bitchy little comment in the diary section of *Marketing Week* and everyone would laugh themselves silly:

> Which consultant with a tootsie fetish has been dispensing edible shoes to which insight managers of Footsie (boom boom!) companies?

Actually, that wasn't bad. Maybe I should become a columnist – I'd certainly shot myself in the foot in the consultancy world.

I steeled myself and checked my emails. Oh God; there were two from pre-eminent market research buyers. Heart hammering, I opened the first:

> Dear Emma. Thank you for the chocolate 'foot in the door' shoe. However, I'm afraid it's strictly against company policy for employees to use their official position to receive gifts, hospitality or benefits of any kind which might reasonably be seen to compromise the Company's position or the employee's personal integrity...

The message went on for three more paragraphs, the gist being I could expect the imminent return of the offending item. Talk about humiliating! At least I could eat the shoe.

I opened the second:

> Hi, Emma. What a surprise to receive the gorgeous choccie shoe. Thank you so much. We're tied into our current suppliers for the next two years but I'll keep your details on file...

Huh! No project *and* she was going to keep the shoe. What a blooming waste of money.

There was also an email from Mark.

I've got a meeting in Swindon tomorrow so I could drop in at yours on the way and brief you? And guess what? Someone sent a client a chocolate shoe! Bizarre thing to do.

Bizarre.

Chapter Twenty-Two

After drop-off the next day, it was all systems go for my meeting with Mark. Unfortunately, I had only just started dusting the dining room when the house phone rang.

'It's Florrie. From the school office. I'm afraid that Jack has a headache.'

Jack had been fine fifteen minutes ago. I explained as much to Florrie.

'That's as maybe. But he's here with me now and he *is* looking a little peely-wally'.

'Please, Florrie. I have a meeting.'

'I'm sorry. I must ask you to pick him up.'

Outmanoeuvred, I drove to the school, trying to think of a contingency plan. There wasn't one. Daniel had 'people' over from the States. Mum had a hospital appointment. Ness and Mandy were working.

Jack was waiting for me in reception. He *was* slightly pale, but perked up noticeably once we got home. Surprise, that!

I called Mark. Maybe we could have a telephone meeting instead.

'Not possible, Healey,' said Mark. 'I need to take you through some 3D prototypes.'

'Skype?'

'No. You need to handle them. See how they work.'

'What about tomorrow?'

'Tomorrow's Geneva.'

This was embarrassingly unprofessional. Mark would never hire me again. Word of my flakiness would spread among the research community and I'd be blacklisted throughout London.

'OK,' I said. 'Let's stick to Plan A. I'm sure it will be fine.'

I was sure it wouldn't be fine.

I settled Jack in the living room with some DVDs and finished flicking a duster round the dining room. Just as well. The doorbell rang ten minutes before Mark was due.

I flung the door open theatrically. 'Shome mistake shurely—' I started.

It was Mrs Nosey from next door, resplendent in navy slacks and a striped jumper with a red anchor on the breast. *All* her jumpers seemed to have an anchor on the breast. She was clutching a parcel marked 'Foot in Your Door.' Oh God, it was that chocolate shoe being returned. Mark must never, ever see it. He must never know I'd sent them. It would be too humiliating.

'This arrived for you,' said Mrs Nosey, making no attempt to hand it over.

'Thanks.' I smiled pleasantly and held out my hands.

'It looks like a chocolate shoe. It's not your birthday though, is it, dear? That's not until June. Hello, Jack, dearie. Off school again?'

Jack ignored Mrs Nosey. 'What's that?' he demanded.

'Something that Mrs MacBride kindly took in for me while I was picking you up from school.'

'Can I have it?'

'No, you can't. It's for your mother,' said Mrs Nosey. It was fair to say she didn't 'get' Jack.

Mark arrived, almost overshooting the house and bringing his red sporty car to a screeching halt. Mrs Nosey turned to tut and I took the opportunity to wrestle the parcel off her.

'Thank you so much,' I said, 'but I have an important business meeting to attend to.'

Mrs Nosey tutted again and gave Mark a poisonous look as they passed on the path.

'Something I said?' Mark asked, grinning at her generously proportioned rear view.

Jack wrinkled his nose. 'But he didn't say *anything*,' he said.

'It's an expression, sweetie.' I stuffed the chocolate box behind the front door and turned to Mark. In his open-necked striped shirt and glasses and with his short dark hair shot through with grey, he could have been an accountant. Nevertheless, there was something about the slanted blue eyes, high cheek-bones and wide curving mouth that had always done it for me.

Mark kissed me on the cheek. 'Hello to you, too,' he said, turning to Jack and proffering his hand. 'A bit in the wars, I gather?'

Jack ignored Mark. In fact, he went one stage further and physically turned his back. Mark looked taken aback, as well he might, and there was a pause while I tried to think how best to smooth things over. I failed — sometimes there just wasn't an obvious explanation for Jack's behaviour — and the three of us stood in an awkward triangle. I tried to transmit 'do not under any circumstances mention the box in the hall,' to Jack through narrowing my eyes.

'What's in the box in the hall?' asked Jack.

'Nothing.'

'It's not nothing,' said Jack. 'They wouldn't send you a box with nothing in it.'

'It's nothing *important*,' I clarified.

'It must be. You wouldn't have hidden it behind the door if it wasn't important.'

Jack hated secrets. I had to tell him the contents of his Christmas stocking in advance, for goodness' sake. There was no way he was going to let this lie.

Time for emergency action. I shepherded Jack into the hallway and pulled the door shut behind us.

'You can have it,' I whispered.

'*Have* it?' Jack couldn't believe his luck.

'Take it, open it, eat it… whatever you want. Just don't tell Mark what's in it, OK?'

'OK.'

I shepherded Mark into the dining room.

'Sorry about that,' I said. 'Right; let's talk pubes!'

The project was for a razor manufacturer who wanted to explore the potential for a dedicated product for 'down there'. Over the next few months, Mark and I would be criss-crossing the country with a bunch of scary-looking prototypes and asking the Great British public for their views. Mark would interview the men and I would interview the women. It all sounded like enormous fun.

And I was going to be *paid* for it!

At a natural break in proceedings, I went into the kitchen to check on Jack. Cardboard, polystyrene and plastic littered the floor and the boy himself had a mouth full of chocolate. I crammed the most incriminating pieces of packaging into the bin and put the kettle on.

'Why did you do that thing earlier?' I asked.

'Wha' thing?'

'Refusing to shake Mark's hand.'

'I wanted him to think I was ill. I didn't want him to be cross I wasn't at school.'

'But he's not your teacher. Or your mum. And why would refusing to shake his hand make him think you were ill?'

'I don't get it,' said Jack.

Question: laugh or cry?

Answer: a dainty nibble of chocolate instep.

Yum!

Probably not fifty quid's worth of yum, but definitely scrummy. I ate some more; in fact, I shovelled in the whole heel and when Mark arrived in the kitchen a moment later, he found Jack and me with our mouths stretched wide into big chocolate O's.

'Hey guys,' he said. 'I feel like I'm missing the party here!'

I shook my head in a pathetic, 'I'm unable to answer,' way, flapping one hand urgently for good measure. Jack went one better. He walked up to Mark, proffered his hand and shook Mark's with enormous dignity. Then he contorted his features into an agony-infused expression and started rubbing his stomach.

I didn't like to remind him he was supposed to be off school with a headache.

Mark cleared his throat. 'There's someone called Virginia at the door, looking for you. Wasn't sure if you'd want to see her now?'

I started my shaking and flapping again but it was too late. Virginia was wandering into the kitchen, in a short trench coat and high heels.

'Emma, hi!' she said. 'Sorry for barging in.'

She didn't look sorry. In fact, if I wasn't very much mistaken, she was shrugging off her coat to reveal a caramel cardigan worn back to front. On anyone else it would have looked contrived, but on Virginia it looked elegant and witty. It probably wasn't a coincidence it stopped shy of her peachy bottom.

I gulped down the chocolate shoe. 'I'm afraid I'm working,' I said.

'I won't keep you,' said Virginia, giving Mark a radiant smile. 'By the way, did you know you've got chocolate all round your mouth?'

She whipped out a tissue and dabbed my cheek. I hate people touching me uninvited and I swatted her hand away, resisting the temptation to follow through with a swift uppercut.

'Catch you at pick-up?' I said pointedly.

'Sure.' Virginia didn't move. 'Anyway, good news. Paul's agreed to auction off the chance to name a character in his next book.'

Really? He hadn't mentioned it to me and I was only organising the damn auction with him.

'Paul?' asked Mark.

'Paul Archer,' said Virginia, giving Mark another dazzling smile.

'*The* Paul Archer? The Ironmonger Series?'

'Yes. Are you a fan?'

'Absolutely. Bloody good books. I'd quite fancy seeing my name in one.'

'Well, you can always bid remotely.' Virginia perched her bottom on the kitchen table and started rummaging in her handbag. Then she brandished a couple of tenners at me.

'The insurance money from the murder-mystery fire,' she said triumphantly. 'They were quite generous, so this is for your hat.'

The fire was my fault. I didn't deserve recompense. I certainly didn't deserve twenty quid.

'Thank you. I'll donate it to the Lunch Club,' I said.

'Hat? Fire? Murder mystery?' Mark looked intrigued.

'Don't ask!' said Virginia. 'We had a fondue set malfunction. My reputation as a hostess has yet to recover.'

'Fondue. Set. Malfunction. Now I've heard it all.'

'Long story.'

'Do tell.'

So Virginia told Mark about the Lunch Club and the murder-mystery dinner party. Mark seemed in no hurry to continue briefing me. Indeed, he looked far more interested in the idea of debriefing Virginia. I was beginning to feel like a gooseberry.

'Anyway, Emma's fondue set caught fire,' Virginia finished. 'I was a bit heavy-handed with the meths.'

Mark was laughing. 'I think the fondue set was a wedding present from us,' he said.

'Ah, *your* fault then,' said Virginia. 'Should have bought them a toaster instead.'

'Guilty as charged. Except, if I remember correctly, that fondue set wasn't designed for meths.'

Shut up, Mark.

Just shut up.

Virginia looked blank. 'Sorry?' she said.

'You're meant to use a solid gel pack with it. We had the same one.'

Silence. Then Virginia cleared her throat.

'Well, that's a surprise,' she said. Then she laughed. 'I guess it's evens, Emma.'

No.

Don't even *think* about going there.

'Why?' asked Mark.

Oh my God. It was going to come out.

At least I could get in first.

I took a deep breath. 'Virginia asked when my baby was due,' I said.

Mark laughed, not unkindly, but I noticed him sneak a quick look at my belly before I hastily sucked it in.

Virginia smirked. There was no other word for it. 'I was actually thinking of the time I told Jack off at Jamie's party,' she said.

'Right,' I said flatly.

What else was there to say?

'Anyway, I must be off,' said Virginia brightly. 'Lovely to meet you, Mark.'

Speechlessly, I walked her to the front door.

Virginia shrugged on her mac.

'You really could have said sorry,' she said.

Daniel arrived home while I was cooking tea and vaguely supervising Jack and Freddie who were doing homework at the kitchen table. He didn't bother with hellos or comments about Grindstone Cowboys. He stormed straight into the kitchen and said, 'Can we talk about this?' while waving a piece of paper at me. I surmised that any credit I had earned for reuniting him with his phone had well and truly expired.

I took a closer look at the piece of paper. It was a credit card statement.

Oh God.

'It must be you,' persisted Daniel. 'Foot in Your Door?'

Yes.

That.

'Oh yes,' I said brightly. 'Something for work.'

'Work? You *don't* work.'

'My new career as a freelance consultant?'

'What new career? Last I heard you were going to ask for your old job back.'

Surely I'd told Daniel I hadn't got my old job back?

Surely.

I thought about it.

I hadn't.

How and when had things got so bad between us that I hadn't told him something as fundamental as that?

'Far more money in freelance work,' I said breezily, trying to brazen things out.

'Wait.' Daniel's tone was noticeably flat. 'Did you or did you not ask for your old job back?'

'Er, did.'

'And?'

'And they're not recruiting.' I crossed my fingers behind my back. 'So, then I thought I'd—'

'So, then you thought you'd put five hundred quid on our joint credit card for some chocolate *shoes*, so when I try to use it at work, it's bloody rejected.'

It did sound pretty bad when he put it like that.

'I can't believe they're having a fight about chocolate shoes,' said Freddie with a world-weary air.

'Mum and I ate a chocolate shoe today,' said Jack.

Daniel glared at him. 'You *ate* one?' he said. 'You ate a fifty-quid chocolate shoe?'

'Yes. When that man came round, Mum hid it behind the door and later we ate it.'

'Man?' asked Daniel, wearily.

'A man she was talking to about hair on your bottom.'

Daniel turned on his heel and walked out of the room.

'It was only Mark, Daniel. *Mark*,' I yelled after him. 'He's given me some freelance work on *body grooming*.'

Daniel didn't turn round.

The fact it had been Mark really wouldn't have helped my cause.

Daniel had always been funny about Mark.

Ever since the time I'd chosen Mark over him.

–

After university, I didn't see Daniel for several years. I joined a marketing consultancy on a graduate training scheme, was promoted quickly and became quite the girl about town.

It was the Nineties and corporate hospitality was all the rage. That summer, our company hired a marquee at the Henley Regatta. Not many of our clients turned up – it was too far out of London and the same day as the Wimbledon semi-finals. The marquee was on a quiet stretch of the river and, once we'd drunk our fill of Pimm's, there wasn't an awful lot to do. It wasn't as if anyone came to the Regatta to watch the rowing.

Mark decided he could murder a proper pint and I decided it would be a good idea to avail ourselves of one of the little rowing boats at our disposal and join the great unwashed on the other side of the river. Not perhaps the best idea when I was dolled up to the nines in a pink and cream striped blazer and a crushed pink Ghost skirt. By the time we'd moored at the far bank, we'd had a near miss with a dragon boat and were soaked to the skin. We were also weak with laughter.

And that's when I saw Daniel. Casually dressed, pint in hand, he was propping up a makeshift bar. Then he saw me too. He smiled and stretched out an arm.

'Stay, have a drink,' he said.

'She's with me, mate,' Mark intervened. Too loudly. Too aggressively.

I was torn for a second. Then I smiled distractedly and left without a backward glance.

Chapter Twenty-Three

Daniel came round to my freelance venture.

Of course he did. In fact, once he found out how much Mark was paying me, it was safe to say he was fully on board. But every time we rowed, it felt like another tear to the fragile chiffon of our marriage. I wasn't sure how much more it could take.

But I wasn't thinking about Daniel as I took the train up to London for my first focus groups. I was thinking about Paul. I thought about him a lot, anyway, but something had been preying on my mind since Gabriel's non-diagnosis. When Gabriel had said, 'Your mummy's got a baby in her tummy,' I'd taken it at face value. Gabriel thought *I* was pregnant. It was obviously an easy mistake to make.

But there was Gabriel's pronoun reversal to factor into all this. He could have meant that *Hanna* had a baby in her tummy. Of course, it might have been *tense* reversal… but I knew I was clutching at straws. As fields gave way to serried ranks of housing, I acknowledged that Hanna was almost certainly pregnant.

Why hadn't Paul told me? I mean, Hanna was still whippet-thin, so maybe they hadn't told anyone. But surely I wasn't 'anyone'. Paul and I had become quite close.

Hadn't we?

Anyway, regardless of why he had or hadn't told me, it made all the difference. Despite the fact that Paul was already a dad – and I had *three* children, for goodness sake – the fact that Hanna was pregnant completely tipped the balance. Somehow it was understandable for everything to go belly-up during the rough-and-ready tween and teen years but it was so, so wrong when a new life was beginning. I couldn't be a part of that, even tangentially. I couldn't do that to Hanna – no matter how much I disliked her.

By the time the train pulled into Paddington, I had resolved that that was that.

No more hand-holding.

No more little tête-à-têtes.

From now on, I was going to be absolutely squeaky clean.

–

Mark's offices were in Soho, sandwiched between a sex shop and a Greek restaurant. Open-plan and reassuringly scruffy, they had an air of busy enterprise bordering on panic. Some researchers were gesticulating furiously over large polystyrene boards. Others were typing furiously. I could feel my energy levels move up a gear. I'd been stuck in neutral far too long.

Mark came over, wreathed in smiles.

'Thank God you're here, Healey,' he said, kissing me on the cheek. 'I've got three presentations to get out this afternoon, so I'll have to leave the groups to you.'

'That's fine,' I said.

'Oh, and they're being streamed live to some bigwig in the States so the UK guy's very nervy.'

'OK.'

Suddenly I felt nervous. Why couldn't I be interviewing people about gravy or chocolate or something *normal*?

A guy of twelve in a tight, striped jumper showed me to the viewing studio. There wasn't much to do before the clients arrived, so I killed time checking Facebook and eating the crisps intended for the respondents.

Then my phone buzzed. It was a text from Virginia.

A quick drink later would be lovely. Gx

I stared at it, bemused. When, exactly, had I arranged to meet her for a drink? Had something been said when she'd popped round the other day? Did I have early stage dementia?

Then the penny dropped. The text wasn't intended for me. The Gx' was proof of that – I'd never made it onto 'Ginny' terms with her. I shovelled in some more crisps and bashed out a reply:

I think you sent this to me in error? Ex

The reply came back almost immediately.

Sorry! Too many Emmas in my address book!

'Are you the moderator?'

Another guy of twelve in another tight, striped jumper was standing in front of me. This one pushed heavy-framed glasses back onto his nose and repeated, a touch impatiently, 'The moderator?'

'Yes. Sorry.'

I stuffed my phone into my pocket. This was, presumably, the client. Time to ooze professionalism and gravitas.

'I'm James. The brand manager.'

'Hello, James,' I said gravely.

'This is a very important project for us,' said James. 'The key thing is to get down to brass tacks with these women. We don't want them pussyfooting round the subject.'

Ah, so our James was a something of a wit.

'Boom boom,' I said sycophantically.

'Pardon?' James looked blank.

'*Pussy*footing? You know… with us talking about the bikini line?'

'Oh!' James looked aghast.

Bollocks. Totally misread that one.

'Sorry,' I said. 'Not funny. I'll get my bits sorted. Not *my* bits, of course. My bits and bobs – for the group.'

'Right.'

James disappeared to the viewing room. Aware he could see me through the mirror, I put on my reading glasses and leafed through the discussion guide in a belated attempt to look poised and professional.

Hopefully I could claw this back.

Ten minutes later, the group was under way. Qualitative research isn't rocket science but there's a definite knack to it and a lot can go wrong, especially when you're talking about something sensitive. You need to steer participants through a series of stages. Firstly. the group needs to 'form', followed by 'storming', where participants vie for position, and 'norming', when people relax. Only then can the group move on to 'performing', where everyone is working productively together. Miss or skimp on any of those stages and the whole thing can go belly-up.

To my relief, moderating turned out to be like riding a bike and the session was an absolute dream. The seven young women who'd been bussed in from Finchley were bright and articulate and made the very most of their moment in the spotlight. I felt like a conductor, masterfully leading my finely tuned orchestra to a swelling crescendo.

You wanted Brazilian horror stories, James? Tick.

The trend toward Colombians – a few 'freedom fighters'? Tick.

Vajazzling and pejazzling? Tick.

Objectives met? Absolutely, James. Every single one.

Group over, I grabbed a Diet Coke and opened the door to the observation room. My nostrils were hit by a wave of burnt coffee, congealed pizza and hot bodies.

'I hope I didn't pussyfoot around too much, James?' I said cheekily into the darkness.

'You certainly didn't,' said an amused female voice. 'That was quite a show.'

I snapped on the light.

Blimey.

James had been joined by at least twelve colleagues, all now blinking stupidly at the light. It was like a surprise party, only it wasn't. At least the faces were friendly.

A large lady, wearing a purple wrap dress, held out her hand. 'I'm the planner from Coles-Print-Wermann,' she said. 'That was a wonderful group. I'm in awe at how you got those women to open up.'

'Thank you,' I said. To say I was thrilled would be an understatement. Wait until Mark heard about this.

'I'm not sure I caught your name?' the purple lady said.

'It's Emma,' I said.

'Hello, Emma,' said the purple lady. 'I'm Fenella.'

Fenella?

Fenella?

I'd sent a chocolate shoe to a Fenella.

And she'd sent it back!

Oh, my goodness.

Emma was a fairly common name. But what if Fenella asked for my surname? I couldn't admit to it. Not in front of all these people.

'So, when I said my name was Emma, I meant it's actually Emma-Jane,' I said carefully.

'Right.'

'But everyone calls me EJ.'

'EJ it is, then,' said Fenella.

'That was quite a show, EJ,' a disembodied voice boomed from the ether. 'We weren't expecting you Brits to be quite so candid. So, team, what are the main takeouts?'

A lively conversation about landing strips followed and, before long, the next group arrived and I started the process all over again.

Two successful groups later, I was done for the day. Knackered, I went into the viewing room for the last time. Most of the clients had gone but Fenella and James were still there and Mark had pitched up.

'Hear you nailed it, Healey,' he said, slapping me on the back. 'Knew you would.'

Healey.

My skin prickled. I tried to communicate 'My name is now EJ,' through scratching my cheek, but I'm not sure he cottoned on.

Luckily, Fenella hadn't heard. 'That was brilliant,' she said, stretching. 'I feel like a pube guru now. EJ, you're a star.'

James gave us both a gangster-style handshake and they were gone.

Mark turned to me. 'EJ?' he said with exaggerated incredulity.

'Yes. It's my new working name,' I said.

'Is it now?'

'Yes. Like a stage name.'

'A *stage* name?'

'Absolutely,' I said, warming to my theme. 'I find it useful to separate my career and home personas. Helps me achieve a better work–life balance. You should try it some time.'

Chapter Twenty-Four

I was on a real high after the groups and, when Mark suggested
a quick drink, I jumped at the chance. We walked through Soho
and across Charing Cross Road, kicking through the leaves and
litter.

I'd moderated three hugely successful groups and I was *back*!

Mark led me down a side street and into the warmth of a
tiny, stylishly gloomy wine bar.

Hang on.

I *knew* this place.

Daniel and I used to come here when we were courting,
slowly and deliciously teetering on the edge of love. This used
to be one of my favourite places in London. It was just the
same. It was still crammed with French paraphernalia and the
atmosphere was still as authentically Gallic as if it had been
transported lock, stock and barrel from *la Rive Gauche*.

How bittersweet to be back.

Mark grabbed a table. Gesticulating for me to sit down, he
headed to the bar and I could hear his appalling Franglais as he
debated wines with the barman.

Feeling sentimental, I sent Daniel a text.

> **Emma:** Remember the wine bar we used to go
> to? I'm there and it's exactly the same! EXACTLY!

I fiddled with a wine label pasted to the shade of our table lamp
while I waited for a reply.

Daniel: What bar? Can you call?

Emma: Near Shaftesbury Ave. You must remember!

Nothing.

Emma: Well?

Daniel: Nope. Call me.

Suddenly I felt utterly deflated. It hadn't crossed my mind that Daniel wouldn't remember. OK, it was only a place and we had, of course, had other haunts. But how dare he tread oh-so-casually over my memories? And *bugger* talking to him. I didn't want to know Jack was playing up or Jack hadn't eaten his tea or Jack was spinning around on a chair refusing to do his homework.

Let Daniel deal with it all for once.

Mark was back. 'Isn't this a great find?' he enthused, plonking down a complicated-looking bottle of red.

I didn't tell him Daniel and I had found it first. I didn't tell him that Daniel had now forgotten it and that that felt like a slap in the face. I just smiled, tucked my hair behind my ears and discovered that two decades on, the old place could still work its magic on me. After one glass, I was feeling as mellow and gorgeous as the wine. After two, I ignored another text from Daniel. After three, I was distinctly squiffy. And after four, I was anyone's.

Mark was at his most charming. 'I'm pleased to see you still do such brilliant focus groups, Healey,' he said.

'Thank you.' I grinned. 'I'm not bad at debriefing either.'

We both dissolved into immature snorts of laughter. 'God, talk about a double entendre,' said Mark.

'Everything in qualitative research is though, isn't it?' I said. 'Debriefing, stimulus material, probing...'

'Ha! Our job should be a whole load more exciting than it is, then.'

'Oh, I don't know. Those pube groups were fun. I quite fancy a vajazzle now.'

'Do you now?' Mark's eyes glittered.

'Yes. Maybe a little percentage symbol…'

'A *percentage* symbol.' Mark laughed. 'You are one crazy chick!'

'I think that's what Daniel thinks,' I said, suddenly morose. 'But not in a good way.'

The miserable git couldn't even remember the wine bar we'd courted in.

The wine label I was fiddling with parted company with the lampshade.

'Sorry,' I said. 'I think I'm pissed.'

'Me too,' said Mark. 'Come on, let's settle up and get you into a cab.

—

I only remembered Daniel had been trying to get hold of me once I was on the train home. Of course, said train was packed with late commuters and merrymakers and I was standing with my hip wedged uncomfortably against someone's seat back. Whatever Daniel wanted could wait until I got home.

Daniel had other ideas.

We'd barely reached Ealing Broadway before my phone starting buzzing. I was all set to ignore it when it crossed my mind that there might be an emergency. I answered, trying to ignore a fat guy in a suit giving me the evil eye.

Yes, I know. I hate people who bark down their phones on the train as well.

'God, Emma,' said Daniel. 'Where the *fuck* have you been?'

There was a scream in the background. My maternal antennae picked up anger rather than emergency.

'I've been working,' I said, inserting a note of indignation into my voice.

The fat man unwrapped a Mars Bar and raised his eyebrows at me. He obviously didn't believe me either. The fact I was three sheets to the wind and swaying independently of the train clearly wasn't helping my cause.

'You finished *hours* ago,' said Daniel.

'I've been debriefing with Mark,' I replied.

The Mars Bar paused en route to Fatman's lips. I gave him a severe look.

'God, how much there is to say about pubes?' said Daniel.

'Stop taking the piss out of my work. Pubes – or lack of them – are big business nowadays.'

Fatman gagged on his Mars Bar. A woman reading the *Evening Standard* glanced up at me. Maybe I had been louder than I'd intended.

'Well, why not debrief by phone or email rather than *in the pub*?'

'Come on, Dan. I never nag *you* about work.'

'Course you don't. Anyway, *I* don't talk about pubic hair in the pub, with an ex-girlfriend.'

'*Pubic hair* is about to be the only thing bringing home the bacon at the moment.'

You could have heard a pin drop.

Or the sound of Fatman choking on his Mars Bar.

I lowered my voice. 'Anyway, what did you want to tell me?' I asked.

'It doesn't matter.' Sulkily. 'The moment's passed.'

'Come on. You've been desperate to get hold of me.'

Fatman was staring at my tits, chewing his Mars Bar, mouth open. I turned my back on him.

'OK. D'you want the good news or the bad news?' said Daniel.

'The good news.' I've never been big on delayed gratification.

'OK. I might be able to stay on at work.'

'Oh, Daniel, that's fantastic.'

It *was* good news. Of course, it was. But did it mean I'd have to give up my freelance career? It was just getting going. It had gone so well tonight.

'It's *fantastic* news,' said Daniel. 'A chance to run a global project on sustainable food sources. It could really make a difference.'

'What's the bad news, then?'

'I'd have to spend three months in the States getting things kicked off.'

'Three *months*?'

'Yeah.'

The train lurched into Slough. Fatman hauled himself to his feet and, as he squeezed past me, pushed a business card into my hand.

'Text me,' he said in a low voice.

There was sweat on his upper lip and a globule of toffee on his brightly patterned tie. Still, it's always flattering when a stranger finds you attractive, isn't it?

Fatman glanced over his shoulder. 'Let me know if you charge extra for a threesome,' he leered.

Chapter Twenty-Five

I tried not to get too worked up in the taxi home.

Of *course* Daniel wasn't seriously considering three months in the States. It was a ridiculous proposition. Completely ludicrous. But when I pushed open the front door, Daniel was in the hallway. That's when I knew he was serious.

Daniel gave me a peck on the cheek. 'Can I get you a drink?' he asked. He sounded nervous, almost formal.

'Coffee please,' I said. I needed to clear my head. 'And I'll just check on the kids.'

As I went upstairs, everything was thrown into stark relief. The grubby wall. The chipped bannister spindles. The slightly threadbare carpet. All the things we thought we had forever to get round to. Rather like working on our marriage—

No.

Stop it, Emma.

The kids were still awake. None of them asked how my first day back at work had been. None of them asked if I'd nailed the focus groups, pretended my name was EJ or been mistaken for a whore. In fact, none of them looked particularly interested to see me.

Little sods!

I went back downstairs. Daniel had made me a proper latte with frothed milk. He'd also added sugar. I only take sugar when I'm tired and emotional. My nerves ratcheted up a gear.

'So, about this job?' I said, as soon as we'd sat down on the sofa.

I was about to add 'you're not seriously thinking about taking it, are you?' when Daniel held up a hand.

'I'm seriously thinking about taking it,' he said.

For a moment, I was stunned into silence.

He couldn't just *take* it.

He couldn't just *go*.

Not when Jack…

Not when *we*…

What about *me*!

Daniel was still talking, quickly, earnestly, filling up the space between the words. 'It's a good job, Em,' he said leaning forward earnestly and gesticulating with his hands. 'In fact, it's a great job. A *dream* job. It just needs to be kicked off in Texas.'

I thought back to the chippy, idealistic boy who'd crashed the May Ball all those years ago. All Daniel had ever wanted was to make a difference. There was an energy and excitement to his voice I hadn't heard for ages.

He *wanted* to go.

He *definitely* wanted to go.

The question was, where did that leave me?

Leave us?

'So, you're just going to bugger off and leave us, are you?' I said. I tried to keep my tone of voice light and non-judgemental but I'm pretty sure I failed.

'Come on, Em, don't be like that,' said Daniel. 'I wouldn't just dump you in it. Maybe your mum could move in. Or there are agencies…'

Oh God.

Daniel had clearly given this a lot of thought.

He really did mean business.

And then a thought occurred to me…

'You've already said yes, haven't you?'

Daniel's silence spoke volumes.

'You've already accepted, haven't you?' I persisted.

Daniel sighed and ran his hands through his hair. 'What choice do we have, Em?' he said.

'There are always choices,' I said. 'I could go back to work. You could get another job. Preferably one on the same continent.'

'But this is a *brilliant* job,' said Daniel.

'I know,' I said, getting to my feet. 'You've already said. And so you're just going to up and off and leave me all on my own, are you, looking after three children?'

'For goodness sake,' said Daniel, standing up too. 'People do it all the time.'

'But they don't all have a Jack,' I practically yelled.

'Virginia does it,' said Daniel coldly. 'And *she* has a Jack.'

'Virginia hasn't got a Jack,' said a quizzical voice from the doorway. 'She's got a Josh and a Jamie.'

It was Jack, of course it was, all clean and shiny in the Reading United strip he wore as pyjamas.

'It's an expression, Jacko,' I said.

Oh God.

How much had he heard?

'I'm an expression?' said Jack, wrinkling his nose. 'Anyway, why's Dad going away? Are you marrying new people?'

Daniel laughed. 'Who'd have a couple of old has-beens like us?'

Jack nodded thoughtfully. 'True,' he said.

'There's a chance Dad might have to go to America for a few months,' I said. 'Nothing's decided,' I added, shooting Daniel a poisonous glance.

'How many months exactly?' said Jack.

'Three,' said Daniel. 'January to March.'

'*If Daddy* goes,' I interjected pointedly.

'That's only about ninety sleeps,' said Jack. 'Two thousand, one hundred and sixty hours. D'you want to know how many minutes?'

'We're good, thanks,' I said. 'Come on, Jacko. Back to bed please and I'll bring you up some water in a few minutes.'

Jack disappeared and I took a deep breath. I needed to compose myself. I needed to try to get things in perspective. At least Daniel wasn't suggesting we separate.

This wasn't a judgement on the state of our union.

It was just a business trip.

'I hope you come round to the idea,' said Daniel when I'd got to the lounge door. 'And, after the last couple of months, maybe it will do us good to have a little time apart.'

I turned round and stared at him, open-mouthed.

I couldn't think of a thing to say.

Daniel gave me the ghost of a smile. 'After all, absence makes the heart grow fonder,' he said.

Except when it doesn't.

—

I settled Jack and, deciding I had nothing more to say to Daniel for the time being, I decamped to the office and Spider Solitaire.

Was Daniel *leaving* me?

Coward that I was, I didn't dare ask outright.

Not now.

Not tonight.

But suppose he wasn't planning to come home? I rolled the prospect round my mind. Was I scared? Definitely. Sad? That too. Cut adrift, anchorless and rudderless? Yup. To mix metaphors, it felt as though I had been pootling around on green ski runs for ages and suddenly I was poised at the top of my first black, unsure I'd make it down unscathed.

The game ground to a halt, cards stuck in their unforgiving rows, and I batted away a strong desire to call Paul. If only he wasn't in America. If only I knew how he felt about, well... *me*.

But I couldn't call him. He would think it was strange. Wonder what it had to do with him. After all, we'd only kissed a few times and, despite his cryptic comment on the way back from Oxford, it didn't necessarily *mean* anything.

Instead, I texted Ness. She was out but she told me not to panic. We'd meet for coffee the next morning and she'd help me put the world to rights.

Thank goodness for besties.

Thank goodness for Ness.

Chapter Twenty-Six

'Mummy, come and stand with me.' said Lily the next morning at drop-off.

She put her hot little hand in mine and led me over to the ragged line of Year Four lunchboxes and book-bags. There was no one else actually in the queue.

'Why don't you go and play with your friends, flower?' I said. I could see them doing somersaults over a bar.

Lily didn't answer, but her bottom lip trembled.

I crouched down. 'What's wrong?' I asked.

'Izzie's telling everyone Jack's weird,' said Lily, all luminous eyes and unchecked tears.

I hugged her to me and she rested her head against my hair. 'Does Izzie know Jack's your brother?' I asked.

'Yes. That's why she's saying it.'

'Then Izzie is being very mean,' I said. 'If she carries on doing it, I'll have a word with the teacher.'

The school bell rang. I helped Lily to wipe her eyes, gave her another hug and she was off, looking sadly over her shoulder at me.

Ness came over to me and gave me a hug. 'Ready for our coffee?' she said.

'God, yeah,' I said. 'I so need this.'

'Emma, hi.' It was Virginia, Sian in tow. 'Did you know you've got something all over your hair?'

I put my hand up and felt around. Lily's snot no doubt. I thought of pretending it was an expensive new hair treatment – or worse – but I really couldn't be bothered.

'Did you come all the way over here to tell me that?' I said, more tartly than I'd intended.

'No, of course not,' said Virginia. 'I wanted to tell you I've found someone to run the Lunch Club. She's a psychotherapist with Asperger's experience *and* she's happy to start after Christmas, even though we won't have raised the money by then.'

'Brilliant.'

Shouldn't we have discussed all this as a team?

Interviewed people, maybe?

'Mr Berry has met her and given her the thumbs-up,' said Virginia. 'I'd like the kids to meet her now.'

'Oh. OK.'

Wrongfooted and outmanoeuvred as usual. Wasn't I meant to be her joint chair?

'Great,' said Virginia. 'Mine a week on Saturday? Paul will be back from his book tour by then.'

'That would be lovely.'

'Right, I'm off to the physio,' said Sian, arching backward with a little 'ooof'.

'Where do you go?' asked Ness, radiating interest.

'That place off Market Street. I've got a new guy today.'

'My stepson's started doing shifts there,' said Virginia. 'Harry?'

So, hottie of the figure-hugging T-shirt was a physio. Who knew? He could sort out my inner thighs any time…

'Yes, that's him,' said Sian. 'How funny.'

'Watch out,' said Virginia with a little laugh. 'He's a great physio but he's got the gift of the gab and an eye for the older lady.'

'Hey – who are you calling older?' said Sian with a laugh.

I suddenly noticed Ness. She was still as a statue. Alabaster skin to match. It didn't take a genius to work out what had just happened.

I touched her arm. 'Shall we go?' I said.

Ness gave the ghost of a nod and I led her out of the school gates and down the long avenue toward town. We carried on walking, passed Café Rouge, which always reminded me of Paul, and on to the other place, the one that was always full of babies and buggies and where the coffee was far too strong for my taste.

Only when we were sitting at a corner table, cradling our emergency rations of hot chocolate, did I say, 'OMG! Your crush is Virginia's *stepson*!'

Ness gave a single nod and I scrutinised her with newfound respect, my own problems pushed to one side for the moment. There was no doubt that Harry was very attractive and I'd always seen Ness as... well, one of us. A mum. A yummy mummy, to be sure, but a mum with a good – what? – eight years on Harry and little time to attend to her roots, her nails, her cellulite. Today, though, I saw only the curves under the tight black jumper, the glossy dark hair, the sexy slant to the eyes.

Lucky Ness.

'What's been going on?' I asked.

'He said he couldn't treat me again,' said Ness. 'He said it wasn't professional. But then he called me and we've been on a few dates. I really thought...'

She trailed off and started stirring her hot chocolate, faster and faster until it spilled over onto her saucer.

'Wow, Ness. Why didn't you say?'

Ness shrugged. 'I don't know. Because it was so new. Because of your reaction first time round. God, I've really made a tit of myself. He's probably moving in on Sian as we speak.'

'You haven't made a tit of yourself at all,' I said. 'Virginia said he had the gift of the gab, that's all. She didn't say he tries it one with everyone he meets.'

Ness wrinkled her nose at me. 'How come you're being so supportive all of a sudden?' she asked.

I sighed. I was so tired of keeping the secret – of keeping the excitement, the confusion and the guilt under wraps. It was eating me up.

'I guess I know what it feels like to fall for someone you shouldn't,' I said quietly.

I hadn't intended to tell her.

Not at all.

I'd just wanted to talk about Daniel going to the States.

'What the hell?' Ness sat forward and pushed her mug away from her. 'What on earth's going on, Emma?'

So, I told her about Paul; the whole sorry tale from the fondue through to the Pumpkin Party and Gabriel's diagnosis. I'm not sure what reaction I was expecting but, by the time I'd finished, Ness's mouth had dropped open.

'I don't bloody believe this,' she said. 'What on *earth* are you playing at?'

Ouch!

'Come on, Ness. You can talk.'

'Hardly. I'm not married.'

'Well, Daniel's leaving me,' I said flippantly.

'No, he's not,' said Ness, impatiently. 'He's *considering* going to the States on an extended business trip and you, my girl, are playing with fire.'

'It's not that easy,' I said.

And then it all came out. The months of not getting on. The arguments. Date night. The feeling that Daniel saw me as the hopeless mother of his autistic child. The Statistic.

It sounded pretty bad when I said it out loud. But if I'd expected Ness to say, 'I see what you mean' I'd have been very much mistaken.

'Even more reason you should be concentrating on fixing things with Daniel,' she said. 'You need to keep things together. You more than most people.'

'Why? Why me more than most people?'

As if I couldn't guess...

'Because of Jack. Because you have an autistic son.'

I could feel my cheeks growing hot. Why was I expected to behave differently, *better*, than other people just because my son had Asperger's?

It wasn't fair.

Surely I should have a *choice*.

Chapter Twenty-Seven

That Sunday was one of those gloriously sunny early December days when it should be against the law to fester indoors. Freddie was out playing football with friends and Daniel suggested that the rest of us go down to the boat and clean it up for the winter. Things between us were carefully neutral and stilted but Daniel kept suggesting ideas for 'quality family time' before he left for the States.

Because he was going.

Oh, yes. He was definitely going.

And there wasn't a thing I could do about it.

Anyway, Jack and Lily were less than impressed by the turn of events but Daniel stood firm. They were to wrap up warm and leave all electronics at home.

It was time to enjoy each other and the Great Outdoors.

And, actually, it was rather fun. We tidied up the cabin and then we attached the communal hose to the standpipe to slosh and mop the decks. Before long, we were all laughing and fooling around together and, if *Frejalily* didn't really look very much cleaner, it didn't matter because we felt more like a united family than we had done for *ages* and that was the important thing.

'Having a spruce-up?' It was the man who owned *Lazy-Daze*, the gin palace next door. He was standing on deck in pink slacks and a purple jumper and nursing a glass of amber liquid.

'Yes,' I said. I couldn't for the life of me remember his name.

'Must say the old girl needed it! We're just going to have a snifter and watch the world go by.'

'Lovely,' I said.

We were interrupted by screams from the cabin. Jack and Lily were clearly having some kind of altercation.

Mr Snifter stiffened. 'We have guests arriving soon,' he said. His tone was pleasant enough, but his intention was clear. Frankly, who could blame him?

'Don't worry,' I said. 'We're just leaving.'

I went to find Daniel. He was tinkering with the engine at the rear of the boat.

'Time to go,' I said. 'There's about to be serious sniftering next door.'

Daniel gave me a wary grin. 'Pootle down to the lock?' he suggested. 'Quality family time?'

I made a little face at him but it was tempting. The sun was sparkling on the water and there wasn't a cloud in the sky. It was too good an opportunity to miss.

'Quick one,' I said. 'I'll need to put the roast on soon.'

'Great,' said Daniel. He leant into the cabin. 'We're going for a spin, kids. Who wants an ice cream at the lock?'

Within a couple of minutes, we were off. I untethered the ropes while Daniel started the engine and, while he steered us out, I used the boathook to shove us away from the cabin-cruiser behind. It was a well-oiled routine and, as usual, it went like clockwork.

Mr Snifter was watching us. 'Very smooth,' he said, raising his glass. 'Have a good one.'

I waved back and started coiling the ropes. As we headed out into open water, I couldn't help thinking how harmoniously Daniel and I worked together. We'd always been in sync, walking side by side, watching each other's backs. We'd been a great little team until the past few months had driven a wedge between us.

Maybe this boat trip was a metaphor for our marriage.

Maybe it was a sign that things between us were better than I'd feared.

Maybe everything was going to be OK.

'Fast today,' said Daniel, cutting across my thoughts.

It was. We were fairly scooting down the river. We weren't quite scattering ducks and geese in our wake, but I was pretty sure we were going much faster than the permitted four miles an hour.

'Can't you slow down?' I asked.

'I'm hardly giving it any wellie,' said Daniel. 'It's the current.'

I glanced ahead. The water was calm and unruffled. All the action must be below the surface. What did *that* remind me of?!

'Let's just grab our ice creams and head back,' I said. 'The river's deserted. Maybe they know something we don't.'

Daniel nodded, eyes fixed ahead. We carried on round the familiar bends and, in barely ten minutes, we were at the lock.

The ice cream van wasn't there.

Jack was less than impressed. In fact, he was downright furious. 'You *said*,' he shouted. 'You *said* there would be ice cream.'

'I'm sorry, Jacko,' I replied. 'We can have Viennetta for pudding tonight instead.'

'No!' yelled Jack. 'Viennetta's not the same as a 99.' He ran down the steps to the cabin and flung himself onto the seat in disgust.

'Great,' muttered Daniel. 'Another happy family outing.'

Daniel swung *Frejalily* in a wide arc and started heading back the way we'd come. And that's when the trouble started.

'We're hardly moving,' said Lily, looking up from her DS.

'It's because we're going upstream now, flower,' I said. 'Come on, Captain. Warp speed ahead. I've got a roast to cook!'

'I'm already at warp speed,' said Daniel with a frown. 'This blasted current. And the wind isn't helping...'

He trailed off and I felt the first prickle of unease.

We were stationary.

No, we were starting to drift backward…

'Are we OK?' asked Lily, eyes huge, voice trembling.

'We're fine, flower,' said Daniel. 'I'm going to try tacking across the river.'

'*Tacking?*' My laugh was strained and high-pitched. 'We're not a yacht.'

'OK, smartarse,' snapped Daniel, swinging the boat over toward the far bank. 'Have you got a better idea?'

'Just moor up,' I said. 'Phone for help before we get swept downstream over the weir.'

'*Stop* it, Emma,' said Daniel sharply. 'And we can't moor here.'

He was right. The bank was soft and crumbly and there were too many waterweeds in the way. I hugged Lily to me.

Daniel swung the wheel again. *Frejalily* didn't respond for a moment but then, to my relief, she turned slowly and made a little progress upstream.

Thank God for that.

Jack poked his head out of the cabin. '*Are* we going to be swept over the weir?' he asked matter-of-factly.

'Of course not,' said Daniel. 'We fine now. Anyway, we've a couple of kids we can chuck overboard if we need to lose some weight.'

Jack narrowed his eyes at Daniel and disappeared back into his lair.

Lily giggled. 'Silly Daddy,' she said, affectionately.

Slowly, slowly, we made progress upstream. Round the first bend in the river, and then the second, and finally we could see our mooring in the distance. Caroline and her family were walking along the far bank and they waved gaily at us. I waved back, pushing 'Not Waving but Drowning' firmly from my mind.

We *weren't* drowning, just tackling a heavy current.

We were still together, still working as a team.

It was all OK.

By the time we approached our berth, my breathing had almost returned to normal. Daniel brought *Frejalily* alongside *Lazy-Daze* and prepared to reverse into our berth. I was at the bow, poised with ropes and boathook. Hopefully, mooring would be as smooth as setting off had been – despite the current and the wind. Mr Snifter had been joined on deck by Snifter and their guests – none other than our neighbours Mr and Mrs Nosey.

No pressure there, then.

'Bit fresh out there,' said Mrs Snifter conversationally.

'It's awful,' I said, planting my legs apart and holding onto the handrail as the boat lurched backward. Daniel was coming in at totally the wrong angle. I pushed *Frejalily* off *Lazy-Daze* with a little apologetic smile.

No damage done.

'Sorry,' called Daniel. 'Bloody current caught us. I'll go out and try again.'

His second attempt was no better. This time, *Frejalily* didn't swing round enough and we ended up banging into the boat behind us. Luckily there was no one on board and the fenders would take most of the impact.

I could hear Daniel cursing as he pushed us free.

'Oh dear,' said Mrs Snifter with a tinkly laugh. There was an edge to her voice that I interpreted as 'Don't you dare touch *our* boat'.

'I need a hand back here,' called Daniel as he tried to line up for the third time.

'I can't, Daniel,' I called back. The current was pushing us into *Lazy-Daze* and it was all I could do to keep the two boats apart.

'Get Jack. I need someone to do the ropes back here.' Daniel could usually steer *and* tie us up but he obviously didn't dare leave the wheel unattended.

'OK.' I leant down to the open cabin window. 'Help please, Jack.'

Jack poked his head out. 'No,' he said.

Out of the corner of my eye, I could see Mrs Nosey's eyes widen.

'Come on Jacko, we need you.'

'No!' said Jack more firmly. 'Dad said he would throw me overboard.'

'He was joking.' A note of desperation in my voice. 'Please, Jack.'

'No!' Jack shouted. 'Dad said he'd kill me!'

'Dear, dear,' said Mrs Nosey.

She'd probably call Childline.

'Emma! For God's sake *do* something,' Daniel called.

Oh, for goodness sake!

What the bloody hell did he expect me *to* do?

I abandoned my post and scuttled around the boat to Lily, who was standing by the cabin door looking worried.

'When Daddy gets close enough, could you put this rope round that bollard and hold it really tightly?' I asked.

''K,' said Lily, creasing her brow even more. 'But I'm not sure—'

'Just do it, flower. You'll be fine.'

'Emma, hurry up,' said Daniel urgently. 'I can't hold her much longer.'

I rushed back to the bow, boathook and ropes at the ready. The Snifters and Noseys were all watching us now.

'Need a hand?' asked Mr Snifter.

'We'll be fine, thanks.'

Famous last words.

Daniel swung *Frejalily* in for the third time, but he came in too fast and at far too tight an angle. There was a thud and a horrible scraping noise as the stern hit the river wall. The bow swung out and the side of the boat hit *Lazy-Daze* with such force that I stumbled to my knees and had to grab hold of the guardrail. I staggered to my feet as the boathook slid across the deck and into the river.

'Shit...'

I pushed at *Lazy-Daze* with my hands and Mr Snifter shoved us away with his boathook, but we were obviously completely out of sync with whatever Daniel was doing, because *Frejalily* lurched away from the river wall and then smashed back against it. This time there was a piercing scream from Lily.

I abandoned my post and ran to her. Lily's hand was trapped between *Frejalily* and the river wall. Daniel had left his seat and was desperately reaching out to her but couldn't quite get there without letting go of the wheel.

Our fault.

All our fault.

I pushed on the river wall as hard as I could but *Frejalily* wouldn't budge.

'*Do* something,' I shouted to Daniel.

'I'm fucking trying to,' Daniel shouted, spinning the wheel frantically.

There were two more thuds and *Frejalily* rocked violently. Mr Snifter and Mr Nosey appeared at the stern and, without a word, pushed *Frejalily* away from the wall. As I pulled the still-screaming Lily onto my lap, I was aware of Mr Snifter taking the wheel from Daniel. I took Lily's hand in mine. It was white and limp but there was no blood. That was somehow worse. How could I have put her in that position? I cuddled her to me and whispered soothingly into her ear and, when I looked up again, we were safely moored. I hadn't realised I'd been holding my breath.

Wordlessly and wearily, Daniel and I looked at each other.

If that boat trip *had* represented our marriage, it was well and truly over.

We didn't deserve each other.

We certainly didn't deserve our children.

Mrs Snifter came down the towpath to us. 'Brave little girl,' she said to Lily. 'I think you might need a little trip to the hospital,' she added to me.

'Dreadful current,' added Mr Snifter, kindly.

It wasn't the current.

It was Daniel and me kissing goodbye to our marriage.

If, indeed, there had been any marriage left to save.

I took Lily to the local cottage hospital, leaving Daniel and Jack to shut the boat up and to get a lift back with Mr and Mrs Nosey. The cottage hospital sent us straight up to Oxford for an X-ray.

Inevitably, after the initial triage there was a very long wait. Lily was heartbreakingly stoic. It was her fault, she kept saying; her fault for not keeping her hand in the boat. After a while, she cuddled up to me and fell asleep. I wrapped my arms round her and rocked her slowly backward and forward and watched other people whose Sundays weren't exactly going to plan.

This was it.

I'd decided the boat trip represented our marriage and look at what had happened. The boat had gone completely out of control, one of our children had got hurt and we'd had to rely on the kindness of virtual strangers to get us out of serious trouble.

It was a sign.

Daniel and I were over.

We had to be.

The Statistic had won.

I shut my eyes against Lily's head and, when my phone rang, I answered it without checking the caller.

'It's the Mad Axe Lady!'

It took a moment for me to register the voice. Then I realised. It was Paul. From America.

My heart swooped fifty floors.

'Hello,' I said. 'What's up?'

'Nothing. I was… missing you.'

Suddenly I was all choked up.

'Can I call you later?' I said.

It was time to put Lily first.

—

Lily had broken a bone in her hand. Not badly enough for an operation but it needed a cast and a sling. Lily perked up at this point. A hand in plaster was apparently A Good Thing. By the time we got home, she was positively cheerful.

I waited until the kids were in bed before I closeted myself in the office and returned Paul's call.

I couldn't help wondering if I'd imagined it.

Maybe the stress of the afternoon had got to me.

Had Paul really said he was missing me?

He picked up straight away.

'I thought I'd blown it with the "missing you" bit,' he said. 'Unless you're going to tell me to piss off?'

'No.' I took a deep breath and shut my eyes. 'I miss you too.'

There.

Said it.

Crossed that line.

There was a pause and then Paul laughed. 'Well, thank God for that, you gorgeous girl,' he said. 'The question is what the fuck are we going to do about it?'

I was laughing too.

Relief.

Excitement.

Possibility.

'I have no idea.' I said, 'But just to complicate things further, Daniel's going away,'

Too much?

Way too much?

213

'Going *away*?' said Paul. 'Going where?'

'To the States for three months after Christmas,' I said. 'New job.'

Paul let out a low whistle. 'Wow,' he said. 'That changes everything.'

Did it?

What, exactly, did he want?

What, for that matter, did *I* want?

'So, I guess I'll see you next weekend at Virginia's?' I said.

'Can't wait,' said Paul.

'Me neither.'

Suddenly everything seemed clear.

The Statistic might be claiming my marriage but it didn't say you couldn't have someone else.

Chapter Twenty-Eight

Daniel formally accepted the job and the extended business trip to Texas.

Of course he did.

He'd made his mind up straight away.

For the next few days, Daniel and I hardly spoke at all and, when we did, it was with exaggerated politeness. You could have cut the atmosphere with a knife.

Meanwhile, I waited to see Paul.

Virginia's party finally arrived.

'Why can't I stay at home?' grumbled Jack, as I supervised the putting on of coats.

'Because the party is for *you*,' I said. 'We're going to meet the Lunch-Club lady.'

Jack looked mutinous. 'I don't want to meet a boring teacher,' he said.

'Why do *I* have to come?' complained Lily.

'Because Dad's taking Freddie to football. Anyway, you love parties.'

'Not this one.'

'Why not?'

Because of her hand. Because it would be full of Aspies?

'Because there aren't going to be any girls.'

Ah. Fair point.

Jack tugged my sleeve. 'I'll only come if I can have Pot Noodle for breakfast tomorrow,' he said slyly.

'Done.'

Easy.

Jack looked taken aback. 'For *three* days,' he said quickly.

'Sorry. I can only take your first offer, matey.'

'Pot Noodles aren't a healthy breakfast,' said Lily. 'I'd like us all to watch *Frozen* together.'

'*Frozen*'s lame,' said Jack. '*The Inbetweeners* is much better.'

—

I hadn't been to Virginia's apartment since the murder-mystery party. Since that kiss...

Lily perked up when she saw the mirrored hallway. She attempted a one-handed handstand, all legs and knickers, giggling at her many reflections. Jack didn't laugh. He had a face like thunder.

Virginia opened her front door, stunning in tight jeans and a faux-fur gilet. My new wrap dress and high-heeled boots — so stylish in the mirror at home — suddenly seemed overdressed and fussy.

Never mind.

Heart in mouth, I followed Virginia into the main room and...

Paul was there.

Right there.

Standing by the fireplace, glass of red in hand and looking at me very much as he had done the first time we'd been in that room. My stomach plummeted, my breath quickened.

Surely it was obvious to everyone.

'What can I get you guys to drink?' asked Virginia.

'Mulled wine would be lovely,' I said. 'Thanks.'

God, I wanted to kiss him.

'Apple juice, please,' said Lily.

'Dunno,' said Jack.

'Come on, Jacko,' I said impatiently.

'How can I choose?' Jack was indignant. 'I don't know what she has.'

A tight smile from Virginia. '"She" has got all the usuals. Apple juice, OJ, Coke…'

'Coke, please,' said Jack.

Virginia disappeared and I turned my attention to Paul. He had a fidgeting Gabriel by his side and was talking to a lady I didn't recognise. The Lunch Club teacher presumably. Petite with cropped dark hair, she looked like a little smiley pixie.

Paul gave me his lovely crinkly smile. 'Emma, this is Ally O'Reilly,' he said.

Ally O'Reilly?

Wasn't she the psychotherapist whose card Virginia had given me?

Better be on my best behaviour in case Virginia had put the boot in.

'Hello, Ally,' I said warmly. 'These are my children, Jack and Lily.'

Ally crouched down. 'Hey, guys,' she said. She had a soft, Irish burr. 'It's so lovely of you to come and meet me.'

'We didn't want to,' said Jack bluntly.

Ally laughed. 'In that case, it's even nicer you came along.'

'I only came because I'm getting Pot Noodle for breakfast tomorrow,' said Jack. He took his drink from Virginia and took a sip. 'And Lily gets to watch *The Inbetweeners*.'

'I see,' said Ally, with a wink at me. Over her shoulder, I could see Paul laughing.

I was dizzy… giddy… seventeen again.

Jack took a sip of his drink and turned to Virginia. 'You lied,' he said. 'This is Pepsi.'

After that, there was no opportunity to talk to Paul alone because Mandy had arrived and Virginia was clapping her hands for attention.

'I'd like to introduce Ally,' she said in a singsong I'm-talking-to-children voice. 'Ally's going to run the Lunch Club. Has anyone got anything they'd like to ask her?'

'Can we play *Wizard World*?' said Jack with a smirk, clearly playing to the gallery.

God, he really wasn't at his best today.

Little bugger.

Ally was unfazed. 'Playing *Wizard World* is for home,' she said. 'But we can do lots of other fun things. What about putting on a *Wizard World* play?'

I waited for the murmurs of derision, the scornful looks, the exaggerated sighs. Instead there was a muttering of excitement. Gabriel and Dylan leapt to their feet and started miming what I could only assume was a *Wizard World*-inspired fight.

'Can we go into the playground if we want to, though?' asked Dylan when everyone was sitting down again.

'Of course you can.'

'I *want* to go to the Lunch Club.' Jack was more serious now. 'People are mean to me in the playground.'

Ally gave him a sympathetic look. 'Playgrounds can be very difficult,' she said. 'Shall I tell you what you can do when people are being unkind?'

Jack shrugged, unconvinced. 'OK,' he said.

'Just say "whatever".' Ally's tone was casual – surprised but not concerned. Then she turned her shoulder slightly away.

'Is that it?' Jack looked underwhelmed. I didn't blame him and I couldn't help wondering if Ally O'Reilly actually knew her stuff.

'Try it,' Ally suggested.

The kids stood up and started shouting and turning their backs on each other. Ally walked among them, giving advice on tone and body language for all the world as if it was a RADA class. Everyone was smiling and laughing and having such a good time that the adults joined in too, and it really was quite empowering and fun. Then we had tea – little sandwiches and sausage rolls and cakes — and Jack looked as if he'd totally forgotten it was meant to be a boring party with a teacher and Lily looked like she didn't care a jot there were no girls there.

There was no chance to talk to Paul alone though.

When Ally had gone, Virginia threw open the terrace doors and the children scampered outside. The adults followed slowly. It was a lovely day, sunny and crisp, the air fragrant with woodsmoke. The terrace had been tidied and the pile of flowerpots had gone. There was nothing to remind me of that night.

We made our way down the terrace steps and over to the children's playground.

'How's the wacky world of market research?' asked Mandy as we picked our way over crispy grass and slippery worm-casts.

'Well, I'm now a world expert on pubes,' I said.

Paul laughed his boyish laugh. 'Do tell,' he said. 'What are we meant to be doing "down there"?'

I grinned at him. 'Don't tell me there isn't at least a bit of topiary going on in the Archer household?'

'How very dare you,' said Paul with a smirk. 'I'm a proud Neanderthal.'

The conversation moved on and we all chatted easily. The kids were having a whale of a time because nobody was bothering about tedious stuff like body language or eye contact. Lily wasn't letting her broken hand bother her at all and was hanging from the climbing bars by one hand. It wasn't until it began to get dark that the little party began to break up and drift over to the parked cars.

'I've left my bag inside,' I said to Jack and Lily, 'so we'll have to go back that way.' There was general moaning and groaning, so I capitulated. 'OK. See you at the car in *five minutes*.'

I set off across the grass and up the steps to the terrace.

I knew.

I *knew*...

'Emma, wait.'

I turned.

I knew.

Paul grabbed my arm. The momentum spun me round so fast I nearly fell over and Paul put his other hand out to steady me. Then he leant down and kissed me on the mouth.

I shut my eyes, weak with desire.

Paul pushed me gently against the wall, out of sight of the playground and the car park, and kissed me again, more tenderly. Stubble and wine and honey and the same wall hard and rough against my back…

Then he stiffened and peeked behind the wall. 'Quick!' he hissed. 'Virginia's coming.'

He took my hand and, snuffling with giggles, we ran inside. I grabbed my handbag and we legged it out into the mirrored hallway. Panting and laughing, we reached for each other and kissed again. I couldn't resist a glance at the mirrors. At the many 'us' reflected there. How well we fitted together, his dark curls setting off my blond crop…

Eventually, I pulled away. 'We'd better go.' I said.

'Yeah,' said Paul. 'I'm abroad for my book tour again now. But, maybe, after Christmas, we should have a proper chat about… all this. Preferably somewhere out of Hambley.'

Oh!

That was exciting.

And scary.

And not something that I was absolutely sure I wanted.

I was a married woman.

I loved my husband.

'I'm in Manchester the second week of January?' the traitor in me said casually.

Daniel would have left by then and I had my last couple of pube groups before I reverted to being a lady of leisure.

'That could work,' said Paul, equally casually. 'I could arrange a book signing up there at the same time. We could grab something to eat, see the sights, really talk…'

'Great,' I said lightly. 'Chip butties on Coronation Street it is then.'

Chapter Twenty-Nine

Over the next couple of weeks, things started happening with frightening speed.

Daniel was working and sorting out his move. I hardly saw him from one day to the next and, when I did, he was tetchy and offhand. I soldiered on with the pube groups and, as December progressed, threw myself into the Christmas preparations single-handedly. I bought the tree and wrestled it into a roughly upright position. I helped the kids festoon the decorations haphazardly over the branches. I rustled up a cotton-wool sheep costume for the nativity play. I baked batch after batch of wonky mince pies. I beamed and clapped my hands raw at the kids' concerts and plays. I told myself doing these things on my own would be good practice for when Daniel was away but, actually, I didn't mind. I've always loved the gentle Christmas rhythms and routines and I didn't need a cynical and stressed Daniel by my side.

Then the kids broke up and suddenly it felt as though I was being tumbled about in a washing machine; no way out until the cycle finished and the machine clicked off. Cook, shop, clean, wrap. Cook, shop, clean, wrap. Don't think about any of it, Emma; just *do*. Laugh when Jack rearranges the Christmas tree ornaments into strict size and colour order. Chuckle when Lily encourages Matt the Mog to climb the tree and the whole thing topples over. And smile delightedly when Daniel's parents' boiler packs in and they announce they're coming for Christmas too.

Oh yes.

They really did.

After that, Christmas just happened.

That's pretty much all I can say about it. It wasn't *bad*. I think all the parents enjoyed it and, if they noticed Daniel and I were barely on speaking terms, they didn't comment. There were no real disasters. The kids had a great time.

When it was all over and I emerged the other side, wrung dry and disorientated, I realised I'd hardly said a word of import to my husband.

And now it was too late.

–

Departure day was upon us before we knew it. We all went to Heathrow with Daniel, even though airports could unsettle Jack. How could we not? We stood outside the terminal building, breathing in aeroplane fuel and watching passengers disgorge from cars and taxis, and I wondered if I should be wishing I was going too.

'Don't come in,' said Daniel.

'No.' I felt awful that I didn't feel more upset. Did that make me a terrible person?

'Well, this is goodbye, then,' said Daniel. He opened his arms to us all, briefcase at his feet.

Jack turned his back.

Freddie gave him a high five, followed by an awkward stab of a hug.

Lily burst into tears.

My turn. I hugged Daniel self-consciously and kissed him on the cheek.

'Have a good time,' I said.

'Yep,' he said. 'Take care of yourself.'

Then Lily wrapped herself round Daniel's legs and started wailing loudly. We extracted her gently, Daniel picked up his stuff and I watched, my arms round Lily, as he crossed the service road and went through the automatic doors into the terminal building. Then he turned, bobbed his head with his boarding card in his mouth and was gone.

He was gone and I had no idea where I stood.

But. as we drove home along the M4, I still didn't feel sad. I felt unsettled, untethered, excited – the same feeling I'd had when my parents dropped me at university for the first time.

But I didn't feel sad.

It was the start of a new chapter.

–

The next chapter was *awful*.

It was, I found, really hard being a single mum. Not that anything particularly went wrong. The kids weren't being any worse than usual. It was just the relentless drudgery of it all. To say it was exhausting would be an understatement. And there was no one to compare notes with or give me moral support at the end of the day. Even though Daniel and I hadn't been getting on, he'd still been there and, grudgingly, I acknowledged that he'd been more hands-on than I'd given him credit for.

And I still had work to do. Two more rounds of focus groups looking at the clumsy crocodile-shaped pube-trimmers that would never catch on...

Daniel had been gone less than a week when the first 'incident' happened. I'd been in Slough doing daytime focus groups and the respondents had hated everything I'd shown them. This had sent the clients behind the mirror into a tailspin. Urgent changes were needed before the next round of groups.

I'd barely got home and dashed to the loo than my phone started up.

'Mum?' It was Jack. 'Your phone's ringing.'

'It's OK, sweetie,' I called from the smallest room.

The phone stopped ringing.

'Hello?' said Jack.

Crap!

There was a brief pause and then Jack's crystal-clear tones. 'Mum doesn't want to talk to you because she's having a poo.'

Oh God!

I finished my business in record time and burst out of the cloakroom still doing up my jeans. Maybe I could wrestle the phone off Jack and improvise. But Jack had already hung up. A quick glance at the screen and...

The caller had been James; the client of the stripy jumpers and sense-of-humour bypass.

Couldn't be better.

I rounded on Jack furiously. 'I told you not to touch it!' I said.

'No, you didn't.'

'I did! And why on earth did you say *that*?'

'Because you were in there too long to be doing a wee.'

'Oh *God*.'

The phone rang again. I pushed past Jack into the living room to answer it in peace.

'James. I am *so* sorry,' I said.

'Ha!' said James. 'I now know more about your movements than I might wish.'

Was that meant to be a joke?

Should I laugh gaily at his witticism or would that be 'pussy-footing' all over again? I erred on the side of caution by giving a non-committal grunt and James filled me in on the boring work-related reason he'd called. As I was saying goodbye and contemplating my first glass of wine, I saw Freddie and Bethany sidling downstairs.

'What's going on, guys?' I asked sharply.

'Nothing,' said Freddie.

'Does your mum know you're here, Bethany?'

'Yeah,' said Bethany.

Really?

Alone with Freddie in an adult-less house. I took in the smudged kohl, the tiny skirt, the midriff-skimming top.

Frankly, she looked like a slapper. Ness really should be keeping a closer eye on her.

Freddie turned on me as soon as she'd left. 'Why don't you like her?' he asked.

'It's not that,' I said. 'I just don't want you two alone upstairs in your room.'

'But I needed to—'

'You *needed* to be doing your homework and looking after your brother and sister.'

'Mum, you're not listening—'

'No; *you're* not listening.'

'God. I wish Dad was here.'

—

When the kids had finally gone to bed, I took my glass of wine into the living room. But I didn't switch the telly on. I didn't even turn on the lights. I lay on the sofa in the darkness and stared at the ceiling.

I didn't wish Daniel was there. Despite the constant drama, there was something liberating about being on my own, making my own decisions. I could parent the children my way, watch what I liked, eat what I liked, starfish in the bed…

It was all rather wonderful.

And I had a feeling the best was yet to come.

Chapter Thirty

Finally, it was the much-anticipated trip to Manchester.

I left copious instructions for Mum, who was babysitting, and duly caught a train up north. By mid-afternoon I'd checked into the impersonal hotel in the city centre booked for me by Mark's company. I'd had only the most cursory of text communication with Paul, so I had no idea when his book signing was finishing or even if I'd see him before my groups that evening.

I was so full of fizzing anticipation, I couldn't relax into anything. I paced around the executive room, switching the TV on and off, faffing around with the temperature controls and half-heartedly reading through the discussion guide.

What was going to happen?

What did I *want*?

Finally, my phone beeped.

Paul: Hotel bar in 10? MAM

Suddenly I felt queasy.

This was it.

The moment I made my choice.

Could I really do this?

It was so wrong on so many levels.

It felt so right.

I fiddled with my hair and make-up and was in the lift precisely twelve minutes later. Paul was the only customer at the sparkly-marbled bar. Hunched over a glass of wine in a baggy black jumper, he looked deliciously rumpled next to the teenage bar staff in their sharp charcoal suits.

As soon as he saw me, Paul uncurled himself and stood up. 'This feels weird, seeing you out of context,' he said, kissing me chastely on the cheek. 'You look lovely, by the way.'

He ordered me a glass of 'my' wine. It was hardly sensible to start drinking at half past three in the afternoon, but I was so enchanted by the way he'd taken control and remembered my favourite tipple that I let it pass. It was so lovely to be looked after for once. I watched his calm, controlled movements as he paid the barman and I wished I could be more like him. I knew I was always a fizzing ball of unfocussed energy, twirling my earrings, waggling my feet, picking my cuticles...

Paul was just there: a solid, reassuring presence.

Anyway, he handed me my glass and raised his own in a toast.

'What was so hideous about the book signing then?' I asked, toasting him back.

'Nothing really. My heart was just somewhere else. How was your journey?'

And we were off, chatting easily – that lovely, relaxed conversation you have when you don't have to vet what you're about to say. One glass of wine became three and Paul moved onto the sofa next to me; too close, our thighs touching, his hand brushing oh-so-casually against mine.

So, this was how you slipped into adultery—

'Afternoon, Healey.'

Wait a minute.

It sounded like Mark.

It looked like Mark.

Yup. Definitely Mark.

What the *hell* was he doing here?

'Hi there,' I replied, sliding away from Paul. I sounded, I thought, pretty cool for someone who was three sheets to the wind on a school night and sitting rather too close to a man who wasn't her husband. 'I didn't realise you were coming tonight.'

'Evidently.'

Mark bent to kiss my cheek, then offered his hand to Paul, who hauled himself unsteadily to his feet. I introduced the two.

'Ah,' said Mark. 'The writer dad who's been setting a certain Buckinghamshire town a-flutter. I'm a big fan.'

'Thank you,' said Paul.

'Paul's here on a book tour,' I explained hastily.

'A delightful coincidence,' said Mark. 'Where have you been today?'

'Book signing in Waterstones.'

'Really? I've just been in there.'

'Sadly, I was tucked away in a little corner on the second floor,' said Paul.

He sat down looking flushed. He must be more pickled than I'd realised.

That made two of us.

Mark sat down opposite us. 'The reason I'm here, Healey,' he said, 'is because the pube project has disintegrated into a mire of political back-stabbing.'

'Oh no,' I said. 'What's happened?'

'Same old,' said Mark. 'The States want one thing, the UK office another. The ad agency is pumping one route, which everyone else hates. The PR agency thinks the whole caboodle is just too risky. I thought I'd better come up and manage things behind the mirror for you.'

'Thank you.'

'No worries. In the meantime, I'm going to have a shower and make a couple of calls.'

'OK.'

'And Healey?'

'Yes?'

'Go steady, won't you?'

'Of course.'

Paul and I sat down again but the intimate spell between us had been broken. I was rattled by Mark's appearance and

228

worried I might have come across as a bit of a slapper. That's never a good thing for us girls, is it? Besides, I had to moderate some particularly tricky groups in a couple of hours and Mark would be watching. Time to sober up and put thoughts of debauchery aside for now.

I ordered a coffee and showed Paul the latest list of auction prizes I'd pinged to Virginia as a courtesy. I hadn't asked for input, but Virginia had emailed it back absolutely smothered with suggested amendments. Basically, she'd rewritten the whole thing. Hopefully Paul would laugh and it would lift the atmosphere.

Only he didn't.

He tutted with irritation and slapped the offending piece of paper onto a suede cube that was masquerading as a table.

'God, she's so bloody patronising,' he said testily.

'Oh!' I said. 'I didn't expect you to say that.'

'Why not?'

'Well…' Why didn't I? 'I suppose I thought you fancied her.'

'What?' Paul's arms clamped across his chest like the restraints on a fairground ride. I couldn't help imagining those arms clamping round *me*.

'It's nothing to be embarrassed about,' I said. 'She's really pretty.'

'If you like china dolls. You're much sexier.'

I filed that away to savour later.

'Thank you,' I said. 'But I remember the first time you clapped eyes on her.'

'How do you know when I first clapped eyes on her?'

'Because I was there! The special needs meeting in the church. Where it all kicked off.'

'Emma, I don't fancy her. And it wasn't the first time I'd set eyes on her. Unfortunately.'

'What do you mean?'

Had he met her before?

Paul hesitated and then gave a bitter laugh. 'She's my ex,' he said.

Chapter Thirty-One

I stared at Paul, trying to process what he'd just said.

Whatever way I looked at it, his words didn't make sense. I must have misheard him. What rhymed with ex? Flex, hex, sex, vex; the permutations were extensive. But he hadn't said any of them. He'd said 'ex'. I'd heard him. He'd said, 'She's my ex.'

Of course Virginia wasn't his ex.

It was impossible.

Absurd.

I mean, surely someone would have *said*.

'For heaven's sake, Emma, stop looking at me like that,' said Paul. 'This was all a long time ago.'

'Right.'

No, actually it wasn't 'right'.

Paul used to go out with Virginia.

Paul used to go out with *Virginia*.

So many questions.

Like, why?

Like, why hadn't he told me?

Like, what was she like in bed?

'How long were you together for?' I asked instead.

'A few months,' said Paul.

'A few months. Quite serious then.' I paused. 'Is this a joke?'

'Absolutely not.'

I blew a frustrated raspberry and shook my head. 'Well, why didn't you all just *say*?'

'You never asked,' said Paul.

I raised my eyebrows severely at him. 'Well, I'm asking now,' I said.

'OK.' Paul stood up and started pacing; a tight little triangle from sofa to bar, over to the sparkly pillar and then back to the sofa. 'So, it was about twelve years ago. I was living in London and trying to get my first novel published.'

'Tortured artist in the garret with nothing to eat but Pot Noodles sort of thing?'

'Not really. I had a bijou flat the wrong side of Islington and a cushy day job in a trendy ad agency.'

'Right.' I adjusted the image accordingly. And ordered another glass of wine.

Needs must.

'Anyway, I met Ginny at a party – friend of a friend – and we went out for a while. Then she dumped me and that's all there is to say about it really.'

'She dumped you?' I asked.

'Yes. For Andrew, the man she married.' Paul stopped pacing, put his hand on the bar and addressed an imaginary witness. 'So, Ms Jones,' he said, 'what attracted you to the millionaire advertising executive, Andrew Kennedy?'

Right.

'But how come you've ended up living so close to each other? That can't have been the plan.'

'Believe me, it wasn't. I was brought up in Hambley. Hanna and I were looking to move out of London, and it was the obvious choice. Quality of life and all that.'

'And Virginia?'

'Her husband apparently bought a flat in Hambley so he could see Harry at weekends. Then, when he died, Virginia had to sell the London house and she decided to move into the flat full-time.'

'And then the kids ended up at the same school. Such a coincidence.'

'Not really,' said Paul. 'Neither of us is in catchment for St John's, of course, but we both appealed because it's so good for special needs. And then I saw Ginny at the meeting. That threw me for six.'

I was quiet for a moment, trying to take it all in. It all seemed totally unreal and yet it really wasn't that big a deal. As Paul said, it had all happened a long time ago.

There was no need to be angry.

No need at all.

But I *was* angry.

And, almost imperceptibly, Paul's hero status wobbled on its plinth.

'But why get involved in the Lunch Club?' I said. 'Why put yourself in a situation where you'd have to see Virginia all the time?'

'Why do you think?' Paul said, resuming his pacing.

'I have no idea.'

Paul swung on his heel. 'Then you're not very bright for a girl who went to Cambridge, are you?' he said quietly. He sat down opposite me. 'For your information, I threw myself into it – quite apart from wanting to do the best by my son – because it gave me the chance to keep seeing this amazing woman. One of the brightest, funniest, most captivating women I've ever met.'

Oh!

Why wasn't I feeling happier?

Why wasn't I *elated*?

And why was a niggly little voice whispering in my ear that I didn't want Virginia's rejects?

'Oh God, Paul. I'm so confused.'

I put my head in my hands for some clarity. None came. Instead I had a vision of poor old forgotten Hanna, all alone at home. I might not like her very much, but I thought about how much I had struggled being a single mum these past couple of weeks and how angry I was at Daniel for abandoning me. Hanna would feel all those things and more if this went any further. Far more.

She was *pregnant*, for goodness sake.

Could Paul really do that to her?

For that matter, could *I* really do that to her?

I looked up.

Over Paul's shoulder, someone had pulled up the slatted blinds and started washing the window. Outside, greasy city rain darkened the dirty redbrick buildings on the other side of the road. The cold light of day seeped into our cosy little cocoon.

It was messy, mucky. A little seedy.

And then the bubble burst – just like that – and I saw it all for what it was.

'What on *earth* have we been playing at?' I said, as much to myself as to Paul.

'Sorry?'

'Look, I know you've had a crap book signing—'

'Emma, there *was* no book signing. You knew that.'

'No, I didn't. God, that's even worse. So, you've just come up here to…?'

'Of course not. I'm trying to tell you how I feel.'

'Please don't. Whatever you're feeling, it doesn't matter.'

'Yes. It does.' Intense, sexy stare. Easy to resist this time.

'It doesn't. Not in the bigger scheme of things. We're both married. We've got autistic sons. OK, I know, strictly speaking, you haven't. But your wife is *pregnant*, for goodness sake. Don't you see? All this,' I waved around, 'it's just deflection.'

Paul ran a hand over his face. 'Is all this just because I told you about Virginia?' he asked.

'Yes. No. I don't know. Partly.'

Who knew?

'Oh, Emma.' He did, it had to be said, look utterly bereft.

I ran my finger down his face. Still gorgeous.

'I'm sorry,' I said.

Paul grabbed hold of my hand and kissed it, softly, fiercely. 'Can't we talk about this?' he said.

'No. Sorry.'
Wrong time. Wrong place.
Wrong life.

Chapter Thirty-Two

And that was that.

No, it really was this time. Things had suddenly become crystal clear. It was like when I had to wear reading glasses for the first time; only once everything had been thrown into sharp relief did I realise how blurry things had been before.

And thank goodness things *had* become clear; I'd been a hair's breadth away from committing adultery with the first man who'd shown an interest in me. A gorgeous, well-meaning man and one I'd fallen deeply for, but – at the end of the day – a man who was as lost and as mixed up as I was.

And I loved Daniel. Of *course* I loved Daniel. I could see it now. He might have been a grumpy git recently but he was essentially a good husband and father. And I'd let him go to the States unsure of my love. That was unforgiveable.

Desperate to make amends, I phoned him.

'Hi, Em. All OK?'

'Yes, fine.'

Nearly shagged another man, but, apart from that, fine.

'Good. I'm about to go on a conference call. Can't really talk.'

'Oh, OK,' I said. 'But you know Paul?'

'Paul? What's this about, Em? I haven't really got time.'

I felt myself getting cross. I didn't want to feel cross. I wanted to feel like the lady in *Brief Encounter*, when her husband thanks her for coming back to him. But honestly, Daniel *knew* Paul.

'Come on,' I said. 'The writer.'

'Oh yes,' said Daniel. 'What about him?'

'Well, wait for this...' I paused dramatically. 'He only went out with Virginia.'

What was the betting that Daniel now asked who *Virginia* was?

'Yeah,' he said.

'Yeah, what?'

'Yeah, I think I knew Paul used to go out with Ginny.'

Did he?

'*How* did you know?'

And why on earth hadn't he thought it worth mentioning?

'I can't remember. The night of the fire? Look, I've really got to go. Talk later?'

And he hung up.

That had all been very unsatisfactory. Somewhat lighter on the reconciliation and bonding than I might have anticipated. And, instead of feeling closer to Daniel, I felt even more distant.

My head was beginning to pound in ominous fashion. I grabbed the complimentary apple and put it on the pillow. Then I lay down and rolled around so that it massaged the pressure points in my neck. Weird I know, but it sometimes worked. There was still time before I was due to meet Mark. A quick snooze and I would be right as rain.

Only I wasn't.

My headache got worse and there was a painful build-up of pressure in my sinuses and eardrums. What I really needed was to go back to sleep but, as that was impossible, I downed a couple of heavy-duty migraine tablets instead. They left me woolly-brained, but better that than throwing up during the group.

You can't have it all.

–

I managed to get down to reception at the appointed time. Luckily, there was no sign of Paul. Mark gave me a pene-trating look but didn't otherwise comment on my appearance,

236

demeanour or earlier behaviour, and together we caught a taxi to the research venue.

As Mark had warned me, the viewing room was packed with observers. I recognised Fenella, James and a couple of others from the earlier groups but half a dozen new, jittery faces turned toward us.

'Hi. I'm the moderator, EJ,' I said.

And I know it's all about the pubes for you guys, but what you *don't* know is the man I thought I was in love with used to shag the woman I hate most in the world.

Pubes schmubes!

There was a babble of noise as everyone started trying to make sure the research best represented their interests. For the first time, I was relieved Mark was with me. I'd never have coped with this on my own. Not in my current state anyway.

Then a woman in a skater-style leather skirt stood up and waved a copy of the discussion guide at us. 'We need to find out how these prototypes fit with brand equity,' she said, voice bristling with stress.

Mark nodded calmly. 'OK,' he said. 'Emma and I will tack a couple of questions onto the end of the discussion guide.'

I nudged Mark. 'We're running out of time,' I hissed. 'I need to go down, get the respondents, explain about the mirror.'

'I know. Let's get this done quickly, then.'

Together, we leant over the discussion guide. As if on cue, a plump woman carrying a load of shopping bags came into the interview room. We watched through the one-way mirror as she dumped her bags on the floor, slung her mac onto the coat stand and walked over to the mirror. Looking at her reflection, she smoothed her rain-frizzed hair and dabbed away a stray speck of mascara. Then, glancing behind her, she pulled up her denim skirt. There was an unedifying flash of gusset, thigh and half-mast tights.

For a moment there was utter silence, and then one of the clients chuckled. 'Good of you to lay on a visual of the target area, Mark,' he drawled.

Skirt-round-waist lady looked shocked to hear shouts of laughter so close by and quickly hoicked up her tights. She was just smoothing her skirt down when the other respondents piled into the room.

'She's going to freak when she finds out about the mirror,' I said gloomily.

'Don't tell her,' said leather-skirted-client tartly.

'We've got to,' Mark said flatly. 'It's the law. You've got to tell people they're being observed.'

–

The group was a disaster from the word go. Well, strictly speaking, it was a disaster from the moment I told the group about the one-way mirror and skirt-round-waist lady fled from the room in tears.

It was always going to be hard to recover after that. And, lo and behold, I had barely completed the warm-up when Mark crept in bearing a note.

> *Please stop the redhead third from the left from taking over. Sorry. Mark.*

Handling dominant respondents was one of the basic skills of moderating, so this was embarrassing. Mark might well say sorry; it was his job to convince the clients that all was proceeding to plan. But I duly went through the motions of shutting the redhead up. I withdrew eye contact. I gave no reaction to her replies. I interrupted her with a raised hand. Finally, I asked her, nicely, to pipe down. The trouble was, everyone else then shut up too, nervous of saying or doing the wrong thing. And the discussion became laboured and superficial, we never got to the 'performing' stage and we certainly never got down to the nitty-gritty.

It was a fiasco.

I could feel the waves of disapproval as soon as I went into the observation room for the break between groups. I ignored the clients and made a beeline for Mark, alone in a corner seat.

'Nice note,' I said sulkily.

'Come on, Healey, what was I supposed to do? You're all over the place this evening. Getting pissed with old Shakespeare before the group clearly wasn't a good idea.'

'I know. I'm sorry.' I was. It had been good of Mark to give me this work and look at how I was repaying him. 'I'm having a bad time tonight.'

Mark sighed. 'Look, why don't I do this group and you stay here and look after the clients?'

I hesitated. The professional part of me wanted to carry on and moderate a fabulous second group to make up for the first. The rest of me didn't think I could do it.

Not now.

Not tonight.

'Oh Mark, would you?' I said. 'That would be wonderful.'

Fenella leant across us. 'What did Mark say your surname was, EJ? Healey? *Emma* Healey? I received a—'

On second thoughts...

'I'll do the group, Mark,' I said sidling toward the door.

'Was it you who tried to get a foot in my door? With a chocolate shoe?'

I scarpered.

—

I arrived in reception, professional smile glued to my face, unprofessional turmoil eating my insides. Problem: only four of the expected eight women had turned up. I waited a couple of minutes and then decided I'd better make a start anyway.

'What about any latecomers?' the studio manager asked.

I hesitated. Latecomers tended to be paid off because they brought the newly bonded group back to the 'storming' phase, but the clients might kick up a fuss about only having four respondents. I couldn't afford to get into any more trouble that evening.

'Show them in, please,' I said.

Ten minutes later, I'd got stuck into a pube word association game when the studio manager knocked on the door. She ushered in two women with the look of hardened groupies about them; yes, there most definitely is such a thing. Their plan had clearly been to arrive fifteen minutes late, pocket the incentive fee and leave. They were livid to have been foiled.

'Delighted you could join us,' I said. 'If I could take your first names...'

The first woman, a glamorous bottle-blonde, gave me a poisonous look. 'I'm Virginia,' she said.

Yes, she would be.

'Hi, Virginia,' I said.

'Actually, I prefer Ginny.'

'Ginny it is, then.'

Wait!

Cogs started whirring in my medication–and–booze addled brain.

Daniel had called Virginia 'Ginny'. *And* there was the small matter of him knowing she was Paul's ex. Maybe, just maybe, it wasn't the wrong *Emma* Virginia had sent that text to all those weeks ago.

Maybe it was the wrong *Healey*.

Could Daniel and Virginia possibly be having an affair?

Surely not.

But I had to know for sure.

Like, right now.

Ignoring the second newcomer, I threw a random pile of razors onto the table and – apropos of nothing – asked the respondents to group them in any way they saw fit. The women obediently pulled their chairs forward and set to work, politely seeking consensus. Slipping out of the room, I leant against the closed door and called Daniel.

He answered on the first ring. 'What's up now?' he said.

'Dan, I need to ask you something and I need you to be completely honest.'

'O-K?'

'Healey?' It was Mark, coming down the corridor toward me. I stuffed my mobile into my back pocket. Abandoning a group to make a phone call was a complete no-no; in fact, there was no acceptable reason to leave the interview room except to go 'backstage' for feedback or clarification.

'What's with all the razors on the table?' Mark asked. 'The clients don't give a crap about competitive products tonight.'

Oh God!

Think, Emma.

'I was giving the group a chance to re-normalise with something non-controversial,' I improvised wildly. 'You know how latecomers can sometimes push things off-balance?'

I held my breath; it was worth a try.

'Ah. Good thinking. And clever to remove yourself to avoid moderator bias.'

'Yes, I thought it best.'

'I'll leave you to it, then.' Mark started walking back to the viewing room. 'This group is going much better, by the way,' he said over his shoulder. 'Clients seem happy.'

I waited until he'd gone and then put the phone back to my ear.

'Dan? Are you still there?'

'Yes,' said Daniel. 'What on earth's going on? Are you halfway through a *group*?'

'Yes. But I need to ask you something.'

'What?'

Deep breath.

'Are you having an affair with Virginia?' There. I'd said it. It was out and I couldn't take it back. 'Because I got a text from her about meeting for a drink and, at first, I thought she'd sent it to the wrong Emma, but then I realised it could be the wrong

241

Healey. And then she was at the Club, wasn't she? And a woman in this group is called Ginny and it got me thinking...'

I felt a bit silly now, standing furtively in the corridor, babbling away. Because of *course* Daniel wasn't having an affair with Virginia. It was one of my daft impulsive ideas and now I'd gone and disrupted the group and Daniel would be upset and—

Hang on.

Why wasn't Daniel speaking?

I'd expected him to say, 'I can't believe you'd even *think* that.' But he didn't.

He didn't say anything.

'So, was that text meant to be to you?' I persisted. 'And *was* Virginia meeting you at the Club?'

'Oh God, Em,' said Daniel.

Icy water down my spine. '"Oh God" to which bit?' I said. Suggestive emails?

Lunch?

Doggy-style?

'Look, we can't discuss this when you're in the middle of a group,' said Daniel. 'Let's talk properly when—'

'Yes or no, Dan?'

'Yes, But—'

I sagged against the wall in shock. And – right on cue – here was Mark, striding down the corridor again.

'I think this exercise has gone long enough,' he said testily. 'The respondents are going off-piste now and they're really laying into the wine.'

I stood up. 'Right. I'll get back in there,' I said.

Mark looked at me more closely. 'Jeez, Healey, are you on the *phone*? In the middle of a *group*?'

'Yes. But—'

'It's that bloody Paul Archer, isn't it? For God's sake! Bringing him up to Manchester for a bit of how's-yer-father is your own business. But calling him during a focus group—'

I clicked disconnect and blundered back into the interviewing room.

—

The conversation in the interview room had turned bawdy. The respondents had abandoned the task I'd set them and moved on to their sex lives, the two-way mirror forgotten.

'Amazing what a bit of topiary can do.'

'Yes, nothing like a nice bit of clipped box to get results.'

Sniggers all around.

Time to wrestle back control. Time to show the prototypes, assess their potential, earn my keep.

On the other hand…

'That's obviously where I've been going wrong,' I said. 'Channelling leylandii all these years.'

There was a stunned silence. Moderators weren't supposed to declare their hand. They certainly weren't supposed to declare their bits. But, once I'd started, I couldn't stop.

'Perhaps if I'd been more attentive to my own personal topiary, my husband wouldn't be shagging some slag.'

The room erupted. A 'performing' group is actually quite difficult to derail and this group was in all-out self-preservation mode now its moderator had lost the plot.

'All men are bastards,' said Ginny, pouring me a glass of wine. 'Who is she?'

'A fucking milkmaid,' I replied, downing the glass in one.

—

I suppose I shouldn't have been surprised when Mark burst into the interview room a moment later. I was disappointed though – I was just starting to enjoy myself.

'Thank you, Emma,' he said. 'I'll take over now.'

A chorus of support followed me as he virtually wrestled me into the corridor.

'Go straight back to the hotel,' he said. 'Do *not* go back behind the mirror.'

'Go directly to jail. Do not pass go. Do not collect two hundred pounds.'

'And do *not* go and shag old Shakespeare.'

I made my way outside.

That had all gone rather well.

Considering.

Chapter Thirty-Three

I did as I was told.

I went back to the hotel and shut myself in my room. I got into a piping hot bubble bath. And I ignored my constantly buzzing phone.

This, I thought, is how marriages fail.

How the world tilts on its axis.

Happens all the time.

But Daniel? With *Virginia*? How on earth had that happened? Virginia was the most beautiful woman in the playground. If Daniel hadn't been my husband, I'd have been almost impressed. But Daniel *was* my husband and so, of course, I was devastated. And humiliated. And livid. After all, I'd had my own chance to stray and I'd chosen the moral high ground.

When the heat started making me even more lightheaded, I hauled myself out of the bath. I wrapped myself in a towel, put my hair into a towel turban and lay on the bed. Then there was a knock at the door. I didn't want to talk to anyone, so I slid off the bed, before I remembered I couldn't actually be seen. I stayed there all the same. It felt safe and surprisingly comfortable. And it was conveniently close to the minibar.

Another knock. Whoever it was wasn't giving up easily. I pulled a pillow off the bed, divested the minibar of a small bottle of red and settled down for the long haul.

I woke up to knocking that had increased hugely in volume. Presumably it was from someone who had gone away and come back again. Unless they were very persistent and patient. Or someone else entirely.

'Healey? Open up!'

Oh God. It was Mark. He was bound to be furious. I'd completely mucked up his group.

I ignored him.

'Healey, if you don't open the door by the time I count to three, I'm calling reception.'

Oh no. Now, what to do?

Maybe I should *let* him call reception. Let him 'discover' me reclining on the bed in my towel turban like a young and lovely Elizabeth Taylor. Maybe it might distract him from my appalling behaviour. But, as I struggled to my feet, the turban toppled to one side and uncoiled damply around my shoulders.

It was a rubbish turban.

A rubbish plan.

I looked nothing like Elizabeth Taylor anyway.

I opened the door slowly, waiting for a tirade. But Mark just came in and sat on the bed.

'What's going on?' he asked gently.

'Nothing. Everything.' I sat down next to him, looking at my feet. 'Sorry about the group.'

Mark snorted with laughter. 'God, that leylandii comment!'

I stole a glance at him. 'You're not mad, then?'

'Not really,' said Mark. 'The clients will be dining out on it for years. But Daniel…?'

'Don't. Don't say it. I can't believe it.'

'Me neither. Do you know who it is?'

'Virginia.' There was bile in my throat.

'The Virginia who was round at yours?'

'Yes. Cow. Bitch. Whore.'

Mark let out a low whistle. It seemed to suggest Daniel was punching above his weight and, by inference, that I was significantly less attractive than Virginia. I hit him on the arm. Hard.

246

'Ouch!' he said. 'But doesn't this leave the door open for you and old Shakespeare?'

'*No!* You don't get it at all.'

'Come on, Healey,' said Mark. 'It's not a coincidence you're both up here, is it?'

'No,' I conceded. 'But then I found out Virginia's his ex.'

'What? The same Virginia?'

'Yes.'

Mark laughed. 'Doesn't compute, Healey,' he said. 'I think you're very, very drunk.'

He ran his finger gently down my cheek and it was like flicking a switch. Suddenly I remembered why I'd always found him so attractive. Suddenly I felt horny as hell. And suddenly we were snogging. Arms round each other, proper old-fashioned snogging. To be honest, I think I might have jumped on him. In fact, I'm almost sure I did. But I must say he rose to the occasion quite magnificently.

After a while, we overbalanced and toppled onto the bed. I think I might have engineered that as well. Emboldened, I sprawled back on the pillows.

'Come on, Viking!' I said, letting the towel slip seductively. 'Do your worst.'

I smiled up at him, waiting.

But Mark just hauled himself to a sitting position and started tucking in his shirt. 'I don't think this is a very good idea,' he said.

'Why not? Seems like a very good idea to me.'

Revenge? Spite? Booze? Whatever it was, I knew exactly what I was doing. No one could accuse Mark of taking advantage of me.

'Look, you're very drunk and very confused...'

'Bollocks.'

I was *up* for this. If Daniel could do it, so could I.

'Sorry, Emma. No.'

Was Mark *rejecting* me?

I shuffled to a sitting position and the room started spinning. Before I could do anything, waves of nausea washed over me and, to my eternal humiliation, I was violently sick all over the bed. I retched over and over, lost in my misery, vaguely aware of Mark holding both my head and my towel to preserve what was left of my dignity.

I ended up in his bed after all. Mine was past redemption and neither of us could face calling housekeeping. So Mark took me to his room, made me tea, cajoled me into having another bath, and finally tucked me up next to him.

Before I went to sleep, I checked my phone. Among all the messages from Paul was a jaunty little text from Mum.

All fine here.

Well, all certainly wasn't fine here.

Chapter Thirty-Four

I slept quite well, all things considering. Somebody really should market the medication/booze combination to insomniacs. By the time I woke, Mark had left to get the early train and I had to face facts.

Daniel had had an affair.

I went back to my own room to shower and get my stuff. God, it stank! I left a tenner for housekeeping and checked out. Part of me – a big part – wanted to find Paul, fling myself into his arms and tell him I hadn't meant what I'd said.

But I didn't.

Couldn't.

I *had* meant it. To go to him now, tempting as it was, would be to delay the inevitable.

It was over.

I cried all the way home on the train, hunched in a little snotty huddle of self-pity, watching the dreary landscape flash past. The lovely catering person plied me with coffee and little packets of Golden Crumble biscuits but even they didn't help.

Nothing helped.

Nothing could.

Daniel had had a 'thing' with *Virginia* and I hadn't had a clue. Apart from the mis-sent text, the clues had been few and far between. A frisson of interest when they'd met at the murder-mystery evening. Some banter at the fireworks party. Planning to meet at the Club? Beyond that, nothing obvious.

And – crucially – was it still going on? I mean, I knew Virginia wasn't in the States with Daniel, but were they planning to carry on when he got home? Were they chatting, texting, having phone sex? It was ghastly. Ghastly and humiliating.

And heartbreaking.

Oh, I know what you're thinking. Hardly squeaky clean herself, is she? Mooning after Paul. Practically begging Mark to shag her. And you're right. Of course you're right. I can see that now.

But Daniel was mine. Naïvely, I'd assumed he always would be. That, even when I pushed the boundaries, he'd be quietly in the background, waiting for the moment when – if – I returned to him. I know that sounds stupid and childish and altogether unfair, but that was how I'd felt. Subconsciously at least.

Consciously I don't think I'd really given Daniel much thought at all.

And now look at what had happened. Daniel was on the other side of the world and it might be too late to tell him I was sorry. It might be too late for anything at all.

I was a fool of monumental proportions.

–

It was only midday when I got home.

Mum had gone. The kids were at school. The house was silent.

I was utterly exhausted but way too het up to sleep. I wandered from room to room, picking things up, tidying a little. Why was everything always such a *mess*? I seemed to be permanently engulfed in a tidal wave of chaos, in my home and in my head. And what was that *smell*? The familiar sweet-sour teenage-boy aroma. Stronger than usual.

I tracked it down to a sports bag in Freddie's room. Yup; festering football kit. Nice. Wrinkling my nose, I emptied the bag. There was a soggy envelope in there too, addressed to Mr and Mrs Healey. Boring school stuff, no doubt. Maybe the bill for Freddie's drum lessons.

I pulled the letter out and scanned it. It was from Mrs Sharp. *'Persistent poor work… unacceptable…'* Freddie had been given an after-school detention and a day in Gateway. In fact, both had already happened.

How come I hadn't known? Surely I should have signed something? I was his *mother…*

I sat on the floor, letter dangling from my fingers.

Why were the men in my life always letting me down?

Suddenly I was livid at the lot of them. Freddie had messed up. Daniel had betrayed me. Mark had refused to shag me. And Paul had the temerity to be Virginia's ex…

The rage grew in waves, pulsing and throbbing until I could feel the blood pounding in my temples. Throwing the letter aside, I blundered downstairs into the kitchen in search of solace. Wine or tablets; it didn't matter; it just needed to be *now*. With shaking fingers, I grabbed a glass. It was meant to be for wine, it really was, but, without thinking about it, without thinking about *anything*, I opened my hand and let the glass drop. It shattered violently, shards skittering across the stone floor, and it felt so good I did it again. And again. And again.

I finished off the wine glasses and the everyday tumblers and then started on Daniel's beer glasses, throwing them down with extra venom. Then the two sherry glasses, the three brandy balloons and the novelty glass shaped like a jam jar. All gone. Far away, someone was shouting and, for a fleeting second, I wondered who and why.

Then I moved on to the mugs. The plain cream ones, the spotty ones and Freddie's football mug. The one with the photo of the Matt the Mog on it and the one with the whole family posing happily on *Frejalily*. I even smashed my own special bone-china cup with the golden rim.

I only stopped when a large piece of glass ricocheted and opened the scar on my hand.

Enough.

The shouting stopped.

I wrapped some kitchen paper round my hand and surveyed the damage. There was quite a lot of dark, oozy blood dripping down my fingers and onto the floor. And boy, was there a lot of mess to clear up.

Physically, metaphorically, glassily and bloodily.

But there was one last thing I had to do. One person I hated most of all.

I grabbed my car keys and stormed out of the front door.

I screeched my car to a halt on the gravel, stormed to Virginia's front door and jabbed my finger onto the buzzer.

'You *fucking* bitch,' I said when she answered.

'Emma. Hi.' Virginia's disembodied voice was calm. 'I'll buzz you in.'

I stormed through the mirrored hallway and round the corner to the apartment. Virginia was waiting by the door. She was wearing a white waffle dressing gown and slippers, her hair wrapped in a towel turban. I took an instant dislike to the turban. Like its owner, I just knew, it wouldn't unravel under pressure.

'You fucking *bitch*,' I said again, fury rendering me incapable of a wider and more interesting vocabulary.

'What have you done to your hand?' said Virginia. 'You'd better come in.'

'I don't want to come in. I want you to keep your fucking hands off my husband!'

Virginia stood a little straighter and pursed her lips. 'Shouldn't you should be talking to Daniel about this?' she said.

No denial. No surprise even. Daniel had obviously warned her in advance. This enraged me almost more than the infidelity.

'Stay away from my husband,' I said. Some of the fight was going out of me.

'I heard you the first time. And shouldn't you have thought about your *husband* before you started playing around with Paul?'

What?

'You knew?'

'Of course I bloody knew. It was the worst kept secret in Buckinghamshire. Canoodling at the firework night. Snogging here. Holding hands at Gabriel's diagnosis. Oh yes, Gabriel does talk, you know and it was all round the playground. Honestly, if you're going to conduct an affair, at least *try* to do it subtly.'

I was stunned. *Stunned.*

'Does Daniel know?' I whispered.

'Probably,' said Virginia.

Oh God.

'But nothing actually happened,' I whispered.

'Yeah, yeah, yeah.'

'It didn't. And, anyway, he's your *ex*.'

'What's that got to do with anything?' said Virginia.

I hesitated. Now I came to think of it, I wasn't entirely sure.

'Anyway, it's over between Daniel and me,' I blustered. 'Completely over. When he gets back from the States, he'll be slinging his hook. You can schmooze on in there with your mincing little arse but he'll soon realise what a Class-A cow you are.'

'Emma,' Virginia said calmly. 'I think you'll find *I* haven't cheated on anyone. And, if you don't mind, your hand is bleeding all over my carpet.'

That was the final straw. I gave the turban a vicious little tweak. I knew it was childish but I couldn't help it.

The turban didn't budge, so I gave it a little pull. And then a slightly harder one. The towel started to unravel and Virginia grabbed hold of one end of it. There was an unseemly scuffle but then I gave a particularly impressive yank and victory was mine. Throwing the towel over one shoulder, I strode away without a backward glance.

Take that, Virginia!

Victory was short-lived.

By the time I got outside, I wasn't sure I'd won at all. Worse, I was still holding the damn towel, now liberally streaked with blood. It wouldn't do to be accused of stealing, so I left it nicely displayed over a privet hedge.

The shaking started as I drove home. First my hands, and then, as I swung into the driveway, my teeth started chattering too. This was awful.

Awful.

My marriage was in tatters, I was guilty of turban-related assault, and if I didn't get sweeping up pretty damn quick, the kids were going to get back from school to find all the glassware and mugs in smithereens on the kitchen floor. And if anyone official found out about *that* – and Jack would make absolutely sure they did – the kids would most likely end up in care.

The tears came as I surveyed the damage.

It was all too much.

Too overwhelming.

And my hand was bloody killing me.

Defeated, I called Ness.

Ten minutes later, I silently led Ness into the kitchen. I'd tried to sweep the detritus into a pile but succeeded only in smearing the blood across the floor. It looked like a murder scene. Without a body.

Ness's mouth dropped open. 'What the fuck?' she said. 'Have you been attacked?'

I shook my head. 'It was me.' It was almost a relief to admit it.

'*You.*' Her eyes widened. 'Christ. The hand too?'

'That was an accident. I've got to clear it all up before... before...'

My breath was coming in raggedy little snatches. I wanted to scream, I *had* to scream but, if I did, I might not be able to stop.

'Calm down,' said Ness. 'We'll sort it out and then we'll get you some help.'

'Help?'

Oh God, she was going to get me sectioned.

'The Minor Injuries Unit. Your hand might need stitching.'

'Promise me the kids won't see this?' I said, waving at the mess.

Suddenly that seemed of the utmost importance.

'I promise.'

Ness was as good as her word. She helped me sweep up the shards of glass and crockery – actually, she did most of it – and then she mopped the floor.

'So, what's on earth going on?' she asked en route to the hospital.

'I don't know,' I said. 'I wasn't being myself.'

'You can say that again. But there must have been a reason?'

There were a multitude of reasons.

'Daniel's been having an affair,' I whispered.

Maybe she already knew. Maybe *everyone* knew; maybe they'd all been whispering behind my back, passing judgement, feeling sorry for me.

But Ness looked genuinely shocked. 'No *way*,' she said. 'Who on earth with?'

'Virginia.' I felt easy tears threaten again.

'I don't believe it.' Ness stopped at a red and yanked the handbrake on. 'The fucking cow! How did you find out?'

'Last night.' Was it only last night? 'I was up in Manchester with Paul—'

'Hold your horses. *Paul* was there?'

'Yes. But that's not really relevant—'

'Er, I think it might be. You can't expect me to believe Paul just *happened* to be there?'

'No, but nothing happened.'

'Yeah, yeah, yeah.' Ness turned into the car park. 'It sounds like you and Daniel are as bad as each other. Sometimes I wonder who has the real special needs round here.'

–

Later, with me glued and cleaned up, we had a quick whizz round Cargo to buy some emergency tumblers and mugs. Then Ness went to get Jack, Lily and Noah from school and told Bethany to come back to ours with Freddie. I must have done something spectacularly lovely in a former life to deserve a bestie like her.

We all sat down to a fish and chip dinner. The children were enchanted by the way the afternoon had unfurled and I was content to let the waves of chatter roll over me. It was all so surreal I didn't really know what to think. I just wanted to feel comfortably numb.

'Do we have to go to Dad's this weekend?' Bethany was asking, jabbing a chip into the ketchup.

'That's the plan, Beth,' said Ness.

'It's so lame there. One day I'll escape and come home.'

Bastard Towers, where Ness's ex lived with his new wife and new wife's teenage daughter Megan, was only a couple of miles up the river, so this was eminently possible.

'That would make Dad very sad,' said Ness. '*You* like it there, don't you, Noah?'

'S'OK,' said Noah. He was feeding flakes of fish to Matt the Mog under the table and thought I couldn't see him. 'I want them to get a Nintendo Switch though.'

'They won't,' said Bethany. 'Dad doesn't care about us any more.'

Suddenly I had a lump in my throat. This was the reality of marriages breaking down, of families splitting up. Was this what I had wanted for us all?

Was this what Daniel wanted?

'Why do you hate it there so much?' asked Jack. He picked up his saveloy and tipped his head back like a fire-eater to eat it. I let it pass.

'Megan pinches my stuff. She took my new Adidas hoodie the last time I was there.'

'That was ridiculous,' said Freddie. 'Everyone knew it was yours.'

'I know, right. But she told her mum she'd bought it with her own money. Luckily, I'd spilled nail polish on it, so I could prove it was mine.'

'You've got nail polish on your new seventy-pound hoodie,' said Ness mildly.

'It's a good thing,' said Jack. 'Put a blob of polish on every-thing you own, Bethany.'

Everybody roared with laughter and Jack gave a little bow.

'Something's different in here,' said Lily, suddenly.

Wham!

Just when I was beginning to relax.

My children would know I was a nutcase. They'd never be able to trust me again…

'The floor's really clean,' said Lily.

‐

My phone rang as I was crawling into bed.

Daniel.

I might as well take it. The day could hardly get worse.

'Em?' His West Country burr more pronounced than I remembered.

Almost a stranger.

'About what I said last night,' he said. 'That thing with Virginia…'

Time to sound like the saintly character in *Gone with the Wind*. The one whose wimpy husband copped off with Scarlett O'Hara. Wounded but dignified.

'Well, obviously, I'm gutted, Dan. *Gutted*. But—'

'Excuse me,' said Daniel. 'How *dare* you? I know that writer chap was up in Manchester yesterday. I heard what Mark said.'

Only yesterday...

'Yes, but nothing happened.'

'Emma, you arranged to meet another man in Manchester. Since when was that nothing?'

Fair point.

But it all seemed so irrelevant now. Like when you get back from holiday and you can't recapture what the air smelled like or how warm it was. Like looking the wrong way through a telescope and then finding out the telescope's actually a kaleidoscope.

It was like that with Paul.

But how to convince Daniel?

I couldn't.

Not today.

Not when I was so goddamn tired.

I leant back against the pillows and shut my eyes. 'Can we talk about this later?' I said. 'I've had one hell of a day.'

'Fine.' Daniel's tone was clipped. 'Perhaps you'd let me know when it's convenient.'

And the phone went dead.

Bloody marvellous.

Chapter Thirty-Five

Somehow, I got Jack and Lily to school the next morning. I was just late enough for the other parents to have dispersed.

Ness was lurking, waiting for me. 'You're late, missus,' she said, following me to my car. 'And you look bloody awful.'

'Thanks very much,' I replied. 'And do I get the impression you're coming home with me?'

'Quick cuppa?'

'Go on then.'

I was pleased really. Even though I had the mother of all headaches brewing, I didn't want to be alone. I was frightened. Proper heart-pounding, stomach-prickling, skin-crawling frightened. Frightened I was losing it. Frightened I couldn't cope. Frightened I needed Daniel more than I had ever realised.

No sooner were we home than the phone rang. My heart leapt. Maybe it was Daniel. Right on cue.

No, it was the wee small hours in Texas.

It was Mum.

'So silly, darling,' she said. 'I've slipped getting out of the bath.'

'Oh no!'

'I'm fine. But I've twisted my ankle and I'm finding it difficult to get about. I know it's a lot to ask with Daniel away but I was wondering if I could come and stay for a few days.'

The logical answer, of course, was 'out of the question'. I could hardly look after myself, let alone anyone else.

But this was my lovely mum. How *could* I say no?

'Of *course*.'

I expected Ness to be horrified. But she just said, 'it'll be great for you to have some company.'

Then she helped me to tidy the office and make up the guest bed. At the last moment, I decided I should sleep there and donate my room with its en suite to Mum. It was only polite.

Mum arrived, all smiles and apologies. Her ankle didn't seem that bad to me – in fact, she was barely hobbling at all – but she did make a little 'oomph' sound every time she got up or sat down, so it obviously was really painful.

Poor Mum.

I'd take care of her as best I could.

The trouble was that, shortly after Ness left, the migraine that had been threatening ever since Manchester caught up with me. Pounding head, nausea, sensitivity to light – the full works. I felt *rubbish*. Despite my best intentions, Mum ended up tucking *me* into bed.

The single bed.

The pink flowery bedspread pinched from my childhood bedroom.

The darkened room.

The damp flannel on my forehead.

I was thirteen again.

All day I battled the waves of pain and misery that beat a tattoo on my brain.

Jack, Daniel, Virginia, *Paul*...

Jack, Daniel, Virginia, *Paul*...

Jack, Daniel, Virginia, *Paul*...

Then I realised Jack was innocent in all this. He was the least of my worries. Weird but true.

I adjusted the words accordingly.

Mark, Daniel, Virginia, *Paul*...

Mark, Daniel, Virginia, *Paul*...

Mark, Daniel, Virginia, *Paul*...

The throb in my hand. The throb in my head. Too much had happened.

Too much for me to process.

It was all too much.

—

Next morning, the migraine had gone but I stayed in bed. I wanted to be alone. I tossed and turned, heavy-hearted, woolly-brained. I ignored the text from Mark checking I was OK. I ignored the calls from Paul. And, most of all, I waited for the text from Daniel telling me he was coming home.

It didn't come.

I was tempted to stay in bed the next morning as well. But Jack burst into my room before school and stood over me, hands on hips.

'You're coming to the Lunch Club play at lunchtime,' he stated.

I looked at him, my heart swelling with love and confusion and anxiety and heartbreak.

My precious boy.

And I got out of bed.

—

The Lunch Club play took place in the Lilac Classroom — the politically correct name for the Special Needs Room. The name, of course, referred only to the colour of the walls, but as soon as I walked through the door the scar on my temple began to itch. The scabs on my hand joined in for good measure.

The good news was Paul wasn't there. The bad news was that Virginia and Hanna were. I could feel two pairs of censorious eyes boring into the back of my head as I took my seat at the front. Thank goodness my lovely mum had come with me. It was all I could do not to clutch hold of her hand.

The play was wonderful. It had been written by the children and was a jolly romp based around *Wizard World*. Everyone wore a dressing gown and a brightly coloured turban and there were lots of complicated fight scenes and much vigorous waving of light-sabres. The children were having a whale of a time until Josh's turban unravelled and he stropped off in tears. Even then, the rest of the cast rallied gamely.

It was all a million miles from playground hell.

Jack had a starring role as Wizard Master. I watched him as objectively as I could; a small, purposeful boy with a sweet intensity and a perfect sense of comic timing. A wave of guilt swept over me. Far from fighting to keep the family together, Daniel and I had been hell-bent on sabotaging our marriage. Poor Jack.

Once the play finished, I felt totally exposed. If I'd been on my own, I'd have boycotted the refreshments and gone straight back to bed. But Mum, holding Jack's hand, was chatting to Ally, so I couldn't really. Or maybe I could...

No, Emma.

Stop being pathetic.

Thank goodness Mandy was there, busy pouring squash into plastic cups. At least I hadn't tried to shag her husband or pull a towel turban off her head. I went to join her.

'Hey, doll,' she said. 'Put the biscuits out for me?'

I tipped a packet of economy custard creams haphazardly onto a paper plate, relieved that at least Mandy was treating me normally.

Jack flung himself against me. 'Did you like my evil wizard?' he said, laughing up at me.

I bent down so our heads were level. 'I thought you were absolutely brilliant,' I said honestly.

'Good. Can I have some peach squash?'

'Sorry,' said Mandy. 'No peach. Only orange and blackcurrant.'

'But Ally said there was peach.'

'There was,' said Mandy. 'But it'd gone really thick and yucky in the PTA cupboard.'

'Have blackcurrant, sweetie,' I said, 'and we'll buy peach on the way home.'

'How come you're so nice to me at school,' said Jack. 'But you scream and shout like a loony at home?'

I laughed, embarrassed. 'I'm not—'

'You *are*. And I want peach!'

'Jack!' I put my hand on his shoulder. I know – who tries to touch an Aspie in potential meltdown? Predictably, Jack lashed out at me. Over his shoulder, I could see Hanna staring at me with that she-can't-even-control-her-own-kid look. Next to her, Virginia was carrying Josh. She couldn't have looked more sodding maternal if she'd tried.

'I've an idea, Jacko,' said Mum, bustling over. 'What about if we mix orange and blackcurrant *together*? We could call it black-orange. Shall we give that a go?'

Jack, the little traitor, allowed himself to be shepherded away.

Absolutely brilliant.

I was completely redundant.

My vision blurred and my throat tightened. I was crying. Here. In front of all these people. I walked over to the wall and pretended to be interested in some pictures of lions drawn by Year 2. Limbs at unfeasible angles, unlikely colour schemes, terrible perspective—

'Are you OK?'

It was Hanna, looking at me with concern.

Maybe pregnancy had blurred the angular lines of her face, but she looked softer and her eyes weren't the ice-cold gimlets I remembered. Suddenly I felt terrible. I wondered if Hanna knew I'd spent the past few months relentlessly pursuing her husband. I wondered if she knew what a weak and pathetic person I was to boot. The kind of person who threw glasses when things didn't go her way and pulled towel turbans off people and disintegrated into a snivelling wreck whenever her son had a meltdown.

263

The kind of person who couldn't last five minutes without her husband...

The school bell rang and Hanna patted my shoulder and left. Mum came over hand in hand with Jack.

'I'll take Jacko back to his classroom, poppet,' she said, 'and then I've got a couple of things to do in town. Why don't you stay here? I'll be back in half an hour.'

There was a plethora of reasons why not. Because *I* was Jack's mum. Because Mum had a dodgy ankle. Because I was meant to be the one looking after *her*.

But Mum had gone. Jack left without a backward glance.

'You're very welcome to stay,' said Ally. 'Would you like a cup of tea? No one's due in here for an hour.'

'Thank you,' I said gratefully, sitting down and wiping my eyes. 'Unless you're going to programme me to shout "knickers" every time the school bell rings.'

Ally laughed. 'I think that's a hypnotherapist, not a psychologist,' she said.

At least I could still make people laugh.

I must try harder to be a nicer person and not just a funny one.

'It was a brilliant show,' I said.

'Thank you. Jack was wonderful.'

'He was,' I said. 'I was so proud of him.'

'So why the tears?' asked Ally gently.

'Because he lost it afterwards and spoiled everything.'

Ally raised her pixie eyebrows. 'He didn't spoil anything,' she said. 'And they were *all* losing it. Josh wouldn't let Virginia put him down after his turban fell off.'

'Really?' And I'd thought Virginia had been posing as Madonna and Child just to make me feel inadequate. 'But Jack's *always* losing it. How's he going to cope in the future?'

'Oh, Emma,' said Ally. 'Jack has everything going for him. The world's his oyster.'

'Yes. What about his Asperger's?'

264

'It's only mild. It doesn't need to define him.'

I was so surprised I slopped my tea all over my lap. No one at Jack's diagnosis had talked like that. It had been all doom, gloom and despondency then. Portentous tones and 'helpful' leaflets. And look at the chain reaction it had set off...

'You can't just dismiss Asperger's,' I said defensively.

I couldn't dismiss it.

'I'm not dismissing it. But Asperger's is just one aspect of his personality.'

'The most important aspect!'

'Is that how you see it?'

'That's how it *is*. My cousin Teddy has autism...'

And I told her everything. All of it. The rock. The institution. The marriage break-up. The Statistic. I waited for the sharp intake of breath. The shake of the head.

But Ally just laughed.

'That was your cousin. It wasn't Jack. It wasn't your marriage.'

'But...'

'But if it's still haunting you after all this time, maybe you should find out what *did* happen. Lay the ghost to rest.'

—

That evening, Jack could talk about nothing but the play. The peach juice debacle was forgotten.

'It was epic,' he said, mouth full of macaroni cheese. 'All the mums were crying even though it was funny. And then Josh's turban fell off and he had a meltdown so we had to say his words and Dylan had to stab himself because Josh was meant to do it...'

I don't think any of us could follow exactly what he was saying but his excitement was infectious and soon his brother and sister were hanging on to every word. Then Jack wound a tea towel round his head and acted the whole thing out. Mum, Freddie and Lily laughed until tears ran down their faces and even my shoulders relaxed from their usual position around my ears.

Such a roller-coaster.

Then my mobile rang. It was Mark.

'Where the *fuck* have you been!' he said. 'I've been trying to get hold of you for three days.'

I was not expecting that.

Although I probably should have been after my performance in Manchester and the fact that I'd been ignoring his calls. I went into the hallway and pulled the door shut behind me.

'I'm sorry, Mark,' I said. 'I've been… sick.'

'I'm not surprised with the amount of booze you sank in Manchester,' said Mark sourly.

Through the kitchen door I could hear the laptop buzzing. It would be Daniel, Skyping the family. He did so every evening but tonight I really wanted to talk to him.

'Mark, any chance I could call you back?'

'No, you sodding can't. God knows when I'd be able to get hold of you again.'

I could hear Mum and the kids laughing. I could even hear Daniel chuckling across the ether. From what I gathered, Matt the Mog was on the kitchen table playing to the gallery.

'Look, Mark. I'm sorry about the groups and I'm sorry about what happened afterwards,' I said. 'I promise to be on my best behaviour next time.'

There was a pause.

'Healey, there is no way I'm letting you near those clients again.'

'Oh.'

Sacked. From my first freelance job.

How humiliating.

Unsurprising but humiliating.

'But I would like you to listen back to the recordings and take notes,' added Mark. 'I think hearing that leylandii comment will be apt punishment.'

266

There, finally, was a hint of laughter.

Maybe I was forgiven.

We said goodbye and I ran into the kitchen. The kids were clearing the table and Mum was stacking the dishwasher. The call with Dan was obviously over.

'Did Dad ask to speak to me?' I asked casually.

'No,' said Jack.

'You told him you'd call when you were less busy,' said Freddie.

Oh God. I had said that, hadn't I?

And then I hadn't.

'And now he's in meetings all day,' added Jack, holding out his empty yoghurt pot out to Matt the Mog.

'I miss Daddy,' said Lily.

Chapter Thirty-Six

On Saturday morning, Freddie had a football match in the arse end of Reading.

Jack came with me and Lily stayed at home. That was one of the great things about having Mum at home. Lily wasn't dragged cross-country for footie and I got to spend quality time with the boys. Sadly, the weather was ghastly: grey and drizzly with a real bite to the wind. Jack flatly refused to get out of the car to watch the match and, frankly, I didn't blame him. I left him with my phone and headed over to the touchline alone, even thought my jacket was too flimsy for the elements and my fashion boots were getting trashed by the mud. The other parents were chatting in smug little groups and shouting unintelligible things to the players. I went and stood by the nearest group. No one spoke to me and I couldn't think of anything to say to them, so I rubbed my hands together and beamed like an idiot. As you do. Then I yelled encouragement to the players, but Freddie turned and gave me a look that could have curdled milk.

Defeated, I went back to the car.

This was better.

Nice and toasty.

Protected.

Jack was sprawled out on the back seat, tapping. Just a happy little boy playing a computer game. Ally had said that Asperger's didn't have to define his life. Oh, how I wanted to that to be true. But, if it was, what about Teddy? What about the little boy who had been sent away?

I woke with my mind swimming and my mouth surrounded by crusty drool. Freddie was getting back into the car.

'How did you get on?' I asked brightly, running my hands through my hair.

'We lost.' Freddie snapped himself in. 'As you'd know if you'd bothered to stay and watch.'

'You had a face like thunder...'

'*You* shouted, "Up the Falcons!"'.'

'You *are* the Falcons.'

'Yes, but you don't say, "up the",' said Freddie.

'What *do* you say?'

'"Come on".'

'Anyway, none of the spectators were talking to me. Very snooty lot.'

'You were standing with the other team's supporters,' said Freddie. 'Dad always stands with the right people and stays for the whole match. *He* knows what to shout.'

He flicked on Capital and turned to look out of the window.

—

No one said a word all the way home.

Mum came to the front door to greet us. 'How did you get on?' she asked.

'Not good,' said Freddie. He gave his bag a kick for emphasis. 'We lost and Mum and Jack sat in the car.'

It's never good being shown up in front of your mum, is it?

'Wanna play *Wizard World*?' Jack asked Freddie.

Freddie gave him a withering glance. 'Why would I want to play with a loser like you?' he said.

I sighed, ready to intervene. Ready to shout, if I'm honest.

'Whatever,' said Jack with a small shrug. And he turned away.

Freddie looked thrown. He just stood there. 'Okay. I'll play,' he said finally.

The two ran inside. I watched them go with a lump in my throat.

Ally O'Reilly, I think I love you.

'Lily and I have been busy,' said Mum as she led the way indoors. 'We caught a cab back to my flat for some bits and bobs and Lily's brought back some of the photo albums I'd been sorting.'

Lily was giggling at the kitchen table. 'You were so *cute*, Mum,' she said.

'Still am.' I grinned. I clicked the kettle and went to take a look. There I was; a five-year-old moppet making a daisy chain in the back garden and looking very like Lily with my blond bob and blunt fringe. The photo was labelled *Emma, Portland Road, '76* in Dad's neat hand and suddenly I was back there, hearing the ru-hoo of the wood pigeons and the drone of planes going to Gatwick and Mum calling me in to tea at exactly quarter to six.

Freddie poked his head round the kitchen door. He was already showered and changed, spiky hair, spiky manner.

'I'm off to Bethany's,' he said.

I was confused. 'Isn't she at her dad's this weekend?'

'Yeah. That's where I'm going.'

So, Freddie had been invited to Bastard Towers. A huge monstrosity, it must have been bought by Mrs Bastard's alimony because Ness and Bastard had never had that sort of money.

'Have fun,' I said.

I was smiling as Lily turned the page of the photo album and then—

Teddy!

Teddy transposed from my imagination into a photo of a playground I didn't recognise.

My heart started to thump like crazy.

Did Mum and Lily realise?

Couldn't they see that I was radiating interest?

I took a closer look. I was sitting on a wooden climbing frame and Teddy was leaning against the bottom in flares and a brown jumper. Just a little boy grinning at the camera. He didn't *look* unhinged.

'Who's that boy?' asked Lily. 'He looks just like Jack.'

Bloody hell.

Mum peered over Lily's shoulder. 'That's your mum's cousin, Teddy,' she said with a tut. Or did I imagine the tut? 'Lily, just *look* at the hash I'd made of Mum's hair.'

Mum and Lily started laughing at my rakish fringe.

But, wait!

Look at Dad's caption.

Welwyn with the Myers – July '78.

Myers. Not Miles.

Myers.

Teddy *Myers.*

That evening, I made sure I spoke to Daniel. In fact, for once, I Skyped *him*. As his image flickered up, I had to admit he looked gorgeous; his hair had been bleached by the sun and his slight frown as he focussed on the screen was really quite sexy. To say nothing of the navy polo shirt showing off tanned and muscular forearms...

Why had I had been so tempted to pop out for burger when I had steak at home? Except, of course, the steak had also popped out for burger, which maybe made the steak a burger himself...

We chatted briefly about the kids and I was about to move the conversation on to more personal and conciliatory grounds when Daniel suddenly said, 'So... where are we?'

I was thrown.

'Where were we with what?' I asked.

'The writer chap, for starters.'

That was a very provocative starter for ten. Despite my intentions, the blood started pounding in my temples.

'It's over,' I said shortly. 'And nothing happened.'

Daniel glanced over his shoulder. It looked like he was in a Starbucks or something, not slumped on the spare room bed like me. He turned back to the camera. 'Aren't those two sentences contradictory?' he asked.

'Come on Dan. I might as well ask you the same thing about Virginia.'

'Going up to Manchester with Paul Archer isn't nothing.'

'Neither is shagging the St John's bike!'

I know, I know.

'She is *not* the St John's bike.'

'Don't you *dare* stick up for that slapper.'

Daniel's eyes narrowed. 'If you're going to throw ridiculous comments about Virginia into my face every time we have a conversation, there's not much point, is there?' he said.

'How's that fair? You mentioned Paul first!'

Lily ran into the room. 'Daddy,' she squealed. 'I didn't know Mummy was talking to you.'

I was on borrowed time.

'Is it over, Dan?' I asked.

I had to know.

'Yeah,' said Daniel. 'Yeah, it is. And how's my lovely flower?'

Dismissed, I left the room to get Jack and Freddie. And I realised that I had no idea if Daniel had meant it was over between him and Virginia.

Or between him and me.

—

The more I thought about it, the more devastating and, well, *fundamental* that seemed. There was a huge difference between the two interpretations. A life-changing difference. I agonised over what exactly what he had meant while I made the bangers and mash. I considered calling Daniel back.

But it was difficult.

Scary.

Best to do it when we'd both calmed down a little.

Best to wait.

Once supper was cleared away, I closeted myself in my office-cum-bedroom. I very, very nearly Skyped Daniel, but then I googled Edward Myers instead. Like before, I didn't really plan to. I just did. And, as before, there was nothing. Nothing relevant, at least.

How very disappointing.

Then my eye was caught by a small photo of a *Theo* Myers. Quite a blurry selfie of a middle-aged man, but there was no mistaking the red hair and a goofy grin. Was it possible? Could Teddy actually be short for *Theodore*? Heart in overdrive, I clicked on the picture. It led to a LinkedIn profile. Theo Myers was a Constellation Program Transition Manager (whatever that was) at NASA, working out of Houston. Surely it couldn't be? I scanned his profile in more detail. Theo Myers had attended Oxford University. He'd gone to school in Welwyn Garden City. The town where that photo had been taken.

Theo Myers.

It had to be Teddy.

It couldn't be.

It was.

Impossible.

No other explanation.

Suddenly I felt lightheaded. This was huge.

Confusing but *huge*!

I mean, what about the institution?

What about being locked away?

What about lobbing stones at me and almost knocking me out!!

I still had loads of questions, but it was undoubtedly Good News as far as Jack was concerned.

Far from a stunted life, Teddy – Theo – was living in America and working for *NASA*!

And if Teddy could do that, so could Jack. Well, not NASA necessarily, but you get my drift. Ally was right. Jack *didn't* have to be defined by his Asperger's.

Lightheadedness morphed to lightheartedness.

Halle-bloody-lujah!

It showed that no one got to give you a label except yourself.
And Teddy had clearly chosen the label 'NASA Constellation
Program Transition Manager'.

Bloody brilliant.

As the nuns at my old school used to say, 'All shall be well
and all shall be well and all manner of things shall be well.'

Chapter Thirty-Seven

I continued to feel fab over the next few days. I was calm and centred yet bubbling over with optimism; the sort of feeling you get on a lovely spring day when everything seems possible. Even though this was January and the weather was relentlessly dull and drizzly.

'What do you want to be when you grow up?' I asked the kids one evening. 'You could do anything. Go to America and join NASA.'

'Space is boring,' said Jack. 'I want to be a football pundit.'

'I want to be play for Wycombe Wanderers,' said Freddie.

'I want to be a backing dancer for Harry Styles,' said Lily.

Right!

Nothing could dampen my optimism.

I tidied the house, got up to date with the laundry and took Mum out for lunch in her favourite garden centre. And then I set to work on the audio files Mark had sent me. I listened to them diligently, cringing when I got to the Manchester groups. Was it really only a week ago? How drunk I sounded. How *unhinged*. I put my hands over my ears when I got to the leylandii bit. What on earth had I been thinking?

Then I went back through my notes, sifting and sorting. I pulled out the main themes and put together the outline of a presentation, making sure my story was tightly argued and the recommendations watertight. This took me a good couple of days but I was delighted with the results. It was the least I could do to put things right.

An hour after I'd sent it off, Mark called.

'This is bloody good, Healey,' he said. 'You've gone above and beyond. I'd go so far as to say you're forgiven.'

'Thank you. And I *am* sorry about Manchester.'

'Ha! It's not every day a gorgeous woman launches herself at me.'

'And if it wasn't for your marriage vows...'

A pause.

'Actually, Lucia and I are "on a break",' said Mark.

The laughter had disappeared from his voice.

My turn to pause.

'Seriously?'

'Yeah. She's been seeing someone from work.'

I was knocked for six. I'd always assumed Mark and Lucia would stay the distance.

'I'm so sorry.'

'Thanks. How are things between you and Daniel?'

'He's still in the States.'

'Well, if he's not back for the ball, I'd love to escort you. As friends, of course.'

I decided I rather liked the idea.

—

There!

I could do this.

I was back in control and rocking it.

I picked up the children that afternoon with a spring in my step. As I stood shivering in the playground, Virginia came up to me with some bumf for the auction. Damn it, the woman even looked good in a cagoule.

I was in such a good mood I decided to be the bigger person.

'I'm sorry about the turban,' I said. It seemed a reasonable place to start. 'I'm sorry about the fondue set, too,' I said. 'I should have apologised ages ago.'

'Well, thanks for doing so now. I thought Jack was brilliant at the play, by the way.'

Wow.

Somehow, we'd morphed into a mutual appreciation society.

'Thank you. I wish Mr Berry had been there. We need him to cough up for the Lunch Club next year.'

'I'm sure he will anyway,' said Virginia. 'Not that we'll be here to see it.'

What?

'Why not?'

Virginia gave a pretty shrug. 'Moving on,' she said, wiping a tendril of hair off her face.

I was gobsmacked. 'You've only just got here,' I said.

'I'm not sure life in a country town is for us,' she said. 'As soon as I can sell the flat, we're off.'

'Right.'

'And I'm sorry if I overstepped the mark with Daniel. I was just a bit worried about you and wanted to see if I could help.'

She gave me a bright smile and tripped off.

–

What?!

Was that true?

Virginia hadn't looked like she was lying.

She had looked completely genuine.

And, of course, that still made her an interfering old mare but it didn't make her an adulteress.

Maybe, just maybe, I had got the wrong end of the stick and overreacted.

Maybe, just maybe, I owed Daniel an apology.

That night I made my special fajitas to mark the fact that everything seemed to be going so well.

Everyone's favourite.

I was pulling together the guacamole when the doorbell rang. I went to answer it, wooden spoon in hand.

There were two huge policemen standing there, radios crackling.

'Are you Frederick Healey's mother?' the bigger and burlier asked.

I nodded, not too worried. Freddie was inside, doing his homework. Not hurt. Not worse.

The policeman shifted his weight. 'I'm afraid we need to come in,' he said. 'Frederick's wanted on charges of theft.'

Chapter Thirty-Eight

Oh Emma!

You stupid, *stupid* woman.

Obsessed by Jack. Obsessed by Teddy.

Blind to the needs of your other children.

You utter, *utter* fool!

The police were in the living room. I was sure they hadn't pushed me bodily out of the way and barged in, but I had no recollection of how they'd got there. Our lounge wasn't small — indeed an estate agent would probably describe it as spacious — but they seemed *huge*, all boots and helmets and scary officialdom. They diminished the space. Diminished *us*. Those ghastly walkie-talkies, taking our humiliation, broadcasting it around town…

'Have you got guns?' asked Jack. He looked interested rather than alarmed.

'*Jack!*' I hissed.

Jack ignored me. 'Have you come to arrest Mum?' he asked, matter-of-factly. 'She shouts a lot but she's OK really.'

The policemen suppressed grins. 'Could we have a word with Frederick, please?' asked the one with sandy hair and freckles.

'Of course. I'll go and get him. But I'm sure…'

Mum came in, an arm round Lily. '*I'll* get Freddie,' she said, smiling pleasantly at the policemen. She held out a hand to Jack. 'Come with me, Jacko. Let's go and finish making tea.'

Jack complied. And here was Freddie, as white as his school shirt and looking about eight. He perched on the arm of my chair, avoiding my eyes. I patted his shoulder awkwardly.

The sandy-haired policeman cleared his throat. 'So, Frederick,' he said. 'Apparently last Sunday you unlawfully entered a property and stole an iPad.'

'What?' I had visions of Freddie in a black balaclava, shinning up a drainpipe, knife between his teeth.

My son, the cat burglar.

It was preposterous.

Freddie was talking. 'I *did* take it,' he said. 'But I didn't steal it. And I didn't go in unlawfully.'

Oh God.

'What house?' I said. '*Where?*'

'A house on the Riverhead estate called The Trees,' said Sandy-Haired-Policeman. He glanced at his notes. 'The complaint was made by a… Mrs Beverley Richardson.'

I wrinkled my nose. The names were vaguely familiar…

'Bastard Towers!' I exclaimed, just as Freddie said, 'Bethany's.'

Relief bubbled through me as I slumped back against the cushions. 'The Black Panther was invited round for tea,' I said. 'It's obviously a silly misunderstanding.'

I smiled at the policemen, waiting for them to laugh or apologise. Or *something*.

'Is this true, Freddie?' said Sandy-Haired-Policeman.

'Sort of,' said Freddie. 'I know the girl who lives there. Well, she lives there sometimes. But I wasn't exactly invited round for tea.'

'Freddie! You s*aid*—'

'No, I didn't. Bethany invited me round. I didn't know no one else was going to be in.'

'Whatever.' I'd have it out with Freddie later. 'But that's hardly breaking and entering, is it, Inspector?'

Was he an inspector? Had he said? How did people on murder-mystery programmes always know the rank of the official-looking person they were addressing?

'What about the iPad?' asked Sandy-Haired-Policeman.

'I took it from Megan's room...'

'Megan?'

'Bethany's stepsister.'

'Nasty piece of work,' I added, *sotto voce*.

Everyone ignored me.

'But I thought it was Bethany's,' said Freddie. 'Megan's always stealing her things. I was just getting it back for her.'

More bubbles of relief. 'I can vouch for that,' I said. 'If anyone's in trouble, it should be Megan.'

'Who's got the iPad now?' said Sandy-Haired-Policeman.

'Me,' said Freddie. For the first time he looked a little furtive.

'Could you get it for us, please?'

Freddie disappeared and came back with an iPad. There was a big blob of metallic blue nail polish on it.

'Ha! My other son suggested Bethany mark her possessions with nail varnish,' I said. 'I'll call Bethany's mum. She'll vouch for Freddie.'

Sandy-Haired-Policeman nodded and I called Ness, willing her to pick up.

She did.

'Ness, I've got the police here.'

Sharp intake of breath. 'No one's hurt?'

'No. But Bastard's accused Freddie of pinching Megan's iPad and Freddie's trying to explain it belongs to Bethany. Can you just confirm Bethany had an iPad round at her dad's?'

Ness didn't say anything for an uncomfortably long time.

'Ness?'

'Of course she didn't, Em. Where would I get the money to buy her a bloody iPad?'

Well, it all kicked off after that.

Ness arrived with Noah and an uncooperative Bethany, and then Bastard and his wife pitched up. Ness and Bastard had a row about parenting. Mrs Bastard said both Freddie and Bethany were little shits who were terrorising her daughter and stealing her possessions. I shouted at Mrs Bastard. Bastard insisted Bethany wasn't involved and that Freddie had instigated the whole thing. I shouted at Bastard.

Neither Freddie nor Bethany said a thing.

There was a tense and awkward stand-off and finally Bethany cracked and admitted it was Megan's iPad and that she'd persuaded Freddie to take it. I was about to shout at her too but I felt more sorry than angry as she stood there sobbing and saying that her dad didn't love her.

Bastard, of course, immediately dropped all charges. The police gave us all a lecture, which I don't think any of us listened to. And then they all left.

I was shaking.

Freddie looked absolutely shell-shocked.

Bethany was still shaking with sobs.

'Right,' said Ness. 'I think this young lady has an apology to make to Freddie before she's grounded forever.'

'*Sorry*,' said Bethany. There was a funny tone to her voice. It wasn't apologetic. Nor was it sulky. It was... passionate. Provocative, even.

Faint alarm bells began to ring.

'It's been a long day,' I said. 'I need to get Jack and Lily to bed.'

And I needed to start remembering I had *three* children.

Not only one.

Chapter Thirty-Nine

The rather congealed fajitas had been eaten, Jack and Lily had been put to bed and Freddie and I were in his room with mugs of hot chocolate.

'So, lots to talk about,' I said.

A nice open-ended starter for ten.

But Freddie just grunted and swung around on his desk chair.

I shouldn't have sat on the squashy beanbag. I was in a semi-prone position and lower than Freddie. Not good for authority.

'I'm sorry about Bethany,' I persisted. 'How dare she tell you the iPad was hers and dump you in it like that?'

Freddie kept swinging. Faster and faster.

'Please stop it, Freddie. You're making me feel sick.'

Freddie brought the chair to an abrupt halt. There were tears running down his cheeks. Freddie never cried.

'Oh, Fred.' I touched his shoulder.

Freddie shrugged me away. 'I knew,' he said fiercely. 'I *knew* it was Megan's iPad. OK?'

Bloody hell.

'OK.'

'We were hiding it to pay Megan back for taking Bethany's stuff. But then Jack put nail varnish on it and we couldn't get it off...'

He trailed off, looking very far from the Black Panther.

'Why didn't you tell the police that?' I said.

283

Freddie coloured. 'I dunno,' he said. 'I was mad. Bethany had obviously told her dad I took it, so I was paying her back. But then she took the beef and now I feel awful...'

'You're both as bad as each other,' I said. 'We'd better go and say sorry to Megan tomorrow.'

''K,' said Freddie. He looked almost relieved.

'In the meantime, you're grounded for a fortnight.'

Freddie stood up and then threw himself face down on his rumpled bed, all spiky hair and sharp shoulder blades. 'You can't stop me seeing Bethany,' he mumbled.

'I bloody can.'

'I love her!'

My lovely boy.

My lovely, thieving, lying, conniving boy.

I resisted the temptation to tell him not to be so silly. I resisted the temptation to say he was too young to know about love. I reminded myself that I'd only been a few years older when I'd met Daniel.

Freddie twisted onto his back. 'And do you know what?' he added. 'She loves me a lot more than you do.'

'Now you're just being ridiculous.'

'No I'm not. You don't give a shit about me. It's always Jack, Jack, Jack. Lily and I don't get a look-in.'

—

I was still shaking by the time I got into bed and there was only one person I wanted to share it with.

Daniel.

He would understand. Reassure me. Centre me.

Or, at least, he would have done in the old days.

I Skyped him and he answered straight away.

'I've been waiting for you to call,' he said.

'Have you?'

'Of course I have! When the police pitch up to arrest your son, you're generally interested in finding out more.'

'Right.'

Jack or Lily had obviously got to him first. I gave him the adult version as best I could.

'Who took Freddie to and from this house, then?' asked Daniel.

I thought about it.

I wasn't sure.

And what did *that* have to do with anything, anyway?

'I guess he walked,' I said. 'It's not far along the river.'

'Did you check he'd been invited for tea?'

'Of course not. He's fourteen, not four.'

'Did you check an adult was going to be in?'

'*No.* It's Ness's daughter. Freddie hangs out with her all the time.'

'Isn't it your responsibility to keep more of an eye on him?'

Now I was really cross. So much for Daniel keeping me calm.

'Don't talk to me about responsibilities,' I snapped. '*You* had a responsibility not to see Virginia.'

I know.

I'm not proud of myself.

I mean, I was just coming around to the fact that *maybe* there had been nothing going on between him and Virginia and that *maybe* I had overacted...

'Virginia asked to talk to me because she was worried about you,' said Daniel. 'And that's all there was to it.'

'Yes, that's what she said,' I admitted grudgingly. Say sorry, Emma. Say sorry. 'But don't you think that's a bit patronising and interfering. I mean, why should she be worried—'

'Something about losing it in the post office?'

'Oh, for God's sake!'

'And you've been so erratic recently—'

'No, I haven't!'

'You bloody have,' said Daniel. 'Always flying off the handle, yelling blue murder at the kids.'

'Not "always", Dan. And that hardly gives Virginia carte blanche to get involved.'

'Don't change the subject. You've been losing it big time. You lost it at Jack's diagnosis—'

'This is ridiculous, Dan. Stop flinging this *stuff* at me.'

'And how about that lunch with our parents?'

'I couldn't let Jack get away with talking to your father like that.'

'Agreed. But it's possible to tell a child off without liberal usage of the "f" word.'

'I didn—'

'We all heard you!'

'I wasn't being myself!'

Daniel hadn't finished. 'We've been walking on eggshells around you, Em,' he said. 'It's been a bloody nightmare.'

Now I was furious. 'Well, if I'm so terrible, why have you buggered off to the States?' I shouted. 'Surely you shouldn't have left someone so *unstable* in sole charge of the kids?'

There was a pause. 'Why do you think your mum's there?' Daniel asked softly.

What?

'Because she's hurt her leg,' I said. Obvs.

'Yup,' said Daniel. 'That's the official story.'

Oh. My. God.

'So, you know about the glasses?' I whispered.

'Yup.'

'Did Ness tell you?'

'She had your best interests at heart,' said Daniel.

So, Daniel, Mum and Ness had been plotting behind my back and even Virginia had been trying to get a look-in. (I'd *thought* Mum's leg didn't seem that bad.)

I didn't want to talk to Daniel after that.

I was too shocked. Too tired.

He wasn't making me feel calm and reassured.

He'd made everything ten times worse.

I sat for a long time thinking about what Daniel had said, the accusations he had made. I thought about the occasions he'd mentioned and how I hadn't remembered them as they obviously had been.

The shouting.

The red mist.

The swearing.

Calming down and carrying on as if nothing had happened.

Why hadn't I remembered behaving like that?

There was one other person I knew who behaved like that. Who had a meltdown and then denied it ever happened.

Who said, 'I hadn't been being me.'

And that person was Jack.

Chapter Forty

Maybe there is a moment in the life of every Aspie parent when they question if they have Asperger's too. For me, that moment was now. Perhaps the thought had been planted by that conversation with Mum, ages ago. Maybe it had grown silently, a stealthy tumour, ever since...

All I knew was that it was suddenly bursting from me like the thing in *Alien* and I couldn't ignore it any longer.

'What was I like as a child?' I asked Mum the next morning.

Mum paused with a new china cup halfway to her mouth. 'Lovely. You were in your own world a lot of the time,' she said. '"Emma's away with the fairies," we used to say.'

'What else?'

'You'd line your teddies up in size order. Rather like Jack used to do with his trains.'

'Really?'

I'd heard similar stories over the years, of course, but now I was passing them through a different filter.

'And everything had to be just so or you'd get terribly upset.'

'Ha! You were always moaning my room was a tip!'

Mum laughed. 'We had to keep playing the same records in the same order. "Delilah", followed by "Lily the Pink", followed by "Wichita Lineman". There would be merry hell if two dropped down together.'

She was smiling, a faraway look on her face.

'Crimes against music,' I said. 'I was probably yelling at you to turn them off.'

We laughed easily together but my brain was in overdrive.

Was that conclusive? Was it *enough*?

'You know about the glasses, don't you?' I said. I could feel myself flushing.

Mum nodded.

'I'm mortified they thought you needed to come and stay,' I said. 'I mean, it's been lovely to have you but—'

'You've got a lot on your plate,' said Mum firmly.

'Yes, but all those *glasses*.'

Mum patted my hand with her powdery-soft one. 'It wasn't the first time,' she said gently.

What?!

'I'm sorry?' I said.

'The plates? When you were sixteen?'

Oh God.

I'd totally blanked it from my mind, but it was all coming back to me now.

'Something to do with not getting a lift to Youth Group?' I asked, physically cringing in my seat.

'Yes.'

I'd fancied some guy. Was looking forward to playing Twister. Then I couldn't get a lift.

I'd done it before.

I'd done it before and blanked it.

Was *that* conclusive?

I called Ness and arranged to meet her by the river.

'I'm absolutely mortified about the whole iPad thing,' said Ness as soon as we'd started walking.

'Don't be,' I said. 'Freddie knew the iPad was Megan's. They were in on it together.'

'Really?' said Ness. 'Well, that makes me feel a bit better. Bethany's grounded for a couple of weeks but I'm going to give the doctor a tinkle. She's really not been herself.'

'We have a grovelling trip to Bastard Towers tonight,' I said. 'I've never actually met Megan.'

'Her mum spoils her rotten. Has done ever since her first marriage broke down.'

More fallout from fractured families.

Was that really what I wanted for mine?

But in the meantime, I had a question that really couldn't wait.

'Ness, can you answer me something honestly?' I said.

'Sure.'

'Have you ever thought I might be autistic?'

There.

Said it.

Now Ness could put my mind at rest and I'd have one less thing to worry about.

'Oh Emma! Stop being such a drama queen.'

Ouch! That stung.

I hadn't been being a drama queen.

It had been a genuine question.

'Have you ever thought it, though?' I persisted.

'I *thought* we were in the middle of a conversation about Freddie and Bethany.'

That was true.

The trouble was, it was the answer to a totally different question.

'Please, Ness. It's important.'

Ness stopped. 'Of course you're not *autistic*,' she said.

Thank bloody goodness for that.

'You might have a few traits but...'

Oh.

Oh!

'What traits?'

'Stop it, Em,' said Ness.

'Come on. You can't just say something like that and then change the subject.'

'I just meant you're very intelligent. You went to Cambridge, for goodness sake.'

'So, you think everyone who goes to Cambridge has got Asperger's?'

'I have no idea. Can we stop talking about this?'

'No!' I exclaimed, close to tears. A nearby jogger glanced at us curiously.

Ness exhaled noisily. 'Why's this all suddenly about you?' she said. 'OK, OK. Your eye contact isn't always brilliant. Happy now?'

I wasn't happy.

'How do you mean?' I asked.

'Well, sometimes you glance at people and look away again quickly.'

Did I?

Sure, I don't like to *stare* at people.

It's rude anyway.

'What else?' I asked.

'God!' said Ness. She sat down on the arm of a bench. 'OK, sometimes you don't close the loop properly.'

Eh?

'What loop?'

'Like when we were meeting for a run that time and you were running late. You didn't tell me. It wasn't that you forgot or couldn't be bothered. You just didn't think to.'

Hmm.

Ness was still talking. 'You're very black and white. You either love someone or you're completely anti them. Everything's great or completely crap. Paul's a demigod; Virginia's a she–devil.'

Yes.

But didn't everyone else think like that too?

'Has anyone else ever mentioned this?' I asked.

'Not really,' said Ness.

'That clearly means yes.'

'It doesn't.'

'*Who?*'

Ness paused. 'Virginia,' she said.

'*Virginia?*' I kicked the bench. 'What the fuck did she say?'

'Oh, Emma. I've come here to apologise about Bethany—'

'Come on.'

'OK. She said you lack some social skills and get by on humour.'

How *dare* she! How dare *Virginia* belittle and reduce me. And in front of my best friend too.

I pushed away the memory of a tongue-tied teenager hovering on the edge of the popular group. I batted away the relief I'd felt when I realised I could make people laugh.

Was *that* conclusive?

I went to Café Rouge on my own and tried to think things through.

It was hard though. Hard to think objectively about myself, about things I'd done that might suggest I was on the spectrum. I was just me. I mean, there was leaving Ness in the cold for half an hour. That seemed clear enough. But were there more?

Over the course of two lattes, the possibilities came through thick and fast. Some might argue my blind belief in The Statistic was black and white thinking; to me it had just seemed logical. My failure to negotiate a part-time role at work could be down to difficulty in reading social situations. I often relied on my learned interviewing skills to make small talk – maybe other people found those sorts of things came naturally. Then there was not going to Freddie's football matches or booking Lily into her gym club as I'd promised all that time ago. Was that a lack of empathy or just being a harried mum? Dumping poor old Roger at the May Ball and chucking that cushion at Paul? Would most people argue that was inappropriate behaviour in a social situation?

And this was to say nothing of my poor motor skills, with the tattoos and the trampolines and… and…

Was *that* enough?

And did it matter anyway?

Look at Teddy…

—

That summer had been a belter.

So many heavy, hazy days I began to think they'd never end. They'd knocked down an old house along the street. Mum moaned about the noise and mess but I loved playing there. Then Teddy Myers came to stay. He loved it too. We made a den in the lilac bushes and we were having so much fun we didn't bother to go in for lunch. I swept the floor with leaves while Teddy lined the pathway with stones. Each stone had to be exactly the same size so it took him ages, but it was perfect. When he was finished, we lay on the ground and looked out through the tangled boughs and lacy flowers and watched the sun getting bigger and lower until it was balanced on the very edge of the world.

Then Dad and Uncle Robert arrived.

We heard them first, calling us. Then we could see their faces through the branches. They both looked very cross. When we got home there was to be shepherd's pie but no pudding and then we were to go straight to bed.

The dads came in, pulling the branches aside and messing up the stones, and then everything went wrong. The sun started jumping around, and the flowers were sickly sweet and the shouting was so loud I had to put my hands over my ears. Teddy started whirling around and picking up the stones and throwing them. Spin. Throw. Spin. Throw. Pain in my head and stickiness on my face and metal in my mouth and suddenly the screaming was coming from me…

Chapter Forty-One

I paid the bill and walked home in a tizzy.

An accident!

The 'rock throwing' had been an *accident*?

But, everyone had said…

Or had they? Maybe it was just my memory. My imagination.

There was only one person who could tell me for sure.

—

As soon as I got home, I put the kettle on and set my laptop up on the kitchen table. Then, in that casual way you sometimes do when something is important but you are too tired and overwhelmed to think about it any more, I sent Teddy an 'invitation to connect' on LinkedIn. It wouldn't come to anything, anyway. I made a pot of tea, took Mum a cup, came back downstairs, poured one for myself and – *wow!* – did that really say 'Theo is typing'? I blinked hard in case I'd imagined it but, no, it was still there.

Mesmerised, I watched the little dots flickering across the screen. This had been almost ridiculously easy. Why hadn't I done it years ago? Well, unless Teddy was telling me to piss off. Or didn't remember me. Or it wasn't him after all and LinkedIn was about to suspend my account for harassing random Theos.

Theo: Hello, cuz!!

Oh, now, this was *weird*.

In two little words, everything changed. I had no idea how to reply. Of course, what I *wanted* to put was 'I thought you were in an institution, periodically strapped to a table. Why are you... here?'

> **Emma:** I wasn't sure you'd recognise me.

> **Theo:** The school in East Grinstead was the give-away! Otherwise I might have struggled. New surname...

This was all so normal. I'm not sure what I'd been expecting but it wasn't this.

We started to chat about our lives. Thirty-five years summed up in a matter of words. Teddy's job sounded very technical and high-powered and he clearly loved it. Then – even more amazingly – I discovered he was married. To Alfonzo! Teddy was gay and had been in a committed relationship for fifteen years.

A swanky job.

A husband he clearly adored.

A life fully lived.

There was no need to feel sorry for him.

OK, so maybe his conversation was a little too stilted to be neurotypical – or maybe I was imagining it. But whatever label Teddy had or didn't have clearly wasn't holding him back. There was a lesson there for all of us.

Right. Time to address the elephant in the room. I had to do it. I had to...

> **Emma:** This will sound weird but, for some reason, I thought you'd been in an institution.

Too blunt?

Too late.

I held my breath.

>   **Theo:** It does sound weird! What kind of institu-
>   tion?

Oh no!

How hideously embarrassing.

>   **Emma:** I don't know. I just thought I remembered
>   Dad mentioning it.

Dad had also said, 'I hope he rots there.' I decided not to mention that bit.

>   **Theo:** Ha! Your dad was never my biggest fan.
>   Maybe he meant boarding school?

>   **Emma:** You went to boarding school?

>   **Theo:** Yeah. Just for a couple of terms. While my
>   parents were splitting up.

Oh my goodness.

Boarding school!

All that stress.

All that worry.

Bloody family Chinese whispers.

But I had to push on. I had more to ask...

>   **Emma:** I guess Dad blamed you for injuring me
>   with that stone.

I scratched my scar while I waited for the reply.

>   **Theo:** Yes! Totally unfair as you started throwing
>   stones first!!

>   **Emma:** No.

No!

I snapped the laptop shut and exhaled slowly. Nothing had changed. Capital Radio was still playing softly. Matt the Mog was still snoozing twitchily on the kitchen table. Even my tea was still warm. I could just creep away and none of this would ever have happened...

Only it had.

I inched the computer open again. Teddy was typing...

> **Theo:** Don't you remember? When Dad and Uncle Norman started wrecking the den, you freaked out and started chucking stones.

I shut my eyes and put my hands over my ears.

No.

No!

I didn't want to talk about it. I told Teddy I had to pick the kids up and we arranged to talk in a couple of days. I disconnected in turmoil. I'd travelled back to the Seventies and over to the States and those adventures in time and space had changed everything.

Everything.

Because I did remember now.

The dads blundering in, the smell of lilac, the dazzling sun...

Spin, throw... spin, throw...

I really hadn't been being me.

—

There *had* been a monster under the bed, but – oh, sod it – I'd known.

Of course I had.

I'd known ever since Jack's diagnosis.

I'd known for much, *much* longer than that.

I might not have admitted it – even to myself. I might have blocked the stone-throwing and the plate-smashing and the yelling and the screaming, but I'd *known*.

I'm myself and of course I'd known.

I had Asperger's too.

I'd just thought I'd got away with it.

Chapter Forty-Two

One minute, I was philosophical.

Asperger's or not, I was blessed in so many ways. And if I could have a happy and fulfilling life, then so could Jack.

The next minute, I was petrified.

I had Asperger's. This was a big deal. I was different. I didn't fit in. Never had. Never would.

I toyed with getting a diagnosis. Making it formal. I wondered if I should tell Daniel. And what about The Statistic? Did it make a difference if one of the parents also had Asperger's?

So, it went on – thoughts spiralling, dive-bombing, colliding. But a couple of nights later – before I'd decided what, if anything, to do – it all kicked off.

Freddie had ignored me for days.

Each afternoon, he came straight home from school and went upstairs without a word. He was monosyllabic at supper and disappeared upstairs again afterwards. To be honest, I let him get on with it. The poor lad needed space to work through his issues without his mother breathing down his neck every five minutes.

But, that evening, Freddie came downstairs after supper.

'It's Bethany,' he said. 'She's down by the river and she's really upset. I'm going to see her.'

I stopped stacking the dishwasher. 'No, you aren't,' I said.

'But she needs me,' said Freddie. 'I think she's been drinking stuff.'

'For goodness sake!' I said. 'What are her parents *doing*? Whose house is she supposed to be at?'

'Her dad's,' said Freddie. 'But he's not there and she's had a massive row with her stepmum. She's got some vodka and now she's walking into town along the river.'

Wonderful.

Just wonderful.

And, of course, Mum had chosen tonight to have a trial night back at her flat.

'Have you got their number?' I asked. Freddie shook his head. 'OK. I'll have to call Ness.'

I jabbed Ness's number into my phone. No reply. But, as soon as I disconnected, Mandy rang.

'I'm walking a mate's dog down by the river,' she said.

'It's cold. It's dark. That's exactly why I don't have a dog,' I said.

No, I don't know why either.

'Healey, your friend Ness's daughter is down here and she's pissed as a bloody fart.'

'Yeah, Freddie said.'

'Best get Ness to come down. I don't have her number.'

'I've tried. She's not picking up.'

'Well, the girl's pretty pickled. I'd hang around but my ex is about to drop Dylan home.'

'OK. Leave it with me.'

I disconnected and tried Ness's number again.

Still no answer.

'I'm going down,' said Freddie, phone clamped to his ear. 'She's really crying and she's met up with the dodgy gang from Year 11.'

'Let me talk to her.' I took Freddie's phone. 'Bethany?'

The phone went dead.

Now what?

300

The responsible thing would be to go down to the river. Not an altogether enticing prospect; it was cold and dark. But at least Freddie could stay at home with Jack and Lily.

'I'm going, Mum,' said Freddie, shrugging on his jacket. 'You can't stop me.'

I thought about it.

I remembered the old 'choose your battles' mantra from the parenting manuals.

'Right, kids,' I said, clapping my hands. 'Hats and coats on. We're off on an adventure.'

Jack and Lily were unconvinced and progress was slow. Eventually I managed to bundle everyone into the car. We drove down to the river, parked by the children's playground and started walking briskly past the bowling pavilion and onto the towpath. Freddie, phone glued to his ear, led the way.

'Bethany's not answering,' he said and we quickened our pace. As we walked further from town, the dog walkers and joggers thinned out, until there was no one about. Lily slipped her hand into mine and Jack stayed close to my other side. Even I was a little creeped out.

Finally, we heard teenage shouts. The odd scream. And then, as we skirted a little copse, we saw half a dozen ghostly forms on a jetty. Some were standing, some crouched over.

Freddie started running. 'Bethany!' he shouted.

The silhouettes started. A couple melted away into the shadows. The others turned slowly back toward the water.

I ran onto the jetty, panic stabbing at my chest.

'What it is?' I shouted.

One of the youths pointed at the water. It wasn't pitch-black by any means – the moon and the houses further along the riverbank were dappling the water with silver – but, nevertheless, it took a moment for my eyes to adjust. Then I saw something in the water. Some*one*. A head, hair slicked back, mouth a wide O. And then the splashing and the yelling started. The river was deep here. Far too deep to stand.

'Bethany?' I whispered. I'm not sure why I whispered. Except there was something terrible, almost religious, about the little tableau.

The youth shrugged. 'I don't know,' he said. 'She's pretty tanked up and she was larking around and then she tripped.'

I couched down on the jetty and stretched my fingers out to Bethany. She was too far away to take my hand but it might encourage her to swim toward me.

'Come on sweetheart,' I cajoled. 'Swim to the bank.'

But Bethany sank further until only her forehead and her slippery-seal hair were visible. For a horrible moment I wondered if she was dead; if she'd hit her head falling in. But then she re-emerged and the splashing and the shouting started again. She was still alive, but drowning.

'I'm going in,' said Freddie. He was already taking off his jacket.

'*No*, Freddie.'

Freddie pulled his jumper off. 'She's going to die,' he said.

'*I'll* go in,' I said firmly.

For a moment, we were almost wrestling on the jetty. He was much stronger but I was absolutely determined not to let him into the river. He wasn't a strong swimmer and it was far too dangerous. I gave him a shove that took him by surprise and made him lose his balance.

'Right, guys,' I said, pressing home my advantage and stripping off jacket, jumper and shoes. 'My phone's in my jacket pocket. Call 999. And then keep calling Ness. Someone else, run along the towpath and get a life-ring. Look after Lily. And don't come *anywhere* near the water.'

I hesitated, then pulled my jeans off too. They were heavy and this was no time for modesty.

Then I sat on the edge of the jetty and lowered myself into the water.

Once upon a time, a very long time ago, I did lifesaving lessons at university. I knew the basics and I remembered to keep my legs wide apart as I entered the water so I didn't go too far under. Even so, the water hit my chest like a brick wall.

Jeez, it was cold.

Scarily cold.

I trod water, trying to catch my breath and get my bearings. Everything looked different from this perspective and the lights dancing on the water disoriented me. The slap, slap of my T-shirt against my chest was almost as loud as the thudding of my heart. There was a current tugging at my legs.

Don't think about hypothermia.

Don't think about the treacherous eddies.

Don't think about any of it, Emma.

Just do it.

I set off toward Bethany. She was only a few metres away and I was a strong swimmer.

I could do this.

Bethany was bobbing up and down, huge, shiny eyes latched onto mine.

'Help me,' she screamed, limbs flailing. There was terror in her voice. In her movements.

I swam up to her and was trying to remember whether you tow a conscious victim with an outstretched or a bent arm when Bethany made a grab for me. Elementary mistake. *Always approach the victim from behind.* But how to do that when she kept spinning round to face me?

'Bethany, I need you to help me,' I called out, trying to sound authoritative. 'I'm going to swim behind you and put my hand under your chin. Just stay calm.'

God, it was cold. My legs were going numb, my chest was heavy.

Please, Bethany, please…

Bethany lunged at me again. I tried to prise her fingers away from my neck, but she was pushing down on me, panicking, thrashing around.

I felt myself going under.

Going down.

Down… down… down.

Pitch black.

I couldn't see… couldn't feel… couldn't…

I forced myself to go deeper, squirmed away and surfaced, spluttering. But Bethany was there, waiting for me. She clutched at me again and—

Boom.

Something large hit Bethany on the head. She put her hands up and I took the opportunity to wrestle her onto her back. I put my arm across her chest, holding her firm. Now I remembered. *This* was how you towed a struggling, conscious victim.

The object turned out to be a large life-ring. I looped my free arm through it and struck out for the bank. It didn't take long for Bethany to start fighting me, and she fought every inch of the way, but I was finally in control. We inched closer to safety. A moored boat to negotiate around – the chains and ropes slimy, tricky to navigate – and we were at the bank.

'Pass her over to me and let me pull her out,' said an authoritative voice. A man – vaguely familiar – was bending over, reaching out. It was too big a gap, so he lay down on the towpath, leaning over as far as he could. I got my feet onto a boat chain and half lifted Bethany up so he could pull her clear of the water. Then an ambulance came screaming across the grass followed by a couple of police cars, and a man in uniform rushed over and carted Bethany away.

I tried to pull myself out of the river, but my arms and legs had turned to lead, so Rescue-Man yanked me out too. It was an inelegant affair and, knackered though I was, I still managed to feel horribly conscious of my baggy granny-pants. Luckily Uniform-Man reappeared with some silver-foil blanket things and I went from beached whale to Paula Radcliffe in a matter of seconds.

'Is Bethany OK?' I asked.

'We're checking her over,' Uniform-Man said. 'But I think she's fine.' I looked at him more closely. It was the sandy-haired policeman who had come to our house. If he recognised me, he didn't comment. He led the way under a cordon that had sprung from nowhere and over to the emergency vehicles. 'That was a very brave thing you just did,' he said. 'Are *you* OK?'

'Just cold,' I said. My teeth wouldn't stop chattering.

I was desperate to see the children and to check on Bethany, but Uniform-Man was adamant I got changed first. He took me over to the ambulance cab, produced my jeans and jumper and a towel and left me to it. I took off my sodden underwear, skin puckered and clammy, and pulled on the dry clothes. I didn't feel very much warmer, but then a nice Ambulance-Lady came and swathed me in blankets and gave me some coffee from a flask and I began to feel a bit better.

I climbed out of the cab and there was Ness, tears streaming down her face.

'Emma,' she wailed. She flung her arms round me and started sobbing into my hair. 'You saved her life. You bloody saved her life.'

'Thank God she's OK,' I said, trying to extract myself. I wasn't very keen on the physical contact bit. Must be the Aspie in me.

'Thank God,' echoed Ness. 'What was she *thinking* of? Down here with a bunch of louts and pissed as a fart. I'll never forgive Simon and Bev. I'll never forgive myself. And you... you've been a star.'

'Freddie's the one who insisted we came down,' I said. 'Talking of which, where are the kids?'

'Here,' said Jack's voice.

I turned round and there they all were. My three beautiful children in a line, staring at me.

'I called 999,' said Jack proudly.

'Wow. Good for you, Jacko.'

'I went and found the life-ring thing,' said Lily.

'Did you? Well done, flower.'

'Yes. But I was too small to get it down.'

'I got it down for her,' said Jack. 'And then I threw it to you.'

'That was you too, was it Jacko? Cracking shot!'

'I didn't actually *mean* to hit Bethany,' said Jack, wrinkling his nose.

'Of course you didn't.'

'But she *was* being very unhelpful.'

'I called 999 and Bethany's mum,' said Freddie. Of the three, he looked the most shell-shocked.

'Freds, it's OK,' I said.

Freddie nodded. 'You went in the river for me, didn't you? You went in so I didn't have to.'

'Partly,' I said. 'Because I love you. And because that's what parents do for their children.'

'Thank you,' said Freddie. 'But Mum?'

'What?'

'*Everyone* saw your pants.'

I laughed. 'Lucky it wasn't my leopard-skin thong, eh?'

I hugged all three of my children to me. 'I am so, so proud of all of you,' I said.

'You're the real star,' said Freddie. 'You rescued Bethany all by yourself.'

'She didn't do it *all* on her own,' said Jack, wriggling away. 'The ugly man who mended the shower helped her.'

The plumber.

Of *course*.

Only he'd looked different as he'd yanked me out of the river. Not so... aesthetically challenged.

He came and sat next to me in the open estate boot of the paramedic's car while I waited to get checked over.

'You did brilliantly,' he said. 'I'd say you saved the young girl's life.'

'Really? I think I just made her panic.'

306

Maybe I'd made a three-act play out of a crisis. It wouldn't have been the first time.

'She was drowning,' said the plumber. 'I'm a volunteer fire-fighter and she was showing all the signs of the instinctive drowning response.'

'What's that?' I didn't remember it from lifesaving classes. Maybe it hadn't been invented then.

'Upright position, inability to keep the mouth above water, lateral flapping with the arms,' said the plumber. 'You've got less than a minute from that moment until they go.'

'Oh, God.'

I looked at him and, for the first time, saw the bright, clever eyes and the warm, kind smile.

'You know, I never said sorry properly about what Jack said when you were fixing our shower,' I said.

The plumber grinned. 'I wasn't sure you'd recognised me,' he said.

'I didn't immediately. But I am really sorry. I handled it very badly.'

'Me too,' said the plumber. 'I'm sorry I wasn't more gracious.'

'Jack is slightly autistic. That doesn't excuse his rudeness but...'

'I'll give him one thing – he's bloody impressive under pressure. Really kept his head when everyone else was panicking. Just like his mum.'

Ha!

Jack and I might have Asperger's but we were pretty damn hot in a crisis.

–

It seemed to take ages before I was discharged. A check-over from someone medical. A handful of leaflets about nasties I might have picked up from the river. A hug with Ness and Bethany.

Finally, we were free to go.

As we walked back to the car, I felt unexpectedly happy. My lovely family. Lily was clinging on to one of my hands. Freddie – *Freddie* – was holding the other. Jack was grinning and running in circles, rounding us up like a sheepdog. We were a team – a tight little unit – again.

There was only one thing – one person – missing.

'I wish Dad was here,' I said.

I had proved to myself I didn't *need* him.

But that didn't mean I didn't *want* him.

Chapter Forty-Three

I'm not usually a big dreamer – at least, not dreams I can remember. That night was different. Perhaps unsurprisingly, I dreamt I was back in the river, trying to rescue someone. But it wasn't Bethany. It wasn't even Jack.

It was Freddie and Lily.

Freddie was desperately trying to cling on to me and – why, Emma, why? – I was pushing him away. Even more heartbreakingly, Lily was silently floating away from me. I was ignoring her too but I could see her sad, stoic little face as she drifted out of reach...

I woke up with tears running down my face and a lump in my throat.

I know what you're thinking.

She's been ignoring her children for months, hasn't she? She had a wake-up call when the police came round for Freddie. But did she do anything about it? Of course she didn't. She started obsessing about herself, for goodness sake – about whether or not she had Asperger's. It was all me, me, me. The poor kids didn't get a look-in.

That's what you're thinking.

Go on, admit it.

I don't blame you.

But no more.

Today was the day I started to put things right.

At drop-off, I asked Lily's form teacher if I might have a word.

'Of course, Mrs Healey,' said Mrs Brown. Petite with a swinging silver bob, she must be nearing retirement but she still radiated passion for her job. 'Year Four have brass first thing, so we could chat now?'

'Wonderful.'

'I hear you're something of a local hero,' said Mrs Brown as I followed her into the cheerfully scruffy classroom.

Wow, news travelled fast in our little town.

'Not at all,' I said modestly as I eased myself into a tiny chair. 'And I just wanted to check how Lily's getting on.'

'Yes. I'm glad you're here,' said Mrs Brown. 'I've been worried about her.'

The guilt-monster reared its ugly head.

'Why?' I asked.

'She's lost her lovely sparkle, hasn't she? You know the issue with Hellie, of course?'

'Sort of.'

No.

'Hellie was so upset when Lily didn't want to be friends any more. They were so close. Now, of course, Hellie's paired up with Izzie and Lily's been edged out.'

Sadness gnawed at my insides. This was all my fault. There was no getting around it.

'There's been a lot going on at home,' I said feebly. 'And Lily's father isn't around...'

God, I wished he was.

'There's something else,' said Mrs Brown. 'I wasn't going to mention it, but...'

She rummaged in a pile of exercise books and pulled out one with 'Lily Healey – Maths' written on the front. Mrs Brown flicked through it and then slid it silently across the table to me.

A pie-chart.

Nicely drawn and neatly shaded in pencil, it was entitled, 'Time Mum Spends with the Family'. Heart thumping, I looked closer. The segment labelled 'Jack' took up a good two thirds. 'Dad' and 'Freddie' each had a smallish wedge. 'Lily' was a tiny little sliver. Even Matt the Mog's slice was bigger.

'It might be nothing,' said Mrs Brown. 'It might be Lily having fun.'

'It's not,' I said, fighting back tears. 'Poor Lily.'

Mrs Brown stood up and hovered behind me. 'It's difficult,' she said. 'Very difficult to give each child equal billing when one has special needs.'

I looked up. 'I know,' I said. 'But I could have done much, *much* better.'

I was crying now and my tears smudged Lily's pencil marks, blurring the lines on the chart.

If only I could change real life as easily.

–

Maybe I could.

Maybe I could start putting things right.

I drove straight to the industrial estate and went into Bounce. It was much quieter than Launch Day when I'd come with Paul. How long ago that seemed. Despite everything, I felt a pang for Paul – or for the way I'd felt when I thought he held all the answers.

'Can I help you?' asked a petite blonde in Lycra, popping up from behind the reception desk.

'Yes please,' I said. 'I'd like to put my daughter on the waiting list.'

There wasn't a hope, of course. Especially now she'd seen I wasn't small and bendy and that my boobs would give me a black eye as soon as I set foot on a trampoline. Maybe I should pretend Lily was adopted...

'How old is your daughter?' asked the Lycra'd Lovely.

'She's eight.'

'Ah. We're very full in the juniors.'

'I know.' An edge to my voice. 'I just want to put her on the waiting list.'

I couldn't fall at the first hurdle. I *couldn't*.

The LL pulled out a file. 'What's your daughter's name?' she asked.

'Lily Healey.'

The LL started to write, then paused, pen mid-air.

'Does Lily go to St John's?' she asked.

'She does.'

'Small? Blonde? Freckles?'

'Yes.'

'Of course. I *know* Lily.'

'You do? How come?'

'We've started doing a lunch class there.'

Lily had told me about the school gym club, of course. I'd had to sign her up to it. But she hadn't mentioned it was anything to do with Bounce.

'Lily is absolutely fabulous,' the LL was saying.

'Really?'

Was she?

'Yes. A natural gymnast. It was on the tip of my tongue to invite her to Bounce but I assumed she must already belong to a club. We'd absolutely *love* to have her here.'

My innate – Aspie? – sense of fairness reared its ugly head.

'But aren't you full?' I said.

The LL grinned. 'Not in the advanced *academy* class,' she said. 'That's invitation only.'

Sometimes, just sometimes, life can be a fairy tale.

Buoyed up, I drove down to the river. I needed to walk, to think, to process. Everything looked so different from last night.

Clear.

Calm.

Benign.

I phoned Ness to check on Bethany. She was fine except for a raging hangover. The doctor was fast-tracking an application for some urgent counselling.

Then I decided to call Caroline. I'd invite Hellie round for tea, see if I could build a few bridges.

'Caroline, it's Emma.'

'Emma! I've been hearing about your escapades last night.'

'Yes.' It already seemed like an age ago. 'I was actually wondering if Hellie would like to come for tea tomorrow?'

'I'm sure she'd love to,' said Caroline. 'She was so upset when Lily was barred from playing with her.'

The seagulls wheeled and cawed accusingly.

'I've never barred Lily from playing with her,' I said.

'That day in the playground, when Luke didn't want to come to yours...'

'I didn't mean *forever*. I meant that afternoon!'

'Oh! I told Hellie we'd wait for you to instigate the next playdate.'

I sat down on a bench.

'Oh God. And I never did. And now Hellie has gone off with Izzie and Lily thinks they both hate her.'

'They don't hate Lily at all,' said Caroline. 'They were just confused Lily didn't want to be friends. And then there was the whole thing with Jack.'

'What thing with Jack?'

'Oh, just some silliness. Jack told Izzie she was a bastard. Izzie's mum took umbrage. Didn't understand the "situation" with Jack.'

Ah, that might explain why Izzie had said Jack was weird.

'I'm not sure *I* understand the situation with Jack half the time,' I said.

Caroline started laughing. 'I do love him,' she said. 'He's *so* funny. Luke says it's boring at Joyce's without him. We must get the two of them together.'

'Right.' This was very confusing. 'But all this started because Luke *didn't* want to come to ours.'

'That one time,' said Caroline. 'He didn't mean forever.'

This conversation was becoming very surreal.

Caroline was still talking. 'And don't think too badly of Virginia,' she said. 'Nothing happened between her and Daniel. She was worried about you – wanted to talk to Daniel about it. That's all. But you seem to have got things together.'

Yes, I thought.

I have.

And I couldn't stop smiling.

I wasn't naïve enough to think I'd solved all Lily's problems.

It was a start, that was all.

I told Lily about the playdate at pick-up and her answering smile confirmed I was on the right track. She ran over to Hellie and the two of them started dancing around and squealing loudly.

Then Lily said. 'You can come for tea next time, Izzie.'

My lovely little flower.

I couldn't resist playing my trump card.

'By the way, Lily,' I said casually. 'You've been offered a place in the academy at Bounce.'

Lily goggled. 'No way!' she said. 'I'm not even in the *normal* class.'

'Way,' I said with a laugh. 'I popped in and the lady with the blond ponytail said she'd seen you do gym here and she's invited you into the academy.'

Squeals all round, and not just from Lily.

'Lily's brilliant at gym,' said Hellie.

'She's fantastic,' added Izzie. 'The only other person from our year who's in the academy is Mia French and she's the coolest girl in the whole school.'

Lily suddenly looked three inches taller. Almost as tall as her friends.

On the way back to the car, she held my hand for the first time in ages.

'Why didn't you ask if you could play with Hellie before?' I asked.

Lily glanced at me, brow furrowed. 'I thought you'd be cross,' she said. 'You said if Jack couldn't play with Luke…'

'I'm sorry, flower,' I said. 'That was really silly of me.'

'It was a bit silly,' said Lily. She swung our hands a little higher. 'But you're still the best mum in the world.'

Chapter Forty-Four

The next morning it was Freddie's turn for the Super-Mum treatment.

I knew it wouldn't be as easy. But I could make a start.

I began by calling Mrs Sharp at Meadowlands. Of course, I should have called days ago when I'd discovered the bloody letter in Freddie's sports bag. Why on earth hadn't I followed it up? What was the *matter* with me?

Anyway, Mrs Sharp was teaching but she did call me back an hour later.

'How can I help you, Mrs Healey?' she said. She sounded almost pleasant.

'I'm just phoning to check on Freddie,' I said. 'I know he had a detention and a day in Gateway...'

A pause.

'I'm afraid Freddie's been in Gateway for the past week.'

OK. This had not started as well as it had done with Lily yesterday.

'Bloody hell! What on earth for? And how come I didn't know about it?'

'For persistent poor completion of homework and swearing in front of a teacher,' said Mrs Sharp, without a shred of irony.

'And who...?'

'His father's been kept informed and his grandmother has been signing where necessary.'

'But what about *me*?' It came out as a wail.

'I... was led to believe you've been indisposed.'

Right.

I should have waited until I was calmer before I phoned Daniel.

Could have, would have, should have…

There was quite a delay before he picked up.

'Has something happened, Em?' he asked. The urgency in his voice took me by surprise.

'You know what's happened,' I said. 'You've been in cahoots with Mum about Freddie's Gateway and now I look an absolute fool.'

A pause.

'Not cahoots, Em—'

'Why didn't you tell me? I'm his *mum*.'

'We were trying to help.'

'I don't bloody believe you.'

'Don't then. And, actually, it's five in the morning here. Would you mind terribly if I got some kip?'

What I really shouldn't do now was talk to Mum.

It really wouldn't help anything. Not in the mood I was in.

I got into the car and drove to her flat.

Mum opened the door, wreathed in smiles at the unexpected visit. This broke my heart. It also irritated me like hell.

'Hello, poppet. And how's the heroine today?'

'She's annoyed,' I said, following Mum into the kitchen and slumping into a chair. 'How come you didn't tell me about Freddie and Gateway?'

Mum clicked the kettle on. 'Oh, sweetheart,' she said. 'You've got so much on and Freddie specifically asked me not to tell you.'

Huh?

He had?

How come?

Actually, there was no need to ask Mum why.

I was a rubbish mother, that was why. Flinging myself at other men, losing my rag, ignoring my children. I was an utter failure. And I had no one to blame but myself. My own mum was in a different league.

My anger melted away and left me with a lump in my throat.

'Oh, Mum,' I said. 'Why am I so rubbish at everything? Why can't I be more like you?'

Mum looked surprised. 'Why would you want to be more like me?' she asked.

'Because I'm a dreadful mother,' I said, blinking back the tears.

I waved vaguely at the tea things Mum was arranging on the table. The blue chinoiserie teapot. The floral cups and saucers. Milk in a jug. Sugar tongs. *Sugar tongs!* All perfect. I couldn't even tease her for being matchy-matchy. At mine, she had a teabag dunked in a chipped white mug. Well, she had done before I threw the mugs on the floor…

'You're a super mother having a tough time,' said Mum. 'You've got three children at difficult ages and Daniel, for reasons best known to himself, has chosen to go abroad. *Anyone* would find it hard.'

'*You* wouldn't.'

'Of course I would. I only had one child, remember. And I made more than my fair share of mistakes.'

My mum didn't make mistakes.

She was just trying to make me feel better.

'Like what?' I said. 'Not ironing the sheets? Shop-bought cake? Reading the *Daily Mail*?'

Mum laughed. She looked out of the window, twiddling one of her curls. Then she turned, looked me straight in the eye and said, 'How about having a fling with Uncle Robert?'

I did a very good imitation of that GIF where the woman spits out her tea.

Uncle Robert, Teddy's father…

It was preposterous!

'I don't believe you!' I spluttered.

I waited for Mum to laugh and say 'Got you!' but her expression didn't change.

'It's true,' she said. 'To be fair, your dad and I *were* on a break.'

Now the conversation had just got surreal. In many, many ways.

'Hang on. You separated from Dad? You had a fling with Uncle Robert? And did you really just say "on a break"?'

'I did.'

'Mums don't say "on a break"!'

'Of course they do,' she said. 'They have Netflix and watch *Friends* like everyone else.'

I was utterly gobsmacked.

'This is too weird!' I said.

'Well, just remember you lot aren't the first to have marriage and children problems. Old sticks like me had lives that were just as real and complex and messy.'

So Mum, perfect Mum, hadn't sailed through life and marriage without a wobble. Far from it. Her marriage had broken down – at least temporarily – and she'd had a fling with her brother-in-law. Bloody hell! That made my misdemeanours look positively tame by comparison. Maybe it was all going to be OK.

In the meantime, I had *questions*. So many questions.

Mum tipped some bourbons onto a plate. 'Now, quite enough about me,' she said firmly. 'We're here to talk about Freddie.'

Yes, this was about Freddie.

Not Mum.

Not Daniel.

Certainly not me.

Freddie.

319

So, what had been going on with my eldest honey-scented bundle?

He'd certainly been a whole load more trouble than Jack since Daniel had been away. What was normal and what was not? Heaven knew the boundaries were blurred.

Falling in with Bethany probably hadn't been the best idea. Stealing Megan's iPad had definitely crossed the line. He'd been naïve and silly but, frankly, it could have been a whole lot worse.

It was school that really worried me. Detentions. Gateway. To say nothing of skipping homework and falling grades.

Freddie had always been bright; he'd been top of his class at St John's.

Asperger's?

No. He and Lily weren't on the spectrum. It wasn't even a possibility.

So, what was it then?

Dyslexia?

No – I was just trying to hand myself a 'get out of jail free' card.

It was far more likely that Freddie's problems were linked to the disruption at home. His brother had been diagnosed with Asperger's, his dad had moved out and his mum had come perilously close to losing the plot.

More than enough for anyone to be getting on with.

I had a feeling Freddie wasn't going be quite as straightforward as Lily to help.

But I could try.

I called Mandy's Steve…

—

After school, I went to Freddie's room. Freddie was sitting cross-legged on his bed, surrounded by school books, sweet packets and his laptop. He had headphones in and was tapping away on his phone and didn't notice me coming in. I studied him for a moment. He had bumfluff on his chin and a couple of spots on his cheek. He was growing up.

I waved to attract his attention. Freddie looked up, frowned and ripped an earplug out.

'Whayerwan?' he asked suspiciously.

I sat down on his computer chair. 'Just to say sorry, really,' I said.

Freddie took the other earplug out and put his phone down.

'Right.' He was clearly waiting for the catch.

'I know it hasn't been easy for you. You had a point when you said too much of my focus has been on Jack.'

'OK.' Freddie was still looking suspicious.

I pressed on. 'I can't promise things will get better right away, but I will do my best. We'll get you a tutor for your schoolwork and maybe someone to talk to if you'd like.'

''K,' said Freddie.

At least he wasn't dismissing me out of hand.

'But there's one thing I need you to do for me.'

'What?' Freddie's eyes narrowed.

'I need a family representative to go to the Wycombe match a week on Saturday.'

Freddie's head shot up. 'You mean the fourth-round tie against Spurs?' he said.

'Yeah,' I said. 'A friend of mine needs someone who knows their way around a football to help with the Cubs' penalty shoot-out at half-time.'

'Not really?' said Freddie, sitting up straight.

'Really. He also needs someone to interview the Man of the Match for the club magazine afterwards.'

Freddie was standing on his bed now. 'Are you fucking serious?' he asked.

I ignored the bad language. 'I am,' I said.

And I was pleased to see my fourteen-year-old wasn't too grown up to jump up and down on his bed.

'You can take someone with you,' I said, as I got up to leave. 'Maybe Bethany?'

Freddie bounced down into a cross-legged position on his bed.

'Nah,' he said. '*She* doesn't know her way around a football. I'll take Jack.'

Chapter Forty-Five

If this was a film, now would be the time for the montage. You know the sort of thing. Fade into a close-up of Virginia, Mandy and Paul clustered around a computer screen, at least two of them wearing reading glasses, one hand gesticulating at the screen. Dissolve into a soft-focus shot of Mandy and Emma larking around on a sofa, heads thrown back in laughter. Merge into a split screen; the left showing creamy invitations emerging from a printer, the right showing manicured hands slipping them into envelopes. There would be heavy use of an airbrush-type technique to ensure the camera didn't put on ten pounds and some loud, inspirational music, heavy on power chords, the different threads representing our different personalities.

Yes; the ball was getting that close. All the tickets had been sold and there was *masses* to do. Nothing difficult – just very time-consuming. Finalising the auction lots. Deciding which would go on the Tree of Promises. Printing and laminating lists to go on each table. Praying the weather improved…

At least things at home were on an even keel. I was finally getting the hang of this single-parenting lark. I'd even instigated an evening routine and helped Freddie devise a homework chart. Everyone seemed happy and settled and, sod's law, it was now that the long-promised help for Jack seemed to be coming through.

I know!

That night, I had the mother of all headaches. A real humdinger caused, no doubt, by too much of everything. 'Everything' always did it for me! Damn my head. But as I plopped painkillers into a glass of water I remembered that, if it hadn't been for my migraines, I'd never have got together with Daniel.

My life would have turned out entirely differently.

—

I didn't row at Cambridge beyond the obligatory first term, when I was single-handedly responsible for slowing the boat down. But, every year, I made the pilgrimage to the Star and Garter in Putney to watch the start of the Boat Race. I hung out with old acquaintances and we got drunk and reminisced about our glory years. The race was almost incidental to proceedings.

The year after the Henley Regatta, I was just reaching the plastered stage when I spotted Daniel's messy blond hair in the shifting crowds. My first reaction was to hide. The last couple of times I'd seen him had been less than successful and I wasn't about to go looking for a third. Besides, I was going through a grungy-indie phase and I wasn't sure I even fancied him any more.

An hour later and I was feeling really grotty. It was more than just the booze, I had a migraine brewing. And I had no pills. Pills would require being organised.

I needed to get home but north London might as well have been the moon. There was no way I could navigate public transport with all my senses in overdrive, and I had no money for a cab. I'd have to find a chemist, buy my trusty pills – the ones in the bright red packaging – and hope for the best.

There is nothing more isolating than a migraine. I set off up Putney High Street on my own, the sun too bright, the traffic too noisy, my skin stretched taut across my forehead.

The sound of quickening footsteps and Daniel was by my side.

'Em?'

'Hi, Daniel.' I didn't even have the energy to express surprise or to act cool.

'Are you all right? You're very pale.'

'I'm fine.'

Actually, I'm not fine. Your clinking carrier bags are suggesting beer and the thought is making me gag.

'You're not fine. You've got a migraine, haven't you?'

Oh, the bliss of someone who understood.

'Yes,' I said and was promptly sick all over the pavement. Passers-by looked at me in disgust. Just another pissed yuppie.

'Who are you with?' asked Daniel.

'Friends. Down by the river.'

'Shall I go and get them?'

I shook my head. They were only acquaintances. They'd be horrified. 'But if you've got any money for a taxi? Or to call my parents?'

Daniel hesitated. 'I'm living just round the corner,' he said. 'Why not come back with me?'

I looked at him through eyes that could hardly focus. 'Yes please,' I said.

And together we walked back to his flat, which turned out to be a little more than just round the corner.

The next twenty-four hours were hell. I was sick over the fruit bowl on the kitchen table. A dusty yucca plant came in for the same treatment. But I also remember kind hands tucking me into bed. Hot sweet tea when I was starting to recover. Feeling I'd come home.

The grungy-indie phase was definitely over.

When I was better, Daniel drove me home and kissed me chastely on the cheek. I wondered if that was that. I wondered why he hadn't returned my grateful answer-machine message. I wondered if the sight of me with hair on end and lightly flecked with vomit had just been too much.

But, four days later, Daniel called and invited me to a little wine bar he knew not far from Shaftesbury Avenue.

We got married a year later and he'd cared for me ever since.

–

So, here was the thing. The past few weeks had proved I could cope without Daniel.

I just didn't want to.

I couldn't let him go. But what to do to win him back? Every time I tried to speak to him, it came out wrong. How to bridge the space between the words?

I'd write to him.

Of course.

It was the obvious thing to do.

After I'd dropped Jack and Lily at school the next morning, I settled in front of the laptop with painkillers and strong coffee. It was *hard*. My first effort was screeds of heartfelt stuff but, when I read it back, it just seemed ridiculously desperate.

I deleted it and tried again.

And again.

In the end, I just wrote:

> I'm sorry, Daniel. For everything. I still love you but I'm so confused. Can we talk? Em x

Clear, concise and to the point. That should do the trick.

Then I waited.

And waited.

And waited.

Finally, I got an email back:

> I'm confused too. Deffo need to talk. Not at the moment though.

What was that all about?

I know we Aspies struggle with communication, but that was definitely ambiguous. And *definitely* fobbing me off.

It was outrageous.

Outrageous.

And scary as hell.

Emma: Why don't you want to talk about it now?

Daniel: Because I haven't got time to wipe my arse.

Charming!

Now what to do?

I just wanted my husband back.

Talking hadn't worked. Writing hadn't worked.

I'd have to go out to the States.

I could just about do it. It would be a whistle-stop trip but, if I left pretty pronto, I could be out and back before the ball. Daniel and I could talk face to face and surely – *surely* – we'd be able to sort everything out.

OK, there were one or two little obstacles. The kids, for example. But maybe Mum could be persuaded to move back in to look after them. Or Ness? Mandy? Even Caroline wasn't out of the question now. Virginia?

I checked the price of tickets to Austin. They weren't too bad. Actually, they were blooming extortionate, but what price love?

Maybe I'd turn up and surprise Daniel. It would be hot out there and I'd have to slather on the fake tan because I had that lovely British winter blue-white glow, but hot pants and a Stetson and some cowboy boots...

How could he resist?

On second thoughts, I should probably tell Daniel I was coming. It was the grown-up thing to do.

So I told him.

Daniel: Stop being such a drama queen, Em.

Great!

Emma: I'm not. I just want to see you.

Daniel: It's a ridiculous idea. It'd cost a fortune. And I won't be here anyway. I'm about to head off to San Diego and then to that conference in Boston.

Ah.

Daniel had mentioned he'd be criss-crossing the States. I'd forgotten.

Emma: I could join you in one of those places?

I'd always fancied California. A soft-top car, the wind whipping through my hair...

Daniel: Stop it, Em. It's a critical week for me.

And clearly much more important than our marriage.

Emma: Stop fobbing me off. When can we talk?

Daniel: How about a week on Saturday. You'll have my undivided attention then.

Suddenly I had a lump in my throat.

Emma: That's the day of the ball. My deadline.

I'd been planning it for months and it wasn't even on his bloody radar.

Daniel: Sorry, sorry, sorry...

Too late.

I'd obviously lost him.

He'd moved away from me. Physically of course. But emotionally too.

Despite my best efforts, it was over.

The Statistic had won.

–

Dear Emma, thank you so much for the delicious chocolate shoe. Very original! You've certainly got a foot in our door! In fact, we have an upcoming project...

Chapter Forty-Six

I'd love to be able to say the day of the ball dawned bright and sunny. It didn't. It was cold and damp and foggy. Rather like my mood. Even the ridiculously flattering navy dress with the tight bodice and swirly skirt hanging on the cupboard door couldn't cheer me up.

At least, thanks to the dress, no one would be asking when my baby was due.

Virginia and Mandy were meeting mid-morning to start decorating the ballroom. Paul and I weren't on duty until early evening, which at least meant I was on hand to drive the kids to their various activities. Jack and Luke had joined the Cubs and were training for a 10k run in a couple of months' time. Lily needed taking to the academy and then she was going back to Hellie's for lunch. That left me to take Freddie to his football match on the outskirts of Maidenhead. This time I stood with the right parents (very friendly) and shouted the right encouragement, even though it was so foggy I could hardly see across the pitch.

Then my mobile rang. To my surprise, it was Daniel. We still talked every day — we were adults and shared children, after all — but it was normally in the evening when he knew the kids would be around.

'I'm calling to wish you luck for tonight,' he said. His voice was echoey and there was lots of noise in the background. The very important conference, no doubt.

'Thanks. I can't believe it's finally here.'

I walked away from the other parents, squelching though the mud in my new wellies.

'I wish I could be there,' said Daniel.

What was *that* about? Mr I'm-Too-Busy-To-Talk-To-My-Wife.

'You hate balls,' I said. 'Remember?'

'Not all balls. I went at Cambridge. Remember?'

'Only because you could crash it! And don't worry, I'm all sorted with a date for tonight.'

'I see,' said Daniel. 'Well, break a leg, or whatever they say. And when you've recovered from your hangover, maybe we can talk.'

—

Freddie's team won, Jack had had an awesome time running in the woods and Lily had perfected some manoeuvre on the beam. It was a good day for Team Healey and I wasn't going to let Daniel drag my mood down. Not today. Not after all my hard work. I'd enjoy the ball, put Daniel to the back of my mind and face whatever needed to be faced tomorrow.

That afternoon, Mum looked after the kids and it was time for some serious pampering. By the time I'd had a manicure and my hair put into a messy up-do, I was much more excited. I slipped on my dress and some uncharacteristically high heels and presented myself to the children, who were lolling around in the lounge.

'How do I look?' I asked, turning around. The skirt twirled silkily around my legs. I could get used to this. Maybe I'd become the girl who always wore gorgeous dresses...

Freddie shifted so he could see the TV. "K,' he muttered.

'Your hair looks ridiculous,' said Jack. 'You should brush it.'

Lily rolled her eyes at the boys. 'You look peng,' she said.

'You look *beautiful*,' said Mum, coming into the room. 'I haven't seen you look as lovely since your wedding day.'

At five fifteen, Mark arrived and we had a glass of champagne to get in the party mood and to dissipate any awkwardness – after all, I hadn't seen him since that night in Manchester. Mark helped me load the car with the auction prizes and envelopes and together we drove to the Club.

The ballroom looked *stunning*. Virginia and Mandy had tied gold and red heart-shaped balloons to the back of each chair and there were red roses on each table and more rose petals and Love Hearts scattered around. The first Love Heart I looked at said 'Broken-Hearted'.

I wouldn't be broken-hearted tonight.

That could wait until tomorrow.

'Emma, hi!' It was Virginia, predictably the belle of the ball in plunging apricot silk. 'I love your dress. And Mark too! How lovely. Come and help me move these tables?'

Mark disappeared with her and it became abundantly clear exactly why he had offered to squire me. Funnily enough, I didn't care at all.

I went to search out Paul. I found him manoeuvring the Tree of Promises into position near the bar.

Paul looked me up and down. 'You look stunning,' he said simply.

'Thank you,' I replied. 'Right, work to do.'

Working companionably, we attached the small gold envelopes containing the promises to the branches together with some red and gold glass baubles. Finally, we tied a big gold ribbon round the pot. We stood back to admire our handiwork and Paul put his arm round me.

'Well done, us,' he said.

I allowed myself to lean against him for a moment. Like the morning mist, our infatuation hadn't stood a chance in the midday sun. But it had happened. And it had felt real – had *been* real.

'How are things?' I asked.

'Good. I've got a job teaching creative writing in Oxford. It means Hanna can go part-time.'

'Wonderful. Good for you. Where *is* Hanna?'

'Feeling grotty with the pregnancy. She's not going to make it tonight.'

'That's a shame.'

'Yes. And Gabe...'

'What happened?' I asked, moving away from him and adjusting one of the baubles.

'The NHS appointment came through. And they diagnosed him.'

'Ah.'

'It wasn't really much of a surprise. Something hadn't felt quite right after Dr Poole.'

'Nothing's changed,' I said. 'He's still your lovely boy.'

'I know. Thanks for not saying "I told you so".'

'Don't be silly.'

'Hey, guys.' It was Mandy, in slinky black ruffles. 'Quick toast before it all kicks off?'

The four of us gathered in the ballroom and Virginia produced a bottle of champagne.

'Here's to us,' she said. 'And here's to our lovely children.'

'Hear, hear,' said Mandy. 'Let's go and make a mint for the little blighters.'

We clinked glasses and it was all a bit emotional, to be honest. The four of us had been through a lot together.

People started arriving, decked out in their finery and full of anticipation for the evening ahead. Glasses of bubbly were distributed, kisses exchanged, official photos snapped. After months of planning, the ball was finally under way. Here was Ness – sexy as hell in black velvet and finally going public with Harry, Virginia's gorgeous toy-boy stepson. Butterscotch-Bottom was in nude silk and her husband Nigel of the ski chalet donation was sporting a multicoloured bowtie I just knew would light up and spin round when he'd reached a critical alcohol level. Ally O'Neill was an emerald pixie tonight, Caroline was elegant in red lace, Mr Berry was sporting an elaborate paisley waistcoat…

Enough of that.

There was more work to do.

Paul and I headed back to the Tree of Promises. It was disappointingly quiet. Several people were peering at it as they queued to buy drinks but no one was parting with their cash.

'Maybe they'll loosen up when they've had a couple of drinks,' I muttered.

'Bloody hope so,' Paul replied.

Virginia sashayed over. 'How's it going?' she asked.

'Fine,' I said in a positive head–of–fundraising voice.

'Actually, not fine,' conceded Paul. The traitor. 'They're proving a tough sell.'

Virginia tossed her hair over one shoulder. 'Oh God,' she said. 'You've had months to prepare for this. Don't say it's not going to work.'

'It will work,' I said testily. 'Give it time.'

'We haven't got time. Come on, *I'll* fire the punters up.'

She smiled at the milling crowd and made a big play of brandishing her tenner and selecting an envelope. A dozen people gathered round as, smiling coquettishly. Virginia unclipped the envelope and flipped it open, pulling out the card inside.

The crowd pressed forward.

'What have you won?' someone asked.

'A visit to Highdown Hall!'

It was obvious Virginia was feigning excitement. There was a muttering of disappointment, even disapproval, and everyone melted away.

Virginia was furious. 'Highdown Hall?' she spluttered. 'You get in for free if you're a National Trust member. It's a rubbish prize.'

'It's *not* a rubbish prize,' I said hotly. I hadn't spent ages blagging prizes and creating the tree for Virginia to talk to me like that. 'We just need someone to sell them properly.'

'I did—'

'Simpering at the audience *isn't* selling it properly.'

This wasn't going well. The ball had barely started and Virginia and I were already spatting. I touched her hand and drew her away from Paul.

'Why do you hate me so much?' I asked.

Virginia's eyes widened. 'I don't hate you,' she said. I was about to demur when she gave an infuriating little laugh. 'Oh, don't get me wrong, I don't *like* you much either. You with your Oxbridge degree and your perfect marriage that, incidentally, doesn't seem to stop you chasing after other men. And don't get me started on your histrionics if anyone dares to criticise you.'

I debated whether to have histrionics now.

Tempting.

Probably unwise.

'I'm not proud of the way I've behaved,' I said. 'And my marriage certainly hasn't been perfect. Far from it. But it's *my* marriage and I'd rather like to keep it that way. If you don't mind.'

It was probably too late.

And that wasn't Virginia's fault.

It was time for dinner.

The ballroom was crammed with circular tables and the ball committee had commandeered the top table furthest from the entrance. I had a seat between Paul and Mark, with Virginia on Mark's other side. The table was completed by Mandy, Steve and Mr Berry.

There was a lovely hubbub in the room and the salmon mousse seemed to be going down a treat. I couldn't eat a thing. This was partly because my dress was so tight I could hardly

334

sit, let alone eat, but mainly because of the imminent auction. Rather than do the whole thing after the meal, we'd decided it would be more digestible to intersperse the lots between courses. But supposing nobody bid for any of them? Supposing everyone was as apathetic as they had been about the Tree of Promises? Not only would it be publicly humiliating, but the whole ball would have been a waste of time.

I needn't have worried.

There was a palpable air of excitement as Mr Berry announced the first lot. Dinner for eight preceded by canapés on someone's boat.

Bidding was brisk, with Mr Berry whipping up the crowd and Mandy helping out as a 'roving reporter'. Mark was really going for it. Every time someone made a bid, he immediately raised it. Soon we were at £200. And rising.

'Careful,' I cautioned. 'You're going to end up with it and you don't even live here.'

Mark shook his head. 'Don't worry, I'll bale out before it's too late,' he said.

In the end he pulled out at £460, leaving Caroline's husband to win it for a staggering £480. £480! Paul and I looked at each other with wide, breathless smiles. This was beyond our wildest expectations. It was all going to be all right. More than all right...

The next lot was the opportunity to name a character in Paul's book. I squeezed Paul's hand in nervous anticipation but the bids came in thick and fast and quickly climbed to £1,000.

I was so relieved.

Relieved for Paul.

Relieved for *us*.

The most enthusiastic bidder was Butterscotch-Bottom, who kept sticking her hand in the air and saying, 'Ooh, ooh, ooh,' like the class swot.

'Are you a Paul Archer fan?' asked Mandy, waving the microphone under her nose.

335

'Never heard of him,' said Butterscotch-Bottom cheerfully. 'But I'd love to see my daughter's name in print.'

'Ha!' I said to Paul. 'Shouldn't be too hard slipping *that* name into your book.'

'Oh God. What is it?'

'Tallulah Hughes-Jenkins,' I said and dissolved into a fit of giggles.

'For fuck's sake.' Paul put his head in his hands. 'Somebody spare me. Preferably someone called Smith.'

'Allow me,' said Mark and put his hand up for £1,100.

After that, it was a two-horse race. The bidding spiralled upwards: £1,200... £1,300... £1,400... Chatter died away, heads swivelling in anticipation at each new bid.

'Be careful,' I said to Mark. 'This is serious dosh.'

'What's your surname?' asked Paul.

'Fox,' said Mark, putting his hand up for £1,500.

'That I can work with,' said Paul. 'Don't let Emma put you off...'

'£1,600 to Mrs HJ,' said Mr Berry. '£1,700 to Mr Fox.'

£1,800... £1,900... £2,000...

'£2,100 to Mr Fox...'

Butterscotch-Bum shook her head regretfully and the bidding was over. The ballroom erupted into whoops and cheers.

£2,100.

A triumph!

Thrilled, I leapt to my feet and went to stand behind Paul. I put my arms round his shoulders and kissed him on the cheek and he twisted round in his seat to kiss me back. Then I looked up, laughing, straight into the eyes of...

Daniel?

Chapter Forty-Seven

I must be imagining it.

A fantasy?

A mirage?

An adrenaline-induced hallucination?

No.

Definitely Daniel, standing at the entrance to the ballroom. Daniel, in jeans and navy pullover; knackered, dishevelled, gorgeous.

I was about to run to him, fling myself at him, but his expression was changing. Anticipation... shock... disdain? Then I realised how I must look: heaving bosom, smeared lipstick, embracing another man. And not any old 'other man'...

He's leaving. He's leaving.

Mustn't let him go.

Can't get there in time...

Desperately, I grabbed the microphone from Mr Berry.

'Daniel!' My voice boomed out, accompanied by a loud feedback crackle. '*Daniel.*'

The room went quiet. Heads swivelled. Daniel stopped in his tracks but he didn't turn round.

'It's not what it looks like,' I called to him. It sounded feeble, even to me.

Now Daniel did turn. Very politely, he took the microphone from Mandy, who was still standing by Butterscotch-Bottom. 'I think it's exactly what it looks like,' he said, icily.

Absolute silence punctuated only by my amplified breathing.

What to do? What to say?

337

'It's not,' I said, tugging my dress up with my spare hand. 'It's really not.'

Pathetic.

'Yeah, right,' said Daniel, into his microphone. 'Draped over your boyfriend. Sandwiched between *two* of them, in fact. You must be in seventh heaven.'

There was a collective intake of breath that unfurled into a babble of excited chatter. Heads swivelled from Daniel to me and back to Daniel again.

Desperation and despair crackled through me and both scars started itching like billy-o.

'Daniel, please,' I said. 'Don't be like this. This is important. It's our *marriage*. And I know you and Virginia—'

'I don't need to hear this,' said Daniel. He dropped the microphone onto the patterned carpet, turned on his heel and walked out.

There was silence apart from a muffled boom from the microphone.

I stood rooted to the spot.

Oh my God.

I'd been going to say 'I know you and Virginia were trying to help me'!

But he'd gone.

Gone!

And now what to do?

It was Virginia who came to my rescue. She took the microphone from me and then put her hand over mine. 'Go after him,' she said. 'He loves you.'

'Really?' Suddenly there was a lump in my throat.

'Absolutely. And if you feel the same, go after him.'

Some stupid sense of duty – or Aspie inflexibility – kept me rooted to the spot.

'But the ball? The auction? Mark?' I said.

'We'll take care of them. Just *go*. Take it from me – being on your own is no fun at all.'

338

I grabbed my shrug and my bag. And then I think I surprised us both by leaning forward and kissing her gently on the cheek before running out of the hall.

I ran without thinking to the front steps of the Club.

And then I stopped.

It was all very well Virginia telling me to go after Daniel, but I had absolutely no idea where he'd gone. I didn't know how why he was here, how he'd got to the Club or what he was planning to do next. I just knew I mustn't let him go. If he went back to America without sorting this out…

Phone him, Emma.

I whipped out my phone. There were two texts from Mum.

> **Mum:** He's on his way to the ball!
>
> **Mum:** Daniel's shown up!

I hadn't seen them. I'd been too busy. Too damn busy for my marriage, as usual, and now look at what had happened.

I called Daniel's number but he didn't pick up. '*Call me, Daniel. Please,*' I pleaded.

I disconnected and called Mum.

'Hello, poppet,' she said. 'Is Daniel there? All very exciting—'

'Yes. But it's not exciting. He misread a… situation.'

'Oh dear,' said Mum.

Understatement of the century.

'What's going on?' I said desperately. 'Why has he shown up like this?'

'Apparently, he made a last-minute decision to come home for the weekend,' said Mum. 'He was in Boston. Not that it's much closer.'

I wandered down the steps and into the car park. Maybe Daniel was getting into a taxi or a hire car. Maybe I could intercept him...

Nothing.

'But pitching up at the ball without a word of warning,' I said. 'Why didn't he come home first?'

'His plane was diverted to Frankfurt because of the fog. He was stranded there for hours.'

'He could have called.'

'He said he spoke to you this morning.'

'Oh God...'

Daniel had come back to take me to the ball. It was an olive branch, an attempt at reconciliation. But I'd blown it. Totally blown it. Casually telling him I was going with Mark. Draping myself all over Paul.

I was a fool of monumental proportions.

'Is he still there?' Mum was asking.

'He left. Was he planning to come home tonight?'

'He has to fly out first thing in the morning. I *assumed* he was coming back here, but...'

But now he probably wasn't.

The implication was clear.

'I'm going to try to find him,' I said. 'If he arrives back home, please tell him—'

'I'll tell him,' said Mum.

We said goodbye and I ran back up the front steps into the club, panic stabbing my chest. An elderly couple, putting on their coats after an evening of bridge or wife-swapping or whatever, glanced at me curiously.

'Have you seen a man?' I asked them.

The old codger laughed. 'Place is full of them!' he said.

'No. A youngish man. Blond hair. Jeans...'

'There was a young chap heading across the grass a couple of minutes ago,' said the woman. 'I wondered what he was up to.'

'Probably been thrown out,' said the man with satisfaction. 'Jeans are banned here.'

I ran outside again, down the steps and round the side of the building. What was Daniel doing out here on his own? Clearing his head? Calming down? Maybe he would come back inside in a while — jeans notwithstanding — and everything would be OK.

My phone buzzed.

Please let it be Daniel.

It was Mum. 'Daniel left a message while we were talking,' she said. 'He's heading straight to the airport tonight. He asked me to say goodbye to the kids.'

Oh God.

So, Daniel wasn't idly strolling around. He was out of here. We were a few miles from town by road but only a couple along the river. Daniel must be legging it along the towpath back to town — presumably so he could catch a cab to the airport and out of my life as soon as possible.

It was over.

No, Emma.

Stop being so defeatist.

I could head him off at the pass once he got to town. Intercept him before he got to the taxi rank. Not by driving, of course — I was way over the limit and even I wasn't that stupid. But I'd booked a cab for Mark and myself much, much later. I could bring it forward...

Not a hope. The man from the cab company almost laughed at me. 'Nothing for thirty minutes. Not this time on a Saturday evening, love.'

Crap.

I could ask someone to drive me? Paul? Ness? Mandy? No. All pissed.

I'd have to go after Daniel. Chase him along the towpath and hope against slim hope I could catch him. There was no alternative.

No sooner had the thought come into my head than I was off. Across the car park and the manicured lawns and onto the shingled towpath. In the morning it was beautiful here, with tall grasses and the dew illuminating a thousand glittering spiders' webs strung between the stalks. Tonight, however, any webs had been eaten by shadows and it was decidedly creepy. It was also bloody chilly, my shrug no match for the elements.

I started to run.

Bloody dress! Bloody shoes! If only I could pull the bottom of the dress off like Jamie Lee Curtis did in that film about spies. And snap the heels off my shoes while I was about it. I took the shoes off. The ground was too cold. Too stony...

I put them back on and started running again.

No choice but to carry on.

The grasses gave way to trees and the path narrowed and became criss-crossed with roots. Now the going became much more difficult. It wasn't quite the bit in *Snow White* when she runs through the forest with branches pulling at her dress, but it didn't feel far off. This was ridiculous. I was in danger of tripping and twisting my ankle, or worse, and there wasn't a cat in hell's chance I was going to catch up with Daniel. I'd left the ball I was supposed to be running, abandoned Mark and put my safety at risk. I was an idiot.

I ran on.

And now it was raining, the first fat drops pattering off the leaves. I'd be soaked before long.

Now what?

Too late to go back, a good mile until I reached town.

No sign of Daniel.

Marvellous.

Blinking back tears, I carried on, mainly for want of anything better to do. But the rain was getting harder and I was getting wetter and the ground was in danger of turning into a quagmire.

This was awful!

I couldn't run on any more.

Frejalily was moored round the next corner, and the key was on my keyring, and I might as well shelter on board until the rain passed. Better that than triple pneumonia.

I pulled out my phone. Last try. No ruddy signal. We often had crappy reception on the boat. It hadn't mattered before; it was part of the getting-away-from-it-all vibe. Now it was a bloody disaster.

Up ahead I could see the silhouette of the road bridge that led to Hambley. Lights and houses and the sound of a car door slamming. Now I just had to find *Frejalily*. It all looked so different in the dark but I knew she was the twelfth boat beyond the bridge. Yes, there she was, sucking up to *Lazy-Daze*.

There was a little ember of hope in my chest. Maybe Daniel had gone through the same thought process as me. Maybe he was already aboard?

I jogged closer. *Frejalily* had an unloved air – even in the gloaming I could see the thin sheen of slime over her sides. No surprise there; I'd hardly have expected Daniel to get out the power hose. But *Frejalily* was also pitch black. Of course Daniel wasn't there! He was probably already in town, drowning his sorrows or getting the hell away from me as fast as he could.

There was a lump in my throat as I walked the final few yards. This was possibly the worst day of my life. Worse than Dad dying. Worse even than Jack's diagnosis. We'd washed our dirty laundry in front of the whole bloody town and then Daniel had turned his back on me and walked away without a backward glance. And now I was in the middle of nowhere and about to board a freezing, mildew-y boat and that was the best plan open to me...

I was sobbing as I reached out to undo the tarpaulin.

Suddenly I was bathed in light. I stepped back in shock.

Security lights? *Were* there security lights here? There must be. Maybe a burly guard was about to step out of the shadows and arrest me...

Don't be silly, Emma. This is *your* boat. Nothing to feel guilty about.

Then I realised the lights were coming from inside the boat. Which meant Daniel must be in there. My God, how lucky was I?

My heart started pounding in quite a different way.

Relief.

Fear.

A second chance, Emma. Just one. Don't blow it.

For an age, I just stood there.

If I didn't do anything, the hope was still alive.

Then I unclipped the tarpaulin cover and climbed aboard. My weight set the boat rocking and the cabin door swung open before I could rap on it.

I couldn't read Daniel's expression.

That's the trouble with Asperger's.

'You'd better come in,' he said.

Chapter Forty-Eight

We faced off in the tiny thoroughfare between the seating area and the sink. There was a muscle flickering in Daniel's cheek and his hands were lightly clenched by his sides. Even his hair was sharp and spiky from the rain. It didn't take a master of body language to deduce that this did not bode well.

Sure enough…

'Would you like to explain what's going on between you and Paul Archer?' It sounded like another Daniel. This Daniel was cold, his voice clipped. 'And Mark? *Mark!* What the hell was he doing there?'

I'd meant to be calm.

I really had.

I'd meant to state my case with poise and dignity and show Daniel how much I'd changed. But really! Did he have any idea how unfair he was being?

'Don't even think of talking to me like that,' I hissed. 'You've just humiliated me in front of everyone I know!'

'*You* were draped over Paul Archer with your tits half out!'

'*You* stomped off without bothering to find out what was going on!'

'*You* were behaving like a slapper! I wasn't about to hang around—'

Enough.

Enough.

'Well, you know all about not hanging around, don't you, Daniel?' I said.

Out before I could stop it.

345

Daniel took a step back. 'What's that supposed to mean?' he asked.

'You know exactly what it means,' I said. 'You were on that plane to Texas like a shot...'

'Wow!'

I was about to carry on when I started sneezing. Once, twice, three times. I suddenly realised how wet I was. Hair plastered to scalp, rivulets of water running down my back, dress slapping against my leg.

'And *now* you've made me catch cold!' I snapped.

'Bronchitis, at least.' Daniel's expression was mocking. And not in a friendly way.

Was he trying to dismiss me?

Humiliate me?

Well, I wasn't playing the game.

I wasn't slipping into our well-worn routine. Not now.

Not ever.

I grabbed some towels lying on the seats and closeted myself in the tiny bathroom. I let my dress puddle onto the floor, stripped off my undies and dried myself as best I could. I was angry now. Really angry. Because Daniel *had* left me. However you dressed it up, he *had* upped and offed when the going got tough. Mum had seen it for what it was but Daniel had never admitted it. Never said sorry. *Certainly* never been held to account.

I'd thought I'd followed him down the river to reconcile at any cost. But now I wasn't so sure. I'd proved I could survive without him. I didn't need him. I had to *want* him.

But did I?

Did I want him?

I swathed myself in the least soggy towel and flung the door open. Daniel was side-on, fists on the work surface, utterly motionless save that one muscle still flickering in his cheek. We were barely two metres apart but the space between us had never felt wider.

'You *left* me,' I said.

I braced myself for Daniel's reaction. He'd tell me to stop being ridiculous. That it had been his dream job, that I'd agreed to him going. He'd say I was being melodramatic, over the top—

But then Daniel turned and I saw he had tears in his eyes.

'You're absolutely right,' he said.

I'd expected an argument. I'd expected one of us to storm off into the night (Daniel, probably, as I was only wearing a towel). I hadn't anticipated... this.

'I did leave you,' said Daniel. His voice was quiet, measured, but the pulse in his neck told a different story. 'And it was a terrible thing to do. What kind of man just buggers off when things go wrong?'

'I coped,' I said. If this was about my lack of credentials as a parent...

'It's not about that. I shouldn't even have told you about the job offer. I certainly shouldn't have gone. I was scared, Em. I was scared about Jack's diagnosis and about what it would do to us as a family. I was scared about what it seemed to be doing to you. And, instead of trying to help, I pushed you away and then I ran away. I'm so, so very sorry.'

With that simple apology, any doubt melted away. This was Daniel, *my* Daniel, the man I had loved since I was eighteen. He wasn't perfect – he didn't have to be – but he was *sorry*.

And that was all that mattered.

Daniel was still talking. 'I couldn't talk to you, Em. Every time I tried to, it came out all wrong. And, today, when I saw you at the ball, I thought I'd lost you...' He trailed off, his voice cracking.

'Oh, sweetheart.' I said. 'I've hardly been squeaky clean either.'

347

'No. But I can almost understand why you did what you did. Thank you for following me along the towpath in the rain.'

I gave him a crooked smile. 'Would you really have gone back to the States without even *talking* to me?' I asked.

'Of course not. I'd have come back to the ball when I'd calmed down.'

'Oh God. I'm not sure St John's would ever have been ready for that.'

We were inching toward each other and I don't know who made the first move, but the next thing I knew, I was in his arms.

'You haven't lost me,' I whispered.

The arms that felt like home.

Always had. Still did.

After a while, even the warm glow of reconciliation couldn't stop us shivering for Britain. We brewed up hot, sweet tea — luckily, we never cleared the boat's supplies out as well as we should — and, as we pottered around the cabin, I thought how harmoniously we worked together. We'd always been a good team until the events of the last few months had driven a wedge between us.

We put Bruce Springsteen on the speakers and we talked and talked and talked. About Jack, sure, but about Freddie and Lily too. And about us. About what had happened. What we wanted. What we had. What we couldn't have.

Then 'Thunder Road' came on, urging us to show some faith in the magic of the night. So Daniel and I showed a little faith, and it turned out Bruce was right. He knows these things.

That's why he's called The Boss.

'Do you want to go back to the ball?' asked Daniel, much, much later.

I glanced at my watch. Five to eleven. (How had all *that* happened before eleven?)

348

We *could* go back and face the music. Maybe we even should. But, then again…

'No, thanks.'

Eleven meant the auction would be finished but the disco would be in full swing. Eleven meant 'Dancing Queen' would be belting out and the dance floor would be full. Eleven meant Ally O'Reilly would be shaking and shimmying like a pixie on speed. Butterscotch-Bum and her husband would be dirty-dancing. Steve and Mandy would be camping it up a storm and, over to one side, Ness and Harry would be locked in each other's arms – the age difference unnoticeable, irrelevant. Eleven might even mean Virginia and Mark would be having a furtive snog out on the lawn…

I could picture it all.

Everyone would be busy with their own evenings, their own lives, their own stories.

None of it mattered.

I snuggled against Daniel's warm, mildew-y jumper as the opening bars of 'If I Should Fall Behind' came on. The song we'd danced to at our wedding. The song we'd played as each of our three beautiful children was born. The lyrics we'd spectacularly ignored over the past few months.

Who cared what was going on at the ball?

It was not my story.

'There's one more thing,' I said.

'What?' asked Daniel.

'I think I have Asperger's too.'

Daniel grinned and took me into his arms.

'No shit, Sherlock,' he said.

This was my story.

349

Epilogue

Two months later

The day of the races dawned bright and sunny, the breeze soft and fragrant with promise. It seemed like the whole town was there either to run or to support others. Ness and I duly ran our five kilometres along the river, smashing the target we'd set for ourselves and crossing the line together, hands aloft.

I do love it when a plan comes together.

Afterwards I stood at the finish line bathed in satisfaction and sunshine and waited for my boys. Daniel always ran the 10k and this year was no exception – even though he'd done next to no training. He'd gone back to the States after our reconciliation; of course he had – we were mature and responsible adults and Daniel had a job to finish. But we'd stayed in touch and he'd even gone to visit Teddy and Alfonzo.

But he had come back to me as he'd promised and we were starting again.

Jack was running too – little Jack who'd been so late hitting his milestones, who hadn't even walked until he was two. Little Jack was running a 10k with the Cubs.

I stood and waited for my boys. And while I waited, I looked at the river. It looked deep and wise and timeless today. 'You and I have been through quite a lot these past few months, old friend,' I thought. Well, I didn't think that exactly, of course, because who talks to rivers, and calls them 'old friend', even in their thoughts? But you know what I mean. The river had been the backdrop for the boat trip that made me turn my back on my marriage, Bethany's accident, my reunion with Daniel…

It would have witnessed thousands of other stories but these were the only ones that mattered to me.

I had learned a lot these past few months.

Loud cheers from the sizeable crowd heralded the first of the 10k finishers. They had to run round the riverside meadow in a large loop before they crossed the finish line. Round they came: lanky youths, wiry middle-aged men, taut women, a couple of the Cubs... And, wow, here was Jack. I watched, heart bursting, as he ran, clearly knackered, absolutely focussed. Lily on her bike, blond hair flying under her helmet, shadowed him, shouting encouragement. Freddie and Bethany, arms round each other, allowed their carefully ironic expressions to slip as they cheered him on. Somewhere behind him, Daniel was running his own race. And I thought, here we are, we're a *family*. It's going to be OK.

I went and stood a little distance behind the finish line holding Jack's sweatshirt like a good mother. Because I *was* a good mother, for goodness sake. Jack was laughing with the exhilaration of running, the satisfaction of completion – hell, with the joy of being the best version of himself he could be.

And I suppose that was all any of us could aim for.

Jack ran though the finish line. But he didn't stop. He kept running, straight as a die toward me. Laughing and panting, he ran into my waiting arms, honey head against my heart.

'I love you, Jack,' I said.

'I love you too.'

And here was Daniel. He came panting over the finish line and hugged us both to him.

'My lovely family,' I said, as Freddie and Lily came over to join us.

And we all walked slowly home along the river.

Acknowledgements

I am so lucky to have many wonderful people in my life who have helped *Another Us* see the light of day.

Firstly, enormous thanks to my wonderful agent Felicity Trew – advocate, therapist and co-conspirator – for plucking me from the slush pile and for believing in me and my book. You have made my dream come true. To Emily Bedford and whole team at Canelo; thank you for falling in love with Emma's story and for helping to make it better. You've been brilliant – professional, enthusiastic and enormous fun to work with. I really couldn't have done it without you.

Writing can be a lonely old business – so thank goodness for lovely chums who are always there to support, encourage and pour the drinks – virtual or otherwise. Huge thanks to: the LLs – Catherine Boardman, Vanessa Rigg, Jane Ayres, Chris Manby, Maddie Please, Sue Bavin, Christina Banach and Kazzy Coles; the Sister Scribes – Jane Cable, Sue Bavin (again!), Kitty Wilson and Cass Grafton; the Coppa Crew – Claire Dyer, Marilyn Groves and Becci Fearnley. Mine's a Limoncello!

Thank you, too, to all those who read early versions of the book and made such fabulous, constructive suggestions; that's you Debbie Wermann, Debi Alper, (editrix extraordinaire), Alison May and Julie Cordiner. You were all super-helpful and I really appreciate it.

A huge thank you to you, the reader, for choosing *Another Us* and for supporting a debut. I hope you enjoyed it and, if so, that you'll consider reviewing it far and wide.

And finally – most of all – thank you to my wonderful husband, John and my fabulous children, Tom and Charlotte. Thank you so much for your love, your support and all the fun – even during lockdown! I love you all very much xx